c

MORE PRAISE FOR JEAN JOHNSON

"Jean Johnson's writing is fabulously fresh, thoroughly romantic, and wildly entertaining. Terrific—fast, sexy, charming, and utterly engaging. I loved it!"

—Jayne Ann Krentz, *New York Times* bestselling author

"Johnson spins an intriguing tale of destiny and magic."

—Robin D. Owens, RITA Award–winning author

"A must-read for those who enjoy fantasy and romance."

—The Best Reviews

"[It] has everything—love, humor, danger, excitement, trickery, hope, and even sizzling-hot . . . sex."

—Errant Dreams Reviews

"Delightful entertainment."

—Romance Junkies

FIRST SALIK WAR

THE BLOCKADE

JEAN JOHNSON

ACE
New York

ACE

Published by Berkley

An imprint of Penguin Random House LLC

375 Hudson Street, New York, New York 10014

Copyright © 2016 by G. Jean Johnson

Penguin Random House supports copyright. Copyright fuels creativity, encourages diverse voices, promotes free speech, and creates a vibrant culture. Thank you for buying an authorized edition of this book and for complying with copyright laws by not reproducing, scanning, or distributing any part of it in any form without permission. You are supporting writers and allowing Penguin Random House to continue to publish books for every reader.

ACE is a registered trademark and the A colophon is a trademark of Penguin Random House LLC.

ISBN: 9780425276945

First Edition: December 2016

Printed in the United States of America

1   3   5   7   9   10   8   6   4   2

Cover art by Gene Mollica

Cover design by Katie Anderson

Book design by Laura K. Corless

AUTHOR'S NOTE

To start, I would like to thank Penguin/Ace and my editor, Cindy, for putting up with all the delays in getting this book to you, my readers; I wish to thank my beta editors, Buzzy and Stephanie, for helping me get this book polished, and I must thank you, my readers, for your patience in waiting for this book to come out. I'm afraid I've been ill for over a year, struggling with various problems behind the scenes, so it's a relief to be on the mend and finally have it finished and readied for you to enjoy. I do hope you'll enjoy it.

That being said, welcome to Act III of the First Salik War! ·

As the previous story ended on a cliff-hanger of sorts, I will again be providing a synopsis of what happened in the last two books. If you are brand-new to the series and just wish to read the story without any spoilers . . . it might be better to start with book one, *The Terrans*, or try book two, *The V'Dan*, though you are, of course, free to skip ahead. And if you have just finished reading both, then you can skip ahead as well.

For those of you for whom it has been a while, or if you're new to the series but this is the only book in the trilogy you can get your hands on at the moment and you want to know some of what went on before . . . then by all means, read on to know what happened in the previous two volumes.

In the first book of the First Salik War, *The Terrans*, Jacaranda MacKenzie, a former Councilor for the Terran United Planets government and an ex-officer of the Space Force Special Forces, Psi Division, found herself at the center of several precognitive visions by her fellow psychics involving brand-new alien races her people had yet to meet. Recommissioned as an officer and granted the powers of an Ambassador, she was sent into space aboard one of the fledgling new other-than-light ships that were finally allowing the Terrans to explore beyond their own star system.

On one of those exploratory missions, Jackie and her crew found their small vessel captured by a much larger warship crewed by the Salik, a cruel, amphibious race that look like a cross between a frog and an octopus. Scanning the ship to try to read their minds via her xenopathic ability, Jackie discovered five Humans on board, a seeming impossibility. Furthermore, they did not speak any language she—a highly experienced government telepathic translator—knew.

Determining that the Salik were going to eat the five captives, she arranged to rescue them and bring them back to Earth. While waiting through the process of quarantine to isolate and develop vaccines and antigens for what seemed to be nearly ten thousand years of separation between the two branches of humanity, she discovered two more things about these V'Dan, as they called themselves: The first was that one of them was too arrogant and disdainful to deal well with any Terrans; Shi'ol's main problem was that the V'Dan relied upon colorful skin markings acquired during puberty to determine who in their society was an adult and who was not. This caused problems when contrasted against the fact the Terrans had left skin-based prejudices behind them a hundred years before.

The other thing she learned was that their guests' captain was not just their commanding officer but secretly the thirdborn son of the V'Dan Empress. Li'eth was also a powerful psi . . . but a very crudely, poorly, imperfectly trained one. In the process of training him, Jackie and Li'eth realized that the two of them have formed a Gestalt, a rare quantum entanglement of psychic minds. To deny the bond and to separate the pair will only create misery, and if the bond has time to set deeply enough, any enforced separation will only cause depression, despair, and the eventual death of each half of the pair.

The Terrans understand what a Gestalt is, as they have studied the rare phenomenon for nearly two hundred years. The V'Dan, however, do not; their understanding of psychic abilities lies in legends and the religion-cloaked trappings of their main faith system. Bound together but striving to slow the strengthening of that link, the two are faced with the awkwardness of their Gestalt versus his position as an Imperial Prince and her position as an official Ambassador.

Because of this new twist to the situation, the Terran United Planets Council evaluates the circumstances formally. Its members eventually vote to place their trust in Jackie to put the interests of the United Planets ahead of her own personal needs, though they still do not know how the V'Dan will react to Jackie's bond to their prince. Particularly as she will appear markless and thus juvenile to them, despite her being midthirties in age.

While all this has been happening, Terran astronomers have painstakingly located the V'Dan homeworld in the Eternal Empire and plotted a course for the Terrans' unusual and very swift form of interstellar travel, OTL (other-than-light), traveling two seconds to the light-year, if at the cost of nausea and other problems. Coupled with this OTL method is the ability to communicate nearly instantaneously between star systems—tactical advantages which none of the Alliance races, not even the Salik, possess, given their slower interstellar-travel abilities and lack of interstellar communications.

On top of that, the Terrans use common water for their engine fuel instead of dangerous, flammable, limited-in-quantity biofuels. With all of these new technological advantages, Li'eth is eager to get the Terrans into the Alliance so that they can win the war against their foe, as V'Dan precognitive prophecies have foretold. As soon as they conclude their business on Earth, the V'Dan guests and an embassy of Terran diplomats and soldiers under Jackie's leadership depart for the Eternal Empire.

The second novel, *The V'Dan*, begins with the Terrans arriving at V'Dan. Once again, everyone needs to be isolated for medical evaluation, but instead of less than a dozen people, there are now two hundred crammed into the tight confines of V'Dan quarantine. Two V'Dan specialists are added to the mix when discovering the reason for the *jungen* virus—which creates the spots and stripes on V'Dan skin—becomes imperative: Foods native to the planet V'Dan are so high in histaminic triggers, eating them can cause severe anaphylactic shock, and the normal medicines the Terrans brought are inadequate to the task of fending it off.

The Terrans must become inoculated, but Jackie—mindful that she represents billions of Terran Humans—refuses to have the version that creates the colorful markings be the one her people receive. Amusingly enough, the modern specialist in the *jungen* virus, a woman named To-mi Kuna'mi, is secretly the original source of that virus: the Immortal High One, who according to V'Dan legend ruled for five thousand years before finally stepping aside to allow Li'eth's distant ancestor, the War King Kah'el, to take over ruling their world.

Once free of quarantine, the Terrans begin setting up an embassy on V'Dan itself, as guests of the Winter Palace. Everything seems to be going well, but the pervasive problem of the Terrans' lack of *jungen* begins to be felt; not only are the V'Dan, fellow Humans, acting arrogantly and dismissively toward their potential new allies, but so are certain individuals among the other races of sentient species in the Alliance. Even the most trained of Elite Guards, assigned to assist in protecting their embassy zone, have problems now and again at keeping in their minds that these Terrans are all adults worthy of respect and not dismissible or easily overriden juveniles.

Trying to find a way around this roadblock, Jackie challenges Empress Hana'ka to go through her daily routine for one day with all traces of her own burgundy *jungen* marks hidden from her face, hands, and hair. The Empress eventually agrees, and after one full day of altered appearance, begins to understand just how widespread the cultural problem for the Terrans is. While she agreed to it and received enlightenment from it, however, her eldest daughter and heir, Imperial Princess Vi'alla, found the challenge and unmarked appearance of her mother extremely insulting, adding anger to her arrogance and sense of superiority over the markless "children" of the Terran delegation.

And to add injury to insult, the troublemaker Shi'ol has been dating the copilot of their original expedition, Brad Colvers, a self-professed psi hater. Shi'ol manages to smuggle robots into the Terran embassy with his help and sets them loose to carve up anything touched by Jackie's DNA—ostensibly the robots were meant to just destroy her wardrobe, but in actuality, she had circumvented their safety protocols so that they attacked Jackie herself, who was injured in the attack. The machines also attack Li'eth, whose bond with Jackie has been allowed to progress to enough of an intimate level that they assault him, too, for having traces of her DNA on his body.

This, coupled with the ongoing difficulties of the Terrans integrating into V'Dan society even for something as simple as buying food and clothes, causes enough concern that the Terran Council requests that Jackie deliver an ultimatum during Shi'ol's sentencing. Normally, anyone who attacks a member of the Imperial Family, even as merely a secondary target, is sentenced to death. Jackie, however, has stated her government's wishes to impose a different sentence: a telepathically laid mind-block that will prevent Shi'ol from ever seeing *jungen* again. The effect would be a subtle yet completely pervasive punishment, forcing her to see everyone—even herself—as a juvenile for the rest of her life, as a means of trying to get her to change her shallow prejudices.

But not only do the Terrans wish for this sentence to be carried out upon Jackie's hate-filled attacker, they have Jackie, as their Ambassador, deliver an ultimatum to the V'Dan: From this point forward, any V'Dan or Alliance member wishing to conduct any business with the Terrans, such as entering into treaties or cooperating militarily with them, must treat them with the respect and courtesy due to an equal, a fellow adult. Otherwise, they, too, must undergo a similar mind-block procedure.

Before the Empress can give her reply to this ultimatum . . . the Salik attack the V'Dan home planet and the current capital with such swiftness that only the Terrans' hyperrelay-communications ability is able to give them any advanced warning. While the Elite hustle the Empress out of the room and kill the global positioning satellites, which are inadvertently helping the Salik to triangulate their attacks, Jackie, her fellow telepath Clees, Li'eth, and several more V'Dan band together to attempt to use Jackie's powerful holokinetic gift to make the entire Winter City appear to shift ten kilometers westward into the sea. When the Immortal joins their melded efforts, the illusion succeeds; only a few laser shots and projectile bombs actually strike the Palace and the city in the minutes it takes for V'Dan defense systems to engage the enemy fleet thoroughly enough to turn their attention away from the planet.

Unfortunately, the damage is already done; the Empress has been badly injured during the bombing, and Vi'alla takes up the War Crown as Imperial Regent. Under the hyperrelay-connected witness of the Premiere of the Terran United Planets, Jackie offers to let the final decision on her people's ultimatum be put off until the Empress can recover, so long as the V'Dan understand that they must begin treating the Terrans as absolute equals in the interim. Vi'alla refuses, asserting she will never allow Terran telepaths to meddle with V'Dan minds . . . though she still expects to have the full cooperation of the Terrans and use of their technological advances.

Having discussed this possibility in advance, Premiere Callan gives Jackie a set of orders: They are to evacuate all personnel— a task complicated by how the Terran embassy zone was one of the areas of the Palace hit by those few bombs at the start of the attack—plus remove all non-Terran access to the hyperrelay-communication devices, and to refuse to deal further with the V'Dan. Jackie does so though she lets Li'eth know that he is welcome to join her on the last Terran ship out of the system, just as he is equally free to stay with his people . . . regardless of what that would cost both of them personally.

Ignoring Vi'alla's demands that the Terrans come back and reopen their communications devices, and ignoring the personal cost of her orders, Jackie walks out of the throne room with the assertion that the Terran embassy is now closed.

———————

For those keeping score: The Terrans are upset with the skin-based prejudice of the V'Dan. The V'Dan are desperate for Terran tech but not interested in giving the Terrans respect. The Alliance is nervous about the rising tension between the two branches of humanity. The Salik are still hungry and determined to win. Nobody knows quite at this stage how to manage any of these messes . . . so it's time now for us to sit down and finish the final act of the First Salik War.

Enjoy,
Jean

CHAPTER 1

"The Terran embassy to V'Dan is now officially *closed*!"

Ambassador MacKenzie's final words echoed down the shallow-stepped terraces of the Inner Court. Carved from golden granite and lined with padded benches and chairs designed to accommodate a range of alien and native body types, dotted with security and broadcast equipment, the mix of hard and soft surfaces did not diminish her hard-voiced claim. Silence stifled the ancient hall.

Seated on the top step of the highest dais of his mother's court, just a few *mitas* from the empty, pearlescent pink curve of the Eternal Throne, Li'eth felt that silence pressing down on him, squeezing his skin like some sort of congealing plastic film. The officers' uniforms of the Imperial Armed Forces, made from special ballistics cloth, were designed to look formal enough to appear in his mother's court while still being both comfortable and durable enough that he could fight off an enemy attack. Yet all he felt was trapped in its confines.

The uniform no longer fit him. It was still tailored perfectly to his figure, every crimson seam straight, every golden line neat . . . but the loyalty and pride with which Imperial Prince Kah'raman had originally worn it no longer fit the man whom Li'eth had become.

Li'eth still loved his home nation. He loved his people. He loved his family! Mostly . . . Most of the time.

Right now . . . he wanted to smack his eldest sister repeatedly about the head and shoulders with the hardest, heaviest cushion he could find. Or something that would solidly bruise some sense back into her without actually killing or crippling her. Except the absurd idea of smacking his sister—the Imperial Regent Princess Vi'alla V'Daania—about the head and shoulders with a pillow like some common Fifth Tier sibling did not cheer him out of his . . . grief? Regret? Ire? Despair? Desolation.

He had thought he knew Jacaranda MacKenzie, Grand High Ambassador of the Terran United Planets . . . No, he *did* know her. He had *known* that Jackie would choose to serve the needs and protect the rights of her people despite any personal inconvenience, pain, or peril. And she had chosen to do so just now. They were bound in a Gestalt, a holy pairing, his and her psychically gifted minds entangled on a quantum level—the will of the Saints, pure random chance, or fate, he did not know. They were bound, and he could feel her subthoughts of pain and determination and anger just beyond his innermost walls.

She lived within his outermost mental shields, the very same shields she had taught him how to construct, support, and stabilize in ways strong enough to keep her *out* of his head even though he didn't want to do that. He did it right now, though. Jackie was strong enough to do what was right for others even if not best for herself. Li'eth—Imperial Prince Kah'raman, who had been raised from birth to heed his duty to the Eternal Throne—respected and honored that level of dedication.

Ambassador MacKenzie had chosen to refuse to allow his people to continue to insult hers over and over and over again, all because of a simple yet pervasive cultural difference that was literally just skin-deep. Because of those differences, their embassy had been closed. His people had just lost their access to the only form of breathtakingly swift interstellar communication the entire Alliance knew, and he was going to lose personally one way or another *because* the embassy was closed, his Gestalt partner was headed home . . . and either he would have to stay here and suffer without her or abandon his people and go with her into virtual exile.

He didn't know what to do. Which path to choose. And on top of it all, Li'eth didn't know how badly his mother had been injured. He did not know if his mother would live or die.

"An Imperial Prince does not sit on the steps of the Inner Court like a common Fifth Tier in a marketplace."

He twisted, looking up at his sister. Vi'alla clenched her jaw as she stared down at him, her body tight with returning anger. The same anger that had caused her to refuse to even consider the Terrans' demands that they either be treated with respect or that those who disrespected them be punished so that they could no longer see the cause of that disrespect, via something called a mind-block. Her aura had broken into confusion when their Ambassador had closed the embassy, and panic when she discovered that Jackie had ordered the nearest Terran hyperrelay unit destroyed. But now, that look on her face was the look of someone furious, hurt, and looking for a target.

She wanted one? He would give her one. Herself. Li'eth pinned his sister with a hard look. "An Imperial Regent does not treat her desperately needed allies like *u'v'shakk*."

Vi'alla stiffened, her gray eyes widening. "You dare talk to *me* that way?"

"You dared talk to *them* that way. Imperial Regent," Li'eth stated formally, pushing to his feet to face down his eldest sister. "Our people *need* what the Terrans can provide."

"Then they need to provide it!" Vi'alla snapped, frowning at him. "Instead of yanking it away like a child!"

"You don't even see it, do you?" Li'eth asked softly, more to himself than to her. *She* was the one trying to yank it away like a child. A child being deprived of a toy.

"See *what*?" his sister snapped.

Li'eth wracked his brain for a parable that could get her to understand. ". . . Do you remember the story of Saint Ba'nai?"

"A *story*?" she scorned.

"For once in your mind, will you *clear* it?" Li'eth demanded, gesturing at his head. "A *good* Empress listens to the counsel of her people! The story of Saint Ba'nai is about how she tried to get the people of a village she was visiting to listen to her warnings that they were going to be caught in a great fire because of a terrible drought that had plagued the land that year. They were stubborn and set in their ways, proud of their skill in cutting wood, trimming and shaping it, and sending it downriver. The river kept getting lower and lower until they could no longer pole their barges downstream to the cities that needed it, but the villagers kept cutti—"

"—The villagers kept cutting wood until a stray spark set fire to the forest, and only a third of the people managed to escape by heeding Ba'nai's warnings to go deep into the abandoned mines in the mountain while the firestorm raged through, *yes, yes*, I *know* the legend!" Vi'alla overrode him. "I've studied the Book of Saints far more often than you!"

"Did Nanny Ai-sha ever tell you *how* she got a third of the village to listen to her?" Li'eth asked her. "Because Nanny El'cor told *me* how she did it when I asked him." He waited to see if she would dismiss him and his story. When his sister gave him an impatient but silent listening look, Li'eth continued. "El'cor taught me that Ba'nai was of the Fifth Tier, the daughter of a herdsman. A pig herder. She had no training in eloquence, no ability to make fancy speeches, and no real grasp of etiquette, but she was smart, and she occasionally had dreams of the future, what the Terrans call precognition. Those dreams led her to that village.

"That village was filled with skilled laborers, lumberjacks and carpenters, Fourth and Third Tier, higher socially than her place in the Fifth. She was so worried about the firestorms in her dreams, she spoke bluntly, told everyone they had to stop working the lumber, stop leaving sawdust everywhere, stop piling up the bark against their wooden houses and the uncut trees. She demanded that they stop their livelihood, demanded that they leave the area to save their lives. She thought she was doing the right thing, trying to save lives, but *how* she went about it was wrong.

"El'cor taught me that because she was rude, because she did not *show* her respect, Ba'nai could not sway the hearts of the people—she tried urgency, she tried to describe the violence and horror of her visions, but they saw only someone being hysterical over nothing. Finally, one of the village elders spoke to her and reminded her that her words were like too much spice and soured wine in a dish. If she tried speaking sweetly, with respect, speaking of positive things—of gains instead of losses—the people would be more likely to listen to her. And so she went back to the people, and spoke gently, apologizing for her coarse ways, letting them know she understood how valuable their work was, how important their continued livelihoods.

"Saint Ba'nai pointed out how dry everything was, how many piles of dried limbs and sawdust there were, the layers of bark that had been stacked to provide them with fuel for winter fires, the cane poles stacked in bundles and set aside to dry out so they could be light enough to ship downriver when the water rose again and turned into pulp for paper . . . and how much hotter the days were growing. She asked them where they thought would be the safest place in the region to outwait a massive firestorm . . . and some finally listened. Some of the villagers, swayed by her politeness, her logic, told her that there was that abandoned mine in the river ravine.

"She asked them if they would be willing to help her store water and a bit of food deep in those caves, some old rags and other supplies. Some of them actually helped her . . . and when the terrible fire started, she was able to get those people deep into those caves, cover their faces with wet cloths, and stay there while the world far above burned so hot and hard, they could not go near the entrance for three full days. Those whom she had turned into her friends with kind words were willing to cooperate, willing to go with her, and willing to understand that she meant the best for them. They grieved for those who felt too badly disrespected and who had perished, but rejoiced that she had managed to save at least *some* of their lives."

Vi'alla eyed him, her mouth tight, then lifted her chin toward the hall the Ambassador had taken. "Then *she* should have spoken sweetly to *me* instead of with soured wine and too much spice!"

Li'eth felt his shoulders start to slump. She hadn't seen the analogy correctly. "Wrong person, Vi'alla. Ba'nai needed to be kind and respectful to those who had what she wanted because she needed their cooperation. She was willing to come help save them, and she was willing to warn them of all the dangers, and she was willing to help them make a plan to survive . . . but she needed *their* cooperation. *Their* knowledge of the terrain. *Their* help in stockpiling resources.

"*We* need the *Terrans'* technology. Yet all we have done as a nation is be rude to them, like how Ba'nai treated those Third and Fourth Tiers like Fifth Tiers—we have been treating Terran *First* Tiers like Fifth Tiers," he emphasized, pointing at that hallway where Jackie had vanished. "*All* non-V'Dan are to be treated like respected members of the Third Tier, as they are all *experts* in the knowledge of their ways and their people. That is the custom and that is the law. More than that, their leaders are to be treated as equals of the First *and Imperial* Tiers. Yet *we*—the V'Dan Empire—consistently have treated them like *less* than Fifth Tiers.

"The irony in this, Sister, is that without them, *we* are the villagers being burned alive by the Salik and their war," he told her, sweeping his hand out, then upward. "The whole Empire is at stake! You don't get people willing to listen to your needs by being disrespectful to them. You don't encourage people to share what they have by demanding and grabbing and *insulting* their hospitality and their generosity. You don't *close your ears* to their legitimate complaints about being disrespected, insulted, and treated as infants instead of as adult allies, then *expect* them to still like you enough to *want* to stay and help you.

"And you, Imperial *Regent*," he emphasized, pointing at her, "have forgotten that it *is* my job as a member of the Imperial Tier to warn you when *you* are on a path that will destroy the Empire. Which is more important to you, Regent? Your personal pride, refusing to give the Terrans any respect because you believe they are not worthy of it? Or the survival of the Empire, which demands you give it? *Which* is more important, Vi'alla? I demand that you answer that."

"You *dare* make demands of me?" Vi'alla demanded through clenched teeth, her hands tightening into fists at her sides.

"I am obliged to point out that your *pride* is busy making *enemies* of the *allies we need*," he reminded her fiercely. "You were free to be angry at them as a mere princess, yes, but you are now the Regent, and the needs of your people *must* come before everything else! *Including* your own feelings and opinions!"

"If they weren't so stubborn—" she growled, fists rising.

"That's the *jumax'a* flower calling the sky blue!" he retorted, slashing his hands upward. "You have exactly two ways to get your hands on Terran technology, Vi'alla: You can *attempt* to steal it from them, turning them into our enemies . . . and they have *tens of thousands* of highly trained holy ones they can unleash upon us, never mind their ship hulls that cannot be deeply damaged by our energy weapons and that can travel from system to system in mere moments.

"*Or*, you can swallow your pride, seek them out instead of demand they come to you, *apologize sincerely*, and try to make amends, to make *friends* of them." He stared at her, hoping she would understand. "Because the third thing you can do is to continue to *abandon* your duty to your people, and *prove* yourself unfit for the throne. Which is it, Vi'alla? *Think carefully.*"

She glared back at him in anger, not saying a word. Li'eth knew he had backed his sister into a corner, though. Stepping away from her, he bowed, then moved around her to exit through the side door on the dais level.

"While you're busy thinking carefully, I am going to go check on Mother and the rest of our family. With luck, she will pull through, and you won't have to choose between debasing yourself to do the right thing or condemning the Empire to die out of sheer pride. At the hands of one enemy *or* another."

It took her a few moments to find her voice. Just before he reached the side exit on the uppermost dais, she asked, "You honestly think the Terrans can take on the might of the *Empire*? They don't even have any colonies outside their own star system! They don't have any big ships!"

Swinging around to face her, Li'eth pointed at his sister. "Your arrogance and your pride are blinding you to reality, Regent. If you do not reconsider your actions, your words, your beliefs, and your *responses* to all these events, then I *will* have to make a formal recommendation to the Imperial Cabinet that you be *removed* as Regent.

"The War Crown is best worn by the most *competent* member of the Imperial Blood," he reminded her, reciting a law that had stood strong for roughly four thousand years. "*Not* necessarily the eldest-born . . . and your actions today are *not* sufficiently competent!"

It was political suicide to say such things, but Li'eth was too angry. Turning back toward the door, he headed for the hospital wing. He wanted to reach out to Jackie, to find out how she was doing, to learn who, if any, of her staff had been harmed in the attack . . . but her mental shields were tightly sealed at the moment. He couldn't bring himself to knock on that metaphysical wall, not when he didn't know what he could do to help the situation.

Two minutes later, walking down corridors eerily empty, thanks to the need for Palace personnel to be elsewhere at the moment, he finally heard sounds of someone else approaching. A familiar, brown-braided head streaked with hot pink came into view. V'kol looked up from the tablet in his hand, relief dawning in his eyes when he recognized the prince. "Finally. Did you know my clearance to know your whereabouts as your military attaché *doesn't* cover knowing when we're under attack? . . . Who *invents* these rules? I'm your attaché! I *need* to know."

Li'eth rubbed at the bridge of his nose. "I'll see what I can do. I've been in the Inner Court all this time. What news do you have of everything?"

"The Palace is still in lockdown, but the Admirals have confirmed that the Salik Fleet appears to have retreated from the system. They're at a bit of a loss to report more than that, though, because of the broadcasts the Terrans shared, before . . . ending transmission." V'kol gave him a grim, worried look. He glanced around, then moved in close, and whispered, ". . . Is your sister still *sane*? Doing what she did to them?"

"I don't know," Li'eth confessed out loud. "I honestly do not know. I am going to have to log a recommendation to the Imperial Cabinet that she be removed as Regent. Her decisions so far have *not* been good for the Empire."

"Are *you* crazy?" V'kol hissed under his breath, still keeping his voice low while turning to follow his friend and prince. "Li'eth, I am certain that *everything* that takes place in these halls is being recorded, and saying *that* is political suicide."

Their people had a saying: Stealing a spoonful, stealing a barrel. If one was going to be caught for theft—under the old harsh penalties of his foremost ancestor—then one might as well go for a big score rather than just a tiny fraction of it. "I *am* aware everything is being recorded in these halls. Including my sister's insistence upon alienating and chasing away the allies we need out of simple pride and arrogance. Her choices, made rashly out of anger and some aggrandized sense of self-importance, have cost us an *important* alliance.

"The rank of Imperial Regent is temporary. And it rests upon the requirement that the Regent consider and undertake whatever is *best* for the Empire during the period of the Regency. Insulting our allies and disrespecting them to the point that they would rather leave than stay and help us survive is *not* good for the Empire at this point in time, let alone what is best," Li'eth told his fellow officer, cutting his hand through the air. His decision made, his course laid, he added, "I will ensure that these words *are* recorded."

V'kol eyed his friend but said nothing for several seconds. Li'eth started to turn to the left at the next junction, heading toward the bank of lifts that would take him where he wanted to go. The leftenant superior caught his elbow. "Not that way, Your Highness. The hall's a wreck, that way. That's where they pulled Her Eternity out of the rubble. We'll have to take one of the other lift clusters, and that means going around the other way. I'd say take a stairwell to cut down on the distance detoured, but it's seventeen floors down to the tram, then another six back up to get to the Palace infirmary."

Nodding, Li'eth turned to the right. Together, both men walked in grim silence. Twice, V'kol drew in a breath to speak, then fell quiet again. A third time, he merely shook his head, dismissing his thoughts. Thanks to the teachings of Jackie and Master Sonam, Li'eth blissfully didn't hear any of it. Formerly fragile and easily torn in moments of agitation before encountering the Terrans and their training methods, now his mental walls stood strong and resistant to fluctuating emotions and energy levels. He was *tired* from his efforts to help protect the Palace and city, but he didn't have to endure stray thoughts from anyone anymore.

His own thoughts and memories were unpleasant enough as it was.

The next bank of lifts lay down a shallow ramp, around a corner, and at the far end of a long hallway. Two Imperial Elite Guards approached from a side hall just when they neared those lifts. Both gold-and-scarlet-clad men bore grim expressions, their attention focused on the prince. When he squinted a little, checking their auras, they swirled with aggressive reds and determined browns.

Wary, Li'eth slowed. ". . . Is everything alright?"

"Imperial Prince Kah'raman. By order of the Imperial Regent, you are to report immediately to the *Dusk Army* for reassignment back into the Fleet," the right-hand Elite told him.

Li'eth narrowed his eyes. "My assignment is liaison to the Terrans. While the Terrans are still here, I am still their liaison."

"Their embassy is closed," the Elite on the left stated dismissively. "That means your position as liaison has ended. We are to escort you straight to East Hangar Bay 2, where you will be flown to your next duty post."

This was not right. Something was very much not right. "I choose to exercise my right as Imper—"

"—Sorry," the Elite on the left apologized blandly, drawing a small handheld device from his thigh pocket.

Li'eth recognized it instantly, the V'Dan version of a Salik stunner pistol. He had an instant in which to react, and flung out a telekinetic wall, shoving everyone back. Unfortunately, the Elite's aim was true . . . and a holy force that could move physical objects did absolutely nothing to stop an energy-based weapon . . . just as Master Sonam had once warned him, during his lessons on what telekinesis could and could not do. Static snapped over his senses, dropping him out of consciousness.

AUGUST 11, 2287 C.E.
AVRA 4, 9508 V.D.S.

Jackie woke to a throbbing, splitting headache. For a long moment, all she could do was lie there in agony, breathing through her nostrils in an attempt to control the pain. Her breath finally escaped on a faint groan. Noise nearby made her pry her eyes open in time to see Maria reaching for her forehead. Beyond the dark-haired woman, she could see nothing but plain beige walls and the recessed, diffused lighting strips that served the local illumination needs.

Blinking a little, Jackie managed to make a grunt of inquiry.

"Take it easy, *amiga*," the doctor told her. She pressed her left wrist to Jackie's forehead, taking her temperature in the most basic of ways, wrist to brow. "Still no fever . . . How do you feel?"

"Like my head was trampled by an elephant cavorting in a field," Jackie muttered. Dizzy, disoriented, and . . . it felt like the whole room had slanted to the left somehow. "What happened?"

"You dropped like a tree felled by a lumberjack in the Guard Hall halfway past the Imperial Wing. Clees tried to rouse you, and when he couldn't even reach your mind, he ran for the Elite, then for the Marines and me. The Elite in turn were deeply alarmed since they couldn't find a cause. They rushed you to us, since we're closer than their infirmary, and we know more about psychic ailments, but . . . *my* beautiful infirmary was buried under the rubble of three higher floors," Maria told her. "Lieutenant Buraq has a broken leg, Doctor Du has a concussion, and Doctor Kuna'mi . . . Doctor Kuna'mi is dead. I'm sorry."

Jackie blinked at that. She knew that Maria, their chief doctor, knew that the V'Dan woman known as Doctor To-mi Kuna'mi was considered the foremost authority on the *jungen* virus in the entire V'Dan Empire. That was the virus that had altered V'Dan DNA so that their people could survive the high histaminic triggers found in the local plant life on this planet. That virus had given the V'Dan people their distinctive stripes and spots. The doctor was the foremost authority on it, however, because she *was* the Immortal, the being who had originally created it thousands of years ago.

She almost said aloud, *But To-mi is the Immortal; she cannot be dead. She was still* with *us when we deflected the missiles* . . . Maria continued before Jackie could find the strength to speak, however.

"She came by about a quarter hour before Clees did, stating she was there to help dig out survivors, and not two minutes later, a section of ceiling and a pillar collapsed on her. A couple of Elites tugged her out and said she wasn't revivable. Apparently, her chest was crushed, so they carried her off in a V'Dan body bag. I don't know where they put her. Ours have been laid out in the Guard Hall second floor." At an inquiring grunt from Jackie, Maria nodded. "Kuna'mi wasn't the only death, V'Dan or otherwise. I don't think anyone had gotten around to discussing Terran funeral practices, but they're presuming we'll want to do something specifically Terran with them."

"How many of ours?" she asked, head still spinning, making it hard to focus on thinking. Hard to focus on looking at anything around her. Maria's face, she could see, and the ceiling, a bit of the walls, but it was too much effort to move, just yet.

"Seven," Maria stated, and named them: two nurses, two Marines, and three staff members, all Terrans, and ending with, ". . . including Advisor Amatrine, I'm sorry to say. At least it was quick, for her."

Wincing, Jackie rubbed at her forehead. Amatrine Castellas. The most important of the deceased Terrans, a former lawyer and judge, a former regional representative, and the official Advisor appointed to the embassy staff. Amatrine's job involved intercepting would-be lobbyists so that they could not attempt to bribe either Jackie or her Assistant Ambassador, Rosa. Jackie closed her eyes in silent grief.

She had liked Amatrine, quiet, no-nonsense, able to cut through to the heart of a proposal and impervious to bribes. Amatrine would *accept* them—that was her job, after all, with all bribes carefully logged and diverted into various funds and assets reserves—but she hadn't been *swayed* by them. Instead, the other woman had learned the fine art of dangling hope in her would-be lobbyists' hearts with one hand, while using the other hand to delve into the true motivations behind any such offers, sending her agents to delve deeply into the actual consequences of any attempted piece of legislation. Lobbying for a particular action by the Council *could* actually be a good thing . . . though if it came with a bribe or "incentive to examine our request," then that request had to be examined quite closely.

Ironically, these days, groups often tried to bribe Advisors so that their proposals *would* be more deeply investigated and hopefully proved to be sound, safe, and advantageous for all. Amatrine had treated all cases with equanimity and careful inspection. In fact, Rosa had complained good-naturedly that the V'Dan had tried filing complaints about the woman's ". . . obstructing true acts of commerce, which means Amatrine is doing her usual exemplary job of imitating an impassable castle wall."

She would be missed. She would also, Jackie acknowledged, have to be carefully replaced. Advisors were one of the few groups of nonpsis who had to undergo telepathic ethics evaluations twice yearly. Anyone who came to V'Dan would have to be able to resist a barrage of brand-new temptations, many of which would greatly improve Terran life. But the motives for the companies making those offers still had to be carefully scrutinized to make sure they weren't trying to cheat or harm the Terrans in some way.

The others would be missed as well. Jackie had taken the time to get to know each and every person in her embassy, both those on the trip to V'Dan and the personnel who had arrived since. But—callous as it might seem—most staff positions and guard positions and nursing positions could be replaced by someone new. Replacing an Advisor who was trustworthy was more difficult.

Maria stayed silent a long while, head bowed in respect for the dead. Two of them had worked closely with her, the nurses. She had her own pain to manage. Finally, she drew in a breath, and continued, ". . . We had thirteen more injured alongside Buraq and Du, stragglers and a handful of Marines who weren't assigned to go to the bunkers. Fourteen, including you, though technically you're not actually injured.

"We've been able to patch up everyone, but it's all *just* patchwork medicine aside from getting Jasmine's leg set by the V'Dan. They've had around fifty injured, including their Empress, and their infirmary is overloaded. Rumors of five dead, too . . . but not including Her Eternity. Not yet. Nobody's called to say her situation has stabilized, either, so we're still in the dark on how bad it actually is."

"I knew it would be bad," Jackie murmured. "I doubt they'd let Vi'alla make herself Regent over a few cuts and bruises, or even just a few broken bones . . ."

A corner of her brain remained locked on the other information. *To-mi's body was carried off by Elites . . . perhaps by allies? Who reported she died, a Terran or a V'Dan? Was she actually injured, and has she repaired herself somehow? How* does *immortality work, anyway? The odds of a fatal accident or life-threatening injury go up as time goes on, of even just a maiming injury, yet she appeared healthy and well. So she* had *to have suffered some sort of catastrophic injury several times over long before now if she's really lived over ten thousand years . . .*

Maria distracted her from her thoughts. "So that's the list of injured and dead. The only one we weren't sure about, injury-wise, was you. Thankfully, when the news came in about what happened to Prince Li'eth, I realized what *your* problem was."

"Li'eth? What happened to him?" Jackie asked. She tried to sit up. Maria pushed her back down with her left hand, but Jackie finally managed to get her eyes focused well enough to see that the doctor's right arm was in a sling. "And what happened to *you*?"

"I'm *not* one of the fifteen injured by the bombing. I strained a muscle trying to lift patients for evacuation. Du yelled at me a few times when she caught me using my arm without a sling and dragged me to the healing station to personally put one on me," she added, smiling briefly, wryly. "Told me I had to wear it for two days straight, and bossed more Elites into taking my place in shifting around the rubble. They took *her* orders seriously because of her *vitiligo* problem, of course."

Jackie knew the doctor meant the pale patches where the pathologist had lost the natural tan pigmentation in her skin. It wasn't anything like actual V'Dan *jungen* marks, but it was far closer to those marks than the uniform skin tones of the rest of the Terran embassy staff. "So what happened to Li'eth? What *is* my problem? And where are we, exactly?"

The room they were in was sort of bland, her bed a cot, with portable V'Dan diagnostic machines standing near the head of it. No windows, and signs of a bathroom through an open door, but not the sort of disabled-accessible-sized bathroom one normally saw in any sort of medical facility. Definitely not a typical infirmary room for this world. Maria looked around at the cream-hued walls, the polished-stone floor, the plain furnishings, and shrugged.

"We're in an apartment of sorts in an auxiliary section of the Guard Hall just north of the embassy wing. Apparently they have several of these rooms they can convert into emergency quarters; they've handed several of them over to our injured for recuperation. As for what's wrong with you . . . I'd already suspected something along these lines, but Leftenant Superior Kos'q got word to us, confirming that some of the Elite had stunned His Highness off to the north of the central courtyards.

"You dropped in the Guard Halls halfway here from the Inner Court. From what Clees said of the timing of things, and what V'kol said, you apparently dropped at the same moment Li'eth went unconscious, just like you both had dropped unconscious back in the Sol System. Only this time, they used that stunner weapon they got from the enemy instead of a tranquilizer dart. V'kol was apparently smart enough to quickly distance himself from their capture of the prince, so when he didn't try to interfere, and let them take the prince without any contestation, they left him alone. That left him free to come to us while they carted off His Highness."

"They . . . *what*?" Jackie asked. Her skull still throbbed with a dull, spinning ache, making it hard to render Maria's words into some sort of more logical sense. "Why would they do *that*? They're Elites; they're sworn to *protect* the Imperial Tier, not attack them!"

"V'kol said it was on his sister's orders. The new Imperial Regent," Maria explained. "She had him *shanghaied* off-planet. He's reported to us a couple times since, first to warn us of the prince's departure and its circumstances, then it took the pink-striped *hombre* a good six hours to find out what happened to him after that. By then, of course, it was too late.

"Li'eth's been hauled off on a warship headed outsystem," she continued, making Jackie wince. "It's supposed to go contact one of the nearest colonyworlds, where they should have enough of a fleet to spare a few ships for the home system in case the Salik come back, but I don't know if that particular ship will be coming back with him. Or rather, V'kol didn't know and couldn't find out at his clearance level.

"Since *we* aren't sharing our hypercommunications relays anymore, nobody could confirm it with the system in question," Maria added dryly. At Jackie's wince, she raised her good hand quickly. "I don't blame you, or Premiere Callan. Nobody does; we've all seen the recording, and we've all felt the lash of being insulted for the color of our hides. It's also caused an uproar throughout the Winter Palace. Everyone's taking sides for or against the Imperial Regent—politely, civilly, but icily taking sides.

"*We* cannot do anything about that," the doctor reminded Jackie. "It's a V'Dan internal affair, so for the time being, we have to treat it like the common cold and let it run its course. It's politics, and there's nothing I personally can do. I *can* do something about you, however, besides watch you while I'm on the invalid list."

"You can? Like what? If he's gone . . ." Jackie muttered, trying to grasp the idea of Li'eth's being hours and hours away at light-year-traversing speeds.

"Yes, I can. You're going to suffer separation sickness sooner or later, if not already. You're already suffering secondhand from stunner technology. So . . . since I cannot write down any notes without Jai Du yelling at me," Maria stated, picking up a tablet, "I need you to describe for the microphone on this thing exactly how you are feeling right now."

Jackie slumped into the bedding, rolling her eyes. The room still threatened to sway around her, it still felt canted bizarrely to her left however she moved, she felt like she had a gaping hole in her ribs metaphysically, and Doctor de la Santoya wanted to take notes on how she felt? ". . . Really? *That* is your priority, right now?"

"I need to record the progression of your symptoms so that we have a timeline for how badly you're doing and how urgent it is to try to get you and your Gestalt partner reunited," Maria countered. She braced the tablet, thumped it a few times, then held it up. "Start talking, *amiga*."

"Ah. Well . . . like I said, I feel like an elephant trampled on my head. Dizzy, nauseated, and like my skull has been squeezed repeatedly in a vise. My sense of balance is compromised; I feel like the whole room is canted a full fifteen degrees to my left. And I have a burning hole in my mental psyche, on my left side."

"Any panic? Scale of zero to ten, with zero being non-existent?"

"Probably about a four. I'm not happy to hear *any* of this," Jackie told her friend and physician. "But . . . it's like my brain is numb where Li'eth is concerned. I . . . I can't sense his thoughts, so either he's still unconscious, or too far away, or I'm too tired still to try. I'm still trying to process the *rest* of this situation, too. It's a lot to take in, right now. I'm not feeling emotionally well, on top of physically and psychically."

"I don't blame you. Let's move on to the other emotions, such as any anxiety, dread, paranoia . . . ?"

They went through the list of possible symptoms. Jackie endured it with as much patience as she could muster. What she wanted to do was try to reach out to Li'eth, but her head still hurt, and her reserves of mental energy were still low, making it difficult to focus and concentrate. She also suspected that, like the first time he had been knocked unconscious, she had woken up before him since she wasn't the one actually knocked out. Either way . . . it took an hour and a meal before her doctor stopped interrogating her.

Finally, Maria sighed and shifted the dishes and the table they rested upon out of the way, using her good arm and the edge of her foot. "I know you're being very patient, Jackie. I can also tell by the way you're not wincing and frowning anymore that you feel better. When I went to get the food, I asked the others to try to find the KI machine and a generator for it. I want to hook you up to it before you try to reach for Li'eth."

"You want to record the effects of attempting the longest-distance telepathic comm call, I know." Jackie sighed. "I can't blame you for your scientific curiosity."

"That, yes, but we also do not know if this faster-than-light method of travel the V'Dan use blocks or allows telepathic communication. We've already established that you cannot use telepathy in the middle of a hyperspace tunnel," she reminded her patient. "But we don't know how *far* you can reach for a Gestalt partner. He may be out of range."

"The hyperspace thing is more from sheer discomfort than anything else; it's hard to be coherent enough to speak normally when you're being shaken hard, or the metabolic equivalent of it," Jackie said. "I can also wait a little while before contacting him . . . but you said I've been unconscious for a day. I *feel* like it. I've been stewing in my own sweat since the mass Gestalt to shift the city ten klicks west—I didn't notice it at the time, but I can smell it now. Any hope for a bath and a change of clothes?" she inquired hopefully, wrinkling her nose.

"Bath, no. Shower, yes. Change of clothes . . . maybe. Your quarters didn't take much damage, but the easiest path to them did," the doctor told her. "Admiral Nayak's quarters were completely obliterated, and he's still wearing yesterday's uniform. He's also been busy overseeing the logistics of pulling everyone out of here. A pity it was his quarters that took the greatest hit, and partly yours, but not that traitor's rooms."

"Colvers has had his punishment, and he's been shipped home to serve his time being more useful to society," Jackie reminded Maria. "Leave him be and let go of your anger. Though I'd love to know what happened to Shi'ol."

The older woman muttered a few uncomplimentary phrases in Brazilian about the countess—ex-countess—before switching back to V'Dan to add, ". . . but she's survived and is in some holding cell somewhere, awaiting a final decision on her verdict. I can only imagine the Imperial Regent has thankfully forgotten about her, or she'd probably have been executed by now, completely ignoring our Terran wishes on the matter."

"I hope the Empress pulls through . . . That reminds me," Jackie said, distracted. "I thought Spanish was your native tongue, not Brazilian?"

"Eh, my aunt and uncle had custody of me every summer," Maria explained, flicking her hand dismissively. "They're retired now, but they used to run a combination of archaeological dig sites and botanical survey camps on the eastern slopes of the Andes. Primarily in Bolivia, Brazil, and a few other places. Old Incan civilization stuff, and the preservation of rare pockets of plant life, everything from exotic tilandsia air plants to wild potato species. I learned Brazilian at my uncle's side right alongside how to wield all sorts of portable scanning and sampling equipment, along with how to spell words like *polylepsis* and *stomata* at my aunt's."

"Let me see if I can get you a change of clothes, then we can see how steady you are on your feet and see about getting you that shower," Maria added, rising from the chair she had pulled near the bed. "I'll get someone to pick up the tray, too—oh, Admiral Nayak's orders, you are *not* to allow the Elite into your quarters without Terran military supervision. After V'kol told us what the Regent did to her own brother, we're not taking chances that she'll refrain from any hostage-taking. We have no choice but to take the Elite hospitality because of the wreck of the embassy zone, but . . . well, even your clothes will be Terran, if not necessarily *yours*, to make sure they're not slipping anything into your presence that could give you an unhappy day."

Jackie twisted her lips in an approximation of a smile. "I could always steal another curtain for an approximation of another *sari*. I'm certain they wouldn't have put any contact poison on those."

"Even I know it was that K'Katta Commander-of-Hundreds who stole that curtain, not you," Maria quipped. "But let's not get them into deeper trouble by asking for their help again, just yet."

"Aren't I the one who is supposed to set that sort of policy?" Jackie mock-demanded. "The embassy may be closed, but I am still the Ambassador."

Maria smirked. "*You* are currently my patient. That means the doctor's orders get to rule, today."

That made Jackie laugh. More of a chuckle, really, but the absurdity of it did lighten what was otherwise a very serious situation. "Enjoy it while it lasts, because it won't."

"I know. I'll be back in a little bit. Relax and rest, that's an order." Maria palmed open the door and stepped out of sight. The panel slid shut behind her, leaving Jackie alone in the windowless, modestly lit room.

Sighing, she leaned back against the inflatable wedge tucked behind her pillow, brought in to help her sit up for supper. Everything still tried to slant to her side, balance-wise, and her head still spun a little, but she felt better. Physically. Not emotionally or mentally. *Imperial Princess Regent Vi'alla stunned her own brother and shanghaied him out of the system. Why? Why would she do that?*

. . . I need answers. I think I need to speak with V'kol.

She didn't know if he would have all the answers she

needed, but Jackie did know he was Li'eth's friend and confidant. The problem was, given how unstable Vi'alla's choices were, and the closure of the embassy, she couldn't *summon* V'kol to her. But she *could* reach out to him . . . if he was still within the Winter Palace grounds. Maybe. Closing her eyes, she tested her mind. It felt a little sluggish still, but at least most of the ache was gone, and a trickle of energy had returned.

Breathing deep, centering herself, she gave her mental presence a few moments to stabilize, then carefully formed an image of V'kol and his mind. Then, delicately, she sent out tendrils in a rough sphere, seeking for anything similar to his particular methods and patterns of thinking. It wasn't as if she'd had a choice in learning the feel of his mind; Jackie had spent weeks in close proximity with Li'eth, V'kol, Dai'a, and the rest. Like living in an apartment with thin walls that let through medium or louder voices, she had been able to hear the strongest thoughts of the others beyond the boundaries of her shields.

Most of the time, she had ignored it, but she had cataloged the way each person thought. Each mind she brushed against now was quickly discarded based on its surface thoughts. This was purely passive surface scanning, the sort of thoughts that came even as a person spoke aloud. Most of it concerned the attack, the Empress' health—stable, but unconscious, which was worrisome—and the gossip surrounding the news that the Terrans were no longer willing to be their helpful allies.

Since she didn't know how the room she was in was positioned in the maze of the Guard Halls wending their way through the Winter Palace grounds, she kept stretching outward, first this way, then that way, trying to orient herself. She felt the trembling, cold-slime feeling of a recent death in the aether and shied sideways. It always took around three days for the energies to vanish, and according to Maria, it had only been a day.

It was hard to describe the phenomenon since its perception varied from person to person. For Jackie, it felt slick and hard to grasp. At the same time, it shone like a bright, sourceless thing struggling and shimmering, quivering, then fading into dullness. Not darkness, but dullness, before it dissipated.

There were several such spots, actually. Jackie felt fairly

certain the direction of those feelings—to her right and toward her feet as she lay on the bed—meant the Terran embassy. She pulled that tendril sideways even more, wanting to avoid the embassy zone because Leftenant Kos'q wouldn't be there . . . only to catch a glimpse of him uppermost in someone's mind.

Admiral Nayak's mind, to be precise. In fact, the thoughts of Leftenant Superior V'kol Kos'q were so strong, Jackie searched around the man for V'kol's mind. There were a couple others thinking of him, but not himself within Nayak's environs . . . and that meant either a discussion, or a comm call. She could not go out of body like Clees could, but she *could* visualize a location with a bit of holokinesis. And because she did not want to frighten her fellow Terrans, Jackie carefully shaped a three-dimensional version of the Psi League's Radiant Eye, a line drawing of an ellipsoid eye shape, with a circle forming the iris inside, all of it divided by eight lines radiating from the pupil at the very center.

Gasps echoed in the thoughts of those around her projection. She left the thick, metallic black symbol hovering for a few moments, then swirled it into an image of herself in one of her favorite dresses, black with brightly hued flowers along the hemlines of the skirt and the fluted sleeves. Her illusion-self spoke. *"I need to get in touch with V'kol Kos'q."*

Admiral Nayak blinked, then pointed in front of him, making her aware of the commscreen. On the screen, she could see V'kol though she could not sense his mental presence. Jackie had zero electrokinetic ability. She knew a few telepaths who did have that gift, and who could "reach through" a commlink to connect with the mind of the person on the other end. She, however, could not. Thankfully, she did have holokinesis and its attached sonokinesis.

"Can I help you, Grand High Ambassador?" V'kol asked politely through the screen.

She thought about asking him where he was in Terranglo . . . but too many people here on V'Dan knew it by now. *"Do you remember where we played* quon-set*?"*

"Ahhh . . . yes?" V'kol offered, raising his eyebrows in polite inquiry. Or rather, the dark blurs of his brows since her clairvoyant abilities weren't her best by a stretch.

"You were quite good. I would like to play the Terran ver-

sion with you someday soon. Before we leave. Will you play with me?" she asked, and hoped he got the message.

Details were difficult to image with her clairvoyancy. Had she chosen holokinesis as a career path—stage magic or acting were the usual choices—she could have developed her skills to a much finer level of awareness and accuracy. But while this wasn't her best skill, she was fairly sure she saw his eyes narrow slightly, then widen, before he bowed his head in acquiescence. "I would be honored to play one final game of *quon-set* with you, Grand High Ambassador. I am sorry His Imperial Highness is not available to join us. Have you heard . . . ?"

"Yes. It does not change what we must do. We must move swiftly to finish what we started."

"Of course. I wish all of you the best of luck—if you'll excuse me, I need to attend to a few of my lingering duties," V'kol added, bowing on the other end of the link. "The Grand Generals have not yet reassigned me, but then we are still sorting out Terran versus V'Dan military needs in the aftermath of the attack. I am still useful as a liaison for that. I trust you will let me know, Grand High Ambassador, when you are free to play the game?"

"Of course. I would prefer today, if you are free in a little bit." She let her image fade before Admiral Nayak could question her. *He* knew where to find her, or at least how. Nayak could do so without raising any suspicions. Jackie needed to know where to find V'kol and contact him without anyone eavesdropping on them. Since she could guess which room Admiral Nayak was in, all she needed to do was reorient herself on that section of the Palace, figure out where the North Hangar Bay was located, and head down to level 5 and 6.

If V'kol *had* figured out what she was trying to say, he'd make his way to the hangar bay to await contact from her. She'd set her telepathic awareness to lurk around the Terran hangar bays to await the moment when V'kol visited . . . and then she'd send someone to let him know she wasn't going to show. In person, at least.

Cloak-and-dagger tactics were frowned upon when used by a Councilor. Spying was the purview of government agents, military agents, or even, in a pinch, an Advisor. But Jackie needed information. Even though the embassy was closed, she was still responsible for the safety of her people. That included finding out through the grapevine—one way or another—what Princess Regent Vi'alla V'Daania might do.

V'DAN WARSHIP *J'UNG SHAN G'AT*
TON-BEI SYSTEM

Soft hums and beeps of machines lured Li'eth back to consciousness. He placed them vaguely all around him, swimming up out of the blackness cloaking his mind. Next came the sting of disinfectant in the air. Infirmary, he realized after a moment. Lying on his back on an exam bed. Specifically, an infirmary on a starship because he could feel the low, deep thrum of the engines transporting the ship. Not at faster-than-light speeds, that was a different set of harmonics, but at insystem ones.

Knocked unconscious and sent into space. Somehow, he didn't think he was still within their home system. Something was seriously wrong with their gravimetrics system, too. His whole existence felt as if he were being pulled down a strong-suctioning drain hole to his right. Dizzy, determined to get to a comm unit to call back to the planet and lodge a formal protest against his sister, he forced his eyes to open.

The room spun for a moment, then settled. This . . . wasn't the infirmary he was expecting. Not that he'd been in the *Dusk Army*'s infirmary outside of its quarantine sector, but the *Dusk Army* was a space station. It had a fully functional hospital in the normal sector. This . . . this was an open-bay infirmary, of the sort found on a smallish warship. Two classes down in size from the *T'un Tunn G'Deth*, his former warship. Six beds in alcoves with privacy screens that could be moved into place or stored flat against the wall to keep them out of the way.

His walls were partially unfolded around his bed. He was in a hospital gown—V'Dan style, not Terran, tabard and loose shorts with proper overlapping panels—and someone had fitted his arm with an intravenous drip. There wasn't anyone in immediate view. When he tried to roll onto his side to push upright, he felt a wave of disorientation. Suspecting he'd been drugged, Li'eth sagged back onto the bedding, closed his eyes, and focused his mind inward.

Master Sonam Sherap had not been able to teach him everything the Terrans knew about biokinesis; that would have taken a couple years and several medical courses of dedicated instruction. But he had taught the prince how to assess himself biokinetically and how to use biofeedback techniques—meditating, breathing carefully, mental visualizations—to assess damage, to search for unwanted ailments . . . and to metabolize drugs swiftly.

Looking inward, Li'eth groped for an awareness of some sort of sedative in his system. Finding it wasn't too hard; the entry point for its delivery was obvious. Burning it out of his blood caused his heart rate to rise, however. After about a minute, the monitor started beeping a two-tone signal that meant, "Hey, come look at my patient." Not knowing if that meant more sedative was about to be released, Li'eth stopped focusing psychically, grabbed the tape holding the needle in place, and peeled it off.

Footsteps approached. A short, dark-skinned woman with burgundy star-blotches for her *jungen* marks came into view. "I'll check on His Highness," she called over her shoulder to someone out of view. "The mediscanner may have glitched. I . . . oh. You're awake."

Gritting his teeth, he pulled out the shunt. It stung, but the trickle of blood sealed itself within seconds under his focus.

"No! You could have damaged your vein!" the medic protested, hurrying forward.

"It did not glitch, and I am not damaged," he retorted gruffly. "I refuse to be sedated any longer, and I am using my *biokinesis*—my holy healing power—to remove any drugs from my bloodstream, which will also seal the hole in my arm," Li'eth told her. He still felt like the world was tilted to his right even though she appeared to be walking upright. Sitting up, he listed to starboard like a sea ship with bad ballast for a moment, then swung his legs over the side of the bed and glared at her. "Whatever orders Her Highness gave in regard to me, I revoke them under Imperial Tier Jurisprudence Ruling 74, which immediately places me under the jurisdiction of the Tier Advocates. Now, get me proper clothing and the commander of this ship."

That had been what he had tried to tell those damned Imperial Elites, back in the Winter Palace. The Tier Advocates would not sit still nor stand idly aside while his sister *shakked* away the Terran-V'Dan Alliance out of pride. Particularly those who represented the Third, Fourth, and Fifth Tiers, who could overrule the advocates for Second and First Tiers by majority vote on certain matters. Collectively, they also had the right to strip him of his bloodline if he was found at fault for anything, but Li'eth had zero doubts that he was in the right.

Righteous anger was good for burning away some of the dizziness and lethargy, at least. It made him alert and wary of how the nurse might react. The woman, who wore the steel outline of a small triangle, a mere leftenant, pulled something out of her pocket and reached for him. Li'eth flung up his hand even as she started speaking.

"You are clearly hysterical, and—" She broke off with a gasp, shoved across the room by an invisible force. Eyes so wide, he could see the whites all the way around them, she choked out, *"Saints!"*

"Living Saint," Li'eth corrected her, glaring. His body still felt unevenly energized, and he felt a few lingering edges of dizziness, but his mind was clear enough to focus now that the drug had metabolized. Strengthened by anger, even. "You will get me my clothing. You will get me the officer in command of this ship. You will tell me *which* ship this is, and *where* we are. You will *not* anger me. I am now under the legal jurisdiction of the Tier Advocates, *not* the Imperial Regent. She no longer has any authority over me or my situation, and *all* of her orders regarding me are to be *disregarded*."

"But I—"

Fire *whoofed* along his arms, licking upward without burning either him or his hospital robe. "Is. That. Clear?"

Staring at him in fright, the medic nodded shakily and retreated in a scramble. Li'eth let the flames vanish the moment the infirmary fire alarm wailed to life. A moment later, the siren ended. Bracing his palms on the edge of the bed, he tried not to fall off the edge of the infirmary cot while he waited. *Still listing to my right, alone on a ship full of men and women loyal to my sister. I'm going to have to make sure these idiots cannot stun me before I can stop them . . .*

Bored, he looked around the medical cabin while he waited for his demands to be met, squinting at the various cabinet signs and screens. One of the monitors showed the date, one day after the Salik attack on the capital. *I've lost a day. A day's worth of travel, which means we could be transiting at sublight speeds any of a dozen star systems within twelve to thirty light-years from V'Dan.*

The drug's vanishing from my blood, but not the draining feeling. I don't even want to know how much worse things will get if I can't get turned around and sent back home. Not if this is how bad I feel after just one day's travel away at faster-than-light.

An idle thought crossed his mind a few moments later. *I wonder how much that Psi League of theirs, or their Witan Orders, might howl at missing this opportunity to record my half of this forced separation? It has to be the longest distance on record by now.*

CHAPTER 2

V'DAN

By Terran standards, Jackie's telepathy was robust, but she could not sense emotions unless she was deliberately seeking out thoughts, and sensed it in the undercurrents of those thoughts, the subthoughts and underthoughts that echoed and roiled beneath the main message. Empaths sensed it the way skin sensed heat and cold, as a constant radiation. The only ones who didn't radiate emotion constantly—at least, among

Humans—were sociopaths. She hadn't studied enough alien minds yet to know what the ratio of that sort of thing was among non-Humans. But when she touched another being's thoughts, she did receive a vague impression of their emotions.

V'Kol's mind was neatly ordered, his mental composure a sort of shield in and of itself. When she touched his mind, she could sense that he was tense with anxiety, worried as to whether or not he had interpreted her request correctly. If he hadn't, he was going to feel like a fool, and if he had . . . he didn't know what she wanted from him, let alone if he could even provide it. He was . . .

Reaching out, she envisioned inside the edge of his mind the thought of him standing in front of a standard ship cabin door, from the inside of the cabin, and pressed the comm button from the other side.

. . . Oh! Uh . . . Ja'ki? Ambassador? he thought with exaggerated care. The pink-marked soldier was not a psi, but he did have that organized mind of his, a quick-witted mind capable of realizing her projection was not an idle, random mental imagining.

(Yes. Thank you for agreeing to meet with me. I have to know where a mind is to reach out to one in such a crowded location . . . and right now, both of us are probably under surveillance. I dislike going through unofficial channels, but . . . I don't know what happened to Li'eth, I don't know what's going on with your Empress, I don't think I can trust your Princess Regent or anyone loyal to her right now . . . and I feel like steaming shova v'shakk set at a fifteen-degree angle. I can't even walk straight without wobbling over, so I can't go looking for answers personally, as much as I would prefer it.)

Ah, yes, right. Let me remember what happened, he thought, and marshaled his memories. The images collapsed three, four times, but aside from a mental wince and some subthought-muttered apologies, he just scraped it all back together again, from the time that he caught up with and walked next to the prince in the Guard Hall corridor, to the moments after Li'eth had fallen, when the Elites had eyed V'kol, and he had lifted his hands in surrender, shrugging and backing off. *That was the only thing I could think of doing. I didn't think protesting and getting arrested would help anyone, not him and not you,* V'kol insisted, guilt riddling his memories. *You do believe me, right?*

(*Yes, I believe you. And it was very wise of you,*) Jackie reassured him. She reinforced it, and sensed some of his tension easing a little with her sending. (*I do feel it was the right thing. Certainly, I would have done the exact same in your position, backing off to let them take him away. You're not politically or financially powerful, and by keeping yourself clear of any overt resistance or censure, you put yourself in a position to inform us of what actually happened rather than be subjected to rumor. Or worse, propaganda and outright lies. Li'eth may be a V'Dan citizen, not a Terran one, but . . .*)

Someone entered her makeshift infirmary room. Jackie broke off, surprised to see it was Captain Hamza al-Fulan.

Ja'ki? V'kol asked. *Not a Terran one, but . . . ?*

(*One moment, the head of my security force is here.*) Switching to her voice, she asked, "How is everything going?"

"We received a summons from the Empress forty minutes ago," he told her without preamble.

"*Forty* minutes . . . ?" Jackie started to ask. Al-Fulan held up his hand, forestalling her questions.

"I negotiated to go in person with Lieutenant Johnston and a couple others as backup, to see if it really was from her, or if it was a trick of the Regent's. Empress Hana'ka was amenable to the pre-visit, and it really was her. We didn't get a lot of time to see her, but she told us her doctors said she would be able to make a full recovery in due time. Apparently they pulled in some of their biokinetics who were also medically trained. V'Dan holy medics. It's not quite as effective as our own training would have been, but they were able to pull off a few miracles."

"Did she say anything about her heir, or the demand we made just before the attack?" Jackie asked, feeling relieved that the Empress of the Eternal Empire would recover but worried that the other woman might side with her too-proud daughter.

"Yes. She wants to say it to you in person," al-Fulan told her. "But she did give me leave to forewarn you. She intends to apologize for her heir's presumptions, to rescind everything Regent Vi'alla asserted, and to bow to our demands to mind-block those who think our lack of *jungen* equals the right to disrespect us. She also wants to do this formally in a broadcast from her hospital bed, as soon as feasible, which requires your going to see her in person."

Deep relief relaxed Jackie into the bed. It even righted for a moment some of her off-kilter sense of balance . . . but only for a moment. Still dizzy, Jackie asked, "And what of her son's kidnapping?"

". . . We didn't get a chance to discuss that. It was a brief meeting, at the medics' and Elites' insistence," he said.

Jackie knew that there should not be surprises sprung during public broadcasts. "Please get my questions to her *before* I go to see her. Where is Li'eth, how fast can we get him back, and who is she going to pick to be her next heir. Warn her that we will *not* deal with Vi'alla a second time. She becomes Regent again, or even the next Empress outright, and we are *gone*. Warn her also that I cannot pledge we will stay until I have talked to the Council *and* seen good-faith gestures from the V'Dan. The evacuation continues as scheduled, though it will end with me on the last ship out of here."

"Yes, Ambassador. I'll get that handled right away. Now, how are *you* doing?" he asked her. "You look awful, like you're going to be sick."

"It's not actually nausea, just dizziness . . . but I'm missing half my balance. *Getting* to Hana'ka's hospital room is going to be interesting," she muttered. "I can barely make it to the bathroom as it is without help."

"Separation sickness, or a concussion?" he asked.

"Separation. My head is starting to clear, but I'm still left canted at an angle, like the whole world is an aircraft missing an attitude stabilizer. But beyond the psychic side effects, Doctor de la Santoya swears I'm fine. She's still trying to find the KI machine and a portable generator so she can monitor my symptoms for Psi League posterity," Jackie added. "Or she'd be in here now, guarding me."

"I'd not have let her guard you on her own if she hadn't proved herself a pretty deadly shot at close range," al-Fulan told her. "Even with half a Squad outside, checking identities with palmscanners anytime anyone wants to get into this room, I won't let anyone in here without trusting their ability and dedication to protect you."

That made Jackie blink in surprise. Not the paranoid security measures, which were justifiable under the circumstances, but his comment about Maria. "She's a marksman?"

"Not expert rating, but she's more than good enough at short range. Small firearms, good hand-eye coordination, excellent reflexes, and she knows that people underestimate medical types. Even these V'Dan doctors have their own version of the Hippocratic Oath," he allowed wryly. "de la Santoya is pragmatic enough to separate out patients from targets, mentally.

"As it is, there are five Marines stationed outside at all times. Not even the Elites are allowed inside without my personal clearance and a full escort. McCrary is back on the planet and has been handling the rescue and evacuation efforts while you've been unconscious, but you're still senior to her. Oh, and your commission has been reinstated," he added. "Admiral Nayak's orders."

"His orders?" she asked.

"If we have to fight and run, both he and the Premiere want you to have a direct say in the decisions to fire or not to fire. You'll be on the last ship out of the system, in the hopes that the V'Dan will come to their senses at the last minute, but that means you'll be the most vulnerable to an attack at the end. Admiral-General Kurtz would rather keep you a civilian civil servant," al-Fulan explained, "but he's back home, and the Premiere's a man who believes in the leadership at the front lines having the final say, not the ones at the rear. Same as the Admiral, and Admiral Nayak is leaving right about now to oversee the safety of the route home."

"Ugh. Great. What am I now? A Brigadier General? A Rear Admiral? Something with three or four stars?" Jackie asked sarcastically. The first time she'd had her officer's commission resurrected, she had gone from Lieutenant Commander to Major, a lateral move out of Navy designations to avoid being called Captain and being confused with the Navy version, which was technically higher in rank than al-Fulan's Marines version. The second time, she'd been elevated from Major to Colonel.

"I'm afraid it's neither, and yet both, sir."

"What?" she asked, not following along.

"You're still a Colonel . . . but you're also now a Colonel, a Colonel, and a Vice-Commodore, sir," al-Fulan stated blandly.

Jackie gaped at him. She couldn't even form a question; his reply boggled her that much.

Her head of security tipped his head. "To be precise, you have been given a rank in each of the four Branches. Colonel for the other three and Vice-Commodore for the Navy. Scuttlebutt has it the Admiral-General and the Premiere went head to head over the matter. Kurtz says you don't have enough experience to be elevated to three- or four-star, and Callan says you need to be able to command all four Branches at a moment's notice, which only the Command Staff 'tier' can do. Someone, I don't know who, suggested just putting you in charge of each Branch separately, and after a quick review, the DoI approved Vice-Commodore, Colonel, and Colonel, and so here you are, a four-part officer."

Shutting her mouth, Jackie rolled her eyes. ". . . Tell me you did not just make a V'Dan-style joke about *our* military, with that 'tier' bit."

"Is that an order, sir?" he quipped blandly. When she gave him a dirty look, the Marine Corps captain shrugged. "Giving you a rank in all four Branches means you can give direct chain-of-command orders for everyone out here. That is, once Admiral Nayak is gone. Nayak's pulling out right now, McCrary is scheduled to depart at the midpoint with me on board for military oversight, and you're on the last ship out of here with Buraq for your security lead, in the hopes that this charlie foxtrot can be salvaged at the last minute.

"If it *can* be, you'll be in charge of the military forces that are still in transit. If it can't be . . . you're the rear guard. Sorry, sir," he added in apology.

That quirked her brows. "I thought the Empress . . . ?" He shook his head, and she reasoned it through. ". . . Of course not. Not until we *are* back to being allies, firmly and formally recognized as such, *and* enforced as such. Vague reassurances aren't enough. Neither are verbal promises, anymore. Which means the next few hours or days are critical and depend quite a lot on how the V'Dan actually act and react . . . So. When exactly does Her Eternity want to meet with me?"

"Since she knows you're awake, in another two hours," her

head of security told her. "She has a few more treatments to go through, probably some primping before the on-camera stuff begins, and I figured you'd want to have your own self checked over and given time for a shower and a fresh change of clothes. If we can *get* to your things and get them out again in one piece."

"Maria told me the easy path to my quarters was torpedoed," she agreed. Staring up at the bland, golden-beige ceiling, she thought a few moments. "Try Master Sergeant Zinchelle, if her quarters are still intact. She's about the same size and shape as I am, and I should be able to fit into her Dress Blacks if you cannot get ahold of mine. I'll also need a ride there," she said. "My whole world is still canted to the left. I can walk a straight line for a very short distance, but it saps my strength, so it's best to conserve it for as long as possible, and that means strictly for the cameras."

"Yes, you don't want to look weak in front of the V'Dan— the ones watching the broadcast," he concurred. "We need to discuss worst-case scenarios, though. You're feeling weakened and disoriented, no doubt by that Salik weapon they used to stun the prince. But also probably from the distance separating the two of you. At some point, that distance may incapacitate you, Ambassador."

"I know. I need . . ." Jackie trailed off, realizing she needed to do something else. "Give me a few minutes to think," she compromised, and when he nodded and fell silent, she reached out telepathically to V'kol. (*I apologize for the delay. The Empress is awake, aware, and requesting my presence in just a couple hours.*)

That is a huge *relief,* V'kol thought back at her. For a moment, his subthoughts were muddied, then he enunciated mentally, *Wait, are you certain she is awake? Not to malign the Princess Regent, but . . . well, yes, to malign her. She acted like a massive idiot . . . and please don't tell anyone I thought that.*

(*Relax, V'kol, your thoughts are your own; I will not share them with anyone outside of a mandatory mind-scan to make sure I have only used my gifts ethically . . . and this counts as ethically. Captain al-Fulan investigated the Empress' situation personally.*)

Good. So . . . does this mean we don't have to sneak around anymore?

(*I wasn't comfortable with the idea of it, either,*) Jackie agreed quickly. (*But we Terrans still have no idea if we can trust anything that Vi'alla says or does, or even says she isn't doing. And I don't know how badly injured Her Eternity is, including if she's well enough to take back her power full-time. That could leave Vi'alla partially in charge and make things very awkward for V'Dan-Terran relations.*)

She is too full of herself. Too proud of being V'Dan . . . which is an indictment against most of my people, V'kol agreed. The former gunnery officer hesitated, then asked, *Would you like me to keep my ears open to any gossip? I don't want to betray my people, but letting you Terrans leave without at least trying to fix things between us would be a betrayal, too. A deeper one, in a way.*

(*I know. I feel the same way. And yes, keep an ear open for gossip. But . . . don't compromise your oaths of service, V'Kol,*) she told him. (*Nothing actively working against the good of your Empire. You can be our friend without breaking any vows to your people. I wouldn't have asked that much even if the Empress hadn't woken up.*)

V'kol mentally nodded. *Thankfully, she did. You do realize, of course, that you Terrans will have to open up your interstellar comm satellites in order to transmit the orders that will bring the prince home swiftly, right?*

(*That . . . will have to be discussed. Wait in the garage while I send someone to you to say that I'm not coming. That's so no one thinks we've been having a telepathic conversation,*) she directed. (*This is private. No information was shared that wasn't or will not be public knowledge soon, either way, but there's no need to shout it from the rooftops either. So to speak.*)

Right.

(*Thank you, V'kol, for being our friend. I will hopefully be able to talk with you in person later.*)

Hopefully. I'll wait for that messenger, now.

She had the impression of a smile from him, tinged with wistfulness. Focusing her thoughts back on the officer at her side, she shrugged and looked at the patiently waiting Hamza.

"If anything goes wrong with me, we'll just have to continue with Rosa as my second. If anything happens to me, she's in charge. If I turn paranoid and delusional from panic and anxiety . . . sedate me and put her in charge.

"If anything happens to both of us, and Admiral Nayak is immediately reachable for consultation, he is in charge," Jackie instructed her security officer. "And if he is not, *you* are in charge, followed by Lieutenant Buraq . . . because if both McCrary and I go down, it'll probably be a set of problems worthy of a declaration of war. At the very least, a retreat under armed rear guard. You and Jasmine will have seniority for those circumstances, at that point."

Nodding, al-Fulan pulled out an organizer tablet and started tapping in information. "Let's hope it doesn't come to that. I'm going to assign an escort guard wherever you go, with orders to sedate and catch you if you go beyond acceptable anxiety levels."

"Good. Oh, and since I'll be busy visiting the Empress, please send someone down to the hangar bay to let Leftenant Kos'q know that I won't be able to join him for that word game I requested earlier," she added.

"Of course, sir." He didn't question the order though he did shoot her a brief look. Jackie ignored it. Information gathering was not illegal, so long as in doing so, those involved broke no laws . . . and so long as a government official did not bribe anyone or be bribed at any point to invent, accept, or ignore that information. Instead, he had a different question. "Under what circumstances do we unlock the hyperrelay probes?"

"When the V'Dan government accepts and upholds our demands for proper displays of respect, and mind-blocks for those who refuse to give it . . . and for when each of the other Alliance governments agree, including planetary governors per system," she added, thinking of that Solarican planetary leader that had demanded access to their interstellar communications ability while being rude to her delivery crew. "Everything remains in lockdown until then, government by government, system by system.

"Only Terran messages in or out until we get full cooperation, though we *will* deliver news of the ultimatum to all systems, and news of which specific systems have agreed to our demands to each system that has not yet agreed to them. And yes, I know that'll make it difficult to find His Highness. Ensuring that our people are respected is more important than the comfort of one or two mere individuals. Even if one of those individuals is me," she finished, closing her eyes. Still dizzy, she let herself rest, conserving her energy.

"Your dedication is appreciated. I'll make sure those tranquilizers are on standby," Hamza agreed dryly. "Do you need anything?"

"Food, coffee—extrastrength if it's V'Dan *caffen*—and someone to help me shower and change. I'm not standing on a slippery surface and contorting myself to get clean without someone to catch me if I fall."

"I'll get right on that."

V'DAN WARSHIP *J'UNG SHAN G'AT*
TON-BEI SYSTEM

The leftenant returned with the captain in tow. "Captain Del'un Qa-Reez," she announced, "of the Warship *Bounding Cat Roar*."

Captain Del'un Qa-Reez, a middle-aged man with deep-tanned skin, short brown curls, and pale yellow *jungen* crescents, did not look happy about being summoned like a servant. The stunner in his hand was proof of that, as were his surface thoughts and agitated swirl of his aura. The instant Li'eth sensed those in combination, he reacted, mind lashing out the moment the captain brought his weapon up into firing position. Telekinesis smacked into the man's wrist, jerking the muzzle of the stunner up at the ceiling; light and sound pulsed in a *tzzzzz* of energy. It hit the ceiling harmlessly, dissipating within half a heartbeat.

Li'eth shifted his mind, twisting his telekinesis to clamp around the older male's forearm and hand, lifting and bending the limb so that the weapon pointed at its owner's head. It was crudely done, and Li'eth could see the pain being caused in the way the captain bared his teeth in a silent snarl.

"Drop it," Li'eth ordered, carefully keeping ahold of the man's wrist but not his fingers.

Those fingers hesitated, then unfurled from around the weapon. It dropped as requested, bouncing off his shoulder and chest to clatter across the infirmary floor. Li'eth released the captain's arm and quickly scooped up the weapon with his mind. He lifted and set it on the bed next to his still-infirmary-robed body.

"Clothing suitable to my station. The name of this ship. The name of our nearest star system. And a communications link to the nearest V'Dan authority so I can finish registering my claim of Imperial Tier Law 74," Li'eth stated calmly. That was, externally he looked and sounded calm; internally, he nearly shook from dizziness and anger.

Behind the captain and off to one side, the infirmary door slid open, and a woman entered, one with the large hollow triangles of a leftenant superior on her shoulders. So did two other officers, leftenants with smaller triangle outlines. Li'eth was grateful they weren't openly carrying weapons and glad when they stopped just inside the room, eyeing the tableau of their superior and the famous stranger on their infirmary bed.

He knew they recognized him; it was evident in the shocked widening of their eyes, in the quick way they straightened to attentiveness. Particularly the two male newcomers. The surprise, however, meant they hadn't known he—Imperial Prince Kah'raman—was on board until now. *That means their captain intended to keep my presence on board a secret . . . but a secret from the enemy or a secret from anyone sympathetic to me?*

Out loud, he carefully stated, "Your loyalty to my sister is commendable, Captain Qa-Reez, but the law is the *law* and is superior to everyone. It is the law even for the Empress herself, never mind a mere Princess Regent. I am now under the jurisdiction of the Tier Advocates, *not* the Eternal Throne.

"Failure to obey and follow the law will be seen as an act of mutiny . . . at which point *I* will be well within my legal grounds as a Grand Captain, never mind an Imperial Prince, to commandeer this ship and throw you and your fellow mutineers out an airlock. I would rather not have to do that," Li'eth added softly. "I'd like you to prove that you and your crew are intelligent enough to be law-abiding instead. Will you cooperate?"

Captain Qa-Reez narrowed his eyes. "Imperial Tier Rule 74?"

"Invoking Imperial Tier Jurisprudence Ruling 74 remands me into the custody of the Tier Advocates on V'Dan; if they are not available, the nearest colonyworld's Tier Advocates are to be contacted in order to get me to the Advocates on the homeworld. This invocation removes me completely from Imperial jurisdiction," he patiently explained, "which means that *any* order Imperial Princess Regent Vi'alla gave to your crew is now no longer valid.

"Continuing to follow those invalidated orders will be considered treason. Attempting to imprison me through stunning and sedation is now *treason* because you, as a non-Advocate, do not have that authority. Only the Tier Advocates can judge me now," he explained with icy patience.

Their judgment could be quite harsh, historically, but it was necessary. Their power over the royal bloodline—granted when a member of the Tier placed themselves in their jurisdiction, as Li'eth was doing—had evolved to help prevent trading one tyrant for another, as well as to help prevent one tyrant from wiping out all possible alternatives to the throne.

"They can only take jurisdiction over you if they *know* about you," Qa-Reez stated coldly. "I thi—"

"—I wouldn't do that if I were you, Captain," the leftenant superior stated. Qa-Reez turned to face her. One of the two men at his back was frowning at their captain along with her; the other was eyeing her and the man to the left warily. The leftenant medic eyed the trio as well. The leftenant superior leveled her shoulders. "There are enough of us on this ship who believe in the rule of law to overrule you. And as *we* are adamant about upholding that law . . . it would not be mutiny on our side. Any mutiny would be *your* actions."

A muscle flexed in the captain's jaw. He lifted his chin. "Fine. *You* take responsibility for him. Get him off my ship . . . and take yourself as well."

"Me? Why should I go?" she asked, folding her arms across her chest and tipping her head. "Because I challenged you when you were about to take an illegal action, as a law-abiding junior officer should?"

Qa-Reez bared his teeth in a brief, silent snarl. "You will take charge of the Tier Advocate's prisoner and deliver him personally to their authority. To make sure he *does* deliver himself into their authority. Since you're so interested in following through on the letter of the law, that is now your responsibility and your official orders on the matter. Everyone else . . . out of the infirmary!"

Stalking toward the door, he forced the male leftenants to quickly scatter. The one on the right, with the burgundy rosettes, followed his captain out. The leftenant medic disappeared into the infirmary offices. The male on the left, with pink crescents on medium-brown skin and black hair, stared at the brown-haired, green-spotted leftenant superior. "Was that wise, Ka'atieth?"

"I remember he said he'd served as a fellow cadet with Imperial Princess Vi'alla. He's currying favor with her, as the heir and future Empress. I don't give a damn about Imperial politics, but I *do* about upholding the law." Crossing to stand in front of Li'eth, she drew herself up, shoulders square, chin slightly raised. "Leftenant Superior A'sha-rayn Ka'atieth, first officer of the Imperial Warship *Bounding Cat Roar*. Do you remand yourself into my custody, Your Highness, until such time as we can get you to the Advocates?"

"No," Li'eth stated bluntly. It made her blink. "I remand myself into the custody of the Tier Advocates on V'Dan and *only* them. You are not one of them. You *may*, however, escort me to them, assisting me in my journey. I should like clothing to wear. A Grand Captain's uniform will do, size 36-7 top, 36-8 bottom, size 23-3 shoes if you have them."

"I'll go get them," the fellow with the pink crescents said. He backed up toward the doorway, which slid open behind him. "Anything else from storage? Toiletry kit?"

Li'eth nodded. He had to grip the edge of the bed because his world was still listing to his right, and movement threatened to stir the dizziness within him, but he kept himself upright. Seated, but upright. The other man ducked out before he could offer thanks. That left him to consider the woman in front of him. "How far out are we from a transfer point?"

"About two hours, maybe a little less. We're coasting into the system, checking the lightwave backlog," Ka'atieth told him. "So far, all is quiet. You're the most exciting thing in this sector, Highness."

"Grand Captain," Li'eth corrected. "Please refer to me as Grand Captain Li'eth Ma'an-uq'en, and inform the rest of the crew to do so as well. *Any* reference to me as a member of the Imperial Blood that leaves this ship could have it painted for the highest priority in capture, interrogation, and consumption . . . whether or *not* I am still on board. Go warn everyone of that, Leftenant Superior," he ordered, lifting his chin. "Gossip on this one point is worth this ship's weight in *flk*-sauce."

"They'd capture and eat us anyway—" she started to dismiss. Li'eth shook his head hard, cutting her off.

"No. I was captured by the Salik. I know what they would do to a normal crew. I also know what they would do if they thought they could get their tentacles on a member of the Imperial Tier. The *only* thing that kept them from taking me to their homeworld for a grand feast was their ignorance. That ignorance allowed the Terrans to free us, but we had the promises of the Immortal and the Prophet of a Thousand Years to ensure our survival from enemy appetites. But *only* a promise for five of us to survive.

"There are no other guarantees for any other ship's crew," he warned her. "My presence on *this* ship is my sister *deliberately* sabotaging our good relations with the Terrans, contrary to the words of the Prophet . . . and we *need* them to win this war. If the Salik learned I was in this system, they would tear this ship apart and torture every last one of you, just to try to take me prisoner and use me as leverage against Her Eternity."

"I heard they cut off their interstellar communications and have refused to allow us to communicate. How do we need *that* from an ally?" Ka'atieth challenged him. "Their behavior—"

"—Their behavior is a direct consequence of *our* behavior," Li'eth stated, closing his eyes, tired of this argument. "We insulted and disrespected them at nearly every turn. Even those who have been formally *trained* in cross-cultural diplomacy, people trained not to blink an eyelid at the strangeness of the K'Katta or the Gatsugi, have insulted the Terrans based on simple skin color. Would *you* stick around to help someone who had repeatedly disrespected you for months on end?

"*Would* you?" he challenged when she didn't answer right away. "If you weren't forced to remain, would you actually stay and let your supposed allies insult and disrespect you every single day, day upon day? Be honest, Leftenant Superior," he added, opening his eyes to look at her again. "If nothing else, be honest with yourself in silence . . . though I should like a reply."

She didn't look happy, and she didn't look comfortable. In fact, the leftenant superior looked like she was trying to swallow bitter Terran coffee. ". . . No, sir. I would not."

"The Terrans aren't being forced to remain, and they will not allow anyone to force them to remain. To do so would be an act of war. They had every right to demand what they did of the Empress," Li'eth told her. "She was about to answer them when the Salik attacked. I don't know what she would have said, but I would like to think our ruler had the best interests of the nation in mind.

"Unfortunately, Her Eternity was injured, and my sister took up the War Crown . . . but my sister's pride refused to consider that the Terrans' complaints were legitimate. The Terrans were willing to have the answer deferred, but Imperial Regent Vi'alla demanded to continue using their technology without giving them any respect or accommodation for it. *That* is why the Terrans shut off their communications and are in the process of removing their embassy from V'Dan.

"*That* move, Leftenant Superior, is why I refuse to remain under Vi'alla's jurisdiction. My sister turned the Terrans away from us—and when I warned her what she was doing, she did *this* to me, had me knocked out and carted off on a ship with a captain loyal to her rather than to the Empire. I don't have to be there to know that the Terrans will not deal with her. And I will *not* sit still on an outbound ship while she destroys the Empire, and with it the races of the Alliance, out of *pride*," he asserted, his body tight with anger. "I don't care what the Tier Advocates do with me so long as they see how terrible her policies are for our survival."

"I hope they do, Your Hi . . . sir," she corrected herself. "As soon as we're within a few minutes of lightwave, I'll start pinging the ships in orbit around the colony, looking to see which one is headed back to the heart of the Empire. Shi'uln—the pink-marked fellow—can fly us to it in a shuttle, as soon as we find one. Preferably one loyal to the Empire, as you put it. Somehow," she added dryly, "I doubt Captain Qa-Reez would be willing to reverse the *Bounding*'s course even by command of this system's Tier Advocates."

"Wait—which colony are we approaching?" Li'eth asked. His question stopped her midturn to leave.

"V'Ton-Bei, third planet. We stopped briefly at the station at the eighth on our way in to refuel and drop off news," she stated. Ka'atieth hesitated, then said, "I should like to have the Terrans' communication ability. Even if it's only one planet per system, it was amazing, being at V'Du'em-ya and receiving fresh news from earlier that same day on the Motherworld . . . the V'Dan homeworld," she amended, since it was now widespread news that the Terran homeworld was *the* Motherworld for their race. "Rather than four days later by news-courier. I . . ."

"Yes, Leftenant Superior?" Li'eth prodded her when she hesitated.

She lifted her light brown eyes to his, one eye colored on the outer edge with just enough vivid green *jungen* to tint part of her iris, and shrugged. "I just . . . if Her Highness stole the technology on how to communicate between star systems, I'd . . . I'd feel sorry for these Terrans, but we desperately need that technology."

"Not *that* desperately, Leftenant," he countered. "Betraying one ally, even just a mere potential ally, is the same as betraying the entire Alliance. Think about it. If the Terrans could not trust us to be honorable, how could the Solaricans? *We* are not the Salik. If we lose our honor, we lose the right to let the Empire continue to live. *I* am not going to let the Empire die in the name of pride *or* dishonorable expediency."

She blinked a little at the fierceness in his words and lowered her gaze. When she spoke again, Ka'atieth's voice was quiet, too quiet to be easily heard past his ears. "Are you planning to . . . to take over the War Crown if Her Eternity does not recover?"

It was Li'eth's turn to blink. *Take over . . . ? Be the Imperial Heir?* He had considered the question before, but only as an intellectual thing, a passing thought. The extent to which Imperial Princess Vi'alla was willing to be ruthlessly selfish, however, was a fact that made him pause and actually consider the choice seriously for several long moments. Ka'atieth peeked at him, shrugging and lifting her hands in a . . . *well*? gesture; he responded by lifting his own palm toward himself. She sighed and continued waiting patiently while he thought through her question.

His dizziness didn't help his ability to focus, but it did not stop him, either. It also pointed out the strongest consideration. ". . . No," Li'eth finally said. "My holy bond with the Terran Grand High Ambassador would make such a thing too politically awkward."

"If she *is* your holy partner, then she would become your Imperial Consort. I don't see what the problem is," Ka'atieth said. "Unless Terrans and V'Dan, for all we seem the same species, cannot interbreed, but then all you'd have to do is get a Consort Imperial to continue the bloodline. Problem solved."

"Genetically, Terrans and V'Dan can interbreed, though as far as I know, no one has tried just yet," Li'eth admitted under his breath. "But no, that is not the reason. It is that *her* loyalty is tied strongly to her people. As strongly as any I have ever seen. If I took the Eternal Throne, I would have to dedicate *my* loyalty to the Empire."

"Ah. And as your Consort, she would be expected to be equally loyal to the Empire, but she is loyal to her people," the leftenant superior agreed. "So . . . who, then?"

"My elder sister, Imperial Princess Ah'nan. She currently serves as the Grand High Ambassador to the Terrans. I do not know if the Imperial Princess Regent has closed our embassy on their world, but if we can regain formal ties with them, someone else can fill that role. Ah'nan is of the Blood and is well trained in diplomacy, reasonably trained in military strategy . . . and is not overly proud like her elder sister," Li'eth muttered. "*I* would be a last resort because of my situation. Our younger siblings might even be a better choice before me, and even if not, I'd look to a cousin."

"You are a very strange Imperial Prince," Ka'atieth muttered.

That made Li'eth raise a brow. "In what way?" When she hesitated, he added, "Speak bluntly, if you need. We're both in the military. I won't take offense."

Ka'atieth flicked her hand at him. "I thought all Imperials were so blood-conscious, they'd never give up a drop of anything their family could claim. I always pictured all of you, or at least most of you, just clustered around the Eternal Throne all day. Supporting whoever sat on it, but eager to one day maybe have a shot at planting your buttocks on the crimson cushions yourselves."

To be fair, that was an honest assessment of a lot of his ancestors, and even some of his extended relatives. Li'eth shook his head. "Another lifetime, maybe. Not in this one. Not under these circumstances. Some of the others, but not me. The needs of the Empire *must* come first. Unlike many of my Tier, I can see and acknowledge when I am ill suited to a particular task."

She smiled, a slight twist of her lips, and eyed him as he sat there on the edge of the infirmary bed, clad only in V'Dan hospital clothes. "I'm beginning to like you."

"I'm already claimed," he reminded her. He still felt that list of the universe to his right, to the gaping hole at his side where Jacaranda MacKenzie should be.

"Pity. Ah, well. I'll get you back to your . . . claimant. You'll have to promise me something however, Grand Captain," Ka'atieth bargained.

That lifted his brow again. "And what would that be, Leftenant Superior?"

"Make sure Captain Qa-Reez cannot claim I deserted my post in escorting you about," she stated bluntly. "If he was willing to imprison and sedate you, an Imperial Prince, I have no doubt he'll feel free to punish me. Outside the military, I'm merely a Fourth Tier—are you sure you won't need a Consort? That these Terrans can interbreed with us?"

Li'eth carefully did not snap at the woman for presuming he'd be interested in anyone other than his holy partner. "As far as we know, and yes, I am quite sure. Get me a comm channel to the Imperial Army when we're within lightwave reach of V'Ton-Bei, and I'll arrange for your formal transfer to my command," he told her. "But it will only be a military position."

"In that case, you might want to consider taking Leftenant Shi'uln, the fellow with the pink marks, too," the leftenant superior stated, flicking a finger over her shoulder at the door behind her. "Captain Qa-Reez is going to be unhappy with anyone who helps you, and Shi'uln will be the one to help you get washed and dressed in a few *mi-nah*. You look awful, probably the residue of whatever it was that they gave you . . . but since they gave it to you, I wouldn't trust anyone in this infirmary to bathe you, let alone cure you."

"I'll consider his transfer, but the fewer soldiers I commandeer, the easier the Advocates will be on me—I won't ruin the Empire with bad choices, but neither will I ruin *me*," Li'eth warned her.

"Of course not, sir. I wouldn't do that to myself, either," she agreed.

V'DAN

Despite the many advances in V'Dan medicine—or even Terran medicine, in its own separate way—there would always be a need for some sort of mobile chair. The one Jackie stepped out of when she reached the final doorway was self-balancing, self-guiding, and more or less functioned like a sort of battery-powered gyroglider, save that it used wheels and not any sort of thruster-field technology for hovering. It was, after all, designed to be used inside hospitals, and the V'Dan still used petrochemical-like fuel systems for its highest energy needs.

It did earn her several dubious looks from the clustered members of Her Eternity's staff. One of them, a woman with burgundy stripes angling symmetrically down her face, asked not unkindly, "Were you injured?"

"Yes." It was shorter than saying she'd had her other half metaphysically ripped from her left side. Brevity was also necessary, because in order to walk and not stagger, she had to move slowly. Jackie hoped it translated to a sort of ponderous grace, something with an appearance of strength rather than weakness. It wasn't as if any of the dozen soldiers and staff from among her own people, accompanying her, could carry her inside. She had to appear strong on her own.

It didn't fool everyone. An older gentleman, his gray-salted hair striped light blue in an attractive sort of way, sniffed a little. "Are you certain you are up to this? You look . . . weak."

Don't get angry . . . "I am on my feet," she stated blandly in reply. "Is your Empress?"

He stiffened in affront. She stared him down anyway, making the older V'Dan move back two paces and bow his head when she took a single step forward. Straightening her Dress Black jacket subtly—thankfully, her uniforms had been the least-damaged clothes rescued from the rubble of the embassy wing just over half an hour ago, the least in need of immediate cleaning—she turned carefully and paced slowly into the private chamber holding the Empress.

Semiprivate chamber, since several people were inside. It was a large room, the flat walls glossy in that way that said they could be scrubbed clean at a moment's notice, but still decorated in the ornate motifs of the V'Dan Empire, strange plants, animal-things, plus transplanted Terran flora and fauna. Various bits of equipment ringed the room, with more standing on the far side of the tilted bed. The sheets were crimson and silklike, framing their occupant.

Empress Hana'ka did not wear a standard, bleached-cream hospital tabard. Instead, the gown had been crafted from a pale cream brocaded in a slightly richer gold, edged with deep burgundy. Her blond-and-burgundy hair had been shaved on one side, and some sort of bandaging patch covered the injury, but the patch had been decorated with yet more artistry, and her hair swirled halfway over it to give the impression of a deliberate hairstyle rather than a serious injury. Even her nails had been lacquered, burgundy with an overlay of gold, a trait V'Dan and Terrans shared, though Jackie had already noticed that the V'Dan tended to paint their nails, male and female, to match the color of their *jungen* marks rather than the color of their outfits.

The Empress lifted her hand, gesturing toward Jackie. The movement revealed a hint of more bandages down inside her sleeve, along with the shadows of several bruises. Her other arm lay cradled across her ribs, suggesting either it or her ribs needed to stay immobilized. It wasn't as if Jackie could probe into the Empress' state of health, however; the true depth of her injuries was bound to be a state secret, and it would be impolite to pry.

That uplifted hand flexed again. Obedient out of politeness, Jackie moved forward. Those lacquered fingers tilted a little. Taking a guess, Jackie slipped her palm against them, shielding herself firmly against any accidental eavesdropping. This moment would be examined by an ethics inquiry, after all, and Jackie could not afford to have any accusations levied at her of influencing the head of the V'Dan Empire into false favorability toward her fellow Terrans.

"Empress."

Hana'ka gripped her hand. "How are you doing, Ja'ki?" she asked quietly. Of the eight or nine other men and women in the room, none drew close enough to hear. They might have strained their ears, but they left the two women alone while their leader spoke with the Terran Ambassador, her gaze a little unfocused. "Were you injured? I heard about the others . . . I am sorry our war caused their deaths."

Lowering her gaze, Jackie shook her head. "We knew the risks coming here. I'm just grateful you're alive."

"Hmmh. Yes. I've heard about the Imperial Princess Regent and her insults to—"

"—No," Jackie corrected, squeezing the older woman's fingers just a little. Her own hand was starting to heat up, in that way that said her Gestalt-based biokinesis had instinctively triggered. She let it pour through her into the older woman, as she did not allow her telepathy. If it was acting of its own volition, that meant her gift sensed imbalances it could repair, and a distinct need for that repair. Jackie would not withhold it from this woman, so she let the inergies flow. "I like you for your own sake, Hana'ka."

Gray eyes blinked and focused on a point somewhere slightly to the left of Jackie's face. "As do I you. Are *you* injured in any way?"

"Physically, I am . . . technically well."

"Technically?" Hana'ka asked, raising her brows. Her gaze shifted, somewhere just above Jackie's eyes.

Were her eyes injured . . . ? Again, not an inquiry she could safely and politely make, even with a budding friendship between her and this woman.

"Your heir ripped away my left half and flung him dozens of light-years from here," Jackie reminded the older woman.

"Imperial Regent Vi'alla ordered the Elites to stun him, which also knocked me unconscious off on the other side of the Plazas, then she ordered a ship of your fleet to carry him away. This is the farthest any known Gestalt pairing has been separated. To be blunt, I'm surprised I'm still able to stand under these conditions. Walking is problematic, you see, when you have a black hole dwelling half an arm length to your left."

Closing her eyes, Hana'ka frowned faintly in thought, then squeezed her fingers and opened her eyes. She blinked twice . . . and stared at Jackie's right cheek. Definitely something wrong with her vision. "I will send word to get him back. I heard your people shut down your communications satellites. It *would* help speed things along if you reactivated them."

"We are prepared to do so. But we will require a formal promise that we will be treated with respect, first," Jackie told her. On this point, the Council and Premiere were firm. "My personal needs are *nothing* compared to the needs of my people. Not even for diplomacy's sake can your son's health and well-being be placed even close to that need. Let alone overtake it."

"I do understand, Ja'ki, and I cannot blame your people for all that you have done." Her tone hardened a little, turning from the soft-spoken regret of the private woman and mother, Hana'ka, to the public steel of the War Queen, the Eternal Empress. "Imperial Princess Vi'alla acted without consideration or forethought for the needs of *both* our people. I revoke and reverse all of her commands regarding your people while she has been Regent. Furthermore . . . I remember your people's demand of us.

"By my command, the Eternal Empire will comply. Starting with myself. When the formal announcements have been made to the Alliance—with your technological assistance," Hana'ka added, "—and when we are no longer broadcasting . . . you will begin with me, apply this . . . mind-block thing."

"Thank you, Eternity," Jackie said. "However, it is the opinion of the Terran government that *you* do not need the procedure. Imperial Princess Vi'alla, on the other hand . . . she must agree, *and* be placed in a probation period of one year under its effects, to see how she adapts. If she cannot change her ways, I'm afraid my people will not change our stance on working with her. We *will* work with you. However, the moment she takes over again, either as merely your regent or your full successor . . . we will have nothing to do with the V'Dan Empire under her leadership, and the embassy will be closed once again. Either way, understand that our communications and hyperspace technologies will remain ours, and our proprietary secrets will not be shared."

"We understand. Will you at least be willing to broadcast this moment?" Hana'ka asked.

"We are prepared to do so now. For now. Each leader in each individual system, including the *other* nations of the Alliance, must also agree to our demands in order to have full communication capacity restored. But we will exchange broadcasts with them at least partially, so that they understand that the V'Dan here in the home system will comply, and give them a chance to consider our demands."

"We understand," Empress Hana'ka stated. Her mouth twisted slightly, almost into a smile. "But as I said before, we of V'Dan are not them, and I cannot speak completely on our allies' behalf. Temporarily, I can make that decision, but not completely and permanently."

"We of the Terran United Planets understand that and are prepared to await their choice."

Hana'ka let her mouth curve into an actual smile. She closed her eyes for a moment. "Even if it will take days to settle out . . . at least it won't take weeks and *months*, with your help." She cracked open her eyelids and peeked at Jackie. Or rather, at Jackie's vicinity. "Of course, you do realize we will have to repeat all of this, in more or less the same words, for the broadcast?"

"Of course. Let us get our equipment ready." Jackie looked over at Captain al-Fulan, who nodded. Under the watchful eyes of the Elite, two Marines brought in a small communications bot, which expanded itself into a screen at about head height. They adjusted the placement and view with a few murmured consultations with members of the Imperial staff, then moved back.

"Master of Ceremonies. Is everything ready?" Hana'ka asked.

"Yes, Eternity. Grand High Ambassador, if you will please stand a little closer to the head of the bed and turn this way to face the screen?" the ornately robed man directed.

Jackie moved as ordered, shifting this way, moving a little farther back, leaning in slightly—that allowed her to lean against the bed to her right, thankfully, which counteracted the ongoing urge to lean, stumble, and perhaps even faint to her left. After a final squeeze of their joined fingers, Hana'ka withdrew her hand and settled her arm at her side.

Some sort of production servant moved in and fixed the Empress' hair minutely, then gently settled the War Crown on her head, clearly taking care with the bandaged area. The woman then fussed over Jackie a little, even spending a few moments plucking stray loose hairs from the black of her formal Dress uniform. Jackie's dark curls were a bit on the reddish side, but she didn't think the hairs would have shown, so the primping amused her.

It also summoned up images of Lieutenant Brad Colvers doing the same thing, and the memory of his betrayal, using those hairs to program cutting robots to destroy her wardrobe . . . programmed to seek out and destroy *her*. Hopefully, none of these V'Dan were thinking of repeating that same grievous mistake. She would not be gentle with any others who tried.

Everyone moved back, and a technician by the V'Dan screen gave a silent countdown, folding in thumb, forefinger, all the way to littlest finger, which he pointed at them. Master of Ceremonies gave a formal invocation of their names and titles, then stepped back out of the frame of the pickups. Off to one side, Jackie could see herself and Empress Hana'ka projected on a side screen monitored by her fellow Terrans. It wasn't a formal introduction ceremony in front of nearly a million citizens, but they looked good.

Actually, we look like hell, she amended to herself. *Primped and preened hell, but still hell. I'm visibly a bit gray in the face from psychic fatigue with bags under my eyes, looking fresh from a hospital bed, and Hana'ka is in a hos-*

pital bed with who knows what injuries on top of what I've seen . . . but we're alive, we're in control, and we are *going to do damage to our enemies.*

Not to our friends, dammit.

V'TON-BEI ORBIT

"Welcome aboard the *Leaping Kitten*," Leftenant Superior Ka'atieth stated, flicking her left hand as Li'eth, finally properly uniformed, followed her into the shuttlecraft. She tapped on a control panel, opening a storage locker so that both could store their kit bags, then sealed it again.

Li'eth hesitated, thinking over her words, then took a couple careful steps back, hand on the airlock door edge so he could be mindful of his dizziness and balance issues. "It says . . . VDS *J'UNG SHAN G'AT*, SHUTTLE 205-671."

"It's a *joke*," the green-spotted woman huffed, rolling her eyes as she turned to walk backwards. "Since our *mighty warship* is named after a *g'at* of all things, the whole crew has had a tradition of giving its shuttles cute, playful nicknames. The *Leaping Kitten*, the *Pouncing Purr Master*, the *Plays with a Paper Ball* . . ."

"Oh." He blinked and considered that, then grinned. ". . . I like it. On the *T'un Tunn G'Deth*, we just used the designation numbers. It was boring. We also had the 203 series of shuttles though I think our ship was commissioned after yours."

"These are fairly new shuttles," she agreed. "We had most of them replaced about eight months ago. Ah, since it's just the three of us—Leftenant Shi'uln is a good enough pilot for this task, though he's only a third-ranked backup—you can either sit on your own in the back in princely splendor or sit in the navigator's seat up front with the rest us like a fellow officer."

"Fellow officer," Li'eth stated, following her. He entered the cockpit and took the rear seat on the left, behind the other male on board. It was easier to go to his left even though his body wanted to stagger to the right; to the left was more controllable. That, and once down and strapped in place, he could lean somewhat to the right, giving in to the compulsion pulling him that way without sacrificing his ability to see either officer. "Leftenant Shi'uln, thank you for flying us out of here. And for the help with my bath, earlier."

"My pleasure, Grand Captain," Leftenant Shi'uln replied, having been the one to bring Li'eth his Grand Captain insignia as well as his uniform. The pink-marked man looked up from his preflight checks, hesitating. "Although . . . are you sure you don't want to use your title? I mean, I found you some concealer for your marks, but . . . it feels a bit weird, *not* deferring to your Tier. Like the whole universe is off-balance."

"I have discovered in the last several months . . . several years, actually, once I joined the military . . . that I would far rather be called Li'eth than by any rank or title. *If* it's done by a friend," he told both of them. The makeup was the normal kind, temporary and easily wiped off if he wasn't careful how he touched his face, but he felt safer wearing it than not. "At least, I presume you're not an enemy?"

"No. Which means you're *our* kind of officer, rather than the Captain's kind, all stuffy and formal," Ka'atieth stated.

"Formality has its place. Just not on board a shuttle named *Leaping Kitten*, I'd think," Li'eth joked. She chuckled.

"In that case, *Li'eth*, I'm Nakko, and she's A'sha," Shi'uln stated airily, flicking a finger at the two of them in the front seats before going back to his preflight checks.

"It's short for A'sha-rayn," Ka'atieth explained.

Li'eth smiled, amused. "You already told me your personal name, remember?"

"Ah, right. Well . . . no putting your feet up on the back of my seat," she ordered. "I don't care if you outrank me. It's annoying, and you're not going to do it."

"I won't. And I try not to be too annoying. My little brother . . ." He let the implications take over.

"That does raise a good question. Why haven't Their Highnesses gone into the military?" Nakko asked. His hands and eyes moved over the controls of the shuttle, both above and below the main viewscreen. His actions warmed up the engines, making them whine and the bulkheads thrum quietly, but it was clear he was familiar enough with his duties to hold a conversation while getting things ready.

"Policy," Li'eth explained. "One child at a time in the military. That's in case there's a war, and the bloodline is threatened. The Empress, knowing of the passages in the Sh'nai Book of Prophecies about me, delayed my going into the military a few years by having me serve a rotating apprenticeship with various high-ranking officials. I think, now at least, it was because she knew or at least hoped I'd be involved in diplomacy afterward and would need a good feel for how our government works.

"As it was, I was just a few months away from being released from military service when the Salik attacked, and that was that. Mah'nami and Balei'in cannot be considered the most direct heirs because of it, but at the same time, they are free from any obligation of *having* to stay and fight. That would allow them to scatter and preserve the bloodline in distant lands. The rest of us . . . My elder sisters and I have to be under direct orders to flee; otherwise, we *have* to remain in a position that's ready to assume the War Crown and take command."

"Ah, right. Four millennia ago, um . . . during the Internecine Wars," A'sha agreed. "I remember it from my history lessons. The bloodline was almost wiped out because everyone in the immediate Imperial Family was in the military, and they kept dying off in all the fighting. One way or another. Wasn't one of your ancient predecessors hanged for desertion?"

"Beaten, hanged, and set ablaze by his officers, who were not happy that one of the War King's descendants could be such a coward. Our bloodline was almost wiped out because everyone in the immediate Imperial Family were congenital *idiots* and went to war with themselves," Li'eth countered bluntly.

Nakko gaped at him.

Li'eth, seeing his shock, shrugged. "It's the truth. The immediate bloodline withered due to idiocy brought out by inbred congenital defects, and thus eventually passed to a collateral branch that hadn't inbred itself into violent psychopathy. They gained a large enough following, took over the Eternal Throne, and that was when the breeding and inheritance-by-competency laws were established for all the upper Tiers."

"Then I suppose *your* collateral branch is going to get the freshest blood possible added to it, since the Grand High

Amba—" She broke off, frowned at a blinking light on her side of the cockpit screens, and touched a control, activating an open commlink. *"This is Shuttle 205-671. What's up? We're not being denied exit clearance, are we?"*

"Turn on comm channel 3!" a male voice exclaimed through the comm speakers, palpably excited. *"The Terrans have reactivated their communications systems again! We're getting a signal straight from the Winter Palace. Is His Hi . . . Is the Grand Captain on board, yet? He needs to see this!"*

All three of them exchanged startled looks. The leftenant superior quickly switched on the viewscreen and accessed the channel in question. Master of Ceremonies appeared on the screen. Behind him and somewhat obscured but still visible . . . his mother, the Eternal Empress, could be seen. Alive, and with a certain markless, tanned Terran woman lounging at her bedside.

"Thank all the Saints . . ." Li'eth breathed, deeply relieved, studying both females.

"We've just been cleared for takeoff. Hang on, Highness," the leftenant told them, pointing at a green light on one of his lower screens. A moment later, the lighting turned red, indicating the atmosphere had been retracted, and a *chunk* reverberated through the deck plates. The warship had released their docking clamps. Nakko eased up and guided the shuttle in a slow curve forward and to their right, toward the ponderously opening blast doors. "We'll get you back home safe and sound, I promise . . ."

V'DAN

Master of Ceremonies finished his invocation, and Empress Hana'ka began to speak with crisp enunciation, as if to prove she was fully in command of her mental faculties even if she was laid up by her injuries. Jackie subtly leaned a bit more on the bed railing, folding one arm in front of the other. She meant it as an impression of familiarity, and thus of implied friendship and support, but also because as time wore on, her dizziness sapped at her energy.

In the middle of a gesture, Hana'ka touched Jackie's fingers with the backs of her knuckles. On pure instinct, Jackie shifted her hand, clasping the Empress' fingers. A subtle squeeze from Hana'ka and the way her hand lingered let Jackie know that her response was the correct one. It also gave her contact with the Empress' mind; she tried screening it out, but Hana'ka's thoughts were filled with echoes of the younger woman at her side.

For a long moment, the Terran telepath had a hard time sorting out those thoughts. Surface ones held pre-echoes overlapped with what Hana'ka was actually saying. A second layer behind it was her mind racing to make sure each word was laid with the care of a mason mortaring stones in place; Hana'ka believed they had to be perfectly placed for the best strength and impact. A third layer worried over what Jackie and her people would think of such careful phrasing, which had to be stated just so to have an impact in V'Dan law but which had not yet been established solidly in its translated meanings in Terran law.

Underneath that lay a swirling mass of anger and disappointment at her eldest daughter, anxiety for her eldest son's absence, worry for her other children, her mate, her fears for her people in the face of a Salik attack that had gotten through to the Winter Palace itself—that last one terrified her, deep down inside. Admiration for the Terrans, their courage under fire, their courtesies, her personal remorse that they were still being dismissed and disdained . . . but also a constant hesitation, like a mental stumble, over their childlike faces. And a determination *not* to see them as children anymore. That determination within the Empress made her squeeze Jackie's hand subtly once again.

Jackie squeezed back equally gently. She would never speak to anyone of what she sensed, but she did silently acknowledge understanding the older woman for a moment before carefully strengthening her mental walls. It was coming up to her turn to speak, and she readied herself to say what her fellow Terrans wanted her to say, what the V'Dan hoped she would say, and what the Alliance needed to hear.

Master of Ceremonies, standing off camera to one side, pointed at her. Jackie faced the V'Dan commscreen pickups, not the Terran ones.

"The Terran United Planets accepts the apologies of the Eternal Throne for the insults which V'Dan have given to our people," she stated formally. "We are grateful your Empress sees and acknowledges the very real cultural differences between our kind. We strive to be fair in our dealings, to be respectful and understanding, but we will not compromise in requiring respect given in return. This apology and compliance comes from the V'Dan Empire, and to the V'Dan Empire we will give our cooperation and the resumed loan of our communications capabilities.

"To the *other* members of the Alliance, however . . . we are limiting access to those capabilities until each of your governments also agrees to our terms. You will treat us with respect. You will treat us as a sovereign and separate nation, a sovereign and separate culture, and a sovereign and separate power. You will neither assume nor presume we are V'Dan. We respect our own rights and differences as we respect your rights and differences, and we require the same in return.

"You will have our assistance in this war against the Salik. I have touched their minds," Jackie confessed, "and found them to be a very serious threat. I have, with each of their permission, also touched the minds of select K'Katta, Gatsugi, Tlassian, and Solarican envoys over the last few weeks of our stay here on V'Dan, and have *not* found you, as a whole, to be any threat to Terran lives and Terran interests. We appreciate this deeply as one sentient culture to another.

"We understand the necessity of peace because we understand the value of cooperation. The Salik think in terms of deception, stalking, and predation. They will not stop until they are forced to stop. Since I believe in giving others second chances," she added, glancing at the Empress, who smiled slightly, wryly, "and as my government does as well . . . we will coordinate our forces and technologies with the Alliance's efforts to help you win this war and help you contain that Salik threat.

"With that in mind, my government has authorized the following actions, contingent upon *each* system's local leadership agreeing to cooperate with Terran requirements in exchange for Terran communications capabilities . . ."

CHAPTER 3

SHUTTLE *LEAPING KITTEN*
V'TON-BEI ORBIT

"Praise the Moons, they're back on our side! It's not just for being able to talk star to star, either," Nakko told them. The Empress was spending a few moments formally thanking the Grand Ambassador, and the shuttle was on autopilot for this part of the trip. Orbital mechanics were not easy to fly through. "I saw some of those little Terran ships and their bomb-things in action in orbit, back around the Motherworld. They were *amazing*. Giant chunks of Salik warships, just . . . gone! With their communications giving us the chance to coordinate our counterattacks, and their massive firepower—"

"—That firepower *was* their communications devices," Li'eth corrected, cutting off the leftenant's enthusiasm with a grim look. "They blew up more than a dozen of their satellites defending V'Dan from the Salik, and they can't make them all *that* fast. Shipping them to the homeworld takes added time, too."

"No! We *need* those things," the leftenant protested, twisting to look at Li'eth. Trusting to the computers to navigate them between parking orbits via a course plotted by the V'Ton-Bei Orbital Control system, he chose to argue his point. "They can't just blow them up!"

"They can, and they did, and in doing so, they saved the homeworld. Now quiet, please. I want to hear what else the Empress is sayi—"

"—The *Salik*!" Ka'atieth shouted, pointing off to starboard.

The other two in the cockpit snapped their gazes that way. Bright columns of orange light lanced through the night even as they did so, crossing the half-lit curve of the colonyworld on their port side. Nakko whipped back around to grab at the controls and disengage the autopilot, swerving their view and even their inertial momentum with a wild maneuver to try to get away from the incoming ships. He swore with rising fear and volume as he did so. *"V'shova v'shiel v'shakka v'cara u'vieth u'v'shova u'v'kanna u'v'shakk-ath . . . !"*

Li'eth didn't even have time to think about that unholy collection of improper high nouns. The lasers were alarming enough on their own; their shuttle was too small to have hull plating strong enough to ward off those energy cannons. But the lasers were only the start. Projectile weapons would soon follow, ranging from hull-shearing explosives to grappling torpedoes meant to haul a vessel within boarding range.

Small as it was, the *Leaping Kitten* might pass unnoticed by someone choosing to aim for a larger, higher-yield target, but some of those projectiles, if not all, would have proximity detectors.

Some of those—movement! Eyes straining, Li'eth saw little flutters of darkness sweeping across the sky, briefly blocking out the light of the stars—incoming! Horrified, he threw up his hands, pulling up everything he could from within himself to save them from destruction, to save *himself* from—

AVRA 5, 9508 V.D.S.
SIC TRANSIT

". . . Of course, with the Eternal Empire backing these things officially and firmly, the Terran ground troops that were originally promised will be expected to resume their deployment shortly," Empress Hana'ka continued as soon as Jackie finished the short but poignant list of Terran demands. "Our troop transports should be arriving any day, and with the Terrans' inoculation efforts for their *algic* reaction needs focusing on their professional soldiers—"

"Allergic reaction," Jackie corrected smoothly. Automatically, actually; most of her attention strayed now to the increasingly exhausting drain to her left. At least the Empress appeared to be focusing her eyes properly by now, and the biokinetic heat in Jackie's hands had eased and faded com-

pletely. Which meant she had no idea what was causing that drain to her left instead of a drain to her right.

"*Allergic*, thank you," Hana'ka acknowledged smoothly. "With those histaminic needs taken care of, we will be able to feed and house your people's soldiers as they fight for their cousins, and for a chance at a veteran's homestead on each colonyworld defended. As per our earlier negotiations, each veteran's homestead rights will be considered firstworlder-colonist rights, albeit at one-quarter the amount of land normally claimed by firstworlder settlers, in exchange for top veteran care for any . . ."

Panic slammed into Jackie in a gasp and a flex of her hand, releasing the Empress' fingers. It came out of nowhere—it came from her left, like a spear thrust into her side. No, like a *harpoon*, one that flexed out its barbs and yanked her back to her left, toward her missing half. She had a split second to react under the impact of that overwhelming fear, and in that moment of flexing, of grappling, sensed a great peril that *had* to be answered.

Lurching leftward with her mind even more so than her body, Jackie whipped that panic into a packet and flung herself far away. She leaped on instinct through the void between one fraction of a heartbeat and the next, through a gap in reality that flared in blinding white, cloaked everything in streaks of gray, and slammed into a half-dark reality dotted with colored lights and nonmedical angles. Slammed back into reality, she bubbled as big and as hard as she could.

Something roared against her shields, flooding everything in an eye-burning shade of peach-white. An instant later, something else *whommed* into her telekinetic shield, with such force that she had no time and no way in which to find a physical anchor to stabilize the force of the blow. The world tumbled around her, cracking her head and shoulder against a hard surface. Protective instinct threw up a second, smaller bubble within the greater one. A moment later, a hand caught her, dragged her across a lap, hip bruising painfully against the corner of a hard armrest.

She didn't even have to register that the hand made it through her very physical shield; it was attached to the one mind she *needed*. The world—the whole universe—stopped lurching to her left, snapping back into a comfortable, solid whole. Nauseatingly whole, from the force of the psychic jolt. Dragging in a breath of less-than-fresh air, she forced her eyes back open through the dizziness of rejoining her Gestalt partner.

Debris tumbled around them, bouncing off an invisible barrier beyond the forward viewpoint. More explosions struck her outermost shield, the one she had thrown up beyond the ship around them, but it held. For now. There were two others in the cockpit of what had to be a V'Dan ship since they were clearly Humans, a brown-haired, green-spotted woman who wasn't Countess Nanu'oc, and a pink-crescented darker-skinned man with black-and-pink hair. Both gaped, their gazes snapping back and forth from her to the windscreen view of space and back.

"You . . . you . . . !" the man whispered.

"You're the . . . the . . ." the woman stammered, pointing.

"Ambassador?" the man squeaked, twisting to look back over his shoulder at her.

Li'eth, holding her on his lap, regained some of his own energy and wits, but for a different reason. *"Yes!* She's here! And *you* need to fly us *out* of here!"

"Yes! Please!" Jackie managed to add politely, tacked on to the end of his harsh demand and her own fervent wish. Her head still spun with the abrupt change in surroundings, affecting both of their thoughts. Realizing that her own confusion and astonishment wasn't helping, Jackie wrenched her thoughts under the calm control she had learned through years of psychic meditation. "Get us somewhere safe. I *don't* want to have to do that again."

Not that she even thought she could. All Gestalt teleportations were *to* one's partner, whether that was toward or away from whatever grave danger threatened to affect one of them. Now that she and Li'eth were together . . . they were very much vulnerable. Nowhere—and no *one*—to flee to a second time.

The man with the pink curves on his golden-brown skin blinked, shook his head, and faced forward. *"U'v'kenna v'u'v'-shakk-ath* . . . I'll do as you command, meioas!"

"You'd better buckle up, Grand High Ambass . . . Saints, I

can't *believe* you're *here!*" the woman with the green spots exclaimed. "How by the demons did you *get* here?"

About to answer, Jackie reluctantly untangled herself from Li'eth and . . . slumped to the deck plates on her knees, the moment she lost physical contact with him. She almost lost the protective bubble wrapped around the outside of the shuttle, too. Clinging to it, she let her body be a distant second place in her most immediate concerns.

Equally dizzy, Li'eth reached for her shoulder; she had to grab for the edge of the far seat when the shuttlecraft swayed around them, dodging an incoming ship, but could feel his touch through her uniform. That helped somewhat with her sense of balance, allowing her to get to her feet and inch over. She felt blindingly dizzy by the time she got strapped in and flung out her left hand. Li'eth grabbed it firmly, restoring his own equilibrium as well as hers.

(*Saints, but I feel* awful *when we're not touching,*) he muttered.

(*Like we're going to pass out,*) Jackie agreed. (*I've never done anything like this . . . If this happened the last time one of us teleported—when* you *teleported to* me *during that robot attack—then* I *didn't notice it.*)

(*The distance . . . how in the name of physics did you* get *here?*) he demanded. The others could ask, but only he had a right to demand.

Physically, she was exhausted, but mentally, she still felt supercharged. When they touched, and only when they touched. Her left hand curled around his, clasping tightly, the way her mind curled around their spacecraft, allowing her a chance to give his question some serious thought. About half a second's worth in real time. (*My best guess? I was pulled to you by sheer mortal peril, and the energy of the hysterical terror that comes with it, focused through our bond. Plus, the whole argument for our neurons being entangled on a quantum level suggests we're anchored to each other. I simply exchanged my previous location for this one on the farthest leading edge of the probability curve.*)

(*That's a leading edge that—* Look out!) he yelped, seeing a bright yellow beam slicing their way, coming from a tiny dot of a ship soaring past at an angle to them.

She flexed her mental muscles, warping space around their vessel. Nakko, the man piloting the ship, yelped in fear from the sight of the stars, ships, and even the curve of the planet spinning abruptly into a half-blurred swirl.

". . . The *shit*?" the woman breathed, craning her neck off to the side. The stars outside realigned themselves. "That . . . that laser *bent*?"

"Yes, and I can only do that a few more times, and only if I see it coming. That was a *lot* of photons," Jackie added, closing her eyes. She was tired, there were ships firing weapons all around them, and she was literally light-years from . . . well, her previous location. V'Dan wasn't here; she was dead certain of that. It also wasn't home. For a moment, she longed deeply for *home*, for the shores of O'ahu, the white-curling waves and dozens of shades of water, from cerulean to sapphire blue, the plants and buildings and sandy beaches . . .

She remained on board the shuttlecraft, however. Miraculous relocation aside, she was not a teleporter. She didn't even understand *how* she had gotten here, save that it had been eighty-eight parts instinct, eleven parts luck, and one part a strange impression of a supershortened hyperrift, of all things. *Why*, for once, was the easy part. Why was observation and logical reasoning. *How* . . . was still beyond even the best Terran understanding of how psychic abilities worked.

"Okay, meioa . . . where do you want us to go?" Nakko asked. "Because we're almost to the edge of the fighting. We can go to the colonyworld, but that cuts across a nasty patch of it; we can go to one of those three big warships over there to try to dock or at least get behind them for protection, but they've got trouble headed their way; or we can head *out* of the fighting and take a leisurely loop out and around, coming back when it's hopefully over . . . and be a tempting little target for anything tracking us, if they have unoccupied gun crews on that side of their ships."

Jackie and Li'eth thought about it in a swirl of subthoughts, and announced as one, ". . . *Colonyworld*."

"V'Ton-Bei is inhabitable," Li'eth added on his own. "If we get damaged, we can have a hope of surviving a forced landing even if we're undamaged right now."

"Oh, we *are* damaged. Those lovely red lights up there,"

their pilot said, waving his hand up over his head at a bank of half a dozen red, a double handful of yellow, and a sea of green, "are showing that all but one of the forward shields got burned out by the explosion that . . . uh . . . materialized our guest. Which is still far too aberrant for me to even *think* about how she *got* here—we're not going to get arrested for kidnapping you, are we?"

"No, you won't. The only one I'd like to see arrested for kidnapping is a certain stubborn Imperial sibling," Jackie muttered. "Then all of this wouldn't have been necessary."

"Yes, yes, about the vote to go to the colonyworld," the woman interrupted. "If you haven't *noticed*, it's through the worst of the fight!"

"Aim to the upper or lower right," Jackie offered. That was what was displayed on the right-hand viewscreen; she'd stared at enough V'Dan tactical screens in the last few months to figure that much out. "That direction skirts it. Go out a little and come around toward the back side of the planet. Just hug it close enough that we have some shielding on that side. If you don't take forever, I should have enough energy to keep the ship shielded from physical attacks, but the less I have to do, the better.

"Laser-based ones . . . you're going to have a narrow field of view if you want that risk abated, too," she warned the two in the front of the cockpit. "I can either shunt aside an incoming beam, which is exhausting, or I can use a lot less energy to cloak the shuttle, making it extremely hard to hit.

"I have no idea what you're talking about, but if it'll save our skins, do it," the pilot ordered. "This isn't a warship. One direct hit, and we'll be cut in half."

Nodding, Jackie spun a cocoon of holokinesis around the ship. It wasn't a perfect sphere, but rather more like a bowl. Dead ahead, they could see the stars clearly; to either side, the view became a literal blur of gray-smeared stars and blue-white-brown planetary hues on ribbons of black. Unfortunately, that caused the tac screen to start popping up little error labels all around their flanks.

"That is a *very* strange effect. What *is* it?" the man added.

"*Holokinesis*, which is from an ancient Terran language meaning *light-movement*, as in the ability to move and manipulate light. I create illusions with my holy gifts, among other things. I cannot *stop* a laser, but I can redirect it along a different path as if my powers were a mirror. In this case, a spinning mirror, which uses far less energy than a static one," she explained.

He shook his head, his braid sliding over his red-uniformed shoulders. "That doesn't make sense."

"I may be moving nearly massless light—photonic wave packets—but the principles are still the same. A spinning surface deflects an incoming impact by hitting it from the side rather than meeting it head-on. I'm *not* reflecting the lasers straight back to their point of origin," she added. "I'm deflecting them to the right or to the left, depending upon the spin. In other words, it doesn't take nearly as much energy to make a small course correction to one side as it does to make all that energy do an about-face in a head-on confrontation."

"Okay, *that* makes sense. I'm Shi'uln," he added. "Leftenant Nakko Shi'uln. Third Tier, in the civilian sector. That's Leftenant Superior A'sha-rayn Ka'atieth, born to the Fourth."

"Terrans don't believe in Tiers," Li'eth told them. "Jackie, these are Nakko and A'sha. Nakko, A'sha, this is Jackie. We've already decided titles are overblown when we don't *have* to be formal."

"Sounds perfect. And it's nice to meet you," Jackie added.

The leftenant superior snorted. "You think it's *nice* to meet us? We were nearly killed, you were pulled from a live broadcast— *U'v'shakk!*" she swore, twisting in her seat to gape at the two in the back of the cockpit. "That was a *live broadcast*! Everyone saw you vanish! They're going to be *frantic*, trying to figure out where you went."

"The Terrans, not so much as you might think . . . once they calm down and think about it rationally," Jackie amended, forced to be honest by her nature. "I'm sure they panicked for the first few moments, as anyone sane would do. The V'Dan are going to be in a true panic, though. Particularly with our return to an alliance still so new, it's shaky. I'll need to access the Ton-Bei communications probe."

"Jackie, we can't announce your presence while the Salik are in the system. They'll pick up any lightwave broadcast and decode it within moments," Li'eth countered.

"Not if we go *to* the satellite and access it . . . directly . . . which . . . we can't do, because I don't have any Terran communications equipment." She sighed, conceding his point. Clinging to his fingers, she focused her thoughts on finding a way around that problem.

"There *are* two Terran ships in the system, though," A'sha said. "We debated taking His Highness home to V'Dan by way of a Terran ship. Even without a treaty, he was fairly sure your people would agree to help on your behalf . . . except he's turned himself over to the Tier Advocates, and the system Advocates say he has to go home via a V'Dan ship.

"But with *you* here, you can shorten up that route with some diplomacy." She called up something on her main screen, but it was a mess of lines and names, several in V'Dan red, and too much in Salik purple. Scowling, she sighed. ". . . Well, they *were* here. I don't know if they still are."

Something impacted against the bubble-shield wrapped around the ship. Jackie grunted, while the view outside the front windows turned a billowing greenish blue from the heat of whatever chemical mix had been in the bomb, combined with the shifting spin of her holokinesis. She felt Li'eth bolstering her, feeding her his strength. He could tap into her own abilities somewhat, but not to this extent, and freely conceded the flow of kinetic inergy to her, the master in training and skill.

"Was that a random attack, or are we being followed?" Nakko asked, swerving the shuttle to take evasive action. "I think the green fire is from their fighter ships' explosives."

"I believe it is, but I can't see through the blurring-thing out there to confirm," A'sha answered.

"Well, I'm not canceling it until we're out of the hot zone," Jackie told both of them. Her head started to throb. "How much longer?"

"To get out of danger or all the way to land?" Nakko asked. The shuttle jolted, and flames roared past them. Everyone yelped but Jackie; she clenched down with her mind and clung with her fingers. None of the telltale lights for the shuttle flickered, but chunks of metal were flung past their viewpoint, visible only because their edges were bright-hot as they tumbled past.

"I . . . don't think we're being chased anymore," Li'eth muttered, slowly relaxing his shoulders when nothing else happened. "I hope."

"Yes, let us hope that was a pursuing fighter being destroyed by one of *our* meioas," A'sha agreed.

Jackie, thoughts racing, came to an abrupt conclusion. Blinking a little, she asked, "Can you project a comm signal on . . . uh . . . the Ar-tuin wavelength 7534?"

"I'm a bit too busy *flying* to fiddle with the wavelength tuners," Nakko replied, dodging their craft yet again, half his attention on the forward view, half on the tactical screen below it showing the battle to their rear. "A'sha?"

"I'll get it," she said. She worked for a few moments, fitting an earpiece in place, murmuring to herself, then nodded. "What do you need to broadcast, and why on that channel? Most are tuned by lots of ten in the Alliance."

"Because that's a channel that corresponds with one of our Terran wavelengths. Put it on a broadbeam, and hand me the microphone," Jackie told her. She stretched forward with her free hand, touching the red-uniformed woman on her shoulder. "I'm going to send a message to any Terrans in the system. It's important to let my people know I'm still alive."

"Jackie, I told you, you can't do that," Li'eth reminded her, squeezing her fingers. "You send out any sort of a signal, and the Salik will know you're here! I am quite certain they attacked the Winter Palace specifically in the hope of destroying your people, and with it, any chance you would help us against them."

That made her roll her eyes. "Yes, it would, *if* I spoke in V'Dan. But not if I spoke in *Terranglo*."

". . . Oh. Right. Saints, I feel stupid," he added under his breath, wincing.

"Don't," the leftenant superior told him. She handed Jackie the earpiece with its little wire of a microphone. "I feel stupid about not considering that, too, so you're not alone. We *were* briefed at least twice, maybe three times over the last few months on the possibility of Terranglo being used as an unbreakable security code, and even *I* was thinking she'd be speaking in V'Dan—you'll be live in five . . . four . . . three . . ."

Pausing a couple beats after the count reached zero, Jackie

switched to Terranglo and spoke. *"This is Grand High Ambassador Jacaranda MacKenzie, authorization Alpha Juliett Mike, to all Terran ships in the Ton-Bei System. I need you to open a channel to V'Dan and get a message to Captain Hamza al-Fulan. The message is this: Yellow Echo Sierra, India, Alpha Mike, Oscar Kilo. My location is the Ton-Bei System.*

"I repeat, this is Grand High Ambassador Jacaranda MacKenzie with a message for Captain Hamza al-Fulan based on the V'Dan homeworld. The message is Yellow Echo Sierra, India, Alpha Mike, Oscar Kilo; my location is V'Ton-Bei. Please send it via hypercomm immediately to Captain Hamza al-Fulan on V'Dan, over."

Three seconds later, A'sha pointed at a light on her console, and touched a couple buttons. "Whatever you're saying, you're getting a response on the same frequency. But it could be anyone, even the Salik. Do you want to hear it?"

"Yes, please," Jackie confirmed.

The comm system had a cache with a buffer. The audio response replayed from the beginning with just a few more button touches. *"This is Captain Sharon Mamani of the TUPSF Embassy 14. Ambassador, if this is really you, sir, and you really are in the Ton-Bei System, you vanished from the commscreen less than five minutes ago. How the hell did you get out here so fast?"*

"The Gestalt bond was in severe danger, prompting a spontaneous teleport," she replied, and felt Li'eth squeezing her hand in silent support. Even with his psychic inergy augmenting hers, she could feel the dizziness returning. *"We're both close to a KI burnout because of it, and I do not know what the severity of the backlash will be. We are on board a shuttlecraft, headed for the planet to find refuge from the battle. But since I don't want anyone back on V'Dan to have a panic attack at my sudden absence . . ."*

"Understood, sir. We'll get the message sent. I will need today's authorization code, however, and a visual confirmation would be preferred."

(*Dammit . . . what is it, what is the code for this week . . .?*) She dredged her tired mind for the answer.

(*I'll give you more, but I feel like I'm going to collapse again,*) Li'eth warned her.

(*I know. We both are. How well do you trust these two?*) she asked. (*Because right now, I am still feeling rather paranoid about how your fellow V'Dan are going to treat you and me.*)

(*These two, I'd trust,*) Li'eth told her. (*A'sha-rayn stood up to her captain, who was trying to get me back under sedation despite my legal maneuverings otherwise. Nakko's on her side. He brought me clothes and helped me in the shower when I would've been stuck in a hospital tunic otherwise.*)

(*That makes me glad.*) Switching back to V'Dan, she said, "Can you connect me visually, Ka'atieth?"

"I'll need a few moments to find the portable camera and get it up and running," the leftenant superior said, already reaching for a storage compartment. "There should be one on this thing, if nothing else than to check the nooks and crannies in the hold . . ."

The shuttle rocked again, another flare of greenish fire gouting out to the port side, blurred by the still-spinning telekinetic shields. Nakko looked up and wrinkled his nose. "That one got some damage through. It must've been a larger payload."

"More like my strength is waning," Jackie muttered.

"Get us to that planet," Li'eth ordered. "Get us inside its defenses and behind some cover."

"Yes, meioa. I am working on it," Nakko muttered. "It's my marked hide, too, you know . . ."

"Found it!" A few moments later the hovercam was active and humming in front of Jackie's face. "It'll be a close-up. Hope your face isn't pimpled."

"Leftenant Superior!" Li'eth snapped, scowling. "You do *not* treat a Grand High Ambassador like a juvenile!"

"What? No!" the other woman protested, twisting to look at him, then Jackie, with wide eyes. "Adults can have acne, too, you know! My eldest brother's face still looks like a *juzul*, with all the little red dots across it, and he's in his *forties*—a *juzul* is a kind of tropical fruit," she added to Jackie, though she faced forward again. "It looks diseased when it's ripe. I am *not* one of those who underestimates someone just because they look young. Or disrespects them. I can understand why you'd think that, but I am *not*. I'm just . . . thinking of post*jungen* acne, is all.

". . . You'll be live in five seconds," she added, still frowning.

Jackie squeezed Li'eth's hand. (*Thanks for the support, even if it thankfully isn't needed.*) A tiny light snapped to life on the camera—technology was ubiquitous in showing when things were active, it seemed—and she spoke into it, switching to Mandarin, not Terranglo. *"Today's full authorization code should be the Year of the Rabbit. The energy is Yin, and the element is Metal. The month is the Monkey, and the solar phase should be* lìqiū. *Don't ask me what the double hour is back home. My wrist unit is still synched to V'Dan time at the moment."*

Jackie couldn't see the corresponding shuttle screen completely, between the seatback in front of her and the hovering camera between her and the monitor screen, but it was definitely Captain Mamani on the other side; her brown skin and sleek black hair were hallmarks of her Aymara ancestry, different from the rounder faces and curlier locks of Jackie's own Polynesian ancestors. Then again, the Aymara were found thousands of kilometers across the ocean among the snow-capped mountains of the Andes, with a thousand and more years of colonization differences between them.

"Xiè xie," the captain replied, peering at Jackie's face through her end of the connection. *"It is good to see you are alive and well. For the record, the Terran Universal Mean Time is in the second half of the double hour of the Pig; it's officially almost tomorrow. I will get your message sent right out. Will you be needing a relay set up?"*

"Not if I end up speaking in V'Dan, which I'd have to do. Too many wrong ears or ear-equivalents would be listening in. I'd have to be on your ship in person to send it hyper without any lightwave leaking out," Jackie added.

"Considering we're broadcasting this as a potential target moving across the planet's orbit, and that I'm only answering your call because none of the enemy speak Terranglo, never mind Mandarin . . . I would have to agree on that. Tell you what," Captain Mamani offered, looking off to one side as she

did something with her control console. *"There's a northern hemisphere mining and manufacturing town named . . . 'ar eye apostrophe oh kay oh,' if I'm getting the V'Dan phonemes right. I'm not going to say it aloud just in case they can pick it out of everything else we're saying, but we stopped there for fueling and a couple items they could manufacture for some minor repairs. Can you meet us there?"*

Jackie covered her mic pickup and traced the letters in the air with a thread of holokinesis, mouthing her way through them. Either it spelled *rye-oh-ko*, or *ree-oh-koh*. She suspected the latter. ". . . Ree . . . oko? Nakko, do you know where the mining town of Ri'oko is, on V'Ton-Bei?"

"No, but hopefully there can't be *that* many places named *Fire Nut*," the pilot dismissed. "Unless we get unlucky and someone named five separate towns that."

"I know where it is. Vaguely," Li'eth added. Still holding Jackie's hand, he twisted to the other side, touching the controls on his console to call up a map of the planet. "My crew had to pick up some parts with rare minerals that were being manufactured there. And yes, there's only one town named Ri'oko on V'Ton-Bei."

"I found it on the colonial grid," A'sha stated, nodding at the terrain map now on her central screen.

"Want me to set a course for it? Evasive course?" Nakko asked.

"Evasive course, yes," Jackie confirmed, and switched back to Mandarin, releasing the mic wire. *"We've found it, and we're on our way."*

"I'll see you soon, then. Captain Mamani out."

"Ambassador out." Removing the earpiece, she eyed the camera. "I'm done. You can put that away now."

"Right." Programming it to return, the leftenant superior deactivated and tucked it away, then accepted the headset as well. "Thanks. I—Saints!" she yelped as a fighter-sized craft shot past them, skimming the upper layers of the atmosphere at speeds that left a brief blaze of plasma in its wake. "I *much* prefer facing a clean fight from the bridge of a real ship, not the cockpit of something the size of a *kikkai* nut!"

"I don't know; I think I *like* this shuttlecraft," Nakko muttered. Jackie didn't know if he was being sarcastic or not.

"Only because we haven't been cracked open yet. Thank you, by the way," A'sha added over her shoulder. "I'm not super-religious or anything, and I don't understand *how* you're even doing it, but I am definitely glad you're both living Saints, right now."

Jackie didn't respond. They were entering the thermosphere now, and she realized she had to change the shape of their protective shield. The speed they were going meant that even the thinnest of gases at this level were still enough to cause significant drag force, particularly on something cup-shaped.

Closing her eyes, she visualized a network of rooflike shapes, sharp and widespread close to the ship, but flaring out to overlap any holes. That funneled the molecules better though there was still quite a lot of resistance. She let the spinning holokinetic cloak fade, too; the last thing they needed was some friend-or-foe-recognition software down on the surface thinking a blurred sphere was an incoming foe.

Sure enough, Nakko spoke into his own headset, chatting on what had to be an atmospheric traffic channel. He identified their craft and listed their course as "evasive high altitude" in between pauses to listen to whoever manned the other side. After a few more exchanges, he dipped the nose of the shuttle-craft down, diving under the highest of the clouds.

Jackie tried to hold the net-and-wedge grid of a shield, but ten seconds after they dipped into the cloud cover, her strength gave out. She slumped, fingers going slack. Only Li'eth's strength held their hands, their flesh together. As it was, she had to close her eyes and struggle just to breathe against a debilitating, nauseating wave of dizziness. Disorientation followed when the craft zigged and zagged around her.

Clinging to his armrest with his other hand, Li'eth fought his own nausea, muscles trembling in exhaustion. Instinct and Master Sonam's teachings said that if he let go now, they'd both collapse unconscious, so he clung hard. The shuttlecraft bucked, crossing boundary layers of the atmosphere. Clouds obscured the real view through the windows before those windows darkened automatically, dimming the incoming white glow so that the heads-up projections on the viewscreens could be more easily seen.

After a while, their flight leveled out, and Nakko sighed. ". . . Quarter hour without any signs of pursuit. Thank the Saints for some decently thick cloud cover right now. I think we can relax."

Li'eth, still dizzy, struggled to get his eyes open. He was too drained. Sonam had spoken of that, too, while training him. "Need food. Drink . . ."

"There should be some electrolyte packs here somewhere." A'sha twisted in her seat, her tone softening when she peered at the pair. "The two of you look *awful*. I guess there is no such thing as saintly powers without paying a devilish price . . . Nakko, don't bounce the shuttle," she ordered, rustling in the small storage cupboards for snacks.

Li'eth heard her unbuckle her seat restraints and felt her hand on his chin a few seconds later. "Open those lips a little . . . here you go, suck on that straw. It's *grapa* flavored; hope you don't mind."

Feeling the straw poking against his teeth, then his tongue, he closed his mouth and sucked. Salty-sweet, tangy with fruit flavoring. Normally, the stuff tasted weird, but Li'eth sucked it down as greedily as if they'd just come out of a Terran hyperrift.

"That's . . . amazingly thirsty," she muttered, pulling away the straw as soon as the packet was sucked flat. "Oh—I'd better—here, let me get this one for you, Ambassador . . . Ambassador?"

Li'eth, feeling the sugars entering his blood, jolted Jackie with a bit of biokinetic heat. She roused and mumbled, and sucked on the straw the leftenant superior offered to her. Blinking, he managed to get his eyes open this time. "Thank you. We'll need more, and . . . uh . . . solid food. *Psychic* abilities require biological energy to empower them, and we just . . . drained ourselves."

A'sha glanced between them. Jackie still had her eyes closed while she drained the last of the packet being held by the other woman, but some color did return to her tanned face. The leftenant superior lifted one brow. "Actually, from that big welcoming display they had when they arrived, I thought she was the one who could create shields and stuff, not you. Why are *you* so tired, Li'eth?"

"Who do you think was the fuel tank to her flamethrower?" he countered.

A'sha shrugged at that. Peeling open one of the other packages, she pulled the wrapper partway down and handed it to him. Nut cluster bars, popular with V'Dan and K'Katta alike. Sticky-sweet, but loaded with proteins and vitamins. She peeled a second one and offered it to Jackie, who finally forced her eyes open again, accepting the packet.

"Thank you," Jackie muttered, awkwardly taking it with her free hand. Her other fingers tightened around Li'eth's.

"You're welcome, Ambassador," A'sha replied.

Jackie chewed while the other woman returned to her seat and buckled herself in place. She spoke when her mouth was clear. ". . . Why so formal? I thought we all agreed on first names?"

"I'm . . . trying to remind myself you're not a kid. In fact, I just realized you're probably older than me. I'm sorry if that offends you—" she added.

"—No, no," Jackie reassured her. "You're *aware* of the disparity, and you are trying to compensate for a lifetime of social and cultural conditioning. It is those who refuse to even acknowledge that the prejudice exists who make things too disrespectful and difficult for us Terrans to tolerate. We're happy when anyone at least *tries* to overcome their cultural conditioning," she added. "We don't ask for perfection; we just ask that you actively try. So you can call me Ambassador if it helps, but you are also free to call me Jackie."

"Eh. I like Ja'ki," Nakko stated, smiling to himself. "I had a little cousin nicknamed Ja'ki because she was a magnet for gems and jewelry. Give her a polished, shiny stone as a toddler, and she'd stare at and play with it for hours."

"Yes, but are you going to *treat* her like a little toddler, once she's all grown-up?" Li'eth asked.

"My cousin? Just because of her nickname? Moons, no! My cousin grew up to be even bigger than me, and became locally famous on V'Zon A'Gar as a professional gladiator. She'd twist and fold me into a paper bird if I ever treated any namesake of hers like a little girl," he confessed.

"Wait . . . your cousin . . . is she *Ja'ki-eth*?" Li'eth asked, eyes widening. *"V'Ja'ki-eth?"*

"You've heard of her? Wait until she hears that a member of the Imperial Tier has heard of her! She's going to faint!" Nakko crowed, grinning.

Jackie blinked and scrambled to translate what Li'eth was trying to say. It didn't come across until he sent her an underthought of explanation. (*Oh! The Death Diamond?*)

(*The stone type she associates herself with is a topaz, but then "Death Diamond" does sound more alliterative in Terranglo, yes.*) Out loud, he said, "Actually, our chief pilot, Ba'-oul—Leftenant Superior Des'n-yi; he's from the island of Tai-mat back on V'Dan—is a big fan of pro combat."

"Let me guess, a big fan of Verlouss Avern? He's the top gladiator from the archipelago," Nakko added in an aside to Jackie.

Li'eth nodded. "Ba'oul said he liked Verlous Avern, Ja'ki-eth, even Big Pockets Bob—he had recordings of *all* the big matches. He'd regularly bribe the comm teams to make sure they downloaded the gladiator fights within the first half hour after the military news packets came through, as soon as the *T'un Tunn G'Deth* pulled into any inhabited orbit. I enjoyed watching them, too, though I wouldn't say I'm an actual fan of gladiator sports. It was something to watch, though. Ba'oul would always put on a showing in the enlisted lounge, then worked his way up to the officers' lounge."

"That must've been very popular with the crew, doing it that way, rather than making it seem like they were lower on the entertainment chain than the officers," Nakko offered.

"The higher Tiers got first pick at lining up the professional dramas and comedies," Li'eth said. "It actually made sense to hand over sports broadcasts and such to the Fifth Tiers first, so they could then switch later on."

Nakko nodded. "My first assignment, our captain came from the Fifth Tier. He gave the Fifths first choice at *everything*, whenever there was enough to go around. Entertainment programs included. Upper Tiers got paperwork and formal newscasts first."

"Can't say the same for Captain Qa-Reez," A'sha muttered. "Always the best for the officers, and the rest got the scraps and the sludge work. I felt ashamed for having Second Tier privileges more often than not, as an officer in the Imperial Fleet under his command."

(*Qa-Reez?*) Jackie asked her Gestalt partner.

(*The captain of the ship I woke up on, a would-be syco-phant of my sister's.*) He broke off, looking up. "Are we descending?"

Nakko nodded. "Fifteen minutes to landing. It might be a bit bumpy, so either finish those nut bars and grab an airsick-ness bag, or hold off and wait until we land."

(*Food is fuel,*) Jackie decided, and munched away. (*The more I eat, the better I feel. I can put up with some roughness, I think.*)

Li'eth joined her, biting off another chunk and chewing fearlessly. Food did indeed feel like fuel, still desperately needed by both of them. (*How soon until the Terrans show up?*)

(*Depends on how far away they were around the planet, what flight path they could take, whether or not they get en-gaged in battle . . . These nut bars aren't going to last very long,*) she warned him. (*We'll need real food. Not a huge meal all at once, but a steady stream of it.*)

"A'sha?" Li'eth suggested as soon as he cleared his mouth. "Why don't you get on the Ton-Bei matrix and look up which restaurants in Ri'oko deliver, and see if you can get a meal catered to the shuttleport? Something with a lot of local var-iety to it, sample plates and such. We might as well treat the Ambassador to a taste of V'Ton-Bei's delicacies while we're here."

"That's a good idea, though I'm not sure how much variety there is to find in a mining town. Or if they'll deliver," she said. "Of course, if the Empire is financing this, I'm sure they'll deliver us a giant tank of water and men in fish suits to do fin-dances if we pay highly enough."

Li'eth grinned. "*Yes,* I will pay for dinner to be catered, but not for that. I'm not interested in fish suiters, thank you."

"Oh, c'mon, have you seen the *abs* on those men?" A'sha asked, laughing. "The very thought makes me weak at the knees!"

"You said it, sister!" Nakko agreed, holding his fist up and out. She bumped the back of her hand against his, and they both grinned.

(*She has a point, swimming* does *strengthen one's abdominal muscles,*) Jackie pointed out. (*Back home, we have a saying, strong waves make strong bodies. Of course, the trick is to know your own strength and not try to swim when the waves are* too *strong.*)

(*I promise I'll swim every day I can,*) Li'eth joked back. (*And in the waters I know I can handle best.*)

(*You still owe me the time to go surfing on V'Dan, with its three-moon tides,*) she reminded him tartly.

(*Yes, beloved,*) Li'eth agreed. (*We get news back to your people, wait for this attack to go away, then take a Terran ship straight back home—oh, how was Mother?*) he asked her. (*She looked like she's going to be okay, on the screen.*)

(*Officially, the Empress is doing well and is expected to recover fully,*) she told him, and sent him surface memories of what she had observed while in that infirmary room.

(*And unofficially?*) he asked, worry threading through his underthoughts.

(*She needs to be seen by qualified Terran biokinetic medical specialists. I think there was a little bit of fine motor-skill brain damage,*) she said. (*There was that nasty bandage on her head, and her eyes wouldn't focus until after my hands heated up, and I let it pour into her. I hope you don't mind I used our biokinesis. I don't know what I did; I just know I wasn't harming anything by it, and she did focus a lot better afterwards.*)

(*As her very concerned son, I say you did exactly what was right. As an Imperial Prince . . . I'd say "shut it off" to the paranoid people who would want to spout words of worry and condemnation, and* also *say you did the right and proper thing,*) Li'eth sent. (*You're the ally we need,* and *the kind of friend we want.*)

(*Good. I like her. For her own sake. She's very . . . stiffly formal on the surface, but a good person down in her core. She has a solid foundation in honor and compassion. Much like a certain son of hers I know,*) she teased.

(*Balei'in is a very good son, yes,*) he agreed immediately.

She squeezed his hand at the return teasing.

CHAPTER 4

"Fires continue to burn on the Ke-chai Peninsula tonight," the beige-starred, dark-skinned news anchor reported from the monitor in the shuttle's main hold. Like many news broadcasts back among the Terrans, images of the reporter sat to one side of the screen while broadcasts of actual footage from the location in question played on the other half. "There are reports of Salik invaders still lurking in that area, but the Imperial Army has been evacuating families and businesses, and tales of brave colonists fighting to defend their lives and their land have been reaching our news center.

"You can check our news matrix for more details on individual heroes and lists of evacuated residencies. Meanwhile, the last of the enemy forces on board the *Sun's Glory* have been captured, though all compartments are being double-checked for holdouts . . ."

"Try the *k'teli* noodles," Nakko suggested next, tapping the carton in question before picking up one filled with some sort of fruit and meat sautéed together. "Those are the turquoise-colored ones. I liked those a lot."

Distracted from the news, Jackie looked at the dish in question. It looked like spinach noodles to her.

"I don't know," A'sha said, eyeing the dish dubiously. "They tasted a bit bland to me."

Jackie poked her complimentary *umma* into the box and scraped a little bit into her bowl. A tentative taste test reminded her of coconuts with a hint of pepper. "They're not truly bland to me, and they're not bad even though they're mild. Have you tried the one with the purple nuts?"

"Ah . . ." A'sha-rayn checked her printout sheaves, finding the dish on the restaurant's pictorial menu and squinting at the fine print under the label attached to the nuts in question. "They call those . . . *plink-pa*. Apparently, it's a sound the nuts make as they fall from the vine when ripe and bounce on the ground."

"I'm just glad I can eat them," Jackie said. She offered that carton to the other woman. "If we hadn't come up with a version of the *jungen* we could modify and infuse, I'd be afraid to eat *anything* foreign."

"Just remember, fatigue should be checked out medically, and fevers are to be taken very seriously," Li'eth cautioned her. "Thankfully, everyone here on V'Ton-Bei has had over 350 years to figure out what's safe to eat and how best to cook it."

"Personally, I really like this food," Nakko agreed, tucking another sporkful of the fruit-and-meat dish into his mouth. He jumped a little—they all did—when something beeped loudly from the cockpit. Pulling out the *umma*, he dumped it into his bowl even as he scrambled to his feet. "I'll check that. It sounds like the proximity alert."

"Hey, don't talk with your mouth full! We're officers, not Fifth Tiers," A'sha called after him. "It's one thing to be casual about names, but how we behave . . . well, the Terrans aren't the only ones to be affected by cultural expectations. Or do you even know what I'm talking about, Ja'ki?"

"Classism still exists back home," Jackie admitted freely. "Those who have a lot of wealth versus those who have not. Those who are educated versus those who are not. Religions still breed intolerance toward nonbelievers, though there are strict laws these days about how you can express that intolerance. Or rather, *cannot* express it. The core thing to remember, however, is that everyone you meet, *everyone*, is a fellow *Human*—up until we start getting true alien visitors. But even then, everyone has potential to be great, to be awful, to be silly, to be serious . . ."

She broke off as the video screen displaying the local news abruptly shut off. Nakko hurried back, leaning through the open door of the transport hold. "Hey, pay attention! The Terrans have arrived. Well, their uniforms are a little weird, full bodysuit things, but they don't have any marks I can see, so they have to be the Terrans, right?"

Quickly wiping her mouth clean with a paper-like napkin, Jackie cleared her throat with a sip of electrolyte water from yet another packet. She was still drained but no longer feeling as debilitated as she had back when needing that very first sip. ". . . Would you mind letting them in?"

"Sure. There's enough food left to share," he joked. "But you should come with me, so they know they've got the right shuttle."

"Of course," she murmured, and pushed to her feet, wiping her fingers on the napkin thing.

"This is the *only* spacefaring military shuttle in the entire landing zone, so you'd think they got it right," A'sha retorted dryly.

"We still don't know your military designs from civilian ones at a glance," Jackie countered. "To be fair, you wouldn't be able to tell ours apart, either."

"True. And yes, there's enough food left to share. Unless there are a dozen of them."

"No, just two," Nakko said, tipping his head at the side airlock door.

"Wait a moment—just two?" A'sha called after them, misunderstanding the conversation. "Your ships are crewed by just two people?"

"Six, actually. Two pilots, two navigators, two other crew members," Jackie admitted. At the other woman's gaping look, she shrugged and spread her hands. "They're not very big ships."

"You must have a *tiny* army . . ." A'sha muttered, staring in disbelief.

"It's only our interstellar capability that's currently tiny in proportion to the rest." She left the hold, following Nakko to the airlock. He opened the door, extended the ramp, then stepped back so Jackie could step into view and lift her hand in greeting. She switched to Terranglo, addressing them. *"Captain Mamani, yes? And . . . Lieutenant Commander Paroquet?"*

"That's me, the Flying Auk," the short, stocky man responded, poking his thumb at his chest. He mock-flapped his elbows and grinned, his teeth a white line in the circle of his tanned face, visible in the fading light of local sunset. *"Glad to see you alive and safe, Ambassador."*

"If you'll come with us to our ship, Ambassador," Captain Mamani added to Jackie, gesturing behind her with a deep brown hand at the familiar-yet-foreign OTL ship that had landed a short distance away, *"we'll get you broadcasting right away."*

"We can't take off immediately, though," the lieutenant commander warned her, holding up his hand. *"We still need time to process fuel. Maneuvers to avoid all that fighting ate up a chunk of our reserves."*

"I'm still eating supper," Jackie demurred. She switched back to V'Dan. "Why don't the two of you come aboard and have a bite to eat while I finish my meal?"

Mamani eyed her with a touch of skepticism in those dark brown eyes though she moved toward the shuttle readily enough. *"I thought you were in a hurry to get back online, and to get yourself back to V'Dan."*

"I am," Jackie replied in kind, guessing the woman was still speaking Terranglo out of discretion's sake. *"But my partner and I are on the verge of KI-shock. Food and water are more important at the moment. And please speak V'Dan to be polite. I know Aixa transferred it to both of you."*

"Ah. That makes sense. Hello," the captain added in V'Dan, nodding to Nakko as she reached the top of the boarding steps. "I am Captain Sharon Mamani. Ah, you are the captain of this vessel?"

"The pilot, since it's just a shuttle. Leftenant Nakko Shi'uln," he introduced himself.

Mamani glanced at Jackie. "He's related to that green-spotted woman that tried to . . . ?"

Jackie quickly shook her head. "That was Shi'ol Nanu'oc. This is Nakko Shi'uln."

"Ah, my apologies for the confusion," Mamani offered. "The names are similar."

"That's okay. I wouldn't want to be mistaken for her, either. You also say 'ah' a lot," Nakko offered, smiling. "You'll get along fine with my superior. Leftenant Superior A'sha-rayn Ka'atieth. And . . . Thass-mi, Tha Fly-yeeng'ock, was it?" he added to the man following her.

The Terran male gaped for a moment, then laughed, teeth gleaming white in his tanned face. "My *name* is Julio Paroquet.

My family name, Paroquet, means 'auk,' which is a type of seabird. My nickname is the Flying Auk because I am a pilot," he explained. "So, I literally said, translated, 'That's me, the Flying Auk.' It's a pun, since I'm a pilot and my name . . . eh, never mind," the lieutenant dismissed. "I'm a Lieutenant First Grade, the equivalent of one of your Leftenant Superiors. Don't mind the joke."

"No, I get it. I'm sure it's even funnier in the original language," Nakko allowed. "Thank you for explaining. Welcome aboard Shuttle 205-671, nicknamed the *Leaping Kitten*. It's a lot funnier in *our* language when you know the parent ship was named for the roar a wild *g'at* makes when it attacks."

Paroquet smiled warmly. "It's nice to know awkwardness is a species trait—that's a joke as well. It's only funnier in a psychological language, of course."

"I thought it was funnier in a metaphorical language, but that's just my opinion," Nakko retorted. Both men grinned. He gestured at the others, leading the way into the main cabin. "Come on inside. Meioas, these are Captain Ma'mani and Leftenant Par'o-kay."

Li'eth addressed them. "I suggest we continue to use first names, since this is hardly the Winter Palace. Or the Summer. Or even a pleasure yacht. That's Nakko, this is A'sha, you already know Jackie, and of course myself as Li'eth."

"Ah. Sharon, then," Mamani said, flicking her hand at herself, then at her fellow officer. "And he's Jack."

"Any relation?" A'sha asked, digging through the delivery bags for a few more *umma*. "Jackie, Jack?"

"None that we're aware of," Paroquet stated, holding up his hands.

"Nobody's related to anybody closely, in the expedition forces," Jackie added, gesturing for the others to settle picnic style on the deck plates since there was no table. Her fellow Terrans shifted into sitting positions on the floor where indicated without a qualm, allowing her to join them and pick up her spork to continue poking at the much-needed and rather tasty food.

"Why aren't there any relatives?" Nakko asked, curious. "Are you forbidden from having relatives serve at the same time in your military, as the Imperial Tier is?"

"We do have siblings who serve, but they're rarely posted in the same region," Jackie replied. "That minimizes a loss to a bloodline."

"It's similar to the Imperial Tier's ruling of only one prince or princess serving in the military at a time, but in their case, it's mostly because Terrans have very small family sizes," Li'eth added. "*Earth*, the Motherworld, is very crowded. They've been limiting their population sizes for . . . uhh . . . a hundred years?"

"About 137, actually, but we had a two-generation easement, about thirty-six years, to replenish the numbers decimated by the AI War," Jackie stated.

"Artificial Intelligences that got out of hand," Captain Mamani explained at their blank looks. "Between excellent health care, longevity treatments that keep us functioning well into our eighties and nineties, constantly improving safety features in various jobs, and a lack of serious wars, we've been forced to stick strictly to a two-child system, with only an occasional lottery drawing for a third whenever premature deaths have reduced the population pressures."

Both A'sha and Nakko wrinkled their noses. A'sha put her spork back in her bowl, her appetite clearly affected. ". . . That's awful."

"I'll bet your people are eager to sign up for a chance to fight for colony space," Nakko added.

"To a point." Sharon glanced at Jackie, who nodded, giving her permission to be honest. She accepted the spork A'sha handed over with a nod of thanks, and carefully added, "We're not as keen to live under the rules of your Empire as we are to live under the rules of our own. It's what we're used to, after all, and we'll react with instincts attuned to the rhythm of our own culture before any others."

"It's what we know and like best, and for us, it works," Jackie added, making a mental reminder to put a note of praise in the captain's file for her diplomatic phrasing. "Try the dish with the blue lumps. They're a tasty local vine-nut of some sort."

The other two Terrans tried some of the local food. A'sha helped them figure out what everything was by referencing the diagrammed printouts once again, and the conversations revolved around food, exports, imports, colony life, flavors, who got the last scrapings of the last few dishes, and other cheerful topics.

About fifteen minutes later—V'Dan or Terran, it didn't matter—Jackie nodded slowly in a pause between conversations. ". . . That should do it. I think I can keep going another hour or two, before I'll need sleep. You?" she asked Li'eth.

"If I don't fall asleep from the food," he agreed, "then yes, I should be good for a few hours as well."

"This meal *was* good, but we should get you back to our ship, check in, and let everyone know you're okay," Mamani agreed.

"I'm surprised you were so close to our hail," A'sha offered, glancing at the Terran woman.

"We'd gone to one of the Chinsoiy systems to deliver a hyperrelay and were already on our way back to Earth for more via the Gatsugi route, when the recall went out with the closing of the embassy. If that happened, we had standing orders to return to V'Dan to help pack up and pick up everyone still on your capital world," Mamani stated in explanation. "You're just blindly lucky we hadn't left this system yet.

"Captain Charboli and I were both in orbit for our mandatory rest breaks between jumps when the relays came back online and told us the embassy had been reopened. He was on the far side of the planet from the fighting, though, so he was free to go farther out when the fighting started happening. We were debating what to do when we picked up the Ambassador's call since we have no current orders to stay and fight. Just standing orders to cut and run if things go bad," she added.

"Oh?" Nakko asked between bites. "You make that sound like you have to be given specific orders to fight."

"We still have a limited number of ships. The *14*—our ship—decided to stay in close proximity to live-broadcast the battle to the Terran version of your info-matrices, so if nothing else, everyone would have the latest battle intel even if we weren't actively fighting. I'll admit your broadcast caught us off guard, Jackie," she said, twisting to follow Jackie, who had stood to fetch her black uniform jacket.

"That's an understatement," her junior officer told them, swallowing a mouthful of something like cooked greens, only they were purple in hue. "The embassy's *closed* . . . the embassy's *open* . . . the Salik are attacking, and the Ambassador's in the system, when moments ago, she was sixteen light-years away. Bad news followed by good news followed by awful news followed by *weird* news," Paroquet listed, flicking his spork with each point being made. "It's been a very strange past few days."

"Imagine it from *my* end of things," Jackie replied. "I can only imagine how this is going to tangle up everything even more before we can get it all straightened out."

"We can easily get you back to V'Dan if you order it, Ambassador," the captain offered. She twisted the other way to eye Li'eth. "And you, Your Highness . . . unless there's a reason why you're out here? Ah. Wait, you *are* going back to V'Dan, right? Both of you? Or since you're still in their military, are you actually under orders to go elsewhere, Your Highness?"

Li'eth shook his head. "Those orders are . . . It's complicated. But I am going back to V'Dan, yes. I need to hand myself over to the Tier Advocates."

"The who what, now?" Paroquet asked, looking up from scraping out the last scraps of food from one of the delivery boxes.

Jackie twisted to look at Li'eth, buttoning up her jacket. She knew what they were since they were very much a part of the Empire's government system, but she didn't know why he mentioned them now. "Why *are* you handing yourself to the Tier Advocates?"

"It was the only way to get out from under Vi'alla's orders regarding me," he explained. They hadn't had time or energy to discuss these things until now, food being a priority. "Even then, it barely worked."

"Your m . . . the Empress rescinded those orders," Jackie told him, correcting herself. The V'Dan people—including Li'eth himself—tended to refer to Empress Hana'ka formally most of the time. Even when he was talking about her as his own mother. "She revoked and rescinded all orders made by Imperial Princess Regent Vi'alla that affected my people. As you are my Gestalt partner, and deliberate separation of Gestalt partners is against Terran law as well as Terran custom, those orders are also revoked. Both our governments agreed to it before I vanished."

"Well, that's good to know *now*," he retorted sarcastically, flicking a hand skyward. "But I made that decision *hours* ago, to keep from being sedated and hauled even farther away, to Saints know where! That decision cannot be revoked by any outside authority, not even Her Eternity. The Tier Advocates alone must agree to release me from their jurisdiction . . . and they may choose not to do that. It's a small possibility, but a very real one."

"Why wouldn't they do that?" Paroquet asked him.

"Politics," Mamani replied sagely, even though she wasn't V'Dan. "Keeping an Imperial Prince under their jurisdiction would give them clout with the Empress." She shook her head, her black braid sliding over her shoulders. "No matter how far we roam, no matter the star systems we visit, it all boils down to death, taxes, and politics—no offense, Ambassador."

"None taken," Jackie murmured.

A'sha nodded sagely, if mock-sadly. "Ah. We have a similar saying."

Jackie crossed to Li'eth and offered her hands to help him up. "I'm well aware that sometimes a government official has to do something that isn't generous and free. Actions have value as well as consequences, and that value can be a tool for creating leverage in negotiations. A bargaining chip, as we say."

"Then I hope you'll flex some of those political bargaining tools on my behalf, Grand High Ambassador," he replied, accepting her help in rising. He started to say more, then blinked and eyed the shuttle around them a moment. Frowning, he turned his gaze to the two V'Dan. "What's the news from the *J'ung Shan G'at*?"

"Officially, we were detached to go with *you*," Nakko countered. "I don't think it's healthy for us to go against those orders, so don't expect us to want to go back. If you're looking at what to do about this shuttle, which is technically still the *G'at*'s property, *they* can send a spare pilot to come pick it up. Otherwise, wherever you go, *we* go, since we were attached to your command."

"He's right," his superior said. A'sha shrugged and gestured at the mostly empty containers on the floor, continuing in a light, dry tone. "You made the mistake of feeding us. Now you have to bring us home."

That made Jackie, Paroquet, and Mamani all laugh in amusement. The Ambassador grinned at her, speaking. "That's *another* saying we have as well. I'm constantly amazed at the things we still have in common despite ten millennia of difference."

"Even the Chinsoiy have a similar attitude," Nakko told her. "It seems to be a common habit of most sentientkind to have pets and to feel a responsibility for strays." He started gathering up the containers. "Let's take a few moments to secure the shuttle here, then we'll come along. If that's alright? Otherwise, we'll be stuck sitting around doing nothing while you're gone."

"I'll need to have the Ambassador's permission to use one of her vessels," Li'eth pointed out. "I was supposed to go with a local Advocate representative on a V'Dan ship."

"I'll grant you permission, without a doubt," Jackie confirmed. "Where you go, I go, and the other way around. And I'll not leave behind your soldiers if I can help it. There should be room for them."

"If it's just these two, there will be," Mamani confirmed, poking her thumb at the V'Dan.

Jackie nodded. "But let's check in with the Tier Advocates directly, via hyperrelay, as well as with my people, the V'Dan military, the Empress, and I don't know who else at this point. We can use Captain Charboli's ship to relay since he's still up in orbit, yes?"

"Ready and waiting, Ambassador," the captain confirmed.

"Then that's good news. Let's tidy up so we can get going," A'sha agreed, moving to help Nakko with the rubbish of their meal. She paused after a moment, though, craning her neck to look up at Jackie. "You know . . . you're handling all of this rather calmly, Meioa Ambassador. A sudden translocation of light-years within an instant would probably find *me* feeling more than a bit hysterical. Add on top of that all of us nearly dying multiple times on our way down here . . . you are *remarkably* calm, given all of that."

"I'm not too surprised. Terran soldiers are trained to think through and past our emotions," Paroquet told her, gathering up his share of the empty containers and stacking them together.

"So are V'Dan soldiers," A'sha replied dryly, arching her brow. "Do you doubt it? But even the best of training can be forgotten in the face of an unbelievable shock."

"We do believe your people have the same training. But for one, I already knew such a thing was possible, if not necessarily over that distance. For another, I'm also exhausted, too *tired* to react strongly to anything right now," Jackie confessed wryly. "If I stop to think about it, yes, I start to feel extremely weird about it. But as there is literally nothing I can do to change the situation, nothing anyone can do to put things back as they were . . . and several reasons to let things stay as they now are . . .

"Well, the best thing I can do is breathe deeply, let go my unnerved feelings, and just accept that this is my current reality. It is unnerving, yes, but I am here, and I have to deal with what *is*, not what I want to be." She looked at Li'eth. "On the bright side . . . I'm no longer feeling like half of my whole universe was ripped from my side."

"That's . . . actually a little bit romantic," Paroquet offered, tipping his head.

"It's *actually* a pain in the spine, not nearly so romantic," Li'eth replied tartly. He handed over his eating utensils to be tucked into the shuttle's self-cleaning storage compartment.

"Okay, *that* is un-romantic. What do you see in this *v'kon-shin*?" Nakko asked Jackie.

"Uhh . . . I'm not familiar with that word," she hedged. Tired as she was, Jackie could not dredge it up out of her vocabulary

"It's a slang for . . . ah, the closest Terranglo epithet would be 'bastard,' even though it technically means something entirely different," her Gestalt partner explained. "And we both acknowledged long ago that our Gestalt is more problematical than helpful, given our respective political positions."

"Suffers to be you, then," Nakko muttered. "No offense intended, just sympathy."

"None taken," Li'eth replied. "Let's finish getting this shuttle prepped for lockdown, so we *can* take you with us."

———————

After reassuring the Premiere back on Earth that she was alive and well, if several light-years away from where she was supposed to be, Jackie managed a vidcall to the Winter Palace on V'Dan. During that call, the Empress was visibly relieved that Jacaranda was alright. And grateful that her son was safe and sound. Hana'ka confirmed that her daughter's orders regarding Imperial Prince Kah'raman were now officially and fully revoked but agreed grimly that it was up to the Tier Advocates as to what happened next with her thirdborn child.

Hana'ka did, however, expedite the matter by arranging on her end for the Advocates to be gathered as quickly as possible for a group conference. It took over half an hour to be contacted by them, but they did eventually call. While they waited, the Terrans of the *Embassy 14* entertained the two V'Dan officers by giving them a tour of their shuttlecraft. They had to be quiet in the crew cabin because the off-shift pilot and gunner were sleeping on narrow air mattresses on the floor, but Jackie and Li'eth could hear them exchanging questions and answers in low murmurs while moving from cabin to cabin beyond the open cockpit door.

(*Getting tired,*) Li'eth warned her while they waited. He rubbed at his eyes, and stifled a yawn. (*I could sleep for two days, I think. Maybe five.*)

(*We're just one jump out from V'Dan,*) she pointed out, stifling one of her own. (*Two extra seconds won't exceed the safety limits on a single hop.*)

(*I think . . .*) Light flickered on the console in front of her; Li'eth blinked at it, losing his train of thought. Jackie looked as well.

Jackie tapped a few commands on the console, then slid out of her seat, allowing Li'eth to take her place. Leaning over, she tapped a couple more controls. A composite image appeared on the screen. Split vertically in thirds, with the outer thirds split in half again horizontally, each section showed a V'Dan Tier Advocate member.

Two men and three women, all of them visibly middle-aged or older. The youngest, a brown-skinned male with sapphire-blue lightning stripes similar to the forked lines squiggled across Li'eth's skin, looked to be maybe in his mid-forties at most. The eldest, a gray-haired grandmother with large cyan blotches on golden skin, sort of like a colorful cowhide effect in Jackie's eyes. She had to be in her seventies or eighties, if not older, if her many wrinkles were any indication.

The elderly woman was the figure in the center screen. Seniority among the Tier Advocates was not based upon the Tier rank but upon sheer seniority, and this woman had quite a bit of clout. Li'eth greeted her politely. "Third Tier Advocate Che'en Shu-Plik. Thank you for the honor of answering my call."

"Imperial Prince Kah'raman Li'eth Tal'u-ruq Ma'an-uq'en Q'uru-hash V'Daania," she replied, her voice quavering a little with age though her expression was rock-steady sober.

(*She just used your full name,*) Jackie observed silently. (*That's a bad sign in most Terran cultures. I take it you're in deep trouble in V'Dan culture, too?*)

(*Probably.*)

"You claim to have placed yourself under our authority," the Tier Advocate stated flatly. Her companions looked equally sober; the woman with the dark brown skin and short, light gray stripes in the upper-right corner even frowned a little though she stayed silent, letting the eldest speak for all of them.

"Yes, meioa. Imperial Princess Regent Vi'alla acted against the best interests of the V'Dan Empire and interfered with the will of the Saints," Li'eth stated. "She ordered the Imperial Elite Guard to stun me unconscious and drag me out of the home system for no reason other than she did not believe that Grand High Ambassador Jacaranda MacKenzie and I are true holy partners. She did so after refusing to acknowledge the sovereign and separate rights of the Terran nation. She chose to insult the customs, expectations, and courtesies of our prophesied potential allies, causing them to close their embassy and withdraw their support and assistance in our war against the Salik rather than remain and continue to be insulted, dismissed, and bullied by our people under the then-current policies of the Empire.

"The Imperial Princess Regent's orders were to keep me sedated while I was removed far away, causing Imperial officers to bring harm to a member of the Imperial Tier from the initial stunning, and harm again from the separation from my holy partner. All out of nothing more than pride and in ways that caused grave harm to our good relations with the Terran Empire. I place myself under the authority of the Tier Advocates in the name of what is *good* for the Empire," he stressed. "Separating me from my bonded partner, their chief ambassador, is not good. Denying the Terrans their right to be treated with respect is not good. Refusing to heed the needs of *all* of our people by clinging to her rank and her pride is not good for the Empire.

"Empress Hana'ka has since resumed command of the Empire and revoked all of the Imperial Princess Regent's orders regarding not only the Terrans but me as well," Li'eth continued. "She did so by citing that they are not what is best for the Empire at this time, and she is right. I should therefore be released from Advocate jurisdiction to resume my Empress-appointed duties as liaison to the Terrans. Which *is* good for the Empire."

The gray-striped woman spoke, her words crisp and carefully measured. "Imperial Prince, you placed yourself under the jurisdiction of the Tier Advocates in the name of what is good for the Empire. Explain how *not* being a provably competent starship captain is good for the Empire."

It was a fair question. "When the Grand High Ambassador was attacked by those robots," Li'eth stated, "I was within the Imperial Wing, exercising. Sensing her in mortal peril, I somehow transported instantaneously to her exact location in the Guard Hall outside the North Embassy Wing. Palace security footage confirms this instantaneous transfer, which took place over a laser-line distance of approximately 635 *mitas*."

He had looked up the distance while Jackie had been recovering from her wounds. The Tier Advocates frowned a little, two of them looking skeptical, but nodded to let him continue.

"Just a couple hours ago, sensing that I was in mortal peril here in the Ton-Bei System, the Grand High Ambassador transported instantaneously over a distance of roughly sixteen *li-yet* to *my* location. This, too, is confirmable as fact, as she vanished from a live broadcast and reappeared on board the shuttle carrying me," he stated. "I have two Imperial officers as witnesses, the shuttle's internal recordings, and the timing of her broadcasts shortly thereafter to her own people to have them contact the Terrans on V'Dan as confirmation of this event. Additionally, the Ton-Bei System buoys will confirm there were no incoming or outgoing Terran vessels anywhere near the shuttlecraft carrying me at the time. These things verifiably happened."

"What is the point of mentioning them?" the elder of the two gentleman stated. His tight, dark curls were salted with both gray and peach, matching the peach rosettes dotting his brown face.

"My point, Advocates, is that no matter what others may wish, the Saints have ordered the universe so that we *will* be together in times of peril. Since the process seems to exhaust our holy abilities, it makes more sense for the two of us to *stay* together so as to preserve our abilities for more important matters . . . and as she is the Grand High Ambassador of a separate nation, it is not appropriate to expect her to serve in the Imperial Army at my side.

"There are many other officers throughout the Empire who are competent enough to lead a ship. There are only a few citizens who have the social status, grasp of politics, and military competency to serve as a liaison to the Terrans. There is only one, myself, who can communicate in full thoughts as well as mere words, allowing far greater understandings to be exchanged and avoiding a large number of mistranslated misunderstandings. It therefore makes sense in multiple ways for me to be at her side, both for the advantages brought and the disadvantages avoided."

Their gazes shifted slightly, each Tier Advocate looking at one of the others on their own screens. Finally, the eldest, Chu-Plik, spoke. "We are pleased that we have seen similar points. However . . . we do not wish to release you back into the Imperial Tier at this time."

That took Li'eth aback. He blinked twice. "You do not? What reason or purpose do you have?"

Her gaze did not waver. "We would like to appoint you as a subadvocate of the Tier Advocate Council . . . to the Terrans."

(*U'V'Shakk!*)

Jackie, standing in the aisle between seats, jumped a little at that mental yelp. She stared at Li'eth, whose eyes had widened so much, she could see the whites of the sclera all the way around his burgundy-and-gray irises. (*What's wrong? Li'eth?*)

The Tier Advocates did not seem upset or curious at his reaction; they merely waited patiently for a reply. Li'eth knew that *they* knew what they were asking, that they had considered the ramifications in advance. Jackie could tell the five people on the screen were far too politically canny *not* to have considered all the ramifications in advance. No doubt that was the true cause of the half hour it had taken to go from being contacted by the Empress' staff with his whereabouts and claim to actually reaching out to him, time needed to hash out What To Do, and Why.

Whatever those ramifications were, Jackie didn't know. But Li'eth did, and it shocked him to the core. (*I . . . The Advocates . . . They are . . . They're kicking the Prime Root!*)

(*They're . . . what?*) His subthoughts seemed to be some sort of sports analogy, one Jackie didn't grasp.

(*They're cheating politically,*) Li'eth managed to explain, lifting a hand to scrape his hair back from his face. The physical sensations grounded him a little. (*Kicking the Prime Root directly in a guanjiball game to make it chime, instead of letting the* goraball *strike the root post—they're* not *supposed to grasp for political power with outsiders! It's not* illegal,) he added quickly as she started to frown, offended. His subthoughts carried the information that kicking the Prime Root in an actual guanjiball game *was* against the rules, but this technically was not. (*They do have this right . . . but this . . . The Empress* must respond *to this.*)

"Have you nothing to say, Your Highness?" the eldest Advocate finally asked, raising a brow in a skeptical movement shared not only by the Terrans and the V'Dan, but by the Solaricans as well. Even the Gatsugi used it occasionally when talking with those groups though their eyebrow analogs weren't quite as flexible.

"Ah . . . What you want requires careful thought," Li'eth managed to reply, mind still racing. "Would it be permissible for me to discuss this with the Empress before such an advocacy appointment is formally settled on me?"

Chu-Plik smiled slowly. "We have anticipated this request. Please do speak with her. Report back to us immediately. Be well, Highness."

The Advocates vanished from the viewscreen. Li'eth sat there a few moments, just trying to absorb the political implications. He reached for Jackie, appreciating her confused patience but needing her to understand. This was going to affect her government, after all, not just his own. Her people swore daily oaths in their government offices to always consider the needs of those their own people interacted with, after all.

(*The Tier Advocates are . . . are trying to go* around *the authority of the Eternal Throne to negotiate with outworlders. They* do *have authority to . . . to* liaise *with non-V'Dan,*) he added. (*Tier Advocates are the grease that keeps clashing cultures from grinding down and locking up the machinery of our interactions with the rest of the Alliance. Particularly in how our various Tiers are treated by outsiders.*)

(*But . . . ?*) Jackie prompted.

(*But she specifically said* advocate, *not* liaison. *A liaison facilitates, explains, smooths things over. They are fluid in that liaisons can represent both sides to each other in the attempt to translate intentions and meanings, but their words are not the final word in any matter,*) he explained. (*An advocate, on the other hand,* represents. *They are not fluid, they cannot bend to carry out the wishes of the other side without strenuous negotiations, they cannot . . .*

(*No, they are* nothing *like your Advisor's Council,*) he corrected her straying underthoughts. (*They don't act as go-betweens, cushioning your civil servants from special interest groups attempting to lobby or bribe their way toward favorable changes to laws and rulings. They're more like the representatives of the special interest groups themselves, save that this is a political/governmental thing.*)

(*How does that differ from diplomatic envoys?*) Jackie asked. She corrected herself a moment later from his underthoughts. (*Ah, they represent specific points delegated to them by their superiors, and cannot stray outside those boundaries into vastly different or even just more generalized requests.*)

(*Exactly. And that's the danger inherent in this request,*) Li'eth told her. (*They want me to go to my mother and say that the Tier Advocates, who advocate for each Tier they represent—the* population *they represent—these Tier Advocates want me to represent* them *to your people. Not to represent the V'Dan government, which she* represents, *but the people of the Empire.*)

Jackie, knowing he was leading up to that, still sucked in a sharp breath anyway the moment he clearly thought out his explanation. (*That's . . . yeah. That's a damning political move. But they* are *giving her a chance to save face, aren't they? By letting you "discuss" their intentions before actually implementing them?*)

(*Yes, by the Saints' grace. They're giving her a chance to salvage the whole situation, yes,*) he agreed. (*If* she can. *Either she represents the will of the people, not just the will of the government, or* they shall *do it. Instead of her. And Jackie, they* have *that legal power,*) he warned her. (*They can, at the behest of the people* or *on behalf of the people, make alternative arrangements with other governments. They rarely do it, but they do hold that kind of political power, to check and halt uncaring ambitions in the highest Tier of the realm.*)

(*In Terran sports, this would be called an end run, I think,*) she agreed. (*Running around the opposition through their own territory in order to get on a clearer path to their goal, or something like that.*)

(*That . . . is actually a closer analogy than kicking the Prime Root,*) he agreed, sampling her subthoughts. More and more as they interacted telepathically, it was getting easier to share such things. He started to say more, but a yawn cracked his jaw. Smothering it behind his palm, he shook his head—as much to clear out the reflected undercurrents of her own triggered yawn as to remove the dust of sleep settling over his mind. (*I will contact her now, while I still can. Help me stay awake a little bit longer?*)

(*I'll try. Thank goodness Mamani's setting up some air*

mattresses and bedding in the lab compartment for us, so we can sleep undisturbed. Which we can do as soon as you let everyone know what's going on,) she said.

(*Yes,*) he agreed. (*Let's get my mother back on the line, inform her of the facts, tell her to take a day or so to decide, tell the Advocates they'll hear back in roughly a day or so . . . and* then *we can sleep for a week. And make both of them wait a week, not a day, just for putting me through this mess.*)

She chuckled in his mind, agreeing silently with him.

CHAPTER 5

AUGUST 14, 2287 C.E.
AVRA 7, 9508 V.D.S.

"You weren't kidding about sleeping the clock around," Sharon murmured when Jackie emerged from the lab compartment of the *Embassy 14*. The other woman checked her wristwatch. "It's been . . . twenty-three hours and fourteen minutes since you two lay down for your naps."

Jackie managed a grunt, still groggy and exhausted. She had slept with Li'eth spooned at her side, on an air mattress that had filled the floor space in the small compartment. The cramped closet wasn't in use as a lab at the moment, but it had all manner of equipment tucked behind doors on the walls, ceiling, and floor, designed for access in zero gravity. Small, cramped, but blissfully dark and quiet, save for the faint hiss of cycling air.

Thankfully, Captain Mamani interpreted her version of a reply as something polite and continued with the morning news, following Jackie on her way toward the crew cabin. "Let's see . . . five messages from the Empress, three from the Tier Advocates—they're getting a little bit impatient—seven from Captain al-Fulan, twenty-three from the Command

Staff, twelve bearing the stamp of various Council members, eight from your Assistant Ambassador, and six from the Premiere himself."

"Uh?" Jackie grunted, pausing and straightening her stiff, sore back so she could squint at the other woman. Sleeping without moving for twenty-three hours straight had not been kind to her body.

"The V'Dan ships that were en route with masses of Terran soldiers while all the froufraw was happening over the V'Dan attitude problem are about to start arriving on various colony-worlds. The Command Staff and the Council have been issuing new orders—some of them contradictory to each other—every few hours," Sharon told her, not unsympathetically. "When I pointed this out, Premiere Callan said he wants *you* to look all of them over, figure out which ones will work best, *then* get back to him. Including the ones from the V'Dan government. Which ration packet will you want for breakfast?"

"Ugh." She rubbed at her eyes, trying to knuckle away the sleep sand crusted in the corners.

"The Hawai'ian por—?"

"Uh-uh!" The thought of that overseasoned yet tasteless blob made her shudder and find the strength to actually speak. *"No.* I'd rather eat the peppernoodle hash . . . I'll take the, uh . . . Thing. Cheesemac. Something."

". . . Right, anything *but* the Hawai'ian pork, got it."

Jackie managed a thumbs-up and started shuffling again toward the crew quarters and the commode therein. It was designed to be accessible while in a gravitied environment, thankfully, even if far too many of the other amenities on board this class of ship were dependent on a lack of gravity to easily access. As she moved, the hatch to the lab hissed open a second time, disgorging an equally zombie-esque Imperial Prince in a now-rumpled uniform.

"Buh . . . Bright morning," he managed in greeting, hastily smothering a yawn behind his hand.

". . . Make that two packets of anything but the Hawai'ian pork, and two packs of coffee," Sharon murmured, eyeing him. She headed toward the galley.

Li'eth made a face but didn't protest. Out loud, at least. (*I think I actually* need *Terran coffee to wake up, today.*)

(*A bathtub's worth.*) A moment later, her brain caught up with what he had said. (*Poor baby, you* must *have it bad. I know how you hate our version.*)

(*Don't take too long in the toilet,*) he warned her. (*I have a full day's worth backed up. Also, something small and fuzzy died in my mouth.*)

(*You, at least, have a toothbrush in the kit bag you brought,*) she reminded him, waking up a little more. (*Mine is sixteen or so light-years away.*)

He managed a mental grunt, slumping against the door while she was busy in the small closet-like space. (*You can borrow mine. Saints . . . We slept so hard, my whole body is stiff from not moving much . . . but I do remember waking up at some point. A couple of points. Something about a bunch of messages . . . ?*)

(*I don't know. Not clearly; I was out of it, too. Sharon said something just now about the Terran troops getting close to arrival on each appointed colonyworld, and contradictory orders? We have a bunch of messages backed up and waiting to be waded through, at any rate.*)

(. . . *I definitely need your coffee* v'shakk *to deal with all that.*)

She laughed at that, the sound barely audible through the compartment door.

A short time later, seated at the communications station on the bridge with a mouth scrubbed minty-free of small dead fuzzy things thanks to sharing his toothbrush, Jackie didn't feel like laughing. The mashup of orders *was* a mess. In fact, it was more of a headache inducer than a giggle inducer, and a full pack of coffee hadn't helped her yet to figure out what to do. Elbows braced on the console edge, hands manipulating food pack and spork to shovel overseasoned fiesta eggs into her mouth, she shook her head slowly between bites.

Li'eth, leaning against the console while he dug into his own packet of shepherd's pie, shrugged. (*It could be worse.*)

(*How could it be worse?*) she asked, flipping her spork-wielding hand at the screen, with its plethora of opened missives. Many of them indeed contradicted each other, including at least three arguing as to who should be in charge to *give* orders to her so that they wouldn't *be* contradictory anymore.

Nearly every message had a different priority, a different "fire" for her to try to put out, many of them *not* what she'd call a top priority at this moment when viewed from three different angles, even if she could admit that it was a priority when viewed from a fourth. (*What could possibly make this mess worse?*)

(*They could have actually expected you to carry through on* all *of them?*) Li'eth offered. Sticking his spork in his food pouch, he picked up the thermal pack of coffee and sipped cautiously at the straw. He grimaced in the next second and sucked in cool air. (*Saints! That's still a bit too hot . . . but at least with a burned tongue, I can't taste it as much anymore . . . On the bright side, that last message from Callan looks like he has decided to dump the mess in* your *basket and let* you *figure it out.*)

(*That was the bliss of sleeping for a day straight,*) she agreed, along with an undercurrent of apology for the excessive heat. (*I'm glad I opened the most recent one first. But still . . . Callan's orders put* me *in charge as "the only Councilor-General on the front lines" . . . and I'm worried he thinks I* am *a general. I'm only a colonel!*)

(*Didn't Kurtz order you to assess and assign strategic objectives?*) Li'eth asked. He leaned over and swiped his finger over the control pad, awkwardly manipulating the interface. Jackie, reading his subthoughts, took over and found the right message. (*. . . Yes, that's the one. The officers sent with the troops are to determine the tactical methods, and you are to determine the strategic objectives, by liaising with the local governments, planet by planet.*)

She caught on to what he wasn't saying in the caffeine-stirred undercurrents of his thoughts. (*You think I should go to each location, assess and liaise on the spot?*)

(*It makes tactical sense, and political sense,*) he pointed out. (*You're the Grand Ambassador of the Terrans to V'Dan. You'd be backing up the authority of the Terran troops . . . and if any of the local First Tier officers balk at working with "children," you can rewrite their brains. With me at your side, you'd palpably have the backing of the Crown. And that of the Tier Advocates. Which we'll know better how to handle once* you *have an idea of what you'll need to do, whether I have to be their advocate, or if I can convince them to be their liaison.*)

(*That . . . is rather brilliant, actually,*) she mused, spork poking out from her lips while she poked at the console with her finger, shifting messages around. (*And if I combine it with this request here, by making Rosa my de facto representative on the V'Dan homeworld . . . I can fob off most of the administrative stuff on her. Unfortunately, this means zooming from planet to planet as fast as possible because all these ships are bound to arrive all too soon. Some of them within hours of each other, and that means days before I myself can get there. I'll have to be on the comms as much or more as I am on the ground, and I can't do that from here.*)

(*You don't think Captain Mamani and her crew are . . . ? Oh, you don't think this ship is capable of handling those kinds of performance issues,*) he corrected himself, following her subthoughts.

(*Unfortunately. But that's why we built the* Embassy 1, *to be bigger and more useful, with sections of floor and ceiling and bulkhead that could accommodate V'Dan gravity weaves. If you'll remember, they were working on getting that stuff fitted before everything got kicked out an airlock by your sister.*)

(*Call the Palace and ask them about that,*) he urged her. (*Commandeer the 14 here and go from planet to planet until your flagship is retrofitted and ready to serve as your mobile command post. Even if this one ship is inadequate, it's better to be on location to see what the problems are than trying to fix them from hundreds of li-yet away.*)

Jackie admitted silently that his idea did have merit; the Space Force trained its soldiers and its officers to be able to think on their feet. To adapt to the current situation, not the far-distant version of the situation that the Command Staff knew. How *could* they know? Earth was hundreds of light-years away, and despite the willingness of the V'Dan to share plenty of information about their colonyworlds, there simply had not been enough time to transmit all of that data, let alone absorb and assimilate it. Doing so now required having a *mobile* command post, one with civilian authority on the spot to back up the military.

Earth barely had a handful of non-Earth outposts, never mind any real colonies, but even her people could grasp that trying to get the locals to cooperate with a foreign *military* structure would cause more problems than if they had a solid civilian presence to smooth things over. Militaries, after all, were for fighting. Civilian governments were for all the *non-*fighting, peace-minded stuff that most civilizations respected and wanted from their neighbors. Particularly as a reassurance that any military force was *not* going to be fighting *them*, just fighting *for* them in exchange for the right to form a civilian settlement on their colonyworld afterward.

Of course, the trick lay in making her position of civilian and military authority truly mobile, so she could go and assess things in person. Every colonyworld would be different, some by a little, and some by quite a lot. That required being on hand to assess everything from both viewpoints, civilian and military.

(*With Colvers shipped back home to serve his time in prison, we'll need a backup pilot and gunner for the* 1,) she mused, thinking it over. (*Nayak was going to arrange to have one come out. But if we're going to take the flagship out, we'll need a spare pilot* now, *not whenever one can be brought out. At least it's down to a six-day trip for the OTL ships, now that we have the fuel depots set up with V'Dan merchant reserves processing the local ice chunks in each system, using your much bigger ice-capturing systems . . .*

(*Actually, I'm still surprised they agreed so readily to do all the grunt work for us. And grateful, since your people have the gravity weaves to live normal lives on board your ships. We still don't,*) she muttered, thinking about the *Embassy 14*'s needs once it took off from this planet.

(*Building up value in a foreign currency is worth more to spacefaring businesses than to planet-bound ones,*) Li'eth told her. (*It builds up the potential for future trade contracts in foreign territories. It's also literally worth quite a lot money-wise to any business. The Alliance waits about twenty-three years—that is, twenty-three in V'Dan terms; it's only twenty in K'Kattan Standard—to ensure the incoming government and its economic system are stable, before arranging for the newcomer to undergo a full conversion to the Alliance credit-chit system.*)

(*I remember the lecture on having to wait, but I can't remember any doubled value being mentioned,*) she replied, opening the dessert packet accompanying her meal, a brownie bar that was almost more fudge-like in its solidity.

(*The margins jump around a bit, but early investors can make a fortune in the long term when the conversion hits, because early investors get double their money—they get a payout value for value from the incoming government, and a payout value for value from their home government,*) he explained, opening his own dessert pack, also a brownie bar. (*The K'Katta realized that a strong encouragement of early interstellar commerce brings with it a commensurate level of interstellar stability, and thus interstellar peace. They much prefer peace.*)

(*Yes, it's very hard to successfully trade when you're more likely to be shot at than shopped at,*) she joked lightly. The console beeped, drawing her attention. (*Looks like we're getting a signal from the Winter Palace. Li'eth . . . what are we going to do about you?*) Jackie asked, instead of answering the signal. (*My situation is becoming clear, if we are to not only stay allied, but actively help.* Yours*, however . . .*)

(*Answer the call. Maybe Her Eternity has come up with a solution,*) he offered. His subthoughts were a mix of yearning hope and a level of realism that had already braced for possible awkward disappointment.

Tapping the controls, Jackie opened the commlink. Empress Hana'ka appeared on the screen, once again lying in her red-draped hospital bed. She waited a few seconds, then spoke. "Greetings, Grand High Ambassador. I presume you have a means to record this message?"

"Of course, Eternity," Jackie replied. She tapped a few commands and nodded within moments. "This comm call is now being recorded. It will be archived in both Terran and V'Dan programming languages."

"Good. I will now speak with Imperial Prince Kah'raman."

Guessing this was a formal call, Jackie nodded and slipped out of her seat.

Li'eth traded places with her. Settling into the seat, he bowed his head. "Greetings, Eternal Empress."

"Imperial Prince Kah'raman V'Daania, you are instructed to inform the Tier Advocates that the Eternal Throne will not relinquish your service to the Empire to be their advocate to the Terran Embassy. Inform them that you are to be the *joint* liaison between the Empire and the Terran Grand High Ambassador, and the liaison between the Tier Advocates and the Terran Grand High Ambassador, so long as that Grand High Ambassador is Ja'ki Maq'en-zi."

Li'eth drew in a breath, but before he could ask any questions, his mother added dryly, "This means you will be reporting to *both* factions for every step you take, and considering carefully all suggestions made to you to help facilitate our alliance with the Terrans."

"I understand, Eternity," he allowed, bowing his head again.

"Your compliance is more necessary than your understanding, but I will enlighten both you and the Tier Advocates who currently hold jurisdiction over you. The Eternal Throne will *not* allow one of the Imperial Blood to be used as a pawn by anyone." Hana'ka paused again, then switched to Terranglo, of all languages. *"Particularly one who is a potential heir. Until Imperial Princess Ah'nan can be replaced as Grand High Ambassador to the Terrans and come home to serve us as our Imperial Heir . . . you are our Heir Imperial. We are willing to share the uniqueness of your position, perspective, and expertise, Heir Imperial Prince Kah'raman, with those who advocate for the true needs of the vast majority of the Empire."*

"Eternity . . . *I am not suitable as an Imperial Heir,*" Li'eth protested, switching languages as well.

Her Eternity held up her hand, fingers just barely appearing at the edge of the screen. *"We are aware of your long-term unsuitability. It is rare to invoke the temporary rank of an Heir Imperial, but such is a necessity until we can formally confirm Imperial Princess Ah'nan in the role of Imperial Heir. This process is estimated to take at least one month, possibly longer . . . and you will be expected to* remain *her backup.*

"Imperial Princess Vi'alla has been removed from the succession for as long as the Terrans have the potential to be our allies. She retains the rights of a member of the Imperial

Blood, and her children shall be included in the pool of future candidates for the Eternal Throne, but her personal place in the succession has been suspended indefinitely."

(*Wow,*) Jackie breathed mentally, blinking. (*I honestly didn't expect her to go that far.*)

Empress Hana'ka switched back to V'Dan before Li'eth could do more than blink twice. "As I was saying, the Empire does not need a divided front when dealing with our new allies. What *is* needed is the understanding that only a true liaison can bring, someone who can be the diplomatic grease to ease the workings of the cogs and wheels powering the machinery of interstellar cooperation. To that end, we will allow you to liaise between the Tier Advocates and the Terrans . . . with the understanding that you are not to be parted from Ambassador Ja'ki's company. Not even by Tier Advocate order."

"Such an allowance is generous, Empress. Thank you," Li'eth told her.

He knew that *their* people didn't have quite the same strict rules as the Terrans did about preserving such pairings. Indeed, it couldn't even be formally acknowledged that they were a holy pairing until the Sh'nai priesthood did so . . . and the priests were still reluctant, as far as he knew. Having the backing of the Eternal Throne in this matter would help preserve the good health of their Gestalt. The other matter . . . Li'eth hoped his secondborn sister would be recalled smoothly and safely from Earth. (*I am not suitable to be the true Heir, and I am glad Mother knows it.*)

"Inform the Tier Advocates of your position as liaison. If they object, they may study Imperial Tier Jurisdiction Ruling 5. During an official, Tier-Advocate-authorized war, one which is a threat to all six Tiers, both the War Sovereign and the designated Heir outrank *everyone* in all situations. Even so, we can afford to be generous in this case. Instruct the Tier Advocates to deliver their confirmation of your appointment as a dual liaison to the Terrans within the day. They may query the Imperial Secretary for the full details in this matter."

"I will do so, Eternity," Li'eth pledged, guessing she didn't want him broadcasting the news of his temporary heirship in a system all too recently under enemy attack.

"Let the Grand High Ambassador know I look forward to

her safe return." Her image vanished from the screen, replaced by the white, gold, and crimson mark of the Empire.

Li'eth cleared his throat. ". . . I apologize, Ambassador. As you can see, I didn't have time to inform her of your—our—plans to go elsewhere, first. I trust you will not be offended by that, mistaking her assumption for an arrogant command?"

"She didn't put a time limit on it, so how could it be? I *do* eventually plan to return to V'Dan with you at my side," Jackie reminded him. "Eventually."

"Of course. And she did state for the record that I was to stay at your side," he allowed. Taking a moment, he contemplated his mother's . . . his *sovereign's* displeasure at not coming straight home, and stood to inch his way out from behind the console. "Here, have your seat back. You'll need to send that recording to the Tier Advocates for me—and I *do* appreciate your willingness to play comm tech for all of this," he added earnestly. "I'm not taking our interactions for granted."

"I know," she promised, and reinforced it telepathically. (*I do know, Li'eth; I could feel you pause and remind yourself not to do so.*)

(*As natural as it does feel to communicate with you in so many ways, on so many levels . . . I still keep forgetting you're more skilled than I am.*) He sighed, leaning against her workstation console. (*How long will it take for me to catch up in skill? Five, maybe six years?*)

(*Half a year, maybe a year at most. Your telepathic skills in dealing with* other *people will take more than six years, at your current rate of interaction with those who aren't me,*) she replied. (*Sonam said you do have all the right instincts when it comes to interfacing telepathically with me; you just lack practice at sorting out your thoughts from mine and reading the subtle variations. Honestly, you* are *getting better at a remarkable rate. It's just that each mind is a little bit different from every other mind out there. You're learning my quirks far faster than anyone else's, but you're not interacting with other people's minds on a daily and near-hourly basis like you are with mine. It's literally just a matter of practice at this stage.*)

(*Well, I can't exactly practice with anyone else on a regular, hourly basis,*) he returned. Reaching up, he plucked at one of her curls. The reddish-black wayward strands had escaped from her braid. He tugged on it for a moment, then attempted to smooth it back into her braid with fingers and mind. (*Nor do I want to, to be honest. Master Sonam said most telepaths dislike sharing thoughts. He also said the dislike would grow stronger for a Gestalt pair confronted with a nonpartner's mind.*)

(*He is an expert . . . Are you trying to rebraid my hair?*) she asked

(*Yes, without plucking you bald.*) He sent her an image of the lock that had partially escaped.

(*Then ride your mental fingers on top of mine while I fix that. Practicing telekinesis is just as important as practicing telepathy, after all.*) She hesitated, then sent carefully, (*I suspect she spoke in Terranglo about your heir status to keep the Salik from eavesdropping, and not because she expected it to be important to my fellow Terrans. Do you think I should keep it silent from the others?*)

(*I think for security reasons, we should tell at least a few. Leftenant Buraq, for one, if al-Fulan will be remaining at the embassy,*) he allowed, somewhat distracted by trying to follow the movements of her mind in wielding her psychic gifts.

(*I'd want to tell her at the very least so she can ensure heightened security,*) Jackie agreed, before focusing on guiding their shared gifts.

Rebraiding her hair only took a few more moments. Tidying up the video of his mother's announcement for the Advocates took several more, since Li'eth wanted to excise some of the more personal bits, and Jackie wanted to include an unedited version marked for the highest-ranked eyes only to peruse. That required dredging up the security protocol programs in the *Embassy 14*'s computer banks.

Shortly after they sent off the carefully edited dual packets, the Terrans called. Specifically, Secondaire Jorong Que Pong contacted them. Jackie opened the connection, squaring her shoulders in front of the workstation screens to put herself back into a more formal, civil-servant mind-set.

"*Greetings, Jackie. The Premiere asked me to make this call on his behalf; Hurricane Taxaca is pounding its way across the Yucatán Peninsula as we speak, and that's taking up all of his attention right now,"* Pong stated in Terranglo, giving both names the local pronunciation.

"That would make him very busy with all the posthurricane-relief preparations, yes," Jackie agreed, catching on at once.

"Indeed. It's good to see you awake," Pong added. *"You missed a bit of excitement as we all scrambled to figure out where you'd gone and what to do with you."*

"It's good to be awake, Jorong," she agreed. *"I can state for the record that separating Gestalt partners by several light-years is not a healthy idea. It can be survived, but it isn't healthy to subject* anyone *to that much psychic stress."*

"Duly noted. Have you had a chance to review all the requests and order changes that have been made?" Pong asked, lifting his brows. *"I realized they formed a bit of a mess."*

"I realized that, too, reading them," she said. *"Please thank whoever it was who asked Augustus to tack on that final order to, 'Come up with a good solution to this mess.'"*

He smiled. *"That would be me. I spoke literally because it is* a big mess."

She chuckled, then shrugged, flipping a hand in wordless acknowledgment. *"You're good at that, Jorong. You were good when you first represented Taiwan. But now to the meat of the matter,"* she continued, switching to V'Dan. She knew Secondaire Pong spoke V'Dan as well as Premiere Callan because she had given both men the language transfers herself. "What the Council needs—which is for me to return to V'Dan to continue being Grand High Ambassador in the Empress' court—is not what the situations out here, plural, actually need."

"Oh? How so?" he asked. Then added in Mandarin, *"Do we need to switch languages for any of this?"*

She shook her head and replied in V'Dan. "Beyond the information in the classified packet I just sent, no. I reviewed the mess of conflicting orders with His Highness, discussed some of my ideas for a solution, he offered some more of his own, and we have agreed that one of my ideas is the most solid one."

"And what did you come up with?" the Secondaire asked, raising his brows.

"What we have are a bunch of V'Dan transport ships—six, at the moment—crammed with Terran soldiers and Terran supplies, headed toward the six M-class V'Dan colonies. Including this one. Those colonies need more ground troops than the Empire can provide, given they also need troops sent up into space to man a lot more of their ships and space stations, to help fight off Salik boarding parties."

"Yes, we've already discussed this several times over," Pong agreed. "And as you know, we've authorized the continuation of those transported troops and their missions."

"Yes. But while the military is providing officers to manage those troops and who can interface and interact with the local branches of the Imperial Army, *none* of those troops have any civilian authority . . . and all six insertion sites are going to require telepathic oversight in case any of the local V'Dan authorities object to having a bunch of 'children' running around with loaded weapons in their backyards," Jackie stated, lifting her fingers briefly into view of the commscreen pickups for making the air quotes. "We've already seen how damaging that can be to good relations between us."

"True," he allowed. "I'd rather you not have to shut down the embassy again."

"We do now have the Empress' permission to enforce telepathic mind-blocks," Jackie stated. "And enough trained telepaths on staff to help block anyone who willfully protests our unmarked status to the point that it interferes with our autonomy and our objectives as their allies. But most of those are on V'Dan, with only one additional being sent out with each of the six troopships—and those are actually telepathic translators, not necessarily telepaths skilled in mind-block applications. Such a task requires a powerful telepath on hand. Since we have a limited supply of civilians in positions of authority, and a limited supply of telepaths strong enough and trained enough to place mind-blocks . . . and since I qualify on both counts . . . well, I have made the decision to set up a mobile command."

The Secondaire quirked a brow but slowly nodded. "I take it you'll be having McCrary stay on V'Dan to act as Ambassador to the Imperial Court? Rosa offered to take up the Advisor's post on V'Dan since you've lost Amatrine Castrellas, but Callan put his foot down, vetoing that—he said she looked relieved, in their vidcall on it," Pong added. "I don't blame her for offering; you still need someone to cushion you from special-interest-group lobbying and the bribery attempts that have been made by various V'Dan interests. But don't worry, we're sending a career Advisor to V'Dan. Augustus was thinking one of the two Advisors from Argentina, or possibly the Advisor for the Emirates. We'll have a decision in the next few days and ship them out as soon as possible."

"Argentina's been quiet on the Advisory front over the last two years, so I can see that, yes," she agreed. "And I'm not surprised Rosa offered, since it is an important role," Jackie added, "but these V'Dan don't understand what it means, and they certainly don't understand what taking it up would do to her career. I agree wholeheartedly: Keep Rosa pristine so she can become Grand Ambassador to the Alliance at large. Anything else is a waste of her sheer experience. In the meantime, I think Clees should remain at her side as the chief telepath to the world of V'Dan, along with Aixa, to continue to do language transfers, mind-blocks, plus holding classes to continue training the V'Dan psychics, so on and so forth."

"Good choice," Pong said, making a note on his tablet. "You say those two are staying on the V'Dan homeworld. What about the others?"

"Most of the newest ones are dedicated entirely to making language transfers. Of the ones who came out with the initial embassy forces, I was thinking of taking either Lieutenant Johnston or Lieutenant Wang-Kurakawa with me in my mobile command and leaving the other to Rosa to reassign as she sees fit," she added. "I figure I'll only be able to take one of them because I'll have limited space for extra personnel since His Highness has a couple extra bodies of his own he'll need to bring with him. Frankly, Jorong, it makes far more sense for me to be mobile at this stage since I have both military and civilian experience, and matching authority."

"I hadn't considered the need for a civilian authority to be on hand for each of the landing sites," Pong admitted, frowning softly while he mulled it over. He was good at thinking on the fly, and came to a decision fairly quickly. "But . . . it has merit. And a great deal of foresight, invoking both reassurances and absolutes, even if your presence is just part-time.

"Also, given what I've reviewed of each of their files, I'd take Darian Johnston in your position," Jorong added. "I've gone over his personnel file a few times. He has a lot more actual combat training than that junior-grade psi does—if you are going wherever the troops are going, you *are* going into combat zones. I don't think Captain al-Fulan is going to be too happy about that, but your ambassadorial purview *is* an entire, ongoing war zone right now."

Jackie nodded, accepting the grim reminder. "His Highness and I are both aware of that, yes. We will be taking steps to try to stay out of the actual combat zones. Of course, war knows no boundaries, so we won't hold our breath, but for many reasons, we will be taking several extra steps to ensure our safety wherever we go."

Li'eth pulsed a query to her. When she responded in the affirmative, he leaned against her, putting his head into view for the pickups. "Greetings, Secondaire Pong."

"Your Highness," he replied when the few seconds of lag ended. "I hope you are doing well, right now?"

"Reasonably well, now that our Gestalt is no longer parted. I wanted to reassure you from a V'Dan perspective that having the Grand High Ambassador herself visiting each colonyworld should impress upon my people just how seriously you Terrans are taking our difficulties in the war. It will also underscore just how much we need your people's help and how seriously we must in turn take you.

"Honorable Assistant Ambassador McCrary visited the various capital worlds, but this will be visiting the majority of the actual worlds undergoing the brunt of the Salik attacks. To aid you in this, the Empress has appointed me her liaison as the War Queen to the Ambassador's efforts, among other things. I should also have the full backing of each of the Tiers as well, which means a great deal of widespread political clout, as well as official military clout."

That was the diplomatic way of saying the Tier Advocates would not likely let him go back fully to his mother's control even in the face of her rights as the War Sovereign; there was little more to do at this point than resign himself to playing the role of a guanjiball for the foreseeable future.

Secondaire Pong, ignorant of that development, merely nodded. "Your aid as our liaison will definitely grease the wheels of the various bits of machinery we're still scrambling to put into place, yes. Do you have an initial list of priorities? Anything requiring our coordinated help?"

"My plan is to get several authorization papers lined up for various contingencies for each influx of Terran soldiers on each world," Li'eth continued. "This is actually standard operating procedure for whenever a trusted representative is sent out, to have contingencies preplanned and preauthorized already physically on hand. It's beyond useful to have access to your hyperrelay technology, but having the actual, tangibly printed contingency orders in hand will be an even greater reassurance."

"Anything we can reasonably do to reassure our allies in all of this will be of good use," Pong agreed. He glanced down at something below the edge of the screen, probably one of the data tablets Li'eth had often seen him using, then nodded after a few moments. ". . . It looks like the *Embassy 1* will be retrofitted for gravity within another two days. In the meantime, if everything stays on schedule, the first shipment of soldiers will be arriving on Ton-Bei—sorry, V'Ton-Bei, your current location—in about fourteen Terran hours. That's roughly thirteen V'Dan Standard," he allowed, nodding at Li'eth. "After that, the next lot will be arriving on V'Zon A'Gar, followed by the Selkies attempting to take out the Salik colonies on V'Ba-kan-tuu."

"You can call it just Ba-kan-tuu if you like, since that's a Choya place-name. Ba-kan-tuu is a world covered mostly in water," Li'eth added, adjusting his leaning stance to be a little more comfortable while he spoke with the Secondaire. "It's been extremely difficult for anyone but the Choya to fight them there. We can hold the few islands well enough, but not the seas, because the enemy has been systematically taking out all support ships and submarines used by the nonamphibious Alliance colonists. You're the same species as us, and we are not amphibious in the least, let alone aquatic. When *we* get dumped into the oceans, if we aren't rescued quickly or have life rafts on hand, we drown. So why fight them there?"

"Yes, I'm confused as well," Jackie added, frowning softly. "*I* thought Ba-kan-tuu was going to be declared nonviable for troop insertions because it would be too difficult for the Selkie teams to transport all the necessary equipment for repairs and replacement. From what I recall of the process, the manufactories for making new suits are too huge, and transporting giant nutrient tanks for the existing ones would be even more impractical."

The Secondaire smiled just a little bit, the curve of his tan face somewhere between shy and smug. "The Dalphskin Project had a major breakthrough in portable manufacturing six months ago. The information got lost in the excitement of the *Aloha* project. The Selkies—that's our nickname for the Special Forces Underwater Reconnaissance and Response Specialists," he explained in an aside for Li'eth, "—have since managed to practice enough in long-term water ops with the new Dalphskin manufacturing system that Admiral-General Kurtz decided to greenlight the teams for transport. We need you at Ba-kan-tuu to liaise with the Choya and the V'Dan on deploying our troops."

"Yes, but why a Terran counterattack on Ba-kan-tuu?" Li'eth pressed. "The Choya are holding their own in the water, and we're backing them up on the few landmasses."

"Holding, yes, but the information you passed to us as military liaison indicated to us that the situation is in a stalemate at best." Pong lifted his hands into view, tapping one finger against the others to count off the advantages. "It's not as wasteful as you might think. There is already a strong Alliance military presence in place, so we wouldn't be fighting an uphill battle against uneven odds.

"Stalemates are also only acceptable if you can afford to tie up your forces in a particular location," Jorong continued. "The addition of our unfamiliar troops should give your Alliance forces an edge in combat. If nothing else, it *should* give us just enough leverage from surprise and confusion among the enemy so that the more experienced Choya can counterattack effectively.

"Everything you've told us about the Salik ability to move underwater suggests that our Dalphskin biotech may be able to counter many of the amphibious species' maneuverability there," Pong continued. "We can test it in live simulations with the Choya, then run combat with the Salik if those simulations and our impending allies suggest our tech is viable for such situations. If it *is* viable . . . then it will hopefully be a major psychological blow against the Salik, and can be put to use in the oceans of other colonyworlds as well, particularly near shorelines that have come under siege by Salik forces. By the time we get the Selkies over there, they'll be properly experienced."

"The Salik evolved from hunter species, and they did not evolve very far. They might find a nonamphibious underwater opponent all the more enticing," Li'eth warned him.

"That is a risk our troops are willing to take," the Secondaire asserted. "Moreover, the Dalphskin interface is remarkably intuitive for a Human, and the training time is very quick. And since it's individually tailored to each person's body, we should be able to manufacture versions that even the Gatsugi can wear though our technicians are not as sure about the Tlassians or Solaricans," Pong added in an aside. "The existence of arms that have an approximately similar level of movement can be duplicated, or so I've been reassured by the technicians. Even unusual limb lengths can be adjusted for since those are already features encoded into the portable manufactories for adaptation, and thus integratable. Unfortunately, trying to work out the musculature for tails in addition to legs might cause too many hindrances and stress intolerances when it comes to locomotion."

(*Jackie, are you going to explain at some point* what *a Dalphskin is?*) Li'eth asked, glancing at Jackie. (*You didn't seem to have a lot of biotech, from what I saw, and his explanation is confusing me.*)

(*You'll learn by the time we reach Ba-kan-tuu, if nothing else. Biotech hasn't been developed on a widespread scale for several reasons. Ethical laws have slowed down the exploratory progress, including a very lengthy certification process to ensure the newly tinkered artificial biota won't harm the existing natural biota. Feeding the stuff is also exceptionally difficult; we can grow artificial organs and such, but creating a living organism from scratch and getting it to function is nearly impossible.*

(*Dalphskin succeeds because it's already designed to be immersed in fluids and doesn't need an internal circulatory system. It can get all the hydrodynamic movement of the nutrient fluids by attaching electrodes to stimulate the muscles in undulating patterns. Really, in the end, it's just a matter of donning and removing the suit in a nutrient bath, then attaching a couple of electrode leads and letting the computer control the pumping of the muscles . . .*

(. . . *It's one of those things you'll understand better when you see it in person. Especially as there'll be specialist technicians who can explain it far better than I can,*) she demurred, and moved the topic forward by speaking aloud. "Are we going to miss any landings with that schedule?"

"A few, but it cannot be helped. If you head to Zon A'Gar once you're through on Ton-Bei, we can arrange for the *Embassy 1* to meet you there, and from there, when you reach Ba-kan-tuu, the V'Dan warship *V'Goro J'sta* can pick up the *Embassy 1* after dropping off the Selkies," Pong told them. "The *V'Goro J'sta* has agreed in advance to escort any Terran craft if we wish, even into the neighboring territories. They did so because they knew we'd want to check on other areas with a large enough V'Dan population that they can support the needs of several thousand Terrans as well. If for some reason, the *V'Goro J'sta* needs to depart, we'll be able to arrange other transport, but wherever possible, V'Dan faster-than-light starships will be used, so as not to startle anyone when you arrive in a major system nor alert the enemy to your exact location unless you should need to change ships."

"Thank you for that courtesy," Li'eth replied. "Safety will be a concern for the Ambassador and me."

The Secondaire shrugged. "It's actually more that it's simply faster to take a V'Dan ship on a long-distance journey if you don't have to rest every three to four jumps for six to eight hours at a stretch. Our ships have to for biology's sake, plus the processing of fuel in areas where we don't have depots set up. Our ships would be better served if we ran them in relays with fresh crews changed out every so many star hops, but we'd still have to change out the passengers to let them rest, too. Since we can't do that, and certainly cannot change either of you out for anyone else, that means it's more efficient time-wise on longer trips to take a faster-than-light vessel between stars and reserve the other-than-light jumps for within a specific system, or between two close ones.

"A V'Dan ship can also slow down twice a day to sublight

speeds," Jorong continued, "so you can operate the *Embassy*'s hyperrelay to clarify orders. Once within a particular system, you can then go wherever needed, as fast as needed, with our other-than-light drives."

"All of that sounds like a good idea, Jorong. I think I'd like the *14* to accompany us as a backup ship. Do you know if the *V'Goro J'sta* holds the capacity to carry both?" Jackie asked.

"They should, since our ships aren't *that* big . . ." Pong said, though his tone was doubtful. Again, he looked down. This time, the edge of his tablet came into range of the pickups in his office while he tried to look up that information for her. "Give me a few moments . . ."

"Do you have the name of the class of warship for the *V'Goro*?" Li'eth asked him. "I didn't pay attention to the size of its shuttle bays when I was helping assign how many Terrans could be carried aboard each of the ships we sent to your homeworld, but I do know the general cargo capacity for each class of ship."

"Ahh . . . *Tusq'aten*?" the Secondaire offered after a moment of searching on his datapad.

Li'eth nodded. "That's more than big enough. Midclass battle cruisers like that line have three launch bays. Two are big enough to have spare room for something twice the size of the *Embassy 1* though each one of your ships will have to be the last vessel on and first one off, and three of their shuttles will have to be housed in the third bay to do so—they're *designed* to have the extra room, in case one of the bays is damaged and has to store the remaining shuttlecraft."

"That's good to know," Jackie murmured.

He nodded, then tipped his head, grimacing a little. "Commandeering it for additional Terran transport, however, *will* require a writ from the Empress, even if they've offered in advance."

"Your attaché can bring it on the *Embassy 1*, so that it remains in V'Dan control at all times," Pong stated, then looked at Li'eth. "That is, I'm presuming you will want to have Leftenant Superior Kos'q shipped out to travel with you?"

"If there's room for him, yes," Li'eth agreed.

"There will be," Jackie reassured Li'eth. She looked at Jorong on the other side of the commlink. "We just need to pick a pilot and gunner to replace Colvers. We didn't have time to make an official choice, earlier."

"No, not before everything flew off to U'Veh in a balloon," Li'eth agreed. At the Secondaire's blank look, he grasped for the equivalent. "A . . . trip to hell in a . . . basket? Handbasket?"

"Yes, that would be the correct idiom," Secondaire Pong agreed. "As it stands, the Admiral-General already anticipated that need, the moment he heard Colvers had broken the law and knew the fellow would need to be replaced," Pong reassured them. "He has already asked for the ship with Lieutenant Commander Ramirez to be rerouted to meet you at Zon A'Gar. V'Zon A'Gar," he corrected himself, applying the proper pronoun prefix to the name.

"Lieutenant Commander Ramirez . . . *Anjel* Ramirez?" Jackie asked, dredging up the name and the face together by going through her memory of all the pilots she had met here and there through her earlier days in the *Aloha* program. She nodded to herself when she found a match. "Good, I liked her. No-nonsense when working, but a good sense of humor when off duty. She should be flexible enough to work well with our needs."

"Do let the military know how it works out," Jorong told her. "The Department of Innovations is trying to get a grasp on who should best fit where, but it's still a fledgling science in many ways, only a decade or so old . . . and it's clear we missed the mark by several klicks when it came to Lieutenant Colvers."

Jackie blushed. "Yes. I think I was a little too tactful in my evaluations of him."

"You're a diplomat," Jorong allowed graciously. "You're trained to be diplomatic." He flashed her a brief smile. "Try being a soldier next time."

". . . Department of what?" Li'eth asked them both.

"What, the Department of Innovations? It's . . . um . . . They're data-miners," she said, trying to find a way to explain the concept, since it was foreign to the V'Dan way of hierarchical, Tier-based thinking. "They gather and sift through information on all soldiers, from the soldier's own daily reports to battle debriefings from peers, subordinates, and superiors, all of it cross-referenced to other soldiers' observations, and collate and cross-reference it with official psychological evaluations."

Li'eth tipped his head, still confused. He flicked his gaze between her and the man on the screen; how had his attention bent downward once again, multitasking. "Why would you do that? That sounds like a lot of work."

"We want to find out who is most suited to command," Secondaire Pong stated, his attention more on his tablet than on the commlink. Still, he answered in some detail. "We can only learn so much when our soldiers go through Basic Training, or through an officer's Academy. You can only *train* so much. The rest of it has to come from within, an innate understanding, a grasp of principles, a different way of looking at problems, at approaching and solving them. Not mechanically solving them, but in knowing *how* to solve them, and *who* can solve them.

"Most of leadership rises to the surface—or sinks like a rock—when a soldier goes into the field and starts working," Jorong continued, speaking with some passion. "Rather than relying upon training alone—or worse, nepotism—we try to cull through the after-action reports to see who shows leadership skills and potentials, then encourage that. A good leader can come from any walk of life, once they've had basic training, because all it takes is to look at a situation in a different way than the usual sort of person might.

"Because of this," he continued, glancing up briefly, "because we actively look for leadership traits *without* being so close to the subject that we're swayed or even blinded by friendships and favoritisms, the DoI can pick out who might be an effective leader much more efficiently. Or even bar one from rising further. Training does not guarantee good leadership decisions, though it does help immensely," he stated, his attention on the tablet screen again. "As it stands, the DoI is going to be even more important in the coming months because we can train basic soldiers a lot faster than we can officers. Those who have the aptitude for good leadership *need* to be promoted up the ranks to fill in the gaps in those upper ranks."

"They're the reason I was elevated to Colonel and Vice-

Commodore, but no higher—you remember what I explained of our military structure, how Lieutenant Generals and Generals can command any soldier in any of the four Branches, right?" she asked him. Li'eth nodded. "The DoI doesn't think I have what it takes to be a three- or four-star officer. And in my opinion, they're *completely* right," she added bluntly, cutting her hand through the air over the console. "I *don't* have the training and the skills for anything that high. I'm too much of a civilian. But they *do* think I can be a Colonel for the Special Forces, Army, and Marine Corps, and the equivalent rank of Vice-Commodore for the Navy."

"Since everyone other than Admiral Nayak who has been or is going to be sent out at this stage is a Lieutenant Colonel or a Ship's Captain or less in rank," Pong told him, "that means MacKenzie carries the military authority she needs as a *civilian* government official to step in and make decisions that can countermand the orders and the decisions of officers ranked under her.

"The *only* reason the Department of Innovations thinks this is a good idea is because they data-mined her civilian leadership and determined that she *doesn't* step in and overrule those under her jurisdiction unnecessarily . . . unless, of course, she knows that a particular course of action would be bad for the greater good of the situation," he added, giving Jackie a significant look. When she groaned and covered her face with her spread hand, he smiled again. "Yes, the DoI went over the wading-pool incident with a fine-toothed comb for this last round of promotions."

"Boot me back to Basic . . . it was *not* a wading pool, it was a *sacred wellspring*," Jackie mumbled, trying to banish thoughts of that near-disastrous diplomatic mess. She waved her palm quickly, scrubbing the air and her memories. "We're *not* getting into that mess, gentles. Ah . . . I'm getting data on a subchannel," she added, noting the text scrolling across the bottom of the screen. Her hands shifted to copy it to a folder.

"That's a formal proposed itinerary to get you started. I'm lining up the paperwork to authorize it—check the bullet-point list," Jorong added, lifting his data tablet back into view briefly, "and make sure I caught everything on the list?"

"Jorong, you have an incredibly organized mind, and a fast

set of thumbs on a datapad," Jackie quipped. "I'm sure you've thought of everything in advance. At the very least, 98 percent of everything."

"I meant His *Highness* should take a look. You know what the Terrans require, but neither of us are experts at V'Dan requirements," he replied tartly. "As the Secondaire, I'm ultimately responsible for all the paper-pushing on our end of things. It's up to Imperial Prince Kah'raman here to handle the V'Dan side."

"I'll get right on it," Li'eth promised, leaning in to peer at the lower screen displaying the incoming text.

"I'll pass it to the right-hand console, so you don't get a kink in your neck," Jackie told him, remotely activating the workstation directly across from hers. "We'll get back to you as soon as we've looked it over, Secondaire."

"I look forward to hearing from you," Pong replied. "Try not to take too long, or I'll think you've gone to sleep for another day."

"We should be so lucky," Li'eth muttered, settling into his seat.

———

"What do you mean, *you are not coming home?"*

The question thundered over the channel with far more force and indignation than Li'eth had *ever* heard his mother use on him. It made him flinch and blink a little. Thankfully, he had Jackie on hand to lean against for support, both physically and mentally.

(*Stay strong. She knows we cannot be parted,* and *she has no say over what I do in the service of my government,*) Jackie reminded him.

(*Yes, but she does have a say in what I do in the name of mine,*) he retorted. Blinking again, he firmed his jaw. Thankfully, this conversation was taking place in Terranglo at his request, for security reasons. *"I mean, Eternity, exactly what I said. I will be accompanying the Grand High Ambassador of the Terrans as she visits each Terran troop deployment across our various colonyworlds, both here in the Eternal Empire and among several of our other allies."*

"Your duty as the Heir to the Eternal Throne is to come

home!" Empress Hana'ka—or rather, his mother, Hana'ka—
ordered. "*You will not risk yourself, especially by going to
planets that are known points of conflict! That is* why *the Terrans are sending their troops to those worlds.*"

"*Yes, and that is* why *I must go there!*" Li'eth shot back,
brain seizing on her wording. "*These worlds are in a war
zone, and* I *am the* War Prince. *I am an heir in the military
from the start of the war onward. I have the right to claim the
responsibilities as well as the privileges of that title, Mother!
And you are* reacting *as my mother, and not as the War Queen,
who should know* booting *well that I* have *to go where the
Ambassador goes. Not just as her Holy Partner, but as the
War Prince, to lend weight to every decision made on behalf
of our allies' needs.*"

His mother started to say something and broke off, holding
up her hand, palm toward herself in the V'Dan style, though
she looked off to the side and switched to her native language.
". . . Why do you disturb me, Secretary Je-sat? I am in the
middle of an important comm call."

"My apologies, Eternity. I heard shouting. Is everything
alright?"

"No—yes!" she corrected herself. "Everything is fine. And
may the Saints take back the curse my father laid on me to
have children just as stubborn as *I* was," Hana'ka added under
her breath. She switched to staring through the screen, almost
glaring at her son, and resumed speaking in Terranglo. "*I am
very irritated right now. I am annoyed and worried as your
mother that you insist on throwing yourself yet again
into harm's way . . . and I am proud as your mother and
your Empress that you insist on carrying out your duties in
spite of the threat to your personal safety. Now put the Ambassador on.*"

Li'eth hesitated, nudging at Jackie's instinctive movement
closer to forestall her. "*Are you going to yell at her? Because
as the War Prince, your current if temporary heir, I do not
think that would be appropriate behavior for my Empress and
War Queen.*"

"*I am going to threaten her to within an inch of our friendship as a very concerned* mother . . . *and threaten to put*

Vi'alla back in charge if anything happens to you," Hana'ka returned tartly.

"Duly heard and noted, Eternity," Jackie quickly confirmed out loud, though she stayed out of sight of the video pickups. *"My government would have to lodge a protest on our behalf, but I assure you, we already have sufficient motivation to keep His Highness safe."*

"Good. I hope your people can bring about the prophesied victory soon," Hana'ka added. *"I want to know my son is safe and well, and I fully expect our customs experts to argue back and forth over proper marital rituals versus the political tangles of making the highest-ranked ambassador of a foreign nation a member of the Imperial Tier. You will be marrying my son, yes? You do have that custom, of formal legal unions between two people, for discerning various legal rights and lines of inheritance?"*

"Mother, we have already discussed those things," Li'eth interjected firmly. *"And we have agreed that we will make the time to discuss them* after *we have won the war. Or at least are completely certain we are winning. Now, is there anything else we actually* need *to discuss since I will not be coming back home directly? Aside from needing various authorization documents to be shipped out to me, secured in Leftenant V'kol Kos'q's hands."*

His mother rubbed at the bridge of her nose for a moment. *". . . I'm going to have to think about all of that. Especially as I will have to decree you the Interim Heir until Ah'nan can get back, and figure out who to stand in proxy for you during the ceremony. Most of the cousins are either deployed, or in hiding,"* she muttered under her breath. *"The cowards."*

Jackie leaned down into view, arm on the back of Li'eth's seat. *"Why not ask V'kol?"*

Both V'Dan stared at her. Li'eth answered first. *"It would have to be someone with a direct blood relation or an exceptional ceremonial tie,"* he asserted. *"V'kol is merely an attaché in the eyes of Tier custom."*

That made her roll her eyes. *"You both have a very strong bond of having survived nearly dying at the hands of your mutual mortal enemies. He loves you as a brother.*

You have shed blood together metaphorically as soldiers. You are best friends. Declare him your spiritual brother—or do you not have any such customs among any of your peoples?"

Li'eth blinked, looked at his mother, and they both at the same moment said, "Valley of the Artisans!"

"We are *related to their customs within . . . fourteen generations,"* Hana'ka agreed, continuing. *"Which is within the twenty generations needed to claim a cultural observance as legally legitimate."*

"Double-check on the generations for that, and if they pass, then ship him out as my proxy, Eternity," Li'eth informed his Empress.

"And then you'll come home," his mother pressed. He rolled his eyes, and she flicked up a hand. *"—I* am *free to hope, Kah'raman . . . Li'eth. Especially if we invoke Valley customs. But I do expect you—both of you—to come straight back to V'Dan as soon as possible. Preferably the moment Imperial Princess Ah'nan returns, so that we can formally acknowledge her as our next fully invested Heir."*

"We will do what we can, Your Eternity," Jackie promised. *"But we cannot guarantee the results of actions that are also dependent upon the actions of others, including those of our mutual enemy."*

"I could almost wish you were *marrying a Valley girl, Kah'raman . . . Li'eth,"* Hana'ka muttered, rubbing at her temple under the edge of the today far-less-ornate bandaging still covering part of her scalp. *"Their needs and territorial scopes would be so much smaller . . . and yes, I am trying to get your preferred name-choice right."*

"I can only promise you, Eternity, that my own mother has warned me that I shall one day have children who will cause as much trouble for me as I have caused for everyone else," Jackie replied with dry-voiced equanimity. *"And I shall grant you the right to hurl the same curse at me yourself. That will have to suffice as a punishment, for now."*

The Eternal Empress gave a soft huff of a laugh and let her mouth twist into a wry smile. *"May the Saints ensure we* do *get to watch those speculative children of yours tormenting you. And I shall spoil them horridly as a greatmother should. Great . . . ah . . . grandmother?"*

"Grandmother," Jackie confirmed. *"Great-grandmother is the next generation up."*

"Thank you for the clarification; I will eventually have the time to learn the subtle nuances in our linguistic differences. My Secretary is signaling to me that I still have more business on this end to handle. Especially as you will not yet be returning to our side, Imperial Prince," Hana'ka stated, returning to speaking in V'Dan. "Since this is all we needed to discuss, I shall get back to you with all the paperwork handled by Assistant Ambassador M'crari. The physical copies will be sent with Leftenant V'kol as soon as he can be tracked down."

"I do regret not being able to return, Eternity," Li'eth replied, returning to the same formality she had resumed using. "But I shall do my best to represent the Imperial Tier and the Empire in all ways that will bring only glory, honor, and victory to our nation."

His mother nodded, then shifted an annoyed look off to the side. Her image vanished from the screen in the next moment, leaving the sigil of the Eternal Empire in her place. Li'eth sighed and sat back, taking comfort in feeling Jackie's arm near his nape. (*Well, that could've gone a lot worse. She's not happy, but she's accepting it. I think. I couldn't see any of her auras through the link.*)

(*She seemed to be, yes. And I am aware that the Terran nation will owe the V'Dan a political debt of honor for allowing us to haul you off wherever I go, despite your being your mother's current heir,*) Jackie said. (*We try not to forget what we owe to others, as well as what we are owed.*)

(*I'm sure she'll get over it. So long as we survive,*) he sent back. (*Time for another nap, yes?*)

(*Ordinarily, I'd say no, but you just wrestled emotionally as well as mentally and verbally with your mother and your sovereign,*) Jackie allowed, shifting back so he could stand up. (*We'll both take a nap. And set an alarm clock, so we don't oversleep the arrival of Major Slovaskoff and his people, though I'm sure someone will call and wake us up anyway with yet another half-booted piece of minutiae to be handled.*)

CHAPTER 6

The V'Dan equivalent of a community college no longer had access to its many parks and athletics fields, thanks to the incoming Terran presence. Instead of long, flat expanses covered in some sort of local, tough, turquoise stuff that reminded her of tiny, densely packed strawberry leaves, the lawns of the academic facilities now sported row after row of closely packed tents, supply sheds, washroom facilities, and other sturdy yet temporary structures.

It amused Jackie that the V'Dan version of a row of portable commodes looked little different from the ones her fellow Terrans used back home. About the same size, about the same shape, plus even the soothing blue shade of the outer casing looked similar. The chemical smells were a little different, but that was to be expected; the functionality remained the same.

The tents were also similar, again constructed along familiar lines of functionality. Flexible exterior surfaces erected on a thin but sturdy framework, all of it designed to shed rain, provide shelter from hot sunlight, cut off cold winds at night, and bearing sewn-in panels that from their brief tour and explanations would collect solar energy and transfer it to lighting and other internal systems. Inside some of those tents, bunks and lockers awaited occupants, while others contained tables, chairs, workstations, and more. A few had clear purposes, kitchens and eating spaces, makeshift medical facilities with V'Dan medical personnel on loan from the Imperial Army, that sort of thing. Others stood empty in different sizes, ". . . for whatever needs you Terrans might have for a sheltered space."

A rumble of thunder overhead caught her attention. Squinting upward through the early-morning sunlight, she watched a tiny string of five shuttles soar down out of the sky. Their outlines were very different from Terran atmospheric craft; thanks to the *Councilor One* disaster, when hundreds of high-ranked government officials died while traveling in a sabotaged transport, Terran ships were required to have at least some functional aerodynamic flight capacity. By comparison, V'Dan orbital transports looked like blunt bricks. Like they shouldn't be able to fly at all, to the aesthetic eye of a Terran. Aerodynamic bricks, but utterly lacking anything resembling an airfoil or a wing.

An amalgamation of metallic-gray, white striping, and red-and-gold symbols on the side, the shuttlecraft almost made her think of ambulances. White with red or blue markings—usually a cross, a crescent and star, or the Staff of Asclepius with its wings and entwined snakes, that sort of thing—Terran ambulances all had a similar look to them. *Of course, officially the Asclepius symbol for emergency medical services is actually white on a blue six-limbed star. Which makes me wonder what they'll think of our symbols as the V'Dan encounter more and more of them, and if they'll have any unforeseen cultural associations with entirely different subjects.*

I suppose we're just lucky the almost Shinto-shrine-like symbol they use for their government doesn't have any unfortunate association in any Terran language I know. At least, not one openly known in any diplomatic circles back home. That might not be the same for how people would view such symbols away from the political venues, where politeness is expected even when one is offended.

Being stuck in the Winter Palace handling politics hadn't exactly given her a chance to see many daily-life reactions to the mixing of Terran and V'Dan Humans. Her few shopping trips had been focused on deliberately experiencing the negative side of those reactions, so Jackie wasn't certain if that should count. Even in the town of Ri'oko, she hadn't really interacted with the locals; Leftenant Superior Ka'atieth had done that for them.

As it was, capitals on Earth tended to be places where people were much more cosmopolitan and thus much more aware in their daily lives of the need for tact and diplomacy.

The Winter City of V'Dan seemed to be the same way. V'Ton-Bei would be the first world to experience it outside of the capital of V'Dan, thanks to the massive influx of soldiers now descending from the skies.

She had no idea if this colonyworld's capital would follow along similar lines, being cosmopolitan and open-minded, or if they would be more insular, more easily offended, or even if they carried particular cultural quirks that were simply unique to this particular area on this particular world.

One of the commode doors opened, and Imperial Prince Kah'raman Li'eth V'Daania stepped into view. Like her, he wore a fresh, formal military uniform. Both had been express-shipped from V'Dan with the help of the *Embassy 3*, which had brought Lieutenants First Class Baraq and Johnston, and Lieutenant Second Class Paea. At the moment, Baraq slept on the *Embassy 14*, which sat in solitary splendor on a small sports field on a rise a few hundred meters away. In Baraq's place, Lieutenants Johnston and Paea stood off to one side, chatting idly, waiting for the moment when they would be needed to play military aides-de-camp to both Jackie and the incoming Terrans.

Off to Jackie's other side, the local head of the Imperial Army, Grand General Ta-mal I'osha, stood in her own red-and-gold finery. She did so in the V'Dan version of Parade Rest, feet a little closer together than shoulder-width apart, but not actually touching like the Terran pose for Attention. Her hands rested together in front of her belt, not behind it. In all, I'osha looked like a serene, composed statue with her gray-and-blue hair braided and pinned up in twin buns on her tanned and blue-striped head. Panda buns, had she been a Terran.

Behind her, a full two hundred soldiers stood in similar poses. Their uniforms were not nearly as ornate since they wore the local camouflage, shades of turquoise and teal for the foliage mixed with beige and brown for the soil, but their positioning was perfect, and their heads were mostly turned up to watch the incoming shuttles. Their expressions were a mix of curiosity, interest, boredom, and speculation.

(*I'osha seems to be doing well for someone with a brand-new language in her head,*) Li'eth observed, joining Jackie.

(*She's also freshly rested. We're the ones who've been up*

for thirteen hours. Ri'oko's a third of the way around the world from here,) Jackie added. She didn't know much about Ton-Bei's topography, but she did know that much. She'd seen only that much since they had gone into orbital flightspace to make the parabolic trip in as short a time as possible. Most of what she'd seen had been covered in clouds and night-shadow, dotted with a few lights from city clusters. Certainly, local area had been covered in clouds during their landing.

(*True. Then again, she wouldn't be a Grand General of an entire colony's defenses if she couldn't adapt with some flexibility. V'Ton-Bei is the oldest outsystem colony we have, but it still has its share of problems.*) The mental image he sent her, of some sort of teal-and-gold-striped, elephant-sized lobster thing, showed it wasn't just the threat of a Salik invasion the local colonists and soldiers had to worry about.

(*I'm still amazed there are so many M-class—Human inhabitable—worlds out there,*) she sent, looking around her again. Jackie squinted as she did so, for the shuttles were now close enough to kick up dust and bits of turquoise leaves as they circled, homing in on their assigned landing spaces on what looked like a racing track of some sort. Not the guan-jiball field; that had been taken over by personnel tents erected among the curved walls and root posts. (*Thousands of stars, tens of thousands of gas giants and ice planets and lumps of scorched or frozen rock, yet we can find worlds we actually can inhabit, as Humans.*)

(*Not as many as would be nice, but there are some. And* plenty *of places for space stations and dome colonies.*) His underthoughts included a reassuring pulse that—if they won the war—V'Dan would help the Terrans survey their nearest star systems for suitability and help build those dome colonies. (*We might argue over who gets the next few inhabitable worlds, however,*) he teased her. The roaring of those incoming shuttles was no longer so distant, making even telepathically sent thoughts a little difficult to hear.

(*Or we can learn how to share. Looks like they're coming in for the final stages of landing,*) Jackie returned, squinting against the bits of dust and debris kicked up by V'Dan-style thrusters.

One, two, three, four, five, each craft landed with very tight precision, barely a couple meters from the next. Impressed, Jackie started to move forward. Li'eth touched her arm, lifting his chin at the air. Squinting upward, she saw five more coming in, unnoticed in the distraction of her thoughts and their conversation. They, too, landed with equal precision, forming a second row. All ten now sat tucked just within the oval of the running track, while their thrusters whined and slowed, reducing the noise with each engine shutting down. A good thing, too; the ramp-like hatchways cracked open, lowered with pneumatic hisses, and touched down on the gravel-like surface of the track encircling their position.

(*Impressive,*) Jackie murmured. (*Very well done. Remind me to let those pilots know how much that impresses me.*)

(Now *we can move forward,*) Li'eth told her, and moved with her toward the settled ships. (*I checked the specs; the* Tarast V'Tak *holds ten dropships. It makes sense to run all of them at once, to minimize air loss each time the shuttle bays are opened in getting everyone and their gear down to the planet. Since this isn't a combat zone, they can let the autopilot programs do the fancy precision during a landing . . . but they'll still be pleased to know you admire our engineering and programming skills, if not their actual piloting skills.*)

That confession made her grin and nod. (*Doesn't matter. Even if it's programmed, that still doesn't mitigate the awe of such a well-placed landing.*)

Coming up on their right, Grand General I'osha approached, along with a dozen soldiers. Jackie eyed their insignia. Ten were officers of the Second Tier she hadn't seen before; the other two were the pair she had also given Terranglo to earlier: Leftenants Shava and Na'akarra, officially appointed liaisons between the Imperial Army and the Space Force.

Shava had those follow-the-hairline tiny spots like those of Doctor Mi'en Qua, the geneticist who had helped modify the *jungen* virus enough to allow Terran Humans to survive on V'Dan and eat V'Dan-grown foods. Where the doctor's skin had been peach with lavender spots, however, his hide bore golden spots on a rich chocolate brown.

Na'akarra looked even more exotic, with a lovely golden tan of the sort that, back on Earth, came from Southeast Asia; thick, Prussian-blue stripes colored her skin in the usual *jun-*

gen way. A raccoon-like band framed her Prussian-blue eyes, while two more tapered streaks decorated each cheek. Her appearance reminded Jackie of some of the Amazonian tribes back home, how they painted their skin with charcoal and ochre. Compared to her and the other leftenant, the Grand General's light blue spiraling stripes on golden-peach skin looked a bit boring.

(*Careful, you may be growing accustomed to V'Dan versions of beauty,*) Li'eth teased.

(*I'll try not to fetishize the exoticness of it,*) she returned mock-soberly. Semiseriously. (*You do know I like you for your mind, first and foremost?*)

(*Sweet speaker.*) He switched to speaking aloud, greeting the Grand General, and the leftenants and so forth accompanying her.

Jackie turned to check on Darian and Jasmine. "Everything in order on our end?" she asked them. Both nodded. Turning her attention to the shuttles, Jackie lifted her chin. "Do you know which shuttle is the one holding Major Slovaskoff?"

"That will be the center one on this side," Grand General I'osha interjected, joining them in closing the last dozen meters to the running-track area. "That is, if the pilots on that ship are following standard procedure for loading as well as disembarking troops. Which they should be. Their commanding officer would hear from me if they didn't."

Squinting at that ship, Jackie made out a figure in a dark green uniform, sleeves and pant legs striped in black. He descended the ramp to the very edge of the composite materials banding its edge. Halting just a few ceremonial centimeters from the local soil, he held himself at Attention, arms straight at his sides and heels together. Jackie recognized his features from the profile she had perused, and nodded. "I see him now."

Slovaskoff lifted his arm when she came close enough to speak, his eyes on her, his tanned fingers flattened and held at an angle at his brow. "Colonel MacKenzie. I have been given V'Dan, sir; you may converse with me in the local tongue."

Halting in front of him, Jackie returned the salute. "Major Slovaskoff. Good to know." Lowering her arm in tandem with his, she gestured to her left, then to her right. "These are His Highness, Grand Captain V'Daania, and Grand General I'osha, who is the head of the V'Dan Imperial Army here on V'Ton-Bei. Your troops will be liaising directly with Leftenants Na'akarra and Shava, here, as both have been given Terranglo *telepathically* and have been appointed to work with you. The Grand General has been given a transfer as well, to facilitate matters in the case of a dispute."

"It's good to meet you, Grand General, Leftenants. Full translation transfers will definitely smooth things over. My troops have been studying V'Dan the hard way from the training manuals our translators made," Slovaskoff stated, nodding at the Grand General. "We've been focusing on basic nouns, verbs, directions, distances, and common military commands, based on what we've learned from each other over the last few months." Turning, he gestured, raising his voice in a carrying shout. "Lieutenant Dagim! Front and center!"

A young woman detached herself from the other troops. She wore camouflage clothes vaguely similar to what the V'Dan troops wore, but they hung a bit loosely on her short, slender frame. With her tight black curls cut close to her scalp, teeth white against her dark brown lips where she bit them nervously, she looked rather young.

Li'eth shifted uncomfortably. (*I know I'm supposed to view all Terrans as adults, but . . .*)

(*Yes, she looks rather young to me as well,*) Jackie reassured him.

"Grand General, this is Lieutenant Junior Grade Mulunesh Dagim," Slovaskoff introduced. "She is a *telepath* Rank 6, among other things, and will be performing language transfers for key personnel."

"I am not very strong, meioas," the young woman stated, flicking her eyes briefly to Jackie before squaring her shoulders a little. "I am not the Ambassador. But I can do one transfer a day. It takes several hours, but it is an accurate transfer."

Grand General I'osha hesitated. She looked at the other Terrans before cautiously saying, "Forgive me for this, but . . . even for someone unmarked, you look very young. May I know your age, Lieutenant, so that I may reassure my troops you are indeed an adult?"

Jackie relaxed subtly. That was *exactly* the right way to handle the subject. She nodded permission at the younger psi.

Lieutenant Dagim grinned. "I *always* look young, Grand General. I am small and skinny and only nineteen in Terran years—even to our own people, I look fifteen or so, which I understand is about the same in your own years. My grandmother is in her seventies, and she still looks to be in her forties. I assure you, though, I am well trained; I graduated three years early at the age of fifteen, and have since earned a master's degree in Cryptoanalytic Linguistics in a military academy. I also speak six languages without transfers. I don't count the five that I learned *telepathically.*

"I am just . . . I am overwhelmed by being here. On another world," she finished, gesturing beyond them, dark eyes gleaming with wonder in the early-morning light and a returning touch of nervousness. "Breathing the air . . . worrying if any of the local bugs will be dangerous . . . It is one thing to whack one's boots for *scorpions* in the morning, but what if you have things that won't fall out when the boot is turned over and struck?"

Her commanding officer shrugged. "Considering *I* feel the same way, as will many of our troops . . . we will be staring at a *lot* of things, looking and feeling a little lost inside until we get used to this place." Major Slovaskoff lifted his chin briefly at the tent-strewn fields, then looked at Jackie and the Grand General. "With that said, permission to disembark, meioas? We have a lot of work to get done if we *are* to get used to this world well enough and fast enough to defend it."

I'osha gestured to Jackie, who lifted the two tablets in her hand, one V'Dan in style, one Terran. "I have all the paperwork right here, Major."

"How many troops did you bring?" I'osha asked him, curious.

"Exactly eight thousand," Slovaskoff stated, skimming through the Terran paperwork and pressing his thumb to the screen wherever indicated. "That includes me as the man in charge."

"Forgive my ignorance of Terran ways," the Grand General said next, "but you are a *may-jore*, which seems like it should be a Second Tier rank, yet you command eight thousand? That is not a small number."

"We're a little short on officers at the moment," Jackie filled in, since he was busy with thumb-signing for everything.

"We're still shuffling around everyone and everything so that the war effort has properly trained and experienced soldiers sent to your worlds, but it's faster to train an enlisted soldier—"

"—than to train a properly educated officer, yes. Learning tactics alone takes a great deal of time," I'osha agreed.

"We get it from day one, sir," Lieutenant Dagim said. Then corrected herself. "Well, day four. The first three days are for orientation and evaluation. Day four onward, everyone gets daily drills in tactical assessment, deployment, and postcombat evaluation. Even the Psi Division, though it's not our main focus. Obviously."

". . . There, that should be everything," Major Slovaskoff stated. He handed the tablet back to Jackie. "Double-check, sir?"

Nodding, she scrolled down through the paperwork. I'osha moved closer, so she tilted the screen to show that everything had been signed. The older woman sighed. "Please don't be offended when I say I'm having to trust you when you say you're getting everything right. I'm not very good at reading your Terranglo symbols yet. I can read it, but I don't *know* it just yet, so I'm not very fast at it."

"That will come with practice, Grand General, never fear. Grand Captain, please duplicate this so the General can review all of it at her leisure," Jackie told Li'eth, handing him the tablet. Nodding, he fished a V'Dan-style data crystal out of his pocket and worked on that. "General, if you are satisfied with the paperwork as it stands, we request permission to begin disembarking and off-loading our troops and supplies."

General Ta-mal I'osha stared at the ten shuttles a long moment, then nodded. "Permission to touch down and unload is granted."

Major Slovaskoff touched the little wire wrapped around his ear, and said in Terranglo, *"Ladies and Gentlemen of the 5th, 6th, 7th, and 8th Legions, 7th Battalion, 1st Brigade, 3rd Division . . . we are Green for Go. Disembark with* discipline, gentlebeings."

A moment later, one figure on board each vessel moved up to the ramp and barked orders, facing the rest. A ragged mass of rote responses—the actual words were garbled by sheer numbers, effort, and timing—roared back. At the same time, a similar echo of five voices followed by mass responses came from the five shuttles on the other side. Once the echoes of that died down, the ten master sergeants in charge of disembarking blew their whistles shrilly and gestured outside.

Dozens and scores and hundreds of boots clomped and shuffled across the deck plates, along with the scraping of boxes, the clicking of latches, the rattling of equipment. Men and women in the Terran equivalent of camouflage, their hues a bit too yellowish for the local foliage, marched down the ramps carrying kit bags and backpacks, and hauling supply boxes in pairs. They peered around with wide eyes when they weren't watching their footing, but didn't joke, didn't run, didn't break formation or discipline.

At the barked orders of their own officers, individual soldiers from the V'Dan contingent detached themselves, trotted over to the cluster of V'Dan and Terrans, and called out somewhat mangled names of companies and platoons, requesting confirmation on berth assignments. At a murmured suggestion from the General, the two main teams of officers spread out as well. Li'eth, I'osha, and her two aides, Shava and Na'akarra, remained on the near side to handle some of the inquiries for those disembarking from those five shuttles, while Jackie, Johnston, and Buraq moved between ships to the other side of the track so they could handle the rest.

V'Dan officers paired up with the Terranglo-speakers, some of them talking into communicators of their own, alerting the troops deeper into the maze of tents spread out all around them. With V'Dan troops manning the perimeter and waiting at strategic crossroads emplacements to help guide the off-loading teams, the shuttles were stripped bare in remarkably short order.

Indeed, within ten minutes, ten supply sergeants hurried back on board, one per shuttle, and strapped into their jump seats even as the ramps hissed and rose back up into place before sealing their atmospheric clamps with hard *clunks*. Thrusters whined, warning everyone on the ground to back up protectively. Within very short order, the white-and-red bricks of the V'Dan Imperial Fleet kicked up dust and bits of turquoise leaf-debris, launching themselves one after the other into the air.

"A very smooth innie-out," I'osha murmured, rejoining Jackie and the prince.

Jackie blushed and cleared her throat, unsure she had heard her counterpart right. "Ah . . . what was that?"

"An innie-out," the Grand General repeated. "Off-loading and disembarking is called an innie-out."

"We would prefer to call it an 'insertion' for a landing and a 'dust-off' for a departure . . . because the equivalent in Terranglo, the 'innie-outie,' has a distinctly *sexual* connotation. It's very crude, in fact, and anyone above the Fifth Tier equivalent in our society would blush to use it."

I'osha arched one of her graying-blond brows. "Does it?"

"Yes, sir, it does."

I'osha looked over at Li'eth. "I'm given to understand Your Highness can sense subthoughts . . . ?"

That was as far as she could delicately press. Li'eth cleared his throat. "They are indeed very crude associations. It hasn't really come up until now, but . . . Ambassador, I suspect *we* are going to be using the term a lot around your Terran soldiers, both here and elsewhere in the Alliance. Perhaps you should explain it to the troops in a broadcast? Like the way you told me that joke about the old cultural differences between '*bastard*' and '*bloody bastard*' . . . ?" he offered, using the Terranglo words.

"May I be let in on the joke?" the Grand General asked, seeing Jackie's lips twitch upward. "I presume this *is* a joke, yes?"

"Only if you promise not to be offended, sir," Jackie replied politely, eyeing the older woman.

"Call me Ta-mal for the moment, and I won't," I'osha countered. "As one soldier to another."

"Call me Jackie, then, Ta-mal. The joke is about two cultures that spoke the same language—a variation on Terranglo—who sprang from similar origins, but whose cultures had evolved differently over a couple centuries because one was a colony of the other that had settled on pretty much the far side of our world from its parent. The two cultures were having a sporting event, something called *rugby* if I remember right. It's not too dissimilar to your guanjiball," Jackie explained in a brief aside, "when one of the captains of the *British* team got very upset when one of the members of the *Australian* team called him a 'bastard.'"

I'osha blinked. "And this leads to a *joke*? Illegitimacy can be a serious issue, particularly among the higher Tiers."

"Well, the captain of the British team went to the captain of the Australian team to complain, and there was some confusion over what, exactly, was meant by one of his men calling the British captain a bastard. When he finally understood what the cultural difference was—the casualness versus the seriousness of it—he marched the British captain into the locker room and yelled at his teammates, 'Alright, you bastards, every time you call *this* bastard a bastard, in *his* culture, it means *bloody* bastard! So which one of you *bloody* bastards needs to apologize to the bastard?'"

I'osha blinked a few times, then puzzled it through. "So . . . the *Os-tral-yans* called the *Brish* . . . wait . . . I'm confused . . ."

"Australians in that era called each other bastards right and left with no offense, compared to the British culture," Jackie explained. "But adding the adjective 'bloody' made it very offensive to the Australians, so he—the Australian team captain—was explaining to his teammates that their casual use of 'bastard' was taken by the British to mean the version with the adjective attached. So essentially what His Highness suggests I do is that I explain that our version of 'innie-outie' is like saying '*bloody* bastard,' and that your version, 'innie-*out*,' is no more serious to you than to an Aussie of a couple hundred years ago calling someone a 'bastard' without any adjectives added to it."

"Ah. That makes sense. I suppose it'll be more funny next time around, now that I know the cultural connotations," I'osha offered dryly. She added a slight smile. "I'll be especially careful not to call anyone a *bloody* anything, just in case."

"That word has been replaced by variations on *boots* and *booting*, General," Major Slovaskoff reassured her. "We've done our best to eliminate a lot of the swearing that tends to accumulate in a military environment," he added. "When I signed up as a raw recruit in the Army—enlisted—my drill instructor caught me swearing and made me stand at Attention and recite one hundred words' worth of absolute absurdities instead of actual swearwords . . . and he made me do that every single morning for a week, at the top of my lungs, before I could go off to get breakfast."

"For a week?" Leftenant Shava asked.

"Their week is seven days long, just like ours," Li'eth explained.

Shava nodded, but arched a dark brow, making the golden-yellow dots dusting his hairline shift a little. "May I ask what some of these absurdities were? Or would that be offensive?"

"It wouldn't be offensive, but it was a long time ago. I remember shouting . . . 'blue-cheese sniffing' . . . and '*klingon* beard-mangling' and . . . umm . . . hm. I believe something about 'dolphin blowholes' getting me an extra day's recitation—dolphins are among what we call the nine-tenths species, almost as sentient as a Human," Slovaskoff added. "Dolphins and whales, the gorillas, chimpanzees . . . so it was stupidly offensive of me to mention them in such a manner."

(*Dolphins, like your dalphskin things?*) Li'eth asked Jackie.

(*Dalphskin suits were inspired by dolphins, yes. I'll share some pictures of the suits later,*) she promised. Out loud, Jackie offered, "Even in the best of possibilities, it will take more than half an hour for those shuttles to load on the next round of supplies and soldiers and come back down. We should probably go tour the camp and make sure there aren't too many problems."

"Yes. Especially as I can see some of the students from the Lesser Academy have come out of their classrooms and are peering past the perimeter fence," Na'avarra agreed, shading her Prussian-striped eyes from the rising sunlight with both tanned hands. "Should we split up further and cover more of the camp, Grand General?"

"An excellent idea, Leftenant. Let's split up. Ambassador, I'm certain you'll be able to handle things with the help of His Highness. Major Slovaskoff, may I walk and talk with you?" I'osha offered. "The rest of you, pair up V'Dan and Terran."

"Grand General, that's an excellent idea, sir. If anyone comes running to find either side in this mess, they'll be presented with a united front," Slovaskoff agreed.

Jackie agreed as well. "Hopefully, that will cut down on complaining and all the headaches attached to such."

Nodding politely at each other, the group split up.

———————

Somewhere around hour seven of the ten or so it would take to bring everyone down from the troop transport, Jackie found her attention drawn to a clutch of soldiers chatting amiably with some local college students. The V'Dan, a clutch of five young women and two young men, were eyeing the Terran men and women working to stow yet more crates into a storage shed. They did so through the gridded metal fence—more like hexagonal chicken wire than the simpler diamonds of wrapped chain link—separating the rest of the college grounds from the gardens and athletic fields set aside for the newcomers' use.

Most of those roughly dozen Terrans were in their early to late twenties, experienced soldiers with the muscles to match. The students seemed to be in their late teens to early twenties at most. Both groups looked relaxed, joking back and forth over the distance between the two troops, a good five or six meters from that fence.

Metaphysically, things seemed to be going fairly well; her ability to see and read auras had gotten stronger, and it looked like both groups were in good humor. Flirtatious humor, even. There were rules about fraternizing with the locals, however, and since she was there in her role as Ambassador, Jackie made sure to stroll a little closer to observe. They weren't speaking too loudly, which meant her ability at reading auras was still more useful than her ears, though the latter picked up sense as she drew near.

They look like they're just having fun. Except that tall fellow . . . Master Sergeant? No, he has only two rockers . . . he's looking a bit more flirtatious than before—

The pinks of the sergeant were counterpointed by a streak of what looked like scornful brown from the young lady he flirted with. She flicked her dark brown hand dismissively, showing off the light blue stripes curling around onto her palm. ". . . Come back when you have some *real* stripes!"

Her girlfriends laughed with her. The sergeant stood up and pointed to the rank patch on his sleeve, his V'Dan heavily accented but still intelligible enough to understand and be understood. "Hey, I *have* stripes! I'm a *First Sergeant*; I have *three*!"

Jackie quickly accessed her pocket tablet as she strode forward. It took less time to call up his personnel file—she could see his name tag from yards away—than it did to reach their side of the shed.

"I meant *real* stripes! *Jungen* stripes!" the girl called back, first cupping her hand to her lips for the catcall, then flipping it dismissively. "Come talk to me when you've grown up!"

The sergeant set down the crate he was heaving off the hoversled and planted his hands on his hips, "Listen, little girl—"

"—Belay that, Sergeant!" she interjected sharply, raising her voice to be heard while she strode a little faster. Ironically, the last patch of sunlight on the area slid away, banished behind one of the hazy clouds drifting into place overhead. From the looks of the weather, it might rain by nightfall. Then again, Ton-Bei was an M-class world.

(*Trouble?*) Li'eth asked. He was still trying to wake up from their nap in one of the officer bunkhouses, doing so by helping the Grand General deal with the mound of V'Dan paperwork that inevitably grew whenever a government or a military force—or unfortunately, both—started doing things in earnest.

(*Probably not.*) Out loud, she addressed the college student. "*Young* lady, how old are you?"

"Twenty-two," the girl asserted, lifting her chin a little. "I'm not *that* young."

"First Sergeant Ivan Khrebet, here, is twenty-eight. Terran and V'Dan years are close enough in length that a single day's variance a year does not matter. He is *older* than you by six full years. He did you the courtesy of presuming you are an adult because you are attending a school of higher learning. Perhaps you should do him the courtesy of realizing that as the equivalent of a High Sergeant, a *Fourth* Tier soldier, he is clearly a competent, educated, highly trained *adult*.

"Considering that we Terrans have traveled hundreds of light-years specifically to protect *you*, perhaps you should do as your own Empress has commanded and strive harder to see us as adults, stripes or no stripes."

"I am a Third Tier! Why should *I* take orders from a stripeless—" the V'Dan student started to argue.

"—Ja'ana, that's the *Grand High Ambassador*," one of the other students interrupted her. The new speaker was a young woman with darker skin splotched with pink stars, including one on her jawline. "Don't you *recognize* her?"

"Yah, don't be a S'Arrocan," one of the two young men added, his Imperial High V'Dan heavily accented. "She's *First Tier*, not Third. Treat her with respect!"

"Don't criticize your friends too much, either," Jackie added. That resnared the attention of the youths on the other side of the fence. "All of you, don't get angry, don't act snobbish, don't be disdainful, and don't dismiss what you do not understand, yet. Accept that we Terrans are the same species but a completely different culture that deserves your full respect.

"As my own people once taught me when *I* was in higher education many years ago, *think before you speak*," she emphasized in V'Dan. "Not just the words you intend to use right now, but the possible repercussions into the future based on what you are going to say.

"Speaking of which . . . go easy on the flirting, *all* of you. Even for a mind-speaker, there are far too many things we still do not know about each other's cultures, yet. But *do* take the time to get to know each other," she added, looking over both groups. "We have a common enemy, and that makes us allies . . . but it would be a lot better for everyone in the Alliance if we could also learn to respect each other as friends."

A couple of the students nodded, and the young woman who had recognized her nudged two of the others. The group moved off, with backwards glances. Jackie turned back to the sergeant and his Squad. They had gone back to quietly opening, checking, and resealing boxes of parts. Idly curious, Jackie squinted at the labels, a jumble of numbers and letters in Terranglo.

The first sergeant answered her without her having to ask. He did so in Terranglo. *"These are replacement parts for the leg joints on the Class IV heavy mechsuits, sir. The Major brought a hundred mech for mobile light artillery, and everyone has ceristeel light armor plating. And . . . I apologize for losing my temper with her. She was cute, but . . . young. I forgot for a moment that our Human brains don't finish maturing until twenty-five or thereabouts, and that means not until after she's out of whatever passes for a V'Dan college in this place."*

"I'm glad to see you paid attention in your psychology sciences classes, in school." Jackie hesitated, then repeated herself from earlier, in Terranglo this time. *"Go easy on the flirting, all of you, and pass the word on that. It's in the manual you were given, on the basics of intercultural interactions—and in my opinion, it should have been listed every few pages in bold lettering to be cautious and reserved whenever you're in doubt on how to act.*

"Even with my Gestalt bond with His Highness, I am still blindsided daily by the little things each side still doesn't know about each other. You don't have telepathy to help you. But do try to make friends. As the old saying goes, the enemy of my enemy is my ally, but it would be even better if I can make him my friend."

"Sir, yes, sir," the first sergeant agreed. The others nodded, still shifting boxes into storage. He lifted his chin off in the direction of the other temporary sheds and warehouses. *"Are you going to be on hand for the mechsuit demonstration they'll be giving this evening, Colonel?"*

She shook her head, smothering the urge to yawn. *"Unfortunately, no. My group has to ship out to get to Zon A'Gar in three more hours—which means leaving as soon as the last pieces of Terran personnel and gear are safely on this planet."*

"Just long enough for a smooth transfer, eh?" he sympathized. *"A pity you can't stay, sir."*

Jackie shrugged. *"You know the military, hurry up and wait, mixed in with long periods of boredom punctuated by way too much excitement. Plus far too much work to do on far too little sleep. Be proactive when talking with the others about this little incident,"* she reminded him. *"The more we Terrans talk it through, figure it out, come to expect it, and know in advance how to handle it, the better off we'll be because we'll carry ourselves with a confidence our fellow Humans will react to instinctively—we have similar physiologies, after all, and that means similar psychological reactions to posture and attitude.*

"Try to remember that yes, they have a lot of technology that's more advanced than ours, whereas we are the more

mature culture, when it comes to things like skin color," she added, giving him a pointed look. *"Don't expect them to know how to get it right on the first try. But do feel free to go up through the chains of command to Grand General I'osha if things start to get out of hand. She is trying hard to treat us right and will be Major Slovaskoff's best ally if you can't handle things internally, once I'm gone.*

". . . I do not want to have to come back here to fix any personnel problems," she added sternly.

"Sir, yes, sir." This time, it came from a smattering of his fellow soldiers, not just from the sergeant.

Pleased with their willing response, Jackie gave the little group a nod. *"Carry on. Or rather,"* she amended, switching back to V'Dan, *". . . carry on, soldiers. Don't forget to practice the local language."*

They eyed each other, puzzling through her words, then one of the privates sucked in a sharp breath, grinned, and held up a finger in mental discovery. ". . . Ah! *Neh-yah-veh!*"

His use of the V'Dan phrase *no-yes-maybe*, which also meant *more or less*, made Jackie laugh. It wasn't completely wrong as a reply, nor all that inappropriate, but as a linguist, she found it funny the private considered it a go-to reply when at a loss for words in the local tongue.

CHAPTER 7

AUGUST 15, 2287 C.E.
AVRA 8, 9508 V.D.S.
PELE-KASTH, PRIME CONTINENT, V'ZON A'GAR

Li'eth had not expected each encampment to be the same from planet to planet and was not disappointed by all the differences when they landed. There were more buildings and fewer tents at the Terran base on V'Zon A'Gar than there had been on V'Ton-Bei. Then again, the Terrans sent here were using an official camping ground designed for large events hosted by the Trinitist faith of V'Dan, not just making do on the athletics grounds of a lesser university. Despite being nowhere near the three moons of V'Dan—and V'Zon A'Gar only having one moon—the symbology of all three moons appeared over and over. Pale full moons, dark new moons, quarter moons and gibbous moons and crescent moons, all were used as a decorative motif for the site.

This time, Li'eth, Jackie, and the Terrans on the *Embassy 14* were met by familiar faces. Robert and Ayinda were two of them, having brought the *Embassy 1* into the makeshift landing site for the campground; both greeted Jackie pleasantly enough, then clustered with Captain Mamani and Lieutenant Paroquet to talk shop with their peers, as was only to be expected after several days of being apart. The others had news on how the embassy staff back on V'Dan fared, and he knew Jackie was hoping for solid good news on how Rosa was handling everything.

The third familiar person turned out to be Leftenant Superior V'kol Kos'q, not at all unexpected. The fourth familiar face, however, belonged to Leftenant Superior Ba'oul Des'n-yi. Or rather, Li'eth noted, Captain Des'n-yi, taking in the fact that the triangular outlines of the pilot's insignia pins were now solid, polished steel instead of hollow outlines.

"Congratulations, Captain," he greeted the other man, holding out his hand in formal congratulations. "May this rise in rank bring honor to your family and glory to the Empire."

Ba'oul clasped it formally, dark brown and turquoise-blue fingers wrapping around the prince's golden, burgundy-striped wrist. "May my sword break before my honor, and may my life burn out long before the glory of the Empire ever dies." He twisted his lips in a wry, almost sheepish look. "Actually, I'm not too sure about how much glory my current round of duty gathers. They've pulled me out of the pilot's chair and stuffed me into a desk chair.

"Instead of sailing between the stars, I've been spending all my time playing amateur linguist since coming home—even when I was officially supposed to be on vacation from any duties right after my return. I've only seen my parents twice since landing here."

"*Aiy!*" V'kol muttered, wincing in sympathy. The brunette wrinkled his nose. "*I* at least have seen mine five times since getting back from Earth . . . though still more over the matrices than in person."

Li'eth nodded. "I knew that *I* wouldn't get a break, thanks to my family and my position among the Terrans, but I did get to see mine every single day. *You* should have been allowed to relax for at least a few days."

"Well, now that the Terran military is here, I'll finally get to do something other than translate block after block of common Terran phrases for the local branch of the Imperial Army to memorize," Ba'oul stated, eyeing the unmarked men and women moving back and forth between cargo sleds and designated buildings. The tall pilot shrugged eloquently. "Of course, that merely means I'll be translating block after block of *living* speeches, but at least I'll be up and moving around. And . . . I find I am a bit terrified of the mere idea of going back into battle in a ship . . . only to be captured again. It's a conflict of urges and duties and best interests."

"*I* still have nightmares of the cells," Li'eth admitted quietly. Ba'oul nodded, as did V'Kol.

"Well . . . If you can't fly anymore, at least you can still run?" V'kol offered, using an old Trinitist proverb. It seemed appropriate, given their location.

"And I'll run my fastest, for as long as I can," Ba'oul agreed, finishing the saying. He eyed the dark blond and pink-spiraled gunnery officer. "So . . . *I* gained a promotion, but V'kol, you did not? Even though you're pulling along on the Captain's coat hem?"

V'kol flipped his light brown and hot-pink braid forward over his shoulder, mock-primping. "I'm decoratively useless."

"*V'shakk* to that," Li'eth muttered. Both men blinked at him over the vulgarity. He shook his head. "They're holding back on promoting you because I pointed out that I wanted you to be seen to be *earning* your solids, not gaining the next pin through being pulled along on my coat hem. You're better than a rank earned through mere cronyism, V'kol. *Your* promotion will come in another month or two. Probably in just a month, once the current mess has settled and someone not directly linked to me has had a chance to review your work."

V'kol eyed his superior, then rubbed for a few seconds at the bridge of his nose. "Saints . . . Cronyism. Nepotism. Inner-*parlor* bargains. I'm beginning to admire the Terrans more and more—Ba'oul, did you know they had a political officer whose job specifically was to intercept attempted bribes and enticements? The poor lady died in the attack on the capital, but her job was to review all offers being sent to the Terrans to look for ethical considerations. The slightest hint of impropriety, and she banned that person from trying to contact the Ambassador directly."

"I only met her twice, maybe three times," Li'eth admitted. "Even when we were in quarantine together, she stayed out of direct contact with the Grand High Ambassador, and by corollary, me. She said it was to keep corruption away from our officials, and that as a liaison, both before and after being officially appointed as one, I was considered to be too important to be pestered by bribery."

Ba'oul snorted and quickly covered his nose and mouth, muffling his wincing laughter. The other two men eyed him in curiosity. Sniffing to clear his sinuses, the pilot grinned as he lowered his blue-and-brown hand. ". . . Can you imagine how *many* such people we'd need, to attempt to push away all the layers of inner-parlor dealings in the Empire?"

"*Aiy!* Maybe *we* should hire the Terrans to do it for us, too, because *we* won't have enough bodies in the whole Empire for the job!" V'kol joked, snickering.

Li'eth choked on a laugh of his own and quickly covered his mouth as he started to cough. Ba'oul snorted again and grinned. A moment later, the prince felt a tendril of curiosity from Jackie.

(. . . *Something amuses you?*)

(*It's . . . complex. A cultural thing. How are you doing?*) he asked, peering around him to look for her. (*Actually, where are you? I don't see Robert or Ayinda anymore, either.*)

(*The ship with the new copilot is coming into orbit; we're on our way to the* Embassy 1 *to work out where they're going to touch down, and when. The landing field is getting a bit crowded—augh! What is that on my . . . ? Ew, is that the equivalent of* dog *poo? Yuck!*)

He received a mental impression of her trying to scrape whatever it was off her boot with the help of the fuzzy yellowish vine that passed for ground cover, locally. (*I'm not a native of V'Zon A'Gar, so I have no idea. You want me to ask Ba'oul?*) he added politely, even if the subject wasn't. (*He's still right here.*)

(*No, it seems to be coming off. Travel the galaxy! Meet new sentients! Step in new forms of feces! Oh, how* glamorous *my life is as an interstellar Ambassador . . . Yuck. Just . . . booting yuck!*)

Li'eth choked on more laughter. He shook his head at the other two men with him, unable to explain what he'd just telepathically heard. Some thoughts—especially not his own—were not meant to be shared.

AUGUST 17, 2287 C.E.
AVRA 10, 9508 V.D.S.
SU-CHELLIS MINING STATION
VLLS-119 SYSTEM

"Woo! Yeah! Look at that!" Lieutenant Commander Ramirez crowed in Brazilian, bouncing a little in her seat. Her restraint harness kept her in place. She had to wear it, as an unexpected design flaw of some sort on the Terrans' part had rendered it impossible to install gravity in the cockpit of the *Embassy 1.* Not without taking the cabin apart and reworking it entirely over a period of weeks that they felt they did not have. She thumped her armrest and pointed at the screen, which streamed a live feed from a heads-up camera on the helmet of a Terran Army soldier back on Ton-Bei. *"You go! You booting go, girls!"*

"Practice your V'Dan, Anjel," Jackie admonished. Part of her felt like cheering, too, as the projectile rifles in the hands of her fellow Terran soldiers spat out smoke and brief flashes of exploding light on her own viewscreens. Those rifles chewed up the Salik forces trying to make a successful landing a thousand or so klicks away from the new Terran base. But this was not a one-sided fight. Bright yellow light seared back in return, nasty laser beams concentrated so bright they were visible even in the gray light of early morning.

That helmet-carried view was not the only one; Jackie had all the screens on both consoles at the pair of back-leftmost cockpit stations running similar streamed images from the hot zone on Ton-Bei. The pocket of Salik on that peninsula, Ke-chai, had been pinpointed by V'Dan forces, and V'Dan transports had been pressed into service, ferrying half the Terran brigade under Slovaskoff's command into striking distance overnight.

One of the camera views suffered a flash of yellow, spun, and pointed up at the sky at an awkward angle. Jackie quickly tapped it with her stylus, marking it with a red outline. That meant it was now inappropriate for broadcast past that point. She didn't know if the soldier bearing that helm had died or was merely injured, but this was a broadcast compilation that was supposed to give the V'Dan and their allies a boost of confidence and hope for the future of the war. That meant minimizing on-screen casualties. That particular footage would not be erased nor hidden, but neither would it be broadcast publicly right now.

She wasn't the only one doing this task, but since they were between Ton Bei and several colonyworlds downstream, such as Ba-kan-tuu, Va'atuu, and Dai'a's dome-strewn colonyworld of Du'em-ya, it was necessary to run censorship checks in a live stream as they passed through. Li'eth sat to the right side of the aisle at the back of the cockpit, strapped into his seat, speaking softly into a headset as he translated into V'Dan some of the commands being transmitted in Terranglo, providing a running commentary. Occasionally, he corrected himself, and sometimes pulsed a query to Jackie, who juggled it as best she could with her other duties.

"*YES!*" Legs thumping in the footwell of her seat, Anjel Ramirez thrust her fists up and out. She bobbled a bit in her seat. Jackie couldn't blame her; she saw the same image that had excited the pilot, a walking cannon vehicle toppling in the aftermath of explosions.

Li'eth frowned, but the copilot fell quiet again, watching the footage from the battle on Ton-Bei. Then he asked his next question. (*What are clay-more mines?*)

(*Directional explosives; if you're behind them, you're relatively safe. If you're in front or ahead to either side, not really.*)

(*Nice understatement,*) he quipped, explaining aloud in Imperial High V'Dan what had just happened.

Seeing blood on her screens, Jackie tapped another image, cutting it off from the feed. She had a question of her own for him. (*Salik have iron-based blood?*)

(*Something close enough to bleed as red as me,*) he agreed. Then added darkly, (*They'll never bleed enough, though.*)

Jackie flinched away from that thought. She *knew* why; Li'eth had the memories of his captivity, the memory of watching one of the aliens eating the severed limb of a former bridge officer, a former friend. It was understandable that he would want to eradicate his enemy. It was not, however, a comfortable position for her.

She was not sure if she could ever explain it to him. Raised multiculturally, to understand the societies in which her parents moved as well as the languages encountered, Jacaranda could not look at anything from just one perspective, one angle, one viewpoint. She did not *agree* with what the Salik were doing—not by any means—but in her mind-set, they still had a right to exist. The trick would be finding the way to get them to stop attacking, stop harming, and stop eating people alive.

The trick to diplomacy, to governing wisely and well across disparate cultures and beliefs, lay in finding the commonalities, the needs that could be simultaneously met. Substitutions and compromises that could further common goals. To deliberately eat another sentient being, to derive deliberately invoked pleasure from it . . .

Her mind shied away from the idea that there was a sentient race out there that was psychopathic. Not just sociopathic, possessing a weak conscience and very little empathy for others, but utterly lacking in a conscience and any empathy for other beings in life.

On an individual level, being instinctively manipulative as a survival trait, the successful sociopaths and psychopaths could climb quite high on the social ladder, to the point where they might even have a chance to set official policy in a moderately corrupt or lackadaisical system. In a vigilant system, however, that chance was lessened. Jackie lived and breathed on the front lines of stopping that from happening. So she was aware of sociopathic individuals, yes, and for the good of cooperative survival, knew they had to be stopped.

But at the same time, she could not—would not—believe it of an entire *race*. It went against common belief on how societies *could* develop under the auspices of intelligence, self-awareness, and comprehension of subjects like species survival and group success. Such things *required* basic species-wide levels of cooperation well above what such individuals would ever bother to give if they didn't have to do it. Cooperation required understanding the other person's viewpoint and needs as well as one's own. It was one of the tenets of even nonpsychic empathy, to put oneself in someone else's shoes metaphorically.

So she had seen Li'eth's nightmares in their shared dreams, but they were not *her* nightmares. They would never be her nightmares. Of course, neither would she try to invalidate them . . . and ugh, that combat camera feed on the upper right was a little too graphic on bloodied body parts. She tapped that one off and turned another one back on, when it looked like the owner was back on their feet and back in combat, wounded but still capable of fighting.

Her headset chirped to life in her left ear, dragging some of her attention away from the combat broadcasts. Paea and Buraq had suited up with Ayinda to maneuver feeding hoses into the *Embassy 1*'s tanks. Those hoses came from the free-floating tank of hopefully purified water left by the V'Dan in a station-tethered orbit since they didn't have any docking facilities large enough for the *Embassy 1*, just the smaller *Embassy 14*.

"*Primary lock engaged. Seal looks green. Cockpit, confirm the green seal,*" Ayinda reported.

Anjel broke off from her enthused viewing and touched her headset. "*Main filter pump seal is . . . green, Mbani. I repeat, you are green for go.*"

"*Confirm that, we are green for go. Beginning fuel processing now.*"

Jackie's right earpiece chirped, and a notification popped

up. Jackie quickly verified the channel codes. "Anjel, can you take over monitoring the combat feed? I have a priority two message coming through."

"I can do it," Li'eth told her. "I've been watching what you cut and reinstate, and I already have the matrix feeds running."

"Do it, thank you," she said, and linked their consoles. Clearing one of her screens, she opened the channel, answering verbally first as she waited for the lines to connect. *"This is Grand High Ambassador Jacaranda MacKenzie. What is your priority two?"*

She waited a few seconds, and got a visual pingback. It unfolded in an image of Rosa McCrary. "Hello, Jackie. This isn't a pleasant call, but they insist upon having an official reaction from you, as well as one from Premiere Callan."

"Okay, you have my attention," Jackie said. That was not the sort of request that boded well for whatever had happened. "I presume something went wrong?"

"Yes. A Tlassian military-sciences team apparently attempted to open one of the two hyperrelay satellites left in their capital system . . . with the inevitable end results," McCrary finished dryly as soon as she finished listening to her end of Jackie's words over the lag between their positions. "I can have you patched through to their government, or send you their contact number. I think you're closer by now, though, so a direct call would have less lag time to it than a rerouted one."

"Contact number," Jackie decided quickly, calling up the star charts the V'Dan had given her people. "We're indeed closer to Tlassian space, and that'll cut down on the lag time by at least a few seconds."

"You know what the Premiere's stance is, right?" Rosa asked dryly, working on her end of the connection. "And . . . there, it's been sent."

". . . Received, and of course I do. We discussed this exact sort of thing in full before leaving Earth. I know what to say to them—I'll chat with you later, Rosa; I've several other things to do as well, but I'll give this a priority call right away. *Embassy 1* out," Jackie finished, ending that call. Double-checking the information, she queued up the correct frequencies, system satellites, and calling code, and sent the call through.

And waited, not only for the lag time involved over the hundreds of light-years, but for the system to work.

For non-V'Dan systems, the V'Dan had cobbled together programming-code-translation units for the Terrans to use; the method was a bit jury-rigged, but the call, sent out under Terran code, would go from relay to relay, feed itself into the externally attached Terran-to-V'Dan code box, and from there, feed into a translator for V'Dan-to-Tlassian, *then* broadcast itself through a third unit in Tlassian digital broadcasting codes.

Thankfully, the whole process only added a fraction of a second. That meant the response on the other end was reasonably prompt. The smooth-skulled Tlassian who appeared on the far end had greenish scales; V'Dan lettering along the bottom of the image gave a name and gender, MEIOA-E T'SSARGESS, SECRETARY OF ALLIANCE AFFAIRS. The alien bowed her head slightly. "Grannd High Ambassador Ma-Ken-Zee. It isss amazing to tallk with you so sswiftly."

"Secretary T'ssargess," Jackie replied, dipping her own head.

Nodding heads was a trait Humans and Tlassians and Choya all shared, which according to her history lectures had led the Gatsugi and even the Chinsoiy to use it in greeting rituals and confer-agreement gestures. Solaricans preferred to flick their ears or lift their chins. The Salik didn't exactly have a neck, and the K'Katta didn't exactly have a head, so they didn't bother. She leveled her gaze on the alien on the other side of the five seconds of lag and continued.

"I understand you wish to discuss the destruction of a Terran hyperrelay satellite by Tlassian personnel? If I may speak bluntly . . . I am not certain what there is to be discussed in this matter."

". . . That iss blunnt," the Secretary stated in return after several seconds of lag. "But, yess. The losss of lives iss most tragic. The losss of an alllied ship iss wasteful in war."

Jackie realized where this was headed and waited patiently for the Secretary to finish, keeping her expression neutrally polite.

"A devicsse of the Terran governnment has caused the losss of severall Tlassian livess, and Tlassian equipment and transportation. Cossstly thingss," T'ssargess continued. "Our government wisshes to know what your government will do to make recompenssse. The inquiries we gave to your sssecond-ranked Ambassssador were not ssatisfactorily replied."

"If you are dissatisfied, meioa, then I suspect it is because you did not like her answer," Jackie returned honestly. Or rather, bluntly. "The families of those who died have our condolences and our sorrow for their loss, but the Terran government does not owe the Tlassian government or its people anything. In fact, it could be successfully argued that the Tlassian people owe *my* people the cost of replacing that rather expensive satellite."

As the seconds ticked away between her opening words and the recording of his reactions being returned, she watched the alien's eyes widen, those slit pupils narrowing a bit in what she guessed was probably shock or affront, but that was to her opening statement. She kept talking as she watched, however, because Jackie needed to make it clear the alien was not going to get very far with her, either.

"That satellite, meioa, was delivered to your people with the warning not to attempt to open it or move it in any way once it was placed in orbit. You were instructed to leave it alone, and that it was designed to detonate in a powerful explosion if tampered with in any way. That is the extent of Terran responsibility in this matter, to warn you of the dangers inherent in those actions. Your people made the choice to tamper anyway.

"I'm sorry if you don't like my answer, but it is *not* the responsibility of the Terran government to monitor and police any actions undertaken by other governments. And if your people continue to destroy our rather expensive equipment through additional attempts at accessing and tampering, we will have to withdraw the remaining communications equipment and send you a bill for replacing the units you destroyed.

"That is a step I am certain neither side wishes to take," Jackie stated dryly. "Now . . . is there anything else you wished to discuss?"

". . . No," the Tlassian Secretary for Alliance Affairs replied. "You have ssaid more than enough."

"Then please pass along my condolences to the families of those who died, Secretary T'ssargess, and I hope you can have a good day." Closing the connection on her end, Jackie slumped in her seat, sighing heavily.

(*That's not exactly what the V'Dan would do,*) Li'eth observed in the back of her mind. (*We'd pay a recompense fee—we call it "spring money," but you would call it "blood money," I think.*)

(*We are not going to be fined for someone else's arrogant and/or very poorly thought-out choices,*) Jackie countered, sitting up again after two deep breaths. She started the program that would beam the recording of that call back to Earth for archiving and analysis. (*I'm sure we'll have enough problems dealing with the aftermaths of our* own *mistakes. We don't need to compound them with others' idiocies.*)

(*You're getting cranky,*) he observed mildly. (*Are you feeling okay?*)

(*I think I need to go get a snack from the galley.*) Out loud, she asked, "Do either of you want anything to eat or drink?"

Anjel shook her head, her brunette braid bobbing in the lack of gravity. "I might be enjoying watching us kick frogtopus buttocks, but I couldn't eat while doing so. It's just a little too graphic. Thank you, though."

"A drink packet would be okay, thank you, but I'd rather have gravity for eating actual food," Li'eth stated politely. He tapped his screen, altering the flow of video feeds. "And one of us has to keep monitoring these broadcasts, so I shall have to stay here for now."

"One drink packet for you, and a snack pack for me, then," Jackie murmured, unstrapping herself from her workstation. "Got it."

Pulling herself free, she floated to the door. Someone had printed out labels and slapped them on the cockpit door in Terranglo and V'Dan in bright yellow on red—the caution-label style of the Empire—that stated, CAUTION! GRAVITY SHELF! MOVE CAREFULLY! The sign included arrows pointing at a line placed below them, and beneath it, the subtext of THIS SIDE IS DOWN!

An excessive use of exclamation marks in her opinion, but remembering to be cautious would always be wiser than forgetting and falling flat on one's face. Opening the door, she oriented and pulled herself carefully forward, using the newly installed handrails. Her feet encountered the gravity well first, swinging downward, then her legs. Jackie wobbled a little, her body adjusting to the strange sensations of going from null gravity to roughly one-quarter Earth's gravity over the space of just a few inches. Pulling herself fully into the floor weave's effects, she steadied herself for a moment, then moved to her left.

The gravity increased to half strength within just a few steps, but no more than half. The V'Dan engineers who had helped install it were fairly sure that the Terran-designed ship could withstand the stresses of full monodirectional gravity during the sorts of maneuvers that came when a ship was wrapped in a thruster field. But both groups of engineers agreed not to stress these ships' designs any more than half strength until they had solid performance numbers. Which meant the *Embassy 1* was their official low-key test vehicle, as well as her home away from home embassy for the time being. Earth's science technicians had done their best to work with the V'Dan and K'Katta scientists to get everything accurately translated, at least, but they still preferred being cautious.

The moment Jackie opened the cupboard drawer that contained the drink packs, a claxon blared through the ship, startling her into jumping and banging her knuckles on the cabinet edge. She hissed, hastily shutting the door again with her free hand while she kissed the throbbing skin, worrying over what had gone wrong in the few moments since departing the cockpit. She didn't have to wait long to find out.

"All hands, we have inbound Salik warships! All hands on deck!" Anjel snapped over the ship-wide intercom.

Jackie, knowing that Robert and the others sleeping on air mattresses in the crew cabin would be stirring and scrambling to get into combat positions, hurried carefully back to the cockpit. Just turning around to do so was enough to remind her of how wobbly half gravity felt. Palming open the door, with its own list of exclamation-peppered warnings about the *lack* of gravity on the other side, she used a touch of telekinesis to swoop carefully back into her seat. As soon as she was in place and reaching for the straps, Li'eth pushed out of the right-hand bank of rear consoles to join her.

(I've forwarded control of the matrix streams to the

Embassy 22 *and told them to start checking it for gore censoring,*) he told her. (*If these weren't headed toward a couple of K'Katta colonies, we wouldn't have to do that. They're very sensitive toward violence.*)

(*Well, we Terrans have a few social taboos about that, too. We're doing it for* our *sake, not just theirs.*) Out loud, she asked, "Anjel, what defenses does this station have?"

"Not very many. Gun turrets and shields, of course, but they're a stationary target," the copilot stated. "Mobile resources . . . Three ships left orbit about an hour ago, and according to the system logs, two more left two hours before that. Plenty of time for the enemy to sit quiet an hour or so out, pick up the lightwaves, and decide to risk an attack.

"Four V'Dan ships are either parked and coupled to the station or at a relative dead stop to it. One more is out there patrolling but off path by about two hundred klicks. And like I said, the station has some point defenses, which they're bringing online and orienting, mostly lasers, a few projectiles . . . *This* is odd," the Brazilian added. "The navicomp says the incoming ships are slowing down. If I got the numbers right, they're decelerating a lot slower than they *should* be for an attack . . .

"No, wait, Colonel," she corrected herself. "One of the ships isn't slowing down as much, but the others will come into an orbital synchronization if they stay on this heading, widely spaced in about a hundred-degree arc from the station as center point, sir."

"Analysis?" Jackie asked. Behind and to her and Li'eth's right, the cockpit hatch opened and the bridge-crew members who had been asleep started hauling themselves inside. None of the three of them bothered to look back; keeping their eyes on the building situation was more important than counting noses right now.

"If what the station is sending me is true . . ." Anjel murmured, evaluating silently for a moment. ". . . They'll be in range in fifteen minutes V'Dan Standard. Seven of those ships will be in a classic dish formation to target everyone at a dead stop, six on the rim and the advancing one in the center, no other cross fires on their own positions."

"*Shakk,*" Li'eth swore, aura stinging with the swirling reds of agitated realization before threading through with yellowish tones. "They're here for the fuel! It's a *fueling* raid!"

Jackie's headset sprang to life in her right ear again, coding-translation programs activating on her console. She held up her hand, cutting him off; the language was V'Dan, the trade tongue of the Alliance, but it was garbled and mushy. After a few moments, though, she nodded, getting the gist of the message; understanding heavily accented languages was merely part and parcel of her job as a translator. ". . . You're right. They're demanding all ships in this area stand down their weapons, and for the station to prepare to be boarded. They're demanding to commandeer the fuel in exchange for our lives."

"*Don't* believe them. Most Salik captains *do* leave refueling hostages alive and alone, but only around four out of five. We *cannot* risk being boarded," Li'eth insisted.

(*Easy, Li'eth. I can see your anxieties streaming out of you like muddy-yellow ribbons,*) Jackie warned him. (*Now is not the time to panic.*)

(I am not going back.) He took two deep breaths, however, and struggled to let his fear go. (*If they don't see any sentients on the way to and from the fueling docks, they usually let people go . . . but they have had enough time pass potentially to learn about this ship. Or at least this shape of it. The crew of the* G'pow Gwish N'pokk Chu-huu *escaped with recordings of what the* Aloha 9 *looked like, and this ship is just like that one, only bigger. The moment they see it, they'll come to claim us as a unique war prize.*)

"*Ayinda, hurry up on disengaging the fueling lines,*" Anjel warned into her headset, before raising her voice so she could be heard by the others. "Heads up, everyone. We can't go anywhere just yet, and the bulk of it is between us and them. All my projections are based on whatever telemetry the station is feeding me, plus the comm satellite we dropped off a few klicks away. We also have that same huge tanker to hide behind, so even if we were armed heavily enough, we don't have a clear shot just yet. On the bright side, neither do they."

"Great, just great . . . Once again, I am stuck in my *underwear* when the enemy attacks," Robert cursed, pulling his floating body into his seat. All he had on were blue exercise shorts, technically not underwear, but near enough to make him feel embarrassed about it. "This is *not* how I wanted to be remembered in the history books."

"*I* could do without any excitement, period," their backup navigator, Lieutenant First Grade Charlize Taan stated, pulling herself into place behind him. She wore shorts, tee shirt, and a pair of socks to keep her tanned feet warm, but otherwise was just as underdressed for the occasion. "I lost my place on the *17* from a little too much excitement."

"*Mbani to Colonel MacKenzie, we have decoupled, boarded, and sealed the aft airlock,*" Jackie heard in her left ear, while negotiations between the station and the Salik were under way. The station seemed to be choosing to risk that one-in-five chance of being eaten alive. "*All personnel are accounted for. The fueling hoses are being autoretracted now. We have an estimated twenty-five seconds for the Alliance's automatic systems to secure them and seal the hatches.*"

"Acknowledged, Lieutenant Commander," Jackie replied. Her left earpiece came to life with a query from Mamani on board the *Embassy 14*. She switched channels and replied. "*Sit tight, 14, but prep for launch just in case. I don't want you out where they can see you unless we have no other choice. You're docked inside the station, and the station contains the fuel they need, so hopefully they won't attack it directly. You're safer than we are right now.*"

Even as Captain Mamani sent back an acknowledgment, Jackie felt Li'eth's emotions spike upward in a rising panic as his thoughts circled around the last time he'd been captured. This time, his subthoughts fretted, he wasn't wearing that V'Dan concealer stuff to hide his highly valuable identity. To his credit, his fears were wrapped up in thoughts of her vulnerability, too, and the rest of the crew, but those feelings were starting to raise anxiety within her mind, too.

(*Calm yourself, Li'eth. We* will *get out of this,*) she reassured him.

"Hey, Jackie!" Robert called out. "I just had a thought—you remember that transforming robot-ship thing you did?"

"The what I *what*?" Jackie asked him, confused.

"On board that Salik ship! You did a holokinetic thing, beat them up telekinetically with a little light-and-dance show, remember?" he prodded her. "Turned the *Aloha* into a giant robot? Can you use your holokinesis to get us out of this?"

"Oh. *Oh!*" She considered it, blinking. "I . . . I'm not sure if I'm strong enough to cloak any of the ships out here without several more psis, even with Li'eth's help. I don't know the surface of that gas giant well enough to get an illusion of invisibility right . . . and I certainly don't know enough of the other vessels to convincingly project an attack robot onto the space they occupy."

"Stop thinking *hide*, sir, and start thinking *fight*," Taan countered. "With respect to your station as an Ambassador, you *are* still a soldier in the Space Force, sir. No offense, but . . ."

"No, no, you're right, Lieutenant," Jackie agreed, staring at her screen projections, trying to wrest an answer out of what she was seeing. "I don't want to go down without a fight, either. I just need to think of a way to back them off. If I knew what their cultural demons were, I'd shove one of *those* in their face, fifty kilometers high . . ."

"*Can* you actually project anything that high?" Anjel asked, twisting in her seat to look at Jackie.

"No, but it's a pleasant thought, isn't it?" she murmured. "Okay . . . I think I know what I can do to scare them off. Anjel, prep and launch two hydrobombs, authorization Juliette Mike. Give me a one-minute warning before you launch both, so I can cloak them holokinetically. I also want you to plot a debris vector for the explosions that will do the least amount of damage to the station and our allies, and send me a view of the paths involved, so I don't lose track of what I'm cloaking. I'm not the expert at out-of-body that Heracles is, so get the projected paths right the first time. *And* I want to know exactly how long to the second it'll take to get those bombs to their point of no return, either to continue on to target or to get them navigated off to the side."

"Sweet Mary, Mother of God," Anjel muttered. "You don't ask for much, do you, sir? Charlize, I'll take launch number one; you prep and project launch number two. How much time do we have, Colonel?" their chief gunner asked.

"Five minutes to launch," Jackie decided, eyeing the projected arrival of the incoming single Salik ship.

"Shakk," their engineer and backup navigator swore. "I'm going to need your help, too, Robert—I *can't* do on-the-fly calcs *and* prep the weapon! I don't have those kinds of specs in my head!"

"Unless the boss says so, I'm not goin' anywhere," their chief pilot quipped back. *"Are* we going anywhere, boss?"

"With luck, no, but I am going to have to wing this a little," she murmured, thinking quickly through all possible choices.

"I'm on it, then," Robert promised. "ETA on that inbound ship, nineteen minutes, and it'll be in docking range."

"We should've grabbed that Flying Auk fellow for this ship," Li'eth quipped. At Jackie's quick blank look of confusion, he flapped his elbows a little. "He'd have wings, yes? To 'wing' it?"

Robert snorted, hands flicking switches and tapping controls. "Your sense of humor is *almost* there, meioa, but not quite far enough. Still don't quit your day job just yet."

Jackie adjusted her headset and spoke in Terranglo, since part of her broadcast had to reach the *14* inside the fueling station. *"Attention all hands. We are about to run a big giant bluff on the encroaching Salik forces. Get to your stations as soon as you can."*

A chorus of affirmations reached her, both in the cabin and through her left earpiece. Ayinda's voice followed. *"Permission to enter the bridge when ready, sir?"*

She switched to internal audio only. *"Permission granted, Mbani. Just be quiet about it. Additionally, I am going to need silence in the cabin for broadcast. I don't want even a hint of what you're doing to be heard on my audio 'cast. Send any information to my screens, text only. You can still speak for now, but I will give you a twenty-second warning for silence before I open a channel to the incoming ships."*

Watching the chronometer at the lower right edge of her central screen ticking down, Jackie breathed deep and let it out slowly, centering herself until it was time to give the twenty-second warning. As she waited, she eyed the closest approaching ship, captured from three different angles. The others were hanging back, gliding slowly into an excellent parabolic crossfire position, silent threat and testament to how badly the station and its visiting ships were outgunned.

"Hydrobomb one programmed and ready to launch," Ramirez announced, with half a minute to spare on her five-minute window. "I'm aiming it to swoop in from the side on the Salik ship closest to our zero dead ahead, so the debris field will hopefully hit the other enemy vessels. I just need to input a projected speed. *When* do you want it to impact, sir?"

"And . . . my Fat Man is ready to launch, right on the heels of your Little Boy," Taan added.

"Lieutenant Taan, that is historically insensitive," Jackie chided softly. She felt Li'eth pulse her a subthought inquiry following Taan's subdued apology, and sent him back a *Not right now* pulse of her own. "I want Taan's to strike the lead ship, then yours to hit its target one to two minutes after. Prep a third for launch, while we're at it, and aim it at the next in the hexagon."

"Sir, that still doesn't tell me *when*," Anjel protested.

"How soon can all three hit their targets, one-two-three, over a two-minute span?" Jackie asked.

"Approximately . . . eight minutes from now at the earliest," Robert answered. "It'll take me one minute to finish prepping the third for launch, and the rest is all acceleration versus travel time. Anjel, the program?"

"I'm on it. Adjusting target coordinates . . . Do you want a fourth one launched?" she asked. "We only have four, but we could send all four if you just want them launched at regular intervals."

"Oh, sure, why not?" Jackie quipped. "But be prepared to pull it off trajectory if it isn't needed. Someone give me a countdown to the first impact on my screen. I'm going to have to time this—lightwave lag time to the farthest Salik vessel is . . . huh. Negligible. Good. I keep thinking they're farther out than they actually are. Gunners, you may launch when ready."

Silence filled the cockpit until the door opened, and Ayinda pulled herself through, exiting the low-gravity deck of the central corridor. "Everyone is strapped in."

". . . Launching hydrobomb number two in forty-five seconds, sir," Anjel reported. "It goes first because it'll have the farthest to travel of all four hydrobombs, since it needs to circle around to hit the far side—position east, as it were.

Once it launches, we'll have one and a half minutes to launching numbers three and four for targets on the north and south rims, and then four minutes seventeen seconds to launching missile number one to hit the west side, sir. It's all programmed in."

"Confirmed, Lieutenant Commander. You may launch when ready, again under authorization Juliett Mike. I am Colonel Jacaranda MacKenzie, and I take responsibility for the decision to launch hydrobombs at our enemy outside of a formal declaration of war. Let us hope we don't have to use them to get the Salik to back down."

A set of timers appeared on Jackie's screen, each one bearing a corresponding number. Beside her, Li'eth forced himself to breathe. He reached out for her mind again, tightening his grip a little on their Gestalt. (*I do hope you know what you're doing, love . . . and that you'll explain the "historically insensitive" part. The names you used are familiar, but I can't place them.*)

(*Feel free to search the onboard archives for information when this is over. Keywords, World War II, the Manhattan Project, Fat Man, Little Boy, Hiroshima, Nagasaki. And don't feel bad you can't remember them. They're not your manmade disasters.*)

Feeling the *chunk* of the first, or rather, bomb number two launching, Jackie sent her senses outward, found the metal, and wrapped a pod of bent light around the projectile. To her surprise, she felt Li'eth joining his efforts to hers, then, (*. . . Got it. I can shield this one, and . . . that one, too,*) he told her. (*Can't talk for long, though . . . must concentrate . . .*)

Grateful, Jackie handled the third and fourth launching with one corner of her mind and estimated when to begin her broadcast with another corner. She gave the twenty-second call for silence on the intercom, then set up a broadcast using the Alliance standard lightwave-communication equipment the V'Dan had given to each of their ships. Eyeing the chronometers to try to time things just right, she spoke into her headset, audio broadcast only.

"*Attention, Salik vessels,*" she stated crisply and clearly in V'Dan. "*Our allies, in their alarm at your presence and your threats, have forgotten that we, the members of the Terran*

Empire, have pledged to lend our aid and protection to their people wherever we may travel. While we admire our allies' willingness to cooperate with your demands, we have been informed that in roughly one out of every five such attacks of this sort, your race lies to its hostages and slaughters or takes prisoners anyway. We do not care to cooperate with the demands of treacherous liars.

"*However, all of our actions so far have been defensive. We have only reacted to your nation's aggressions,*" she continued in a neutral-pleasant tone, while data streamed in from the station, picking up lightwave transmissions in what was presumably Sallhash, the Salik main language. Not aimed at her, just yet, but definitely some cross-ship communications going on. "*With that in mind, if you agree immediately to withdraw, and actually do so within the next five mi-nah V'Dan Standard time units, we will not harm you. If you continue on course to steal fuel from this station, or attempt to attack anyone, we will destroy you. One ship at a time, to give you a chance to reconsider and withdraw. This broadcast will be your only warning. You will not see our weapons until it is too late.*

"*You can stay to fight, and die today, or you can run away and maybe survive for some other fight another day. The choice is yours. You have exactly five V'Dan mi-nah in which to decide to live or die . . . starting . . . Now.*"

A message popped up on her screen from Ayinda even as she closed her end of the link and awaited the Salik's response. *Colonel, we are coming into firing arc for two of the widest-spaced ships in that cross-fire dish. Orders?*

She felt the *chunk* of the last probe launching, and wrapped her mind around it carefully, juggling the need to protect the missiles with an illusion of invisibility versus typing a reply to both her and Robert. *Keep behind the water tank for cover.*

Aye, sir.

A ping came through for a visual link. Jackie set it up to be one-way. Showing her face would not be wise, in case the Salik had learned by now the identity of the Grand High Ambassador of the new family on the Alliance block. Sure enough, the muddy beige alien with a frog-like face, stubby thick eyestalks, and whistling nostril-flaps was the same type of alien as those she had seen on that very first ship several months ago.

The perspective of that camera view disturbed Jackie a little bit; the camera had been placed up high, and looked down at a steep angle on the alien, giving her a touch of vertigo from trying to reconcile it with the much more level view she was accustomed to seeing when speaking with the other races.

"Hhheww are bluffing," the alien scorned. "Surrender, or we will desstroy efferyonne!"

"My people have a saying. 'It takes one to know one,'" Jackie quipped dryly, one corner of her mind tracking two missiles, another keeping an eye on the timer for the first impact. "You cannot attack this station because you *need* the chemical fuel it holds. Those chemicals are explosive. They will burn. Attacking the station would therefore destroy what you need. More than that, it would ruin your chance to return at a later time to attempt a second theft, or a third.

"I repeat, the Terran Empire does not wish to damage any Salik person, settlement, or vessel . . . but we will destroy you if you choose to attack this facility and its allied ships. Really, I don't see what advantage there is in this for you. I'm even giving you multiple chances for your survivors to retreat . . . but my patience is not infinite. Neither are your ships. I would consider that carefully if I were you."

The Salik on her center screen vanished, replaced by the image of a circle of rippling lines spewing up and out, depicting a fountain. That was the symbol of the Salik Empire, whose founding homeworld name meant *Fountain*. Medium lavender on a beige background, it looked oddly soothing compared to the aggressive nature of its owners.

Their ship swayed a little under faint, thrumming pulses from the attitude thrusters. As requested, their chief pilot trimmed their position relative to the large V'Dan tanker containing the purified water they needed, keeping it between the Terrans and the Salik as much as Robert could. It meant hovering rather close to the bulky, boxy pod, but that pod loomed ten times as big as the *Embassy 1*, adequate cover in close proximity. Maybe.

Jackie still wasn't completely sure how strong Salik weapons were; the last battle she had participated in, she hadn't paid the slightest bit of attention to the actual damage capacity of Salik lasers and munitions. She hadn't been in a position to pay attention. But water—at least, without a catalytic conversion—was not prone to explode, unlike the petrochemical-style fuels used by the Alliance. Even if a rupture occurred, when it spilled out into space, water would merely freeze, harmlessly sealing over any hull breach. A superior fuel from a safety standpoint, as well as a caloric one.

Movement, Ayinda warned her in text at the bottom of her screen. *Allied ships are adjusting position to drift behind the station.*

Acknowledged, Jackie typed back.

If that thing gets hit, it could blow up those ships as well as take out the 14, Robert typed to her. *Are you sure this is the right course?*

We cannot risk being captured. Might as well save the others, Jackie typed back.

The Salik came back on-screen just as the timer countdown started flashing, accompanied by a message from Ayinda. *They have not changed course, sir. Fifteen seconds to no return.*

"We outnnnumber hhyew," the Salik on the screen started to say, nostril-flaps flexing as he pronounced the V'Dan words as best he could. "Hhyew are sssoft, like the K'hn Khatta. We willll attack annyway—"

"No. You do not outnumber us," Jackie countered, typing, *Stay on target.* "I gave you fair warning. *You* chose to stay and advance, rather than flee and live. *You* are out of time."

Two seconds later, light flared back at them from three different angles, station cameras sharing the view of the lead ship exploding with silent, deadly, brilliant orange force. Chunks spun and tumbled outward, all of them blasted away from the station. It was hard to tell sizes, but she was fairly certain the largest chunks weren't more than a couple decks deep. Hydrobombs were ruthlessly efficient.

Unfortunately, they were also limited in supply. She needed to get the enemy to go away, not stay and slug it out.

The Salik on her viewscreen was not one of those on the destroyed vessels. The alien ranted and rasped, whistled and snorted in his native tongue, no doubt cursing her and making yet more threats. The V'Dan had reassured them that it was safe to assume all Salik encountered were male, for reasons of biology and reproduction, so she had no problems labeling him a *him*. Jackie ignored his ranting, speaking over the alien.

"To the remaining Salik ships, I give you fair warning," she calmly stated into her headset mic. "You have less than one *mi-nah* to depart before the next vessel is destroyed. Please leave immediately."

The Salik switched back to heavily accented V'Dan, slitted pupils wide and fixed on her face, strange, split-jointed tentacle-arms flailing violently as he ranted up at the camera. *"I will dessstrrroy hhyu! I will* perssonally *bite off your fffingerlingsss!"*

"Please leave immediately," she repeated, speaking over him, "so that I do not have to deal with the mess and tedium of wrecking our allies' shipping lanes for months to come with chunks of *your* debris. Your refusal to leave is making things very untidy."

Stay on target? Anjel typed to her screen.

Confirmed, Jackie typed back. *Stay on target until they actually move away.*

Light lanced out from one of the enemy ships. Robert yelped and clutched at the controls; the beam struck the tank module they hid behind. Water spewed out rapidly, evaporating into a fine mist . . . that slowed . . . and stopped. No explosion, and the laser did not actually penetrate the near side; the tanker was thin-hulled compared to a warship, but not *that* thin-hulled.

On her screen, the chief alien blinked, stubby eyestalks swiveling up and to the side, no doubt to peer at a secondary screen of his own. Nictitating membranes flicked out twice, sliding over those bulbous lenses and back, clearing his vision. "It . . . it did not *explo*—"

Light flared through both the viewports and the monitor screens in the cockpit currently watching the external views of the five-lobed enemy ships. The video feed connecting her to the Salik vessel snapped with static and went blank. Jackie tapped the broadband-broadcast control and addressed the remaining vessels, transmitting blind.

". . . I dislike repeating myself, gentlebeings, but I shall do so one more time. Please remove your ships from this star system. Please do so *immediately*. And please stop shooting at our fueling unit. It will not explode because it is just *water*. If you remain and continue to approach or attack, I will continue to destroy your ships one after the next until there is nothing left but grief and debris.

"You do *not* outnumber us. Your ships and your strengths dwindle, while my firepower remains the same. You have roughly one-third of a *mi-nah* left to decide whether you want to live or die." She closed the link on her end. ". . . I think that's all the negotiating I care to do for now. Thank you, everyone, for maintaining bridge silence."

"We have movement!" Ayinda announced a moment later. "Lateral movement."

"Colonel?" Anjel asked quickly, since they were almost out of time on missile number three.

"Abort target. Loop around just in case it's a feint, though," Jackie ordered.

"Looping the remaining missiles, aye, sir . . ." the copilot and gunnery officer muttered. The others remained silent on the bridge. "They do seem to be going away . . ."

". . . Confirmed, sir. They're headed *away* from the station," Ayinda stated several seconds later.

"Colonel MacKenzie?" Anjel asked her again, this time a different unspoken question.

Jackie knew what the other woman wanted. "Break off the attack, but keep pathing those last two missiles between us and them. Just in case." She started to say more, but her console chimed. The Salik, pinging them again. She glanced at Li'eth. (*Psychologically, would it be better for me to stay silent, or to answer them?*)

He mulled that over, then spoke aloud. "Stay silent. Don't answer them, Colonel. If you answer, they could consider it a taunt, a reason to turn back around and attack all of us anyway."

"Acknowledged," she replied. "Thank you for the advice, Grand Captain."

(*I want to crush in their teeth and break all their bones . . . but I know we don't have the resources for a prolonged fight,*) Li'eth admitted.

(*No, we don't,*) she agreed. Easing her shoulders with a

little movement, Jackie breathed deep and slow to ease some of the tension. Everyone in the cockpit watched the Salik leave, until they were moving too fast and too far away to easily track.

The station pinged her. So did three of the other ships. Jackie sighed. "And now comes the part where I apologize for not obeying the majority choice of the others in this system to cooperate with the enemy's demands."

"Oh, the joys of diplomacy," Robert quipped, adjusting their trim to continue to keep the tanker between them and the retreating Salik. "That's why *I'm* a pilot. You do realize we're going to be stuck in this system while the locals get around to doing a survey of the water tanker's hull, to make sure it's safe to continue extracting water from it, right?"

"Yes, I do realize that, Robert. We also have to bring the torpedoes back and get them stored for launch again. But let me see if I can soothe some frazzled nerves and coax them into cooperating with the fueling checks since we still don't know what we'd have to look for," Jackie murmured, hands moving to answer the station's call. *"Greetings,* Su-Chellis *Mining Station. You have reached the Terran vessel* Embassy *1. Now that the enemy is gone, with no loss of Alliance life, what would you like to discuss with us . . . ?"*

CHAPTER 8

SEPTEMBER 6, 2287 C.E.
AVRA 28, 9508 V.D.S.
KAI KUUL ISLE V'DAN IMPERIAL ARMY BASE
BA-KAN-TUU

Freshly showered, freshly clothed, and freshly fed—with fresh *food*, which had tasted blissful after sixteen days of transiting space with nothing but prepackaged Terran meals to eat—Li'eth joined Jackie in exiting their temporary quarters. It was time for their tour of the facility granted to the Terrans who had set down on this world a few weeks ago. The actual buildings were pure V'Dan Imperial Army in their construction, gray-painted, no-nonsense, and functional, but the temperature and humidity were Choya-comfortable, warm and damp, which meant they had elected to leave their formal jackets behind.

Though they had only been here six or so days in advance of the *Embassy 1*'s arrival, the Terrans had already plastered colorful printouts on the walls to liven up the military monotony. Not just of local maps, or signs written in Terran underneath the ones in V'Dan, or to explain what some of the objects around them were, but lots of images from their homeworld. Trees wreathed in morning-lit mists, lakes surrounded by snowcapped mountains, some sort of bird soaring on the wind, that sort of thing. Walking up the hall, the two of them passed a corner marked with a picture of a huge, bulbous, vaguely familiar white-and-black creature jumping up out of a deep blue sea.

(*That's a picture of an orca,*) Jackie reminded him, catching his brief confusion at the edge of her thoughts. (*You should remember them; I know you met a few. They're members of Cetacea, the whales and dolphins, one of the nine-tenths species on Earth. Orcas are nicknamed "killer whales," but technically . . .*)

(*But technically they're actually a* dolphin, *yes. I remember now. I was distracted at that point in the tour because I was missing you,*) he recalled. (*Oh . . . Saints preserve me, I forgot the name of the V'Dan officer. Help me remember it before we get there?*)

(*Captain Superior Ro-Shel, and Captain Agneau is the Terran counterpart taking us on our tour,*) Jackie supplied.

(*How do you even* remember *all these names?*) he asked her, subthoughts tinged with both awe and annoyance, most of the latter aimed at himself. (*We've dealt with thousands of people, literally thousands since you and I first met, but you manage to remember everyone. I know I've dealt with a lot of people as a prince and an officer, but I am amazed at your prodigious memory. How do you do it?*)

(*Part of being a polyglot is an epic memory for words,*) Jackie reminded him. (*Names are words, and they often have an attached meaning—Jacaranda is a type of flowering tree, Mac means Son and Kenzie means Fair One, so MacKenzie means Son of the Fair One. Some people have a prodigious memory for sports scores and statistics, but I can barely remember what the different sports are like, never mind keep in mind more than a mere handful of team names attached to sports types. I somehow saved all of my memory's recall capacity for laws and customs and the names and faces of people. That, and in public service, it is vital to remember who someone is and why they should be remembered. They* appreciate *being remembered.*)

(*I do know that. It's a strong diplomatic tool. I used to be better at it, before heading into the military, where everyone gets to wear a name tag,*) he added, touching the bit of scarlet-and-cream ribbon that actually had his makeshift name, Ma'an-uq'en, woven into it. Vertically, unlike the Terrans' horizontal version. They reached the lobby area where their two guides awaited them, one V'Dan and one Terran. Li'eth switched from internal musings to handling the business of the day, greeting the two officers out loud. "Captain Superior Ro-Shel. Captain Agneau. Thank you for waiting while we got some sleep."

"It sounded last night like you had a long flight of, what, sixteen days?" the short, green-spotted V'Dan officer stated. The blotchy marks staggered here and there on Ro-Shel's hide were only a few centimeters across, and were an olive drab on his light brown skin; the two colors clashed a little with his Dress uniform. Li'eth thought the other man would have looked better in the V'Dan version of camouflage than in a formal uniform, or even in a cream version more suited for a post that dealt with the Gatsugi on a regular basis. Unfortunately, both of them were stuck in full crimson.

"Their transit took sixteen days, with more time spent resting than in actually moving," Captain Agneau confirmed. She stood there at Parade Rest with her hands tucked behind her mottled-gray-clad back, her felted, rounded cap tilted at an angle on her head. Her own complexion was more olive than Jackie's, and her dark curls had been cropped short in a fea-

thered wave under her gray wool cap. If the grays of her camouflage uniform hadn't been so varied, her own skin tone
would have looked odd against the most predominant color,
too. "It's always better to start new tasks when rested.

"By the way, thank you for that language transfer yesterday, Colonel. It's already helped immensely, as you can tell,"
Agneau added.

Jackie nodded. "That's one of the reasons why I'm here. As
for the flight, it would've only been twelve days by one of your
faster-than-light ships, Captain Superior, but there weren't any
V'Dan ships headed between V'Zon A'Gar and Ba-kan-tuu of
a size that could carry us."

"You're lucky you could get so many of our ships to carry
your soldiers everywhere," Ro-Shel stated. He tipped his head.
"I don't know if either of you heard since the news just came
across about fifteen *mi-nah* ago, but Grand General I'osha on
V'Ton-Bei has declared a victory in rounding up and neutral-
izing the Salik insurgents on that planet. We have *your* troops
to thank for it, and everyone knows it."

"The message came through while the Ambassador was
showering," Li'eth stated. "I told her as soon as she came out.
Speaking of possible victories . . . ?"

"Yes, let's go see if your troops on *this* world can pull off
another one," the captain superior agreed. He turned, gesturing for them to follow. "This way, please."

Letting the two males take the lead, Jackie eyed Agneau as
they walked. "Romanian?" At Agneau's nod, Jackie switched
to her native tongue. *"So, how have these people been treating
you? Feel free to be completely honest; nobody else here
speaks Romaneşte. Even if they're recording this, the V'Dan
won't be able to translate it for a few more years."*

*"Always a good thing to know—and I love brass who
prefer honesty,"* Agneau added dryly. *"Nothing personal, of
course; I won't spontaneously hug you or anything . . . We've
had disparaging remarks nearly every single day, but very
few of them since landing have had to do with that striping
nonsense—we got some of that on the ship ride over, but
their commanding officer read her crew the riot act on day
five after receiving repeated complaints about it from us, and
it mostly died down. Here, they're more skeptical of the*

Dalphskin's potential . . . and my troops and I find we cannot really fault them for those doubts," Agneau told her, shrugging lightly. *"The brass back home have a great deal of faith in our abilities, but those are based on the conditions found back home.*

"The overall salinity of the oceans on this world is a little lower, the temperature and pressure gradients are therefore different, and, of course, we don't know whether or not the local biome is going to treat the 'skins alright. We certainly don't know if some local thing will come up, sting one of the suits, and dissolve it mid-deployment, or worse, lock it up midcombat with whatever passes for the local version of jellyfish venom. To be bluntly honest . . . I feel like we're selling these people an untested product, and I can't complain about it to anyone because we have *to keep up a positive, helpful spin on everything we do and say."*

"I understand the feeling. We know we can *help,"* Jackie agreed. *"We just don't know how* much, *yet."*

"Exactly. Worst-case scenario, we all die out there on our very first fight," Agneau stated bluntly. *"That's our worst fear because it won't help. In fact, it'll ruin everyone's morale, here and elsewhere. But our V'Dan liaison on the ride over pointed out something very helpful two days into our trip here."*

"Oh?" Jackie asked.

"This world isn't completely surveyed, yet. Even with all their high tech, this planet's about the same size as Earth, it's only been settled about 150 years, and it's 95 percent water, or something. The locals are still *finding new species all the time, including larger and thus potentially dangerous lifeforms."*

Jackie saw the implications immediately. *"So . . . the Salik might* not *realize that a Dalphskin suit is* not *a local lifeform?"*

"Exactly. We've been spending all our spare time watching films of everything the V'Dan planetary scouts have observed, and practicing our movements to look like the local life-forms as they explore new territory and search for food. We have an advantage in that the Dalphskins are designed for movement in a fluidic medium, and that pretty much sums up

*the shape of every fish we've ever seen, including the few alien
versions the V'Dan politely shipped to Earth to help us understand all the various alien ecosystems out here. So with that
in mind, we've broken out the 'natural weapons' packets
when programming the growth of each suit on the way here."*

"I'm not as familiar with what those contain," Jackie
demurred, turning to follow Li'eth and Ro-Shel into a large
bay overlooking a slough of tanks filled with underlit gels and
large lumps of pearlescent-gray torpedo-shaped flesh. She
switched to V'Dan. "Captain Agneau, why don't you outline
what the Dalphskin weapons systems are for Grand Captain
Ma'an-uq'en and me? That way, we can have a better grasp of
what tactics you plan to employ in trying to make the 'suits
look like they're just an unknown local life-form on this
world."

"Certainly, sir. We already have creatures on this world that
have a combination of calcium carbon in their shells—that fact
was confirmed before we took off for this world," Captain
Agneau added, gesturing at the racks of equipment off to one
side. "So we've manufactured spikes and blades blended from
calcium and ceramic composite, strengthened with the aid of
carefully wrapped and layered carbon fibers. Those rolling
lockers over there contain the fin blades and punch spikes,
which can be replaced whenever they inevitably break in
combat . . . provided we can get our Selkies back to base intact.

"That row of tanks over there with the small bladders
growing in it, those contain a special ink that when squeezed
and released can obfuscate most forms of infrared imaging—
it contains the same translucent metallic microcrystals that
are used in standard thermal films for windows, in fact," the
Special Forces officer continued. "It's a bit expensive to pro-
duce, very limited in supply at the moment, and we're still
trying to find a local supplier among the Choya who can duplicate it. But we've already tested some with the local Alliance scanners, and it looks like it'll be excellent for
obfuscating a fast escape. And, of course, it's very easy to
activate when having to make that fast escape since it's tied
into the jet propulsion system."

Li'eth frowned. "Tied into the . . . what? I thought this was
all supposed to be biotech, not engineering."

Agneau smiled. "We mean *biology*-based jet propulsion. It's like an esophagus swallowing something down. In this case, a series of tubes on the body open up and 'swallow' certain volumes of water in order to squirt it out the far end at high pressures and thus high speeds, increasing the Selkie's escape velocity faster than the flukes and fins alone can impart through the artificial muscles. We do incorporate more mechanical means of engineering, of course. Those devices over there, the dive helmets," she stated, pointing at a row of bubbles and curves that looked like old-fashioned bathysphere units, "are integrated into the suits, providing the wearers with portable scanners, communicators, and rebreather functionality."

"Rebreather?" Li'eth asked her.

"Those things process oxygen for breathing, filter drinkable water, and even provide liquid nourishment from bladderpacks located within the torso compartments. All of that allows our soldiers to stay in the water far longer than a regular swimmer—literally, for days. We were a little concerned that the rebreather gills might not be able to process enough oxygen out of the local ocean, but that fear's been put firmly to rest over the last three days of live-ocean tests."

Li'eth nodded. "That might be useful. I can't think of ever hearing about the Salik staying in the water for days at a stretch; they might spend their first few years living with gills, but unlike the Choya, they do lose those gills in favor of lungs before their tenth year. They can *hold* their breath for up to five *mi-nah* or so, and even fight during that time frame, but they do have to carry respirators of some sort for actual underwater maneuvers."

"Yes, the Choya were quite impressed," Ro-Shel agreed. He gestured at the aliens helping the Terrans roll some of the table-sized tanks toward another room. "However, for safety reasons, we haven't had more than a few of these *Dalphskin* things in the water, and mostly only for only a few hours while the Terrans have been testing the oxygenation exchanges and making minor tweaks to adjust them to Ba-kan-tuu's environment. Today will be their first full, mass deployment."

"We *were* going to do a lengthy stress test before full deployment," Agneau added grimly, "but word came through just under five hours ago that the Salik are on the move underwater. They're headed this way in definite numbers." She gestured for them to move along the upper railing and flicked a hand at cases being trundled along the main floor from a storage room. "As you can see, we're packing up extra weaponry for a full engagement. Those boxes contain microgrenades, coated in biofilm for ease of ejection during tail chases. Of course, if we use *those*, they'll *know* we're not normal native life-forms."

"As far as we know, no underwater life-forms *shova v'shakk* literally," Captain Superior Ro-Shel stated. Then blushed a little, glancing at Li'eth. ". . . My apologies for the crudeness of my statement, Highness."

"Since you are being literal in your description, I have no objections to the language used. Though that does bring up the question of what happens to all the, ah, water and . . . liquid nutrients . . . absorbed by the users of these Dalphskin suits," Li'eth said, hoping he wouldn't have to ask more directly than that about a subject that was, well, unpleasant to contemplate.

"It passes into holding bladders fitted with ultraviolet sterilizers, and only then gets squeezed out the rest of the way," Agneau reassured him. "We have delicate *coral* reefs back on Earth where you don't want the wrong biota getting excreted and washed into the ecosystem, so the sterilization treatments have long since been considered and integrated into the whole process—here, let's get you a close-up look at one of the suits."

She led the way down a metal ramp to the main floor of the large chamber and approached one of the tanks. Starting with the information on the side—a string of number and letters in both machine-printed Terranglo and hand-scribed V'Dan declaring it to be the property of the Terran Space Force Special Forces, 1st Cordon, 7th Division, 2nd Brigade, 2nd Battalion, 2nd Legion Underwater Reconnaissance and Response Unit, A Company—she pointed out the many features of the oblong, pearlescent, mostly pale gray blob occupying the long, broad, chest-high tank. She did so by pointing both physically on the blob, and on the sketches visible on the control screen for the equipment monitoring the tank contents.

"This is Sergeant Pian's suit—A Company is on downtime

at the moment, and B Company is asleep. C and D are fully suited and en route, E is suited and swimming in standby pods a few klicks away from C and D, and F Company is our tactical command. If the Salik have dropships that'll be flying out to insertion points to try to ambush any troops on their way back home, A Company will have enough time to get suited up and deploy in the local waters, and B won't be that far behind."

Li'eth eyed the Dalphskin suit, which looked sleek and powerful in the middle, neatly symmetrical and simple at one end, and rather . . . odd . . . at the other. "How do they move through the water? Wouldn't those dangly bits over at that end drag too much?"

"You're looking at a suit that is suspended in a nutrient brine," Agneau explained to him. She pointed to the opposite end from the end with all the weird, awkward angles. "The flukes, which are those big, broad, tapered paddle-things at our far right, provide most of the propulsion through a system of artificial musculature that is triggered through biometric contact sensors lining the interior—to put it in layman's terms, the occupant flexes their own muscles a little bit, and the suit responds by contracting even more along the exterior portions, amplifying their effort in much the same way wearing swim fins on our feet amplifies our speed when we kick as we swim."

"Basically, they act like Salik feet," Ro-Shel added. "But arranged in a different configuration and without separate legs."

Agneau nodded. "The odd flaps at the opposite end, to our left, actually wrap around the diving helm and turn smooth enough to be hydrodynamic when fully suited. They wrap around and adhere to the diving helm with special water-activated adhesives that are preapplied to the helms, so the actual donning of the suit only takes about five minutes, which is pretty close to five V'Dan *mi-nah*," she explained. "That helm in turn is the most current *Tauchersiebe Mark XX* model, military grade, available back on Earth. As we like to say, it has all the bells and whistles an underwater soldier could want, and you will get to see at least some of them in action fairly soon, when C and D Companies engage the enemy."

Li'eth nodded. "I look forward to it, with the hopes they will be effective in combat. What about their operating parameters?" he asked. "I know our species has a limit on how far they can dive and so forth."

"Once they are sealed into a full suit, helm and all, the Selkies are rated to a depth of just shy of forty *meters* in the local waters," Agneau told him. "Your Highness is just a little shy of two Terran meters in height, for comparison. They can do so without needing to worry about decompression whatsoever, so long as they don't spend too long in the water. They can also dive to a depth of just over two hundred meters with minimal worries and minimal time spent decompressing to avoid the bends. The *Tauchersiebe* diving helm automatically compensates in its oxygen mix for hypoxic conditions in pressures found starting below twenty-five meters in all models. We will also have Choya compression ships following along with generously loaned V'Dan medical crews and hyperbaric chambers in case of injuries, but they'll be kept at a distance for safety during combat maneuvers.

"This particular model of Dalphskin suit," Agneau continued, reading the fine print on the display, "has been fitted with composite spikes and blades on the control fins, compartments for escape ink, and transparent metals embedded in the exterior layers to help reduce thermal presence and confuse sensor readings that might otherwise make out a Human-shaped outline through the biomatter."

"What is an M . . . S . . . L?" Jackie asked, squinting at the information on the display screen.

"That's shorthand for *mantis shrimp limbs*," Agneau explained. "If you'll look at those smaller limbs at the middle of the torso portion, the ones folded up and tucked against the underbelly, you can see where they've been grown," she explained. "The mantis shrimp, which is a class of sea crustacean found in Earth's oceans, has an incredibly powerful biomechanical punch. That punch takes advantage not only of spring-tension and muscle contractions to deliver the forces, but also utilizes additional cavitation forces from the water undergoing rapid compression and expansion during each strike.

"Those forces form microscopic bubbles that collapse rapidly and cause additional damage—if you have fast-running propeller blades on a ship, you'll notice them getting pitted and eventually developing holes from a similar process," the Terran captain told them. "Mantis shrimp, despite being incredibly small for their strength, are almost impossible to keep in aquariums because they will punch at the tank walls, breaking them wide open.

"If you'll forgive me for not knowing the V'Dan conversions off the top of my head," she added apologetically to Li'eth, "in Terran measurement terms, the mantis shrimp strikes at a speed of twenty-three *meters* per *second*, or resting heartbeat. The actual creature is only the length of your hand on average; the strike range in a slashing motion covers a distance of roughly the width of your thumb. But it travels so fast, if it kept going for a full second, it could travel over eleven, twelve body lengths in just one modest heartbeat. But that's the sea creature.

"Obviously, if you scale it up to Dalphskin size, we cannot achieve those same speeds simply because of the viscosity of water at that scale. A slashing attack does, however, travel at up to five meters per second over the span of half a meter, or about one-third of the Colonel's body length," Agneau told them. "These suits with the MSL designation have been grown with the design parameters to be hull-piercers, and thus release punching spikes that travel at about nine meters per second over a distance of half a meter. Reloading takes half a minute per spike and consumes a fair bit of nutrients, but it's worthwhile in that they can be reused up to six times per limb."

"Are they effective against Salik hulls?" Li'eth asked her.

Ro-Shel nodded. "Very. We've tested them on hull plates salvaged from the ships the Choya run in these waters—which we've been told are from the same suppliers as the Salik vessels—and these suits can punch right through most models.

"The problem is getting *close* enough to do so," Agneau indicated. "Which is why we've been practicing our biomaneuvers for camouflage. Now, the command center is this way," the Special Forces officer added, gesturing toward a doorway smaller than the large one the tanks were going through. "We'll be running Terran *cetacio* encryption tech for the surveillance relays. It's low-profile, mostly used for out-going broadcasts from the Squads, and will be relayed on bandwidths the Alliance don't use and don't usually monitor."

"What's *seh-tay-shyo* tech?" Li'eth asked.

"Yeah, what is it?" Jackie asked, equally bemused. "I haven't heard of that one, and I've been rated for communications encryption. Junior grade, admittedly, but still."

"It scrambles the signal so that it sounds like *whale* song," Agneau told them. "We're always hesitant to use it on Earth because it confuses the Cetaceans to no end. It'd be like me shouting 'Handbag! Teakettle! Barbecue!' at my target audience while in the vicinity of V'Dan speakers—interspersed with garbage noises between the comprehensible words—instead of stating anything that makes actual sense to a native speaker. But we've revived the old programming tech for these missions because it's a very organic sound that will blend in with the noises the local life-forms already make underwater."

"She explained to me that they will have fish-shaped microphone drones spaced out at a distance, just within audio range," Ro-Shel added. "The noises produced by the suits themselves will mostly be audible transmissions, which will be picked up and relayed back to us via the usual Terran radio frequencies, where they will be fed into her people's translation programs."

"It adds about a second or two of delay to the transmissions, but we'll also be able to receive video broadcasts this way," Agneau told them. They entered a room lined with neatly placed rows of tables bristling with monitors and work-station consoles . . . and a tangle of cables still being taped to the concrete floor by V'Dan soldiers working under Terran direction.

Jackie recognized the bulky boxes the cables all fed into, converter units designed to translate between Terran power needs and the types of energies being supplied by the local V'Dan/Alliance power grids. She also recognized Lieutenant First Class Buraq. Standing at Parade Rest, slightly turned to look their way, the lieutenant nodded the moment their gazes met.

"Good morning, Colonel, Grand Captain," Buraq greeted

them. "*Embassies 1* and *14* are fueled, prepped, and stand ready for launch, sir."

"Prepped for launch?" Captain Superior Ro-Shel asked, frowning. He looked between the two women. "I wasn't informed of an impending departure. I was told you'd be here for the next three days."

Li'eth stepped verbally into the breach of his confusion. "The Terrans have a policy of launching their representative to presumptive safety if the fighting in a war zone gets too close to them."

"Ah. That makes sense; there are a limited number of them in the area, whereas—no offense to the safety of Your Highness—there are plenty of us V'Dan to spare," Ro-shel stated, shrugging fatalistically. "It makes sense to throw us into the fray while you escape. I'd choose to do the same thing if all the roles were reversed."

"Your willingness to fight a rear guard for us is deeply appreciated. Let's hope it doesn't need to happen. So, how close are they, Jasmine?" Jackie asked her security officer.

"Conversion rates are a bit iffy off the top of my head, but they're still at least a hundred klicks out," Buraq reported, gesturing at the screens nearest her.

The screen had Kai Kuul Isle and its nearby landmass neighbors outlined in brown, Choya troop positions outlined in orange, V'Dan in red, and the Salik marked in purple. Gray markers had been added to indicate the Terran troops. It had been weird for Li'eth to learn the Terran military preferred using red to mark enemy vessels; red was the Imperial color, and he didn't want any of the Terrans thinking of his people as the enemy. Culturally stubborn and thus insulting at times, but *not* an enemy of the newest Alliance members.

Thankfully, they seemed willing to adapt to using the Alliance's programming conventions for establishing friends from foes. As it was, just looking at the screen, there were a *lot* of purple marks headed their way. Particularly compared to the tiny blot of silvery-gray Terran units. Buraq pointed at some geometric markings on the islands and on spots scattered around the coastal waters.

"Choya point-defense systems located in these areas, mostly here and over here, are keeping Salik bombardments away from the islands—the locals could definitely teach us a few tricks, Ambassador, from what I've seen of their ground-to-air defensive capacity—so we're safe so long as they stay more than twenty-five kilometers away. But even so, at the forty-mark, I want you in the shuttle, ready to launch," Lieutenant Buraq added.

"Understood," Jackie agreed. "Estimated time to insertion?" she asked Captain Agneau.

"Let me check on that—here, take a seat. Any of them, if they're empty," Agneau added. She gestured for them to take any spare seats available. "Make yourself comfortable while we wait. If a crew member needs you to move, we'll ask; otherwise, it's all open seating."

Just as Li'eth pulled back on a pair of seats for himself and the Ambassador, a cluster of monitors off to the right went black, prompting some rather exasperated exclamations in Terranglo, and awkward commands in pidgin V'Dan to the techs, who had just disrupted the power supplies. He quickly looked down to make sure he had not pulled any wires, but realized there were none around the chair legs; the accident was someone else's fault. On the edge of his mental awareness, he felt Jackie trying to keep track of the exchange between the two groups of soldiers in case they needed her translation abilities. He kept his attention more focused on the displays.

"Here we are . . . twenty minutes, maybe less, depending on how fast the lead scouts push their speed, and whether or not the Salik advance remains steady," Agneau reported. "The Selkies have just hit the water after sliding out of the transport ships. I had the V'Dan send your breakfast with your wake-up call so you'd have plenty of time to get ready and get down here for the show."

"And plenty of time to fill out form after form," Ro-Shel added. He pulled over a couple V'Dan-style workpads. "We're happy for your help, Ambassador, but we have a lot of costs that need authorization. Facilities, infrastructure, vehicles and fuel used, personnel to pay . . ."

"The inevitability of paperwork. I'm used to it," Jackie agreed, reaching for the displayed forms with a sigh. "Occupational hazard, you know."

"I'll take half of those," Li'eth agreed, moving to accept his share of the work.

The two of them put their heads together over the various requests, arguing mentally instead of verbally over what was considered a good price and a fair trade, to help keep distractions in the hall at a minimum. Around them, Terran soldiers worked in their gray uniforms, sober-looking compared to the redder hues of the V'Dan trying to help fix the power issue, which did eventually get fixed.

Several minutes passed as the pair progressed through the forms that way. Li'eth helped Jackie completely clear over half of them, adding his thumbprint authorization and signature wherever needed, particularly on the funding issues. The Empress had granted him broad discretionary powers on Terran-related budget authorizations . . . with the understanding that he would not spend the Eternal Coffers down to the last of the dust motes, of course.

Finally, Agneau's voice broke through their interactive silence, switching from Terranglo to V'Dan. ". . . *Three minutes to insertion, people!* Three *mi-nah* to the encounter point!"

Li'eth looked up and around. Several more V'Dan soldiers had entered the room and were standing in clusters near some of the Terrans manning their makeshift workstations. A pair of Choya lurked nearby as well; he wasn't quite as familiar with their insignia types, but from the looks of things, both were officers. No doubt they had gathered here for observation and stood clad in thermal suits to help keep themselves warm in the relatively cool air preferred by his fellow Humans, wearing the moisture packs their people required when spending extended periods of time on land.

They were an intelligent race, creative, wise, and reasonable to deal with on average. However, it still amazed Li'eth from time to time that they'd gotten into space at all. Indeed, of all the races in the known galaxy, the Salik and the Choya had taken the longest to advance technologically, because of the incompatibilities of needing lots of water for living needs and requiring fire for smelting and forging metals.

Agneau, having switched back to Terranglo, ordered the main screen on the far wall be switched from the real-time map display to the lead scout's view. The image went from bright colors and clearly defined terrain and group features to a slightly murky, bluish view of an underwater world streaked by crepuscular rays from the local sun. From the look of the underside of the ocean surface—oddly distorted by the camera viewpoint—a wind appeared to be stirring a bit of chop, swells and peaks maybe as tall as a forearm, though it was difficult to actually gauge sizes.

The view also included an overlay of tactical blips and Terranglo acronyms in various thinly lined figures and lettering, things that no doubt made sense to the soldier in the suit. Now the colors were Terran in style on the lead swimmer's display screen: green for ally, red for foe, and yellow for neutrals or unknowns, such as the school of fish-analogs they scared into swimming quickly away . . . Apparently, they were only using Alliance coloring conventions for the soldiers staffing the command center. That made sense to Li'eth; when it came to the drilled reflexes necessary for combat, it was best not to change anything without a lot of time for practice, and the Terrans had not had nearly enough time.

Seeing his gaze focused on the main screen, Captain Agneau told Li'eth and their observing guests, "The helmets have camera lenses in several different directions. Normally, when we walk around upright on land, our eyes point ahead in the direction we usually travel. Unfortunately, when we swim, which is usually done horizontally, our eyes point down, which is too awkward for streamlined forward motion. These helmets allow projections onto the face shield from various different angles, which are combined into a single image that provides a nearly complete sphere of awareness for each Selkie.

"So while technically the corporal's eyes point down at the ocean floor, we're actually looking at what he's looking at, a massive, panoramic view morphed into what we call a 'fish-eye wraparound.' Each camera emplacement technically holds two lenses mounted at each location. The best cameras are mounted on the top of the helmet-head, which would be the forward-pointing 'face' of the Dalphskin suit. Special contact lenses worn by the soldiers then combine the dual views into a three-dimensional image they can process with great spatial accuracy—not everyone can become a Selkie, because the stereoscopic version of this all-inclusive view churns a lot of stomachs until one can get used to it, but these soldiers have all passed the test."

"Those cammeras are annn advantage even my ownn peoplle don't have in underwater maneuversss," one of the Choya officers stated. A male, Li'eth realized, for while the Choya was tall and muscular like a female, his somewhat tapered skull boasted only a single crest. "The anngles of our heads and eyes line up for ssstreamlined swimming when we let our heads tilt, but we arrre not a fast sspecies underwater; for milllennia, we have always rrrelied more on technology and don't need to have an easy long-distance view. Thesse helmetss may be better than what the Salik cannn do, even with their eyesstalks."

"We have rrrelllied too much on warrrmsuitss as our only underwater technnnology," the other officer agreed, her four crests flattening a little. She stood only a thumblength taller than him. "Consstantly dealling with land-dwelllers, sssmug in the belief we were borrn for water maneuvers, forgetting we were borrrn toolll users as well . . ."

"I can see where that would lead you to not augmenting anything seriously. For the V'Dan," Ro-Shel stated, glancing at Jackie, "it was quite obvious even before the Terrans' arrival that our joint species evolved to maneuver on land, a nearly two-dimensional setup, not the three dimensions of living underwater. Your people's helmets, Grand High Ambassador, excited everyone here. As soon as our people saw all that these diving helms of yours could do, we put our V'Dan techs to work, and the Choya's, too."

"They are al! frantically sswimming to make dive helmetss for our people with a sssimilar setup, based on the things our joinnnt colonisssts have on hand," the first Choya speaker, the male, added.

"I saw you also put in a request to buy some of this Terran tech," Li'eth observed, nodding at the tablet screen in his hand, and its half-finished requisition forms.

The Choya female spread her slightly webbed hands. "The V'Dann have a sssaying: Why rreinvent a candle flame beyond the shortessst annd most immediate of needs, when sommmeone already has a hearthfire roaring a few doors away?"

"We just need something to fill in the gap between then and now," Ro-Shel confirmed, nodding. "We grew a bit too complacent, relying on surveillance torpedoes, which the Salik can target and destroy far more quickly than beast-looking things they might want to hunt."

"Shh!" Agneau warned them, pointing at the main and lesser screens. "Contact!"

Secondary views along the outer images of the scene being projected showed dorsal, vendral, starboard, and port views, and even a small fluke-cam image from what lay behind. For a moment, they had a glimpse of several oblong, almost beluga-like creatures on those lesser viewpoints, but the main screen held the focus of the watching soldiers.

There was little indication of exactly how fast the Selkie with the camera was moving, other than the fact that tiny pale dots streaked past rapidly. At least, until the first Salik vessel came into view. Splashing through the choppy waters overhead, the hull swelled from a faint pale shadow to an actual large hull within moments. The scout "startled" and shied sideways, swooping and swirling, spinning the view so that they had a glimpse first of darkness below, then watery blue light somewhere above. The others scattered as well, their images swirling and swaying on the lesser screens set up in the command room, their blips on the tactical overlays moving remarkably like schools of aquatic life.

"*Enemy sighted,*" a voice came from one of the speakers, speaking in Terranglo. "*Hull shapes conform to known military oceanic vessels. Sergeant, I have painted the lead ship. Repeat, the enemy's gate is now the lead ship.*"

"*Copy that, and . . . confirmed, Hamsaunsang. I have the lead ship painted as the enemy's gate,*" someone else replied. Li'eth wanted to ask what that meant, other than that it had been targeted for some reason.

"*Sergeant, I am also seeing circles and lines up by the waterline—Salik writing, I think?*" the Selkie reported. "*C First B Beta to Base, can anyone back home translate this stuff?*"

"Ambassador?" Agneau asked Jackie.

"I don't speak Sallhash yet," Jackie replied, shaking her head. "I've touched their minds, but I never did a language transfer; I just went off the images in their heads. But I *can* transcribe what's going on in Terranglo for them if someone else does know it," Jackie replied.

"Can't you just pick up their thoughts?" one of the V'Dan techs asked. "Aren't you like a powerful holy one?"

"I'd have to have a specific visual target at this distance to even try to pick up their thoughts, they're so far away right now. A language transfer with a xenospecies is flat-out impossible at this distance, even for a Gestalt," she explained. "Not with a brand-new species. The only reason why I learned V'Dan in three hours is because the Grand Captain is a fellow *Human* and has a disciplined mind."

That made Li'eth's face grow a bit warm. His mind *hadn't* been disciplined before she had swept in and showed him how to take control of his psychic abilities, rather than be dragged along awkwardly in their intermittent wake.

Ro-Shel pulled out a communicator from his pocket and activated it, murmuring instructions into the pickups. Agneau in turn hissed a name, tapping her ear with one hand and fluttering her other hand at Jackie. An aide came over with a headset and beckoned her to join a crewman at one of the tables. Jackie sat as she fitted it on, and at the tech's nod, began translating into V'Dan. A few moments later, a soldier in V'Dan camouflage hurried into view, oriented, and joined the pair.

Li'eth kept his own attention clear. Skipping from screen to screen among the banks of monitors, he tried to get a sense of what was going on. The Selkies were good; fully wrapped, with the mirror-silvered faces of the helms showing like strange, alien eyes through several gaps in the Dalphskin wraps, they *looked* like a pack or pod of traveling animals. Their darkened helm lenses looked like strangely placed eyes, and what had to be the intake gills for the bathysphere helms kind of looked like mouths.

Strange, exotic beasts, the Selkies swam in and out, some darting closer to their companions than the others; in fact when two got too close, they looked like they made little threat-displays and backed off from each other. The biggest ones also herded the smallest, almost as if they were juveniles. It looked very convincing to him . . . and brought up a new concern. One that prompted him to speak to his allies in Terranglo.

"You do realize that if the Salik think your 'Selkie' beasts look like intriguing enough prey—and they are large and fast enough to be a challenge, so they probably do—then that means the Salik will send out hunting packs," he warned Agneau and the others, using their tongue so as not to alarm their Choya allies. *"Your people are at serious risk of attack."*

"We're actually counting on that, Grand Captain," a new voice stated, a dark-skinned woman with buzz-cut hair and leaf-shaped pins similar to the ones Jackie had worn for a while. A Major, that was the rank.

That made her Major Tai-Khan, head of the Selkies and highest-ranked Terran outside of Jackie on this planet. Captain Agneau technically served as her second-in-command. Li'eth stood politely in respect for her authority, as he had stood when first introduced to her upon their arrival last night. Today, Tai-Khan wore a loose outfit of military-gray tee shirt and pants with slip-on shoes, clearly ready to strip and don her own Dalphskin suit at a moment's notice, and just as clearly not uncomfortable in the cool air of the hall.

She also did not speak much V'Dan, having deferred the telepathic language transfer to her second-in-command last night. Her focus, she had explained, needed to stay on her troops and on her mission, not on being an intermediary between two worlds. Li'eth could respect that and didn't mind sticking with Terranglo to speak with her.

Nodding politely to Li'eth as she moved up beside him, the Major continued. *"The plan is to try to lure out some packs of Salik hunters, try to play with the xenopsychology profiles you gave us against them. This is not just a skirmish sortie to engage and distract the enemy from continuing their attack. This is also a test scenario to discern how well they fight underwater and to see how well we can distract them from their goal."*

"May-jor Tai-Khaann," the second Choya who had spoken stated, four crest ridges flexing briefly in greeting.

Li'eth realized that was a good sign; the Choya tended to be physically conservative around alien races, since a polite gesture toward one species could be a potentially rude one toward another. Smiling with teeth exposed was one such thing. A flexed crest was another; among the Tlassians, it served as a sign of irritability or alarm in the priest caste, much as the neck flares of a warrior caste did, though among the Choya, it was simply a way to greet each other. Seeing it now probably meant the officer considered this friendly territory for such things.

"Second Elbow Turrik," Tai-Khan replied politely in pidgin V'Dan. "You people, ready? We not know good we be today."

"We arre rready," the female said. The officer gestured at one of the larger screens still boasting a map of the region with a webbed, greenish-gray hand. "We havvve deep-lurrkers and mud-stealthed torpedoes on stannndby. The rrrest are out of range. We cannot engage fully just yet. Trroopships are still swimming into positionn. Thirty *mi-nah*."

"We be understand, Second Elbow. *Agneau, I think he said thirty minutes—maybe thirty-four?*" the head of the Selkies asked her first officer, switching back to fluid Terranglo with a hint of an accent Li'eth couldn't place. "*Whatever it converts into. We can hold them off that long, yes?*"

Agneau moved from screen to screen nearby, checking the squiggles and blocks of Terran writing, and nodded, coming back. "*. . . We should be able to hold their attention, provided they're not twice as fast as us. Especially with everyone circling back to 'gawk' at the ships. We might have to bring up the second and third waves, however. ETA on 1st and 2nd C is . . . five minutes, and ETA on 2nd A and B is eight, if they pick up the pace. 3rd Platoon C is twelve minutes out, and everyone in D is roughly fifteen minutes away.*"

"*Send out the* cetacio *call to converge. I want it to seem like the lead pod has encountered something of interest for everyone else to check out,*" Tai-Khan ordered.

"How long will it take the Salik to suit up and go out after them?" Jackie called out in V'Dan before switching to Terranglo. "Does anyone know? *Does anyone have an estimation on when we might possibly engage them, not just encounter them?*"

"Fifteen, maybe twenty *mi-nah* if they don't have anyone ready. Only three more minutes at this point if they do,"

Ro-Shel told her. "But I'd douse myself in *flk* sauce if they didn't. They'll have their equivalent of platoons prepared for an assault."

Nodding, Jackie went back to conversing quietly but urgently into her headset. Several seats away, Li'eth shuddered internally, disconcerted by the junior officer's quip. *Flk* sauce was some sort of acidic-sweet marinade, a dipping sauce the Salik preferred for adding extra flavor to raw strips of meat. Offering to apply it to oneself . . . Not his favorite image. He still had nightmares about seeing that one captain eating his bridge officer's hand in front of him.

Someone came around with a case of flavored drinks. Li'eth chose one that promised a mix of berry flavors. Amused by a memory of a much different bottle, he carefully read the whole label to make sure it wasn't alcoholic, then cracked it open for a sip.

Refusing a drink for herself, Tai-Khan ordered the C Squads to move in even closer and to bring the 2nd Platoon A and B Squads in as well, wanting them to be within just a minute or two of striking distance. Blips on the tactical overlays swerved and moved toward their new positions. More lurked farther out, but they were still going to need several minutes to get into striking range.

In the command center, Humans and Choya alike waited, tense and unable to do anything physically from so far away, while the foremost two Squads circled cautiously around the hulls cutting their way through the water. A couple of the more "daring beasts" even brushed up against those hulls, testing them with a fin, and no doubt scanning with sensors buried underneath that bioengineered skin.

". . . *Movement!*" one of the Terrans in the group announced over his helmet speakers. "*We've got bogeys entering the water!*"

"*Confirmed, three, four . . . five bogeys off the far starboard vessel!*"

"*Five more just launched off the far port side!*" a third Selkie called back.

(*What is a boh-ghee?*) Li'eth asked his Gestalt partner. He looked from image to image on the screen, trying to find what the Selkies were talking about.

It took her a distracted moment to reply. (*Military speak for possible targets . . .*)

"*Sergeant Onata to Base, the Salik fleet has dropped speed by about five knots, but they're still going strong. If they're dropping off soldiers, either they think we have hull mines, they don't need to pick them up for a long while, or they think these frog-fellows can catch up to them.*"

"*Acknowledged, Onata,*" Tai-Kahn spoke into her headset. She leaned over, bracing her hands on the back of an unoccupied chair. "*Stay on target.*"

Li'eth tensed, watching with a mix of dread and hope while the images split and swirled. The nameplate on the upper-leftmost corner of their tactical screen overlay listed that lead scout as CORPORAL M. HASMAUNSANG, C 1ST B ALPHA. The corporal did not drop his own speed but instead kept circling around back to the boats on the starboard side of the Salik fleet. That was, starboard from the direction of the enemy's travel.

The corporal swam around the Salik soldiers now floating in the water, clad in wet suits that would help preserve some of their body heat in the water while allowing them to carry their own version of reoxygenation equipment, tools, and weapons. Corporal Hamsaunsang's view circled every single one of those five alien bodies, appending three sets of numbers to everything even as the cameras tried to figure out what some of their equipment might be.

For a long moment, Li'eth had no idea what those Terran symbols meant. He could read them as letters and numbers, but since they had three clusters of numbers to work with, he recognized at first only one set of them as the readings for latitude, longitude, and depth based on the local positioning satellites. Those numbers hardly changed at all.

Then he figured it out: The foremost ship had been painted as in *targeted*, and *that* was what the second set of numbers meant. They formed an odd spatial partitioning out of three sets of numbers. The first two apparently described two circles, one that sat horizontally, and one vertically. Two zeroes meant dead ahead, which made sense to Li'eth, but the X and Y axis numbers did not dip into the negatives in any direction; they just started with 359 and counted backwards to the left and down, while the numbers counted from 1 forward to the right and up.

The final number was fairly obvious; it was literally just the distance in Terran measurement units to whatever target or object had been identified and outlined by the scout's sensor array. So when those digits dipped into single numbers to the left of the decimal point, he knew just how close Corporal Hasmaunsang swam to the nearest Salik soldier, since a Terran *meter* wasn't that far off from a V'Dan *mita* . . . yet another word apparently carried into their distant past by the time-traveling Immortal.

Compared to the sleek, streamlined Dalphskin suits that dwarfed them by an arm length and more, the Salik seemed stumpy and awkward, like lumps of flesh on sticks, with their bulbous torsos and long, trailing legs. *Fruit ices? Fruit pops?* He couldn't remember what Jackie called them, and—

The Salik slashed at the corporal with a blade wrapped in its tentacle-hand, making half the room gasp and jump. Hasmaunsang gasped, too, jerking away, then jolting—no, jetting—forward, leaving the Salik abruptly rearward, behind a curling cloud of dark, and a rapidly jiggling camera view, along with a shout of, *"—I'm hit! I'm hit!"*

"The enemy has engaged! I repeat, the enemy has engaged!"

"Hasma, report! What is your condition?"

"1st B Alpha, two are in pursuit, on your five and six!— No, make that three! Three are in pursuit on your six!"

"I'm alright! Damn blade got halfway through the suit. I can't turn fast, Sergeant, and it's going to take five minutes to seal the breach. I'm gone for any tight maneuvers. Request permission to fall back to—"

"—Permission granted! Fall back, 1st B Alpha!"

Tai-Khan, pacing, snapped an order into her headset. *"1st B Selkies, attack!"*

The two Salik who had lingered, watching, didn't have time to dodge; a quartet of Selkies sliced right past them— literally sliced, with weapons that scored along their foes' flanks and limbs. Li'eth didn't even know when he'd gained his feet; he just knew he stood stooped over, clutching the tabletop and staring into the screen in front of him, showing another soldier's view of the injured corporal fleeing as fast as he could undulate.

Come now, get away . . . come on, get away! he urged silently, teeth clenched.

(*Li'eth? You're projecting,*) Jackie warned him

(*Sorry.*) Focusing on his shielding wasn't easy; the three aliens were faster than the man in the damaged suit. He knew the Salik were the fastest species in the water, particularly over short distances; their long legs and long flipper-feet worked the water in lunging shoves that allowed them to use the "pause" between beats to turn on a dime. They could spread and flatten their tentacle-limbs, fanning out and—

Blurs flashed across his view, followed by murky red clouds. Something tumbled free and drifted downward, flailing and curling up into four swirls on one end, the other ragged and leaking blood.

"Yes!"

His wasn't the only shout of triumph in the control room, but it was the first and loudest. He crowed again when two more blurs cut through the other Salik, one of the Selkies actually having to twist in a tight circle in order to dislodge the impaled body of their target from one of their spikes. Undignified though it might be, Li'eth hopped a little in place in his excitement. The Terrans were decimating the quintet, and he couldn't be happier.

The other five aliens on the other side of the Salik fleet darted at the Selkies, scattering the nearest ones. Two more were hit by bladed weapons. Two others had their camera feeds spit static. Complaints of *"I can't move!"* and *"The suit won't respond!"* proved to the prince they'd been hit by the electrosonic pulses of stunnerfire. Water greatly reduced the range on the damned things, but the Salik were experts at timing their movement in underwater combat, and deadly in close-range attacks.

Only the fast-slashing attacks from several more Squad members saved the two who'd been stunned and the two who could barely swim away. Trios of swimmers flanked the injured and the stunned, somehow hooking on and undulating *for* them, giving them a boost in speed, though not their top speed. Others circled, making threat-darts at the lone Salik who escaped.

"Incoming! We have incoming! Dozens of bogeys entering the water!"

"C Company, D Company, you are authorized for full deployment!" Tai-Khan ordered. She paced like a hungry hunting *g'at*, long legs and wiry body, her intense brown stare flicking from screen to screen, taking in every image in fractions of seconds. *"E Company, move up into support positions. All E Squads, form an escort for any injured. D Squads, stay on the perimeters of your formations for skirmish strikes! A, B, and C, engage all enemy targets as you see fit."*

If the bloodied, muddied, ink-scattered waters had been mildly chaotic before, within minutes, the battlefield was a mess. Oddly enough, it was the Terrans in the command center who scrambled the fastest, as five or six who had been idly standing by raced to get into their seats. Li'eth, pushed back out of the way by politeness and the necessity to evacuate that particular station, found himself pacing near their commanding officer.

He couldn't make sense of the chaos; aside from her initial orders, Tai-Khan didn't give any further ones. In fact, most of the orders being given came from the soldiers in the chair, most of whom wore the double stripes or stripe-and-rocker of corporals and privates first class on their gray uniform sleeves. Fifth Tier equivalents. *They* directed the battle tactics, not the officers, fingertips scraping over their display screens, which had been shifted into angled positions better suited for viewing and swiping.

It took him several minutes to grasp *why* . . . and when the realization dawned, Li'eth sucked in a breath at the sheer brilliance of it. The actual soldiers carrying out the combat had to focus *on* their combat skills, on swimming and circling and staying alive. Their attention lay on their immediate environs. They could occasionally suggest things, and from the sounds of it they indeed were making suggestions, but they merely implemented the tactics being deployed. Their dryland counterparts, with no need to worry over their direct personal safety, were free to view the bigger picture, analyze it, and carve up fractions of the battle zone for their particular teams to fight their way through.

They decided that the best fighting had to be conducted through hit-and-run tactics, since lingering in the vicinity of the Salik warriors proved to be very dangerous. Once up to speed, a Terran Selkie could outswim a Salik but could not escape if they stayed within range of their deadly lunge-strokes. Most of the fighting had to be done at close quarters to be effective, but that was an advantage as well as a disadvantage.

Projectile weapons and lasers were difficult to fire underwater, stunners required melee range, and the Salik on the ships that had finally slowed to start circling directly over the underwater battle zone proved thankfully reluctant to torpedo an enemy embroiled with their own troops. Twice, the Salik released depth charges on the outer fringes, only to discover that the thick Dalphskin suits cushioned most of the shock waves, leaving the Terrans in far better shape immediately after each concussion wave than their foes.

Just as their stunner weapons did. The prince couldn't help chortling behind a hastily raised palm when one of the enemy accidentally disabled five of his companions, shoved out of aiming alignment by a Selkie bowling into him from behind. Not that the fight was all victories and smiles; dozens of the Terrans picked up yellow-dashed lines on their tactical markers, indicating injuries. Four turned brown and were "rescued" by brutal dashes from their companions, their bodies towed off out of retrieval range by the enemy.

Five . . . six . . . ten. Eleven dead on their side. More, as gray outlines turned yellow and turned red, or flashed straight to red while the Salik fought in vicious earnest. Abruptly, new blips appeared on the edges of the largest-spanning maps, swarming inward and upward. Choya underwater forces riding into battle on their underwater equivalent of something the Terrans called a *jet skee*, individual transports. More forces manning small, sleek submersibles armed with harpoon guns.

At a word from the four-crested female, Tai-Khan gave the order for the Selkies to scatter and retreat. Even as they did so, two of the Salik vessels started to sink. Somewhere in the midst of the chaos, the Selkies had deployed enough of their mantis-shrimp-limb things to turn the hulls sinking into view into virtual collanders.

A strange satisfaction crept warmly through him when he heard the startled exclamations from his fellow V'Dan. The local members of the Imperial Navy knew just how tough those hulls were; somehow, the Terran bioweapons had shredded the reinforced-alloy plating on those two ships. Other hulls also had holes, but not as many as those two. He waited impatiently while the Terrans cleared the field for the much fresher Choya troops to claim, then snagged the major's attention while she had a little break from her intense watchfulness.

"Major Tai-Khan," Li'eth had to ask, *"why did your troops shred those two hulls so much, but not the others quite so much? Is there a tactical reason I'm missing?"*

The short-haired woman shrugged and shook her head. *"I'm not completely sure . . ."*

She looked at Agneau, who replied absently in V'Dan, her attention more on the Choya troop movements to try to cut off escape attempts from the aliens fleeing the sinking ships. "I think I heard one of the techs saying they were picking up a lot of frequency chatter from those two ships. It was a tactical call by the team."

"Mind sharing that with the rest of us who aren't *fluent in V'Dan, yet?"* her CO asked dryly.

Agneau blushed and repeated herself in Terranglo. *"Sorry, sir . . . I said, I think I heard one of the techs saying they were picking up a lot of frequency chatter from those two ships. I'm not sure which one ordered those two ships to be the hardest hit."*

"That was me!" One of the men at a row of tables two up from the back raised his hand high over his felt-capped head. *"I made that call, Major. A lot of comm chatter usually means a tactical command center, so I tagged it as a priority."*

"That, it often does. Thank you, Slawson, good call," Tai-Khan called back. She eyed the rest, their attention still firmly on their workstation screens. *"Bring 'em home, people. Time to put our sealskins back in our chests and let 'em repair and rest before the next storm surge hits."*

Her words were greeted with a surge of strange, barking

noises from her soldiers, somewhere between *ooh ooh ooh* and *oiy oiy oiy!*

That confused Li'eth. Frowning, he reached out to Jackie, asking, (*. . . Sealskin? I thought you said these were Dalph-skins, based on dolphins. Why would they make such a weird noise over a seal? Isn't that a sort of glue or solder?*)

Jackie, listening to his sending and its underthought of confusion, choked on the drink someone had brought her. Mirth spiraled out of her mind, wrapping down around his even as she coughed several times. (Seal, *Li'eth, not seal! Pick up my booting subthoughts, you silly . . .* Seal, *as in the sea mammal . . . ? Don't you remember what I told you a week or so ago, all those Celtic myths about shapeshifters who could turn into seals and back? How they'd take off their seal hides and put them into storage chests for safekeeping while they walked around on two legs like a Human?*)

Li'eth blushed in embarrassment. (*Right. I forgot that. Your people have a lot of legends. Separate from your histories, I mean,*) he added in clarification. (*Ours tend to get wrapped up in our histories until it's hard to separate fact from myth. And the name for the creature is the same word-sound for a completely different thing. At times, Terranglo is very confusing . . .*)

"*Casualty report,*" Major Tai-Khan ordered, distracting him from the mental conversation. "*Have we got a tally yet?*"

"*Eighteen dead, five critically wounded, thirty-three wounded . . . and 67 percent of all 'suits damaged, sir,*" one of the junior officers reported.

"*All bodies have been recovered, sir,*" another stated. "*And all pieces have been recovered or targeted with pocket torpedoes to keep the tech out of enemy hands.*"

Tai-Khan nodded slowly, grimly, hands on her hips. "*Good work, people. Considering we have never fought this foe before, a 25 percent casualty rating is a good day's fight . . . and it looked like you reduced that initial spike once you adapted your tactics. You all get a performance bonus on top of your combat bonuses. I will also personally ensure that those promised colonial rights go to the heirs of our eighteen lost souls. Try to make sure we don't lose more than those eighteen souls after today, soldiers.*"

"Aye, sir!" most of the techs chorused with prompt respect.

"ETA to med-evac, seven minutes or less," someone else called out, and their postcombat operations resumed.

"Try to make it shorter!" Tai-Khan ordered, resuming her pacing while she waited for the three companies to escort all the wounded to the incoming ships. Now that the fighting was over, her movements were slower, a bit more relaxed. More like a hunting *g'at* tempted to go and lie down after successfully chasing down a meal, but still a little agitated.

Eyeing the two Choya observers and their fully upright crests, Li'eth moved over closer to them. They didn't speak Terranglo, but they did speak the Imperial tongue. "Are you pleased with the Terrans' efforts?"

"Yes," the female agreed in V'Dan. "I do not know the casualllty rate, and the battle wasss chaotic, but mmmore of them died in their attack than our sssside."

"If we don't count the damaged suits, just those actually injured or worse, the casualty rate was only about 25 percent," Li'eth translated. "Only about a quarter of them were injured or slain. That number *will* rise, as the Salik get over their surprise. The injured suits were 67 percent, about two-thirds, and they will eventually figure out they have to strike deeper to do actual harm."

"But it willl nnot rise by much," the male officer asserted, flexing his single crest in what looked like a very good mood. "These Terrannsss will learnn as well. They fight wellll, for air kin."

"Good day fight," Tai-Khan agreed, following along somewhat with her bare-bones understanding of V'Dan.

"Yes," the female officer agreed. "A good day'sss fight."

(. . . *Time to get back to that paperwork you were given,*) Jackie nudged him mentally. She no longer needed to cough though he did hear her clearing her throat of leftover phlegm. (*I still have some translating to do, but I should be free in a few more minutes, not much more than a quarter hour.*)

(*I'm on it,*) he promised, and moved back to the station he had used. Picking up his half-drunk bottle of berry drink for a sip, he searched for his abandoned datapad. After a few moments, he realized it was tucked *under* the elbow of the oblivious tech who had taken his place.

Liberating it, he moved off to find an unoccupied chair at the back of the room and turned the device back on. Paperwork could wait, but it bred while it waited, piling up into tedious mountains. It was always best to get the pile scraped down to bedrock wherever possible.

CHAPTER 9

OCTOBER 21, 2287 C.E.
JUNA 12, 9507 V.D.S.
GONN STAA, AU'AURRRAN, COLONY VI
SLLC-9898 SYSTEM, SOLARICAN EMPIRE

The Church of the Spiraling Eye overlooked downtown Gonn Staa. It was not the capital of V'Au'aurrran, but it was their largest city. Set in a long, somewhat broad canyon that suffered from occasional strong storm winds, all of the buildings had reinforced, sloped walls on their north and south sides, stout shields that allowed that wind to pass over and around them whenever it blew that way. The Church, an edifice occupying three of the floors at about the midpoint of the megabuilding they were in, looked out to the east, across the valley.

The great windows of the foyer-like narthex picked up the glow from the city lights as well as the occasional flake of snow that spiraled down out of the overcast sky. Most melted by a dozen *mitas* from the ground. Those snow-bearing clouds marched toward the windows at a steady pace, scraping along from east to west; the winds guiding them pulled on the tops of the steam clouds rising from the natural geyser vents found near the bottom of the valley.

It should have been a beautiful view. It *was* a beautiful view, for despite the sheer functionality of the building shapes for the local climate, the Solaricans believed everything deserved to be beautiful, not just functional. Load-bearing yet elegant arches outlined architectural elements, carvings and reliefwork covered most surfaces, and even many of the windows across the city had been pieced together artistically out of stained and colored glazings.

Beautiful though it was, Li'eth could not bring himself to relax. In the main sanctuary of the Church, Grand High Ambassador MacKenzie, Lieutenant Johnston, and a host of V'Dan and Solarican priests were entangled in a great Gestalt. The Seers of the Solarican race had already developed a crude form of language-learning, imperfect and feeble compared to the Terran version but still quite assistive in learning languages a bit faster. The object of today's lengthy session was for them to observe telepathically while Jackie and Darian worked on language transfers with Solarican Seers, spending the day teaching these people how to begin to make language transfers.

Project Code-Talker had been moved up in importance; the Terrans were now mass-distributing communications satellites to every system via any ship that could carry the satellites and a handful of V'Dan-speaking Terran techs to get them in place and set them up without any of them exploding. More and more of the Salik seemed to be partially aware of what they were, in the sense of thinking they were nothing more than torpedoes, space mines; they steered their ships carefully clear, readjusting their angles of attack whenever approaching a space station, domeworld, or breathable planet.

Like this one . . . except the Salik hadn't attacked this one much. Au'aurrran was a joint colonyworld, predominantly hosting the Solaricans who had founded it three centuries before, a large V'Dan population . . . and a nearly equally large Salik and Choya population. This world was an oddity in the war; within a day of word spreading on this world of the attacks by their brethren elsewhere, the Salik colonists had broadcast their independence from their motherworld government and pledged to reside in peace.

Anyone with any understanding of the planet's geology could guess as to why: Au'aurrran had a series of underground seas and rivers that were thermally heated, ideal conditions for the Choya and the Salik, who preferred warm, wet worlds. Au'aurrran also had a treasure trove of useful minerals, plus precious metals and useful gemstones: malleable gold and silver, platinum and copper, brilliantly colored garnets, beryls, diamonds, topazes. Many caverns kept being uncovered as the inhabitants continued to explore, bringing back thousands of images of underground chambers filled with awe-inspiring crystals the size of skyscrapers.

This world was a haven for gem cutters and goldsmiths, tourists and more . . . underneath the surface. It also occupied the sixth orbit around its sun, making the surface bitterly cold in winter and barely tolerable for the Salik in summer, though the Solaricans found it merely chilly. Neither the Choya nor the Salik wanted to fight on Au'aurrran, and the Solaricans ensured it. The *g'at*-like race that had founded the world had made it quite clear to their first few Salik visitors many years ago that they could and would be shoved onto the surface and left to die of exposure if they did not get along.

The Salik had long memories. They did not forget that threat, and their settlers on this colonyworld had behaved. Li'eth did not expect them to forget the threat. He did not expect them to forgive it, either. No matter how many times the local Salik insisted they would not attack, he could not bring himself to believe them, and that meant he could not relax enough on this world to join the learning Gestalt behind him.

Lieutenant Commander Buraq came out of the side corridor leading to the refreshing-room facilities. Solarican and V'Dan biowaste facilities were designed along very similar lines, making it easy for them to simply share refreshing rooms; Tlassian tails required special seating alterations, and Li'eth had never wanted to know anything about the other races. Not after finding out in his history lessons as a premarked youth that the Chinsoiy "grew" their waste in a sort of crystalline aggregate. Originally, those had been considered quite lovely by the other races, until finding out why the Chinsoiy were so reluctant to sell the fragile lattices as artwork. A rather ignominious day for the Alliance when *that* became widely known.

"Still can't relax?" Buraq asked, moving up beside him to enjoy the windows overlooking the snow-swept city. The V'Dan soldiers who had accompanied them down to the surface from the *V'Goro J'sta* as an escort force looked over at her but otherwise went back to lounging around, watching entertainment programs spooling off the local matrices. A few remained somewhat alert, including Lieutenant Paea, who stood with his rifle cradled across his chest, the muzzle aimed low. But only a few of the dozen in the hall. There simply wasn't anything for them to do but lounge around and wait.

Li'eth shook his head, looking over at the Terran security officer. "There are over half a million Salik on this world. Nearly a hundred thousand live within a day's travel of this city."

"We were reassured they rarely come up to any of the surface zones," she pointed out. "And this building has a shuttle bay on the roof. We can easily . . . get . . ."

She broke off, dark brows pinching together on her tanned face. Peering past him, she moved closer to the windows, trying to see something off to the side. Curious, Li'eth shifted as well, peering through the rising steam clouds and falling snowflakes.

"What are you looking at?" he asked her.

"Is that . . . smoke?" Jasmine murmured, squinting through the pane. "I thought I saw something explode, farther up the valley . . . I think your paranoia has me seeing things. It was probably just light flashing through yet more steam from the geysers," she dismissed. "This city is so damp, I'm surprised the Solaricans don't suffer from arthritis."

Li'eth looked out across the rest of the ribbonlike city. "I'm told it's a common complaint for anyone dwelling on . . . what . . . ?"

The tiny flash he had spotted down below and across the way turned into a gout of white and orange, far too thick to be steam, far too bright to be a normal source of light. It flared again, this time curling black with smoke around the edges.

"Saints!" he exclaimed, backing up a startled step.

Buraq didn't hesitate; she turned and snapped orders to the dozen men and women either standing watch with their eyes on the entrances, or lounging on the benches of the narthex. "On your feet! Be alert! Someone get on the news matrices and find out what is going *on* out there, because we *could* be under attack!"

To their credit, they immediately scrambled to attention;

three kept their display tablets active, and the others grabbed for their weapons. One of them started toward the center of the sanctuary. Li'eth quickly broke away from the window, stretching his strides to catch up to the woman. "Stand down, Corporal!" he ordered. "No one disrupts their session."

"Pardon your Tier, Grand Captain, but if we're under attack, we *have* to get the two of you out of here," the corporal superior countered tartly.

"*I* will contact them," he told her, and flicked his hand to dismiss her back toward the others. "Form a safety perimeter and let nothing through."

"You'd better hurry, Captain," Buraq called out to him, moving away from the window while Paea moved closer. "The faster we can evacuate, the happier I will be."

"I was told these things must be done carefully, to keep from damaging all their minds," he countered. "Now . . . let me work in peace. You find out what is going on out there."

Moving to the edge of the cushion-strewn circle, underneath the great chandelier of tiny pinpoints of light, Li'eth eyed the curly-haired woman at the center of the quietly meditating group. There was no way to get to her without touching one of the others, for they all sat close enough to comfortably clasp hands, some furred, some smooth. Giving up, he found a spare cushion, dropped onto it, crossed his calves, and closed his eyes.

Calming his mind, he slowly, *slowly* opened his innermost shields to Jackie's presence on the inner plane of existence, not the physical one. Let his awareness seep through her shields. Clearing his mind was not easy; he focused on thinking of himself as steam, supersaturated gas seeping into her awareness and condensing into view. He didn't know how long it took for her to notice.

Eventually, she did. Slowing the whirl of information being exchanged, she reached out to him, wrapped him in a bubble that held him away from the others, and asked, (*Li'eth? Why are you in here?*)

(*Danger,*) he sent back, with underflavorings of *explosion* and *fire* and *attack.*

(*Beloved, I* know *you're feeling nerv— What was* that?)

she exclaimed, feeling her body rocking. Their bodies, hers, his, and the others' as well.

Li'eth backed out of the mental plane far enough to hear shouting, which meant so did she. The words "*. . . hangar bay exploded!*" reached his ears, provoking another spike of *Danger!* from him straight into her psyche.

Her reaction satisfied him. (Oh. *Gentlebeings? We are going to end this here and now. Please visualize stepping backwards, until you step safely into your bodies—we will finish the language transfer later, meioa-e. We have a situation outside our heads, and we* need *to go protect our bodies. Visualize releasing each other's hands and stepping back into your own bodies. Be* calm *when releasing physical hands, too . . .*)

Li'eth stepped back with his mind and opened his eyes to the real world. The vast building vibrated slightly but rhythmically, as if something in the distance kept striking it with a giant hammer. Buraq stood near the columns delineating the border between sanctuary and narthex, snapping words into her communicator in that strange language, Man-dah-rin, that the Terrans used for private communications. Beyond her, Lieutenant Paea stood at the windows, hands cupped to the glass to cut down on the reflections from the lighting in the grand chamber. Here on the twenty-third floor, the biggest obstacles to seeing what happened anywhere else in the city were those reflections, wind-whipped clouds of steam, and the now-thickly-falling snow.

Seeing the various holy ones starting to blink and stretch and move, the corporal superior rose from the padded bench she had borrowed during her wait. "Is everyone awake?" she asked the group, her tone brisk and tight with anxiety. "Yes? Good! The city is under attack. We have to get out of here and find a safe place."

"I heard something about the hangar bay?" Li'eth asked.

She shook her head, her short, purple-streaked pigtails sliding across her red uniform coat. "I'm sorry, Grand Captain, but someone's been launching missiles at all the hangar bays. Our shuttles are half-damaged and blocked by the debris. We're going to have to find another way out of here."

"How long was I trancing?" Li'eth asked, alarmed.

The corporal looked down at her chrono and shrugged. "About . . . sixteen *mi-nah*? It's probably a good thing we didn't leave since we might have still been boarding, or just taking off, and been a tempting target. The *V'Goro J'sta*—"

The glazed windows two dozen *mitas* away exploded inward. Lieutenant Paea tumbled and crumpled, flung off his feet by the sheer force of the blow. Li'eth flung up his hand, ears ringing from the concussion, but Jackie was faster, flinging up her mind in a wall of force that stopped the pebbled shards in their tracks. Bits of window glazing pelted off the cringing back and side of Lieutenant Commander Buraq, just a body length beyond that wall.

She turned to look at the bloodied streaks of Paea's path across the floor—and whirled, lunging behind the nearest column for cover as a metallic bulk roared into the great gap made in the formerly beautiful windows. Seers and priests shrieked and scattered, and the Imperial soldiers on either side of the opening yelled and opened fire, adding searing laserfire to the confusion of sights and sounds. Lieutenant Johnston drew his sidearm and hurried forward, only to quickly duck behind a pillar as well when the invader returned fire.

One of the few Seers who did not flee for cover snarled in a mix of V'Dan, Terranglo, and her native tongue, something about the bastard being enclosed in a mechsuit, keeping the damned amphibian warm instead of freezing to death.

Freezing to death . . .

One of Master Sonam's lessons came back to Li'eth now. "*. . . The laws of thermodynamics are* not *broken with pyrokinesis; we expend some of our own energy to ripple light-waves and agitate molecules elsewhere. We don't know* what *kind of energy, precisely, other than kinetic inergy, of course, nor how we can reach across a distance and seemingly manipulate things indirectly . . . but because we are not hampered by* matter *when we do so, a pyrokinetic can also be a* cryokinetic, *someone who* removes *heat by moving it elsewhere. So you will learn to light this birthday candle over here, by shifting the energy from that piping-hot cup of water I just boiled in the microwave, there.*"

(*You have an idea?*) his partner asked, wincing from the

flash of light and sizzling sound shooting out of the little turret-guns on the shoulders of the mechsuited alien. Like the soldiers, her aura was considerably stronger, calmer than the panicked splashes and streaks of the fleeing psis. Scared, but determined. (*If you do,* do *it! I don't know how close he needs to be to stun us all!*)

The V'Dan nearest the Salik warrior were indeed dropping unconscious, considerably more vulnerable to stunnerfire than their attacker was to laserfire, lacking protective armor of their own. Johnston, caught in a moment of sheer bad timing, crumpled to the floor unconscious, his gun tumbling free from his slack fingers. Buraq whipped around the corner of her own pillar and shot at the machine-clad alien, three fast, well-aimed shots . . . that ricocheted off everything, though it did crack that faceplate. The armored marauder tried shooting back at her, but she ducked behind the broad, heavily carved column again before he could turn the nearest gun turret and fire.

Li'eth needed to concentrate, not gape. Squinting, he focused his inner vision, trying to twist his aura-reading abilities into something that could sense thermal energies instead of emotional and psyche-based ones. Trying to look *through* the matter, to the energy states that charged each particle.

The Salik swirled with shades of vicious red, triumphant turquoise, frantic gold. But beneath that . . . it was difficult to find the right viewpoint under pressure. Li'eth had not practiced this twist on his aura-vision recently, though he had tried it several times under Sonam's supervision. It was more of an awareness than a literally visual thing like his aura-reading, so he bent his thoughts to his awareness of where heat *would* be located, to help him focus. The narthex beyond Jackie's telekinetic wall had lost much of its heat out the shattered window, forming a sharp temperature differential. Buraq and the unconscious soldiers made brighter spots, including the barrel of her pistol and the scorch marks from the laser rifles. The Salik, however . . .

Inside the winter-chilled skin, the fully enclosed environment of the combat suit "felt" toasty-warm to Li'eth's inner senses. Breathing deep, in and out, he pictured his mind becoming one with the thermodynamic energies. Saturating it with his strength much as he had saturated Jackie's innermost shields. Becoming one with the heat.

Something exploded in bright-hot golden heat from the alien's armor; it exploded a second time in sharp red kinetic impacts immediately afterward. His eyes were closed, so he didn't see the actual attack, but his ears heard Buraq scream. Li'eth gritted his teeth, wrapped his senses throughout the whole suit of armor, and signaled a subthought to Jackie that he was about to pull. *She* reached out to him, joining some of her strength to his—and suddenly, he felt like he was at the head of a tugging rope, with himself, her, and the Seer who had remained with them in the heart of the sanctuary. (. . . *Three . . . two . . . one . . . PULL!*)

Heat seared the air in a billowing line between them. Li'eth quickly bundled it up inside his shields, not wanting the others to be scorched. Unsquinching his eyes, he held himself still, not daring to move in case he lost control of the thermal energies. The Salik warrior . . . did not move. Could not move. Even as Li'eth stared, the dark alloys of all that carefully jointed armor turned lighter and lighter . . . literally frosting over from the moisture in the air hitting the superchilled statue he had just made.

A moment later, he watched in dawning horror as the alien's aura finished stuttering and snuffed out. A strange emptiness filled the space where the Salik technically stood, a cold that had nothing to do with cryokinesis, thermodynamics, or any normal, rational science. His first kill via his holy skills . . . He had *killed* someone with . . .

(*Snap out of it!*) Jackie ordered. (*I've done it, too, and it's not pleasant, but there are more coming, and Buraq's down, possibly dead! I don't even know about Paea . . . The rest of you get back in here!*) she added in a wider telepathic sending. (*We have injured people in here!*)

(*I . . . I* think *I can convert this to kinetic* inergy,) he muttered, moving forward carefully, step by step closer to the lieutenant commander. The damned bastard had blown up the column, sending her bloodied and sprawling with chunks of stone and metal all over. Stone, and metal, and blood. (*But it's all I can do to hold on to all this thermal energy. I can't heal her without fearing I'd just scorch her.*)

(*Don't bother; we have enough biokinetics coming back out of their hiding holes. I'm moving the kinetic shield up to the opening. Go get near the window and see if you can see what's going on out there,*) she ordered. (*If it looks hostile, fry it.*)

(*I can definitely do that,*) he agreed. Already, sweat beaded on his skin, the air directly around his body quite warm. He compressed more of the energies, pushing on all sides until it formed an oddly glowing ball, faint dull red, like tungsten heating up. (*Maybe I'll get lucky, and—* V'shova!)

He lashed out with the heat-ball just as a new mechanized, tentacle-limbed enemy roared up through the opening with thrusters blasting full bore. The thermal packet scorched the mechsuit with a bang that rattled the remaining windows in their panes. This time, much more sure of his attack, Li'eth sunk his mental hands into the teetering alien, and yanked hard and fast. Frost hissed across the armor. That snuffed off the suit's energies, toppling it out the window and dropping it far out of range before he could sense the swift death of its occupant.

Lights danced around him, golden instead of bluish in hue. Flames, he realized. Flames on his hands, his arms, even his hair from the feel of the fine strands starting to flutter. It did not burn him—it was under *his* conscious control—but the others, the Solaricans and V'Dan who were returning from taking shelter in the two side halls off the sanctuary, slowed and gaped at him. Moving forward, he left Jasmine and Simon to Jackie to check. His place lay at the gaping hole in the outer wall . . . which *he* blocked with a telekinetic wall since he had more than enough energy to spare, now.

He skirted warily around the frost-rimed statue of their first attacker, picking his way carefully across the shard-strewn floor. Not because the pebbled safety glazing could cut through his military boots, but because their scattered presence made footing treacherous. Someone groaned faintly as he approached the windows. Li'eth blinked, twisted to stare at the bloodied Terran male on the floor, realized he was still bleeding in oxygenated red, and called out, (*I think Simon's still alive! Can anyone help?*)

(*I will stabilize him,*) one of the Seers offered, picking his way forward, his brown ears flattened back against his skull, his whiskers down in distress, but still willing to come out of cover and help. (*My body-healing works on outsiders. I have also first medical skills for V'Dan, and he is V'Dan in biology. Keep the Salik away?*)

(*Absolutely,*) Li'eth promised. Stopping a few feet from the opening blasted in the windows, he peered out cautiously.

More explosions peppered the city with brief flares of light and clouds of darkness, too dark to be geyser steam. Their sources came from mechanized Salik soldiers, most of whom were rampaging individually through the city streets. Some from time to time shot up into the air on their suit thrusters, blasting holes at random into the upper levels of the bigger buildings before charging in and wreaking havoc inside. Faint shrill cries wafted up from the fighting, tiny streaks of lasers from those few citizens who had anything for fighting back. But mostly . . . mostly it was death, destruction, and the stunning of hundreds and thousands of victims.

Small, boxy shapes trundled along the roads down below. Squinting, Li'eth realized what they were, as robots moved out, metallic and pale, and came back out of various buildings carrying colorful oblong lumps. Stunned prisoners. A literal roundup of sentient meat for shipping off to the slaughtering pens. Gorge rising, he almost reached down and seared those machines with the heat-energies he clung to mentally . . . but stopped himself. At this distance, he'd be as likely to damage innocent lives as fry those harvester bots.

Do not waste your strength, either, he chided himself mentally, and used a tiny bit of telekinesis to scrape the floor clear of debris. Lowering himself to his knees, he composed his body for comfort and focused on figuring out what he *could* do with a minimal amount of psychic inergy spent, and what he *should* do from among those options. *Those suits probably have thermal sensors, so they might zero in on my location if I try to make another heating orb. I don't want to draw attention up here; our soldiers are down, they could get close enough to stun me, and if I drop, Jackie drops, reducing our defensive strength greatly. I suspect those shoulder cannons were set for a full hour in their strength; he'd not have bothered on a short-duration stunning.*

But . . . I could move the storage orb *out there,* to lure them into a trap as they try to figure it out. There were legends of fire-calling Saints doing things that were not normal, not natural with fire. *Didn't Saint Gile'an once ". . . summon up the summer sun to thaw the snow-buried souls of the army . . ." during his war to help my ancestress wrest the Eternal Throne away from the madness of her kinsman? Isn't that like the thermal sphere Sonam showed me how to make? And . . . and if my strength holds to shift thermal energies, wouldn't it make a lovely trap and weapon?*

Opening his eyes, which had closed automatically during his moment of deep thinking, Li'eth tried to lift his mind up and out of his body. The Terran psi, Heracles, had shown everyone how to do so in that group Gestalt back at the Winter Palace. It took a couple tries, but he lifted up, soared out, shifting his perspective . . . and bringing the heat with him.

The abrupt coldness around his body almost broke his concentration. Quickly parceling the heat he wielded into two portions, with the smaller of the two left behind to keep his body comfortable in the damp cold of the breached building, he moved the greater portion with his awareness over the canyon and condensed the energies into a small but thermally bright marble. Air molecules that intersected with it glowed into the visible spectrum as they absorbed fractions of that energy. They shot outward at high speeds, creating sizzling gusts that swirled the falling snow, rapidly losing their glow but not their velocity.

Splitting his attention a third time, he looked out and down at the robots and mechsuits and waited. Like a *g'at*, stalk-hunting his prey. Sure enough, after what felt like a *mi-nah*, two soldiers blasted upward to investigate Li'eth's thermal anomaly. Splitting his attention again—in the way that he could hold on to something with his elbow and ribs, with each of his hands, with individual fingers, even—Li'eth sank his kinetic awareness into each suit and hauled.

It took more effort than anticipated. Not because it was difficult but because when split, his attention did not provide enough will-backed strength. Letting the thrusters on the left one sputter, he hauled energy up out of the one on the right. That energy, he fed into the tiny, bright sphere, then lashed out and yanked up the energy from the one that had almost reached its position a good seventy or so *mitas* in the air.

(*Not to disturb you or anything, but your hair is on fire again . . .*)

(*Thank you.*) He was still bringing a percentage of energy back to his body to keep it warm; more energy reaved from the enemy meant more energy on his person. Letting the second suit fall, its occupant dying or dead, he siphoned off some of that power around himself and fed it into the growing sphere.

The first suit hit with a *bam* that echoed up from below, no doubt cracking the plaza tiles. Five, six heartbeats after it, the second hit with a softer, crackling splash, striking the edge of one of the geyser pools. That drew attention from the other Salik, and within half a *mi-nah*, half a dozen more had launched themselves skyward. One at a time, Li'eth caught and ripped thermal energy out of their oddly jointed bodies, sending the off-lined suits and their contents crashing downward.

The last of the six struck one of the collection vehicles down below. Li'eth flinched in horror, and almost lost control of the now beach-ball-sized sphere. Jackie surged forward in his mind, catching and holding the fire.

(*This is a war. Casualties are inevitable,*) she soothed in a detached sending, most of her focus on holding in the heat, a trickier, more finicky project for her since this wasn't *her* inborn gift. (*They would have died horrible deaths eaten alive. Right now, they are stunned and feel nothing.*)

(*I know. I know, but I did that to them . . .*) Grimly, he rewrapped his concentration around what he was doing.

A fresh mind, one of the Seers, touched theirs. (*You are shapers of sight? Our people need* hope. *The Fire Lord should appear.*)

(*Got it,*) Jackie sent back, catching the Solarican's subthought images on who and what that Fire Lord was. A moment later, the bright-glowing sphere unfurled into a fiery golden Solarican, half-*g'at*-like in his feral stance, crouching on the air like it was a cliff top. (*I'll challenge the Salik visually—everyone, meld and send your energies to the prince! Li'eth—*)

(*I've got it,*) he reassured her, feeling revitalized by the surge of inner energies rising within him. He was so detached now from his body, he could barely feel it, but took a moment to enclose himself in a pocket of . . . *just so much warmth, and no more*, to keep from searing the air around it. Just in case anyone was touching him to feed him that energy. So when the next group of Salik rose and tried to attack the flame-furred, ten-*mita*-tall Solarican climbing all over the sky, he was able to shift the sphere in tandem with her holokinetic projection, rushing it *through* his targets and first scorching, then siphoning out all the thermal energies.

With each pass, the sphere gained more power than it lost, growing in size both pyrokinetically and holokinetically. Within just a few more waves, the Salik pulled back and launched missiles. Li'eth reached out to suck the heat out of them, only to have Jackie poke his mental hands away.

(*No, don't do it that way—they're* chemical *explosives; they can still explode once they thaw if they survive the landing, and there are stunned civilians on the ground. Blast them out of the sky; it shouldn't take nearly as much energy.*)

She was right. So he peeled off small marbles of heat and flung them into the heart of each roaring missile, exploding them in billowing balls of flames—and *then* stole *that* energy, snuffing the flames like a straw sucking liquid back up into itself, leaving behind dark puffs of chilled clouds that drifted down like tiny soot-stained snow pellets. Three, four, five times he struck the missiles, and the rippling image of the Fire Lord roared and slashed with his fiery fingers splayed, claws fully extended, shooting out bright stars of destruction that the missiles could not evade. Seven, nine, twelve missiles *bamfed* in loud, cracking explosions that were followed by a *whomp* of the air collapsing inward from the sudden shock of lost energy.

No one attacked for a few moments. Gradually, he became aware of several rumbles in the air, and turned his attention skyward. Dozens of ships had descended out of the clouds, triggering a shaft of fear before he realized some were *not* Salik but were instead the soaring bulk of Solarican V'Dan warships . . . and yes, *Terran* ships as well, a full half dozen of their silvery, swept-winged vessels that swooped and spun through the sky, reflecting the Fire Lord illusion in gilded streaks along their silvery hulls.

Still, there were more Salik ships than Solarican, Terran,

or V'Dan, a lot more . . . and then the clouds roiled and scattered around the bulk of an immense hull in the distance. For a moment, only the outline of the clouds let him see it had a five-lobed hull . . . the shape of a Salik capital ship. One designed to *land*, he realized, the kind used for a major invasion of ground forces in an area they believed could be securable with overwhelming force.

Hands touched his shoulders. Fingers slid up to his neck, his scalp, using direct physical touch to augment their powers. (*We cannot stop that by freezing it . . . but we* can *disable it,*) his Gestalt partner murmured. (*The last two dropships of Terran troops has arrived, and if we can get that big ship* down, *then our forces can help mop up what little survives.*)

(*Sear them with the raging blade of the Fire Lord,*) several Seers sent in near unison, their minds enmeshed in a way that allowed them to group-think as one. (*Strike* now*!*)

Li'eth didn't have to think twice; the analytical part of his mind had already realized how if that great ship got any closer, it would crash *in* the city and not far from their own position. So—with a bounding felinoid roar from Jackie, ironically echoing the ship that had forced him into leaving home—the feral Fire Lord image surged through the sky to meet it.

Met it, and torpedoed *through* it with a twist at the last moment that broke the now-massive golden fury into many lesser white-hot lances, like straws on a twig-broom branching out from the main shaft. He tried to pull in extra heat to keep it going, keep each firecone bursting through bulkhead after bulkhead. In the back of his mind, the others shoved their own limbs forward, their own will, using his mind as the tool. Some of the scattered pinpricks resurged to life with sharp stabs that clouded his inner eye with increasing heat and pain, until he heard Jacaranda yelling at the others, shielding him, throwing them back and out of their meld. Keeping them from literally burning him up in their efforts to help.

Coming back to himself, to an awareness of his own body, sensing the flames still dancing over his slightly scorched sleeves, he blinked and looked up with red-clouded eyes in time to see the nose of that massive ship hitting the ground somewhere beyond the far canyon edge. He didn't *see* the actual point of impact, since his physical position sat lower than the rim. But he—and everyone with him—saw the snow and earth slamming upward in a billowing roll of shock-concussed debris. Watched as the great ship teetered bow down, stern slowly rising. *Felt* the shock wave reaching the canyon, bowing the curved wall of nothing sheltering them from the incoming blast, flexing the air pressure against their eardrums with a painful sonic *bang* followed by rumbling stone and crumbling metal.

The great ship continued to slide forward, dual-lobed hindquarters rising higher and higher. Some of the cannons on those giant, turret-like lobes tried to fire, tiny puffs of light and dark. Then the nose of the ship jolted and dropped the whole thing down a visible notch, dozens of *mitas* in depth, some sort of ravine unseen from this angle. Ponderously, slowly, the whole thing shifted, cantilevered up and over that crack in the plateau.

(*Shit!*) Jackie thrust forward, extending a sheet of telekinesis across the top of the whole canyon in a path stretching from their position diagonally across the gap. Knowing she needed help, Li'eth warped the thermal energies still left in his grip, converting them to kinetic inergy. That snuffed out the fire dancing along his sleeves, hands, and hair.

The force of the ship's landing upside down on the cliff shook the whole valley, blurring his vision first from the vibrations, then from the dust clouds raised as parts of that cliff crumpled and gave way. Objects, hard-flung from the impact, soared down into the valley, crashing into buildings and cratering whatever they struck. All save for a cone-shaped path overhead, where they just tumbled across will-hardened air, spinning and bouncing until they parted to either side and did not hit the building containing the remnants of the Church of the Spiraling Eye.

The last few shards dropped short of their position, permitting them to drop the last bit of shielding. Li'eth slumped in place, head bowing. Lifting a shaking hand to his face, he wiped at the cooling wetness on his lip, his cheekbones, and stared at the deep red smears for a long, uncomprehending moment.

(*You have taxed your holy gifts to the precipice and be-*

yond. Much like that abomination above our city,) one of the Solarican Seers stated. The brown-and-cream-furred one, whose warm fingerpads brushed against his temple, bringing with it healing energies. (*I will repair the microscopic tears in your* sa'achen rro faan drrunn.)

He had no idea what those words meant, but they came with an underthought of some sort of barrier thing in his body keeping the blood from bleeding out from between his cells in all the wrong ways. He wasn't medically trained, and he hurt too much right now to care. It took a few minutes before the pain subsided; by that point, someone had found what looked like spare priestly robes to wrap around both him and Jackie while they knelt by the battered opening in the narthex windows.

The great capital ship hung over the edge of the crater by about a hundred *mitas* though it was hard to judge distances from so far away. One curved edge had landed on one of the great, pyramidal buildings, crushing the missile-damaged tip, but the rest of it held. There would have been no danger of the spaceship's dropping into the valley either way as it was, however. Not when the whole ship stretched over a *kila* long and a third that wide, a quarter that tall.

A ship that sat upside down at an awkward angle, with fiery pinpricks lighting up its beige-painted hull, remnants from being reamed by dozens of vicious thermal strikes. Various non-Salik vessels swarmed the thing, shooting at any and all gun turrets, disabling it further in preparation for drop shuttles to innie-out the incoming Terran troops. Salik forces also swarmed that way, including mechanized soldiers, equally determined to defend their own invading cousins.

The "neutral" Salik that had lurked under the surface of this world were clearly neutral no longer. Had clearly *waited* until they were certain they would have massive support to sweep through the greatest city on Au'aurrran, the greatest source of resources and personnel for building up a resistance to any invasion. He hated being right about his paranoia, and just knelt there in awe at what had just happened. Part of him wanted to ask . . . *Did I do that?* But he knew it was more like, *Did we do that?*

Seeing the size of it looming over the large buildings of the valley, realizing just how much psychic inergy had been required to bring it down, Li'eth could see why his brain had started bleeding. (*For the first time in my life . . . I think I see just how much power it takes to wipe out your 'Grey' foes . . . the ones you say are technologically superior by leaps and bounds.*)

(*Like a Human is to an insect,*) Jackie agreed. She had dropped her face onto his shoulder, not bloodied but certainly exhausted by everything they had done. (*Thank god some of us are scorpions and stinkbugs.*)

He chuckled weakly at that, nuzzled her—and flinched as something large, metallic, and holding a big stunner rifle in those servo-tentacles roared up into view. He didn't have the strength left to freeze the marauder, though. (Shakk! *I can't . . . !*)

A loud *bang* hurt his ears, and stung his eyes and nose with a sharp, sulfurous reek. Coughing, he flinched back from the armored figure. Jackie, arm still extended, weapon smoking slightly, shoved telekinetically with a scrap of remaining strength, and the mechsuit swayed outward instead of inward. It wobbled out of sight and vanished, leaving behind crashing, scraping sounds signaling its now-out-of-control fall.

(*It's Johnston's gun. I grabbed it on my way to check Buraq,*) Jackie confessed, lowering the weapon in her hand to his lap, her arm sort of curling around him like a hug. He peeked down, relieved to see her finger was not on the trigger and that she still held it so that the muzzle pointed up and away from his far leg. Sensing his worry, she snorted mentally. (*I have* good *weapon discipline.*)

(*Still glad to see it.*) He shifted his head a little, his cheek nuzzling hers. (*We need to rest while we can. I'm done, pyrokinetically. Cryokinetically. You're going to have to do all the saving until I've recovered, with your Terran projectile weapons that go through Salik armor.*)

(*Deal. And it only goes through the faceplates at close range. Your pistol-sized lasers bounce off that part. I'm seriously regretting agreeing to let the soldiers leave their combat weapons on the shuttle, just for diplomacy's sake.*) She sighed.

Footsteps rattled into audible range. Both of them twisted to peer at the main entrance to the half-shattered Church. The remaining Imperial soldiers from their escort shuttle hurried into view, four soldiers plus the two members of the shuttle crew, Lieutenant Shi'uln and a backup pilot. What Li'eth saw the half dozen men and women carrying made his eyes sting again, this time with relief.

(. . . *Here come those weapons now, thank the Saints.*)

The two men and four women each carried several large, thick-barreled weapons, slung over shoulders as well as cradled in their arms, all of them the heavy-duty laser rifles that the first dozen V'Dan soldiers had not brought down from the shuttlecraft. They had been left in the shuttle's weapons locker at the request of the local government, in the belief that Au'aurrran would be a safe, peaceful colonyworld to visit. These were the weapons that *would* pierce Salik armor, and do so much more reliably than their fading, exhausted psi.

At a few barked orders from Shi'uln, some of the priests hauled over chairs to form impromptu weapon stands and gunnery seats, spaced to create cross-fire cover from both sides of the broken opening. Other chairs scraped across the floor, dragged to watch the three doorways into the Church sanctuary. More bodies moved forward to help urge Jackie and Li'eth to their feet, to pull them out of the firing line and deeper into the sanctuary. The temperature difference felt good once they moved; the building's ventilation system struggled to compensate for the winter cold swirling in through the broken windows by blasting hot air down from ducts hidden beyond the galaxy-chandelier overhead.

"Sorry it took so long to get down here, sir," Lieutenant Shi'uln apologized to Li'eth, following the pair to a padded bench they could share. "We had a lot of debris in front of the stairway. We also armed some of the other pilots with the biggest hand blasters from the armory after making sure they knew what to do with 'em. I hope you don't mind. I had to make a command call when they begged for guns that could penetrate armor but didn't feel right about giving rifles to civilians."

"A good call," Li'eth agreed, nodding. He shivered a little, his holy fire no longer available to combat the freezing draft trying to compete with the ventilation heat. "Any word on the *V'Goro J'sta*, of it coming to the rescue?"

"Not for another hour, most likely. Comm officers said the

Terrans managed to get extra ships into the system, plus they launched every satellite they had to take out the three capital ships in orbit. One got through, but . . ." Shi'uln peered through the opening and off to the side. "I don't know how the fourth came down, but I'm glad to see it *is* down."

"Prophecy!" one of the nearby V'Dan priests asserted, his tone rather reverent, even awed. He lifted tanned arms scattered with burgundy crescents, his eyes wide with his revelations. "Holy Saint Wa'cuna foresaw not just holy Saints, but Great ones, a great Holy Pairing saving a major city on a most-valued world over twelve hundred years before—and I have *participated* in that very same Great Melding of these Great Ones here, casting fiery lances of holy wrath to bring down the Evilest of Evils on my homeworld . . . !"

". . . That's enough, Brother Mei'nar," one of his fellow priestesses asserted, pulling down on the arms he had lifted in supplication to the heavens with his enraptured speech. She gently but insistently tugged him away from Li'eth, Jackie, and the lieutenant with the pink crescents. "They're Living Saints, yes, and they saved us all, yes, but you don't need to dive headfirst into hyperbole."

Shi'uln quirked his brows in dubious amusement but let the woman guide her fellow V'Dan away. He glanced back at Li'eth. "I take it we missed something extraordinary while we were clearing out the stairwell access? Pity. At least from what we could see out the windows of the stairwell, it looks like most of the Salik are headed up to the cliffs to try to save their capital ship.

"From what I saw after it crashed," he continued, "I think they lost two, maybe three of the uppermost decks, crushed under its own weight. Which means the bridge will still be intact, and some hope of finding some of the officers alive and available for questioning. *If* they can get the Generals out alive."

Jackie, shifting a little closer to Li'eth to better share the robe still draped over their laps, quirked her brows. "Still intact? . . . Oh, right. That other ship, the bridge was *down*, not up. They're amphibious, they're used to diving for protection. We came from *monkeys* and *apes*, which liked to dwell up in the trees, so we think of climbing up for safety."

"If those Terran troops coming in can switch from preparing to settle themselves and their gear on this planet, to tackling the task of boarding an enemy ship that's been flipped upside down," the lieutenant said, glancing at the shattered great window again, "then we just might win this battle. If we do . . . you will probably finally be able to work that holy-mind thing on one of them. Read their minds to find out who their leader is, and what they know. They're rather resistant to the lesser interrogation techniques."

(*The Salik will strip off all signs of insignia when they're being captured, so that no one can tell who the leader was. Not without torturing it out of them,*) Li'eth informed her. He felt her flinch and shook his head. (*We don't trust confessions by torture, either . . . but* you *could go into their minds even better than our best alien mind-walkers. If we* can *pick out the leadership from the rest . . . maybe it's not ethical to just take their thoughts and memories from their heads, but it* would *save a lot of lives, if even just one of them knows their entire set of preplanned attacks. They* have *to plan everything weeks and months in advance because it just takes that long to get anyone anywhere.*)

She had wrinkled her nose more and more in distaste at what he was suggesting, until even her lip curled up in disgust. (*I want to protest, but . . . If it ends the war much more quickly, it will save millions of lives. It's not a pleasant burden to take upon my soul.*)

(*I'll do what I can to help,*) her partner promised, hugging her close. (*Just . . . after we've both had a chance to recover. My brain still aches like it was bruised.*)

(*It was. We're both perilously close to burnout,*) she warned him. (*So we shouldn't even talk telepathically . . . except we're Gestalt partners.*)

(*Thank the . . . thank the Saints for that,*) he murmured, resting his cheek on her curly hair. (*I almost said "Thank the Immortal," except I don't know what happened to her.*)

(*You don't doubt she's alive?*) Jackie asked.

(*I have no doubt she survived. The prophecies say she'll be there at the Second Reformation, in five hundred more years. A hundred years* after *her own birth, in an era she has not yet lived.*)

(*Huh . . .*) At his pulsed curiosity, she explained. (*I wonder if that terrifies her, going into a future she doesn't know anything about, not having learned of it in history lessons preparing her to actually live through it.*)

(*Probably. She struck me as fairly normal, despite being immortal.*)

She nodded, nuzzling his cheek with the move. (*Rest now, while we can. We may still have to fight.*)

Reluctantly forced to agree, Li'eth closed his eyes and let the nonstunned members of their security escort handle the watch for another fight. Buraq . . . was badly injured. Paea as well. Either might live, or either might die, depending on how soon they could be rescued. Those Terran soldiers landing somewhere out there had been picked because they understood how to work in harsh winter climates. Had been meant to replace the Solarican and V'Dan ground forces on this world, freeing them up to be shipped elsewhere in the Alliance.

So let them *fight, tonight.*

OCTOBER 23, 2287 C.E.
JUNA 14, 9508 V.D.S.
TANNSNALL, AU'AURRRAN

Jackie had never seen a coffle line outside of a history book. But here they stood, hundreds of Salik prisoners with their backwards knees, backwards flipper-feet, froggish heads, all of them coffled together. Heavy manacles weighted down each ankle analog on the aliens, and their odd tentacle-hands had been forced into weighted-metal spheres.

Coffles back during the darker days of Earth's past had included neck collars, but the Salik didn't really have much of a neck; instead, their eyes sat on finger-length stumps that swiveled. Still, leg and arm chains connected the members of each row to each other, forcing them to shuffle awkwardly along at a slow pace. Those that already stood in place flexed their thighs, their long, webbed toes, and muttered among themselves in quiet whistles and burbles.

Elsewhere on the planet, fighting still reigned. Pockets of

Salik fighters struggled to overcome resistance, heavily armored compared to the civilians, able to knock out dozens at a time with their stun weapons, but the real victory had come at the hands of the Terrans. Someone in the 3rd Cordon Special Forces—also known as Research & Development—had managed to crack the codes used by Salik programmers and cobbled together "code bombs" that short-circuited the enemy's mechanized armor. A different sort of freezing than the disturbingly effective version Li'eth and she had used two days ago.

Now they had hundreds of prisoners whom the Solaricans and V'Dan believed were high in rank. Potentially very high, given the size of those capital ships. Gathered in an underground gymnasium under the watchful eyes of Solaricans armed with Salik-inspired stunners of their own, they waited for the last of the coffled prisoners to take their place on the lines taped on the polished floor.

"Grrrand High Ambassadorr," Naguarr, the Solarican War Prince of Au'aurrran, murmured. He flicked his bluish-gray ears as he did so. An emerald on a platinum chain swung and glittered for a few moments in the overhead lighting, briefly distracting Jackie.

Those ears boasted several ornate earrings, some of them connected to each other by chains. Li'eth had told her and her fellow Terrans before leaving Terran quarantine way back on the *MacArthur* that such adornments were actually rank insignia for both military and civilian matters. Meeting the Solaricans, he said, had changed V'Dan jewelry fashions as a result, banning certain combinations of metals and shapes and gemstones so as to prevent confusion among their felinoid allies. Apparently non-Solaricans could earn similar ranks through meritorious service to their empire, which was why most V'Dan didn't wear earrings anymore.

"The prrrisonners are rready for yourr review," he urged her.

Dragging in a breath, Jackie eyed the rows of aliens. With so many in the hall, they brought with them a sort of murky scent reminiscent of damp straw and lake mud. Not unpleasant, but not what she had expected to smell. Li'eth touched her arm, giving her silent support. Darian touched her other arm, unharmed by being stunned the other day, though a few shards of stone from the shattered column that had injured Buraq had left scratches on his face.

(*You take the twenty on the left, I'll take the twenty on the right,*) she directed her fellow Terran. Li'eth, still psychically sore from his efforts, would be their backup, trained enough by now to pull their minds out if the enemies' thoughts tried to get them lost from too much chaos, too much immersion.

(*On it,*) Darian agreed. (*And cross-check if we think we have a possibility.*)

(*Of course.*)

Focusing her mind, she stared at the prisoner on the far right of the front line. Cold, murky thoughts, alien thoughts with undercurrents and subtexts she didn't understand. Things she wouldn't understand unless and until she did a language transfer. That, however, would take far longer than a few mere hours. Fully sentient alien minds—as she had discovered in transferring Solarican in exchange for Terranglo, and so forth—took anywhere from four to eight hours the very first time. That, unfortunately, was with a willing mind.

Thankfully, all the aliens they had met so far shared similar visual perceptions. Colors were skewed, but a picture of a sphere still came across as a picture of a sphere. Both Terran psis had been briefed in advance with images of Salik insignia, of what bridges and officer quarters looked like. So both skimmed through the thoughts of each alien, looking for memories of seeing lots of bridge workstations, of seeing lots of high-ranking insignia on those around them, on seeing and interacting with lots of officers.

Raising his voice even as they started their scans, Li'eth called out, "We are looking for the security codes for the bridge on your ship! Any prisoner who volunteers that information will be given special compensations. We are looking for bridge officers . . . but we will give the compensations to anyone who can give us what we need. I repeat, we are looking for the security-code authorizations for all bridge systems: communications codes, engineering codes, life-support codes, weaponry codes . . ."

He paced his words, speaking slowly and clearly as well as loudly, so that any of the aliens who spoke V'Dan, the official Alliance Trade Tongue, would be lured into thinking about those codes. Lured into thinking about the conditions in which those codes would be used . . . and the appearances, the identities, of those who *used* such codes. He kept up a steady stream of requests, mentioning ranks, mentioning command structures, mentioning communications officers.

It took the other two until the fifth row out of twenty before Darian and Jackie cross-confirmed four prisoners as crew members who knew bridge officers, and one who might *be* a bridge officer. The seventh row held five more, and the eighth as well. Li'eth directed the soldiers to separate out those rows, to have all forty prisoners in each row shuffle off to the side to wait for further winnowing.

It took over an hour to get all the way to the twentieth row at the back. By silent, mutual consent, the two Terrans returned their attentions to the foremost rows and rechecked every alien brain. By now, they were both much more familiar with sorting through Salik thought-images, and thus faster and more accurate. That took another half hour. Li'eth, gauging their process, requested War Prince Naguarr to dismiss the thirteen rows that weren't soldiers who had a lot of daily contact with their highest-ranked officers, or those highest-ranked officers.

That still left them nearly three hundred prisoners to sift through. Line by coffle line, they were examined silently, stealthily, while Li'eth again spoke slowly and clearly. This time, he attempted to get the remaining Salik to give up the identities of their highest-ranked prisoners.

Confusion and curiosity hampered some of their efforts, since the Salik were not sure of the seemingly random sorting process. Arrogance aided some of it, for the pair of xenopaths were getting rather good at picking out which aliens' thought-images were smug in the belief that they would never buckle under the interrogation efforts of prey species. However, that arrogance eroded and gave way more and more to confusion. At a murmur from Li'eth, monitoring Jackie's and Darian's minds, sometimes an entire coffle line of ten were dismissed. Other times, individual prisoners were picked out, unshackled, and hauled off to join similar sentients, while the others were hooked back together in shorter lines.

(*They're getting worried, I think,*) Darian sent to the other two. (*They're beginning to realize we* are *picking out their higher ranks. The emotions aren't Human, but I'm getting a feeling of "how can they successfully hunt us like this" instead of "they could never successfully hunt me" from several of them.*)

(*Confirmed,*) Jackie shared. (*I'm getting it, too . . . along with horrible images of what they want to do to us, the more accurate we get.*)

(*Wait . . . that one . . . it's not a bridge officer. I get the sense he's just a lowly tech,*) Darian stated. (*He's . . . if it were pack terms, he'd be the omega of all who are left in the hall. He might be, if not cooperative for a language transfer, then at least the least resistant.*)

(*Got it,*) Li'eth told them, and murmured to the War Prince to separate out the soldier, second from the left, of the current line of ten under consideration.

(*Ha!*) Jackie crowed a few moments later. (*They think we've made a mistake. The other separated ones* know *he's not high-ranked.*)

(*I think he's perking up a little, thinking he's been mistaken for a higher-ranked prisoner,*) Darian murmured.

(*Don't get sympathetic to them,*) Li'eth warned the two. (*Our best alien thought-readers among the Sh'nai have always claimed the deeper thoughts of the Salik are disturbing and distressing, even among the least of them.*)

(*I'm sure we can—*) Jackie started to dismiss.

(*—No, beloved, this has nothing to do with* our *skill. It has everything to do with* their *minds. If you learn their words for food like you learned ours, you will find yourself immersed in their thoughts and feelings while eating sentient beings alive.*)

Chastised, Jackie subdued her thoughts, her inner arrogance in her skills. (*. . . You are right. My apologies. I will not take that lightly.*)

He nodded, satisfied that she understood a little better. They worked through the remaining rows, dismissing other nobodies. A final run-through of the remaining sixty-plus reduced their numbers to just seventeen, including the omega-ranked prisoner. At that point, Li'eth gave the War Prince a final set of requests. Under the prodding of the guards, the seventeen were marched to a different part of the capital's underground military base, to be separated into individual cells, given nonsentient, nonliving food and water, and to await the leisure of the Terrans.

Darian and Jackie, debating under Li'eth's warning, chose to have a light meal and to wait an hour and a half for their early lunch to settle before calling for the least-ranked of the seventeen.

Interrogation rooms did not differ much from race to sentient race. That meant the room had nothing but a door, plain walls, floor, and ceiling, a silvered observation window, cameras for recording every angle, a table, and a few chairs. Since the Solaricans ran most of the military base, and since the V'Dan could share similar furnishings, their version of chairs predominated. Each had a supportive span for the upper-back area and a divot cut out at the backs of the seats for tails to slot comfortably through if the sitter did not want to curl that tail along their sides.

Salik physiology required reversing the chair, as their "buttocks" faced forward thanks to their thighs and knees angling backwards. The prisoner, clad in a loose beige uniform, shuffled into the room. The guards seated him in the backwards-facing chair with his leg shackles chained to the floor so that he could not leap up and pounce on anyone, nor use his powerful leg muscles to attack and try to get free.

Those yellow-irised eyes swiveled, looking around the room this way and that, independent of each other. They finally focused forward on Jackie, Li'eth, and Darian. He blinked, nictitating membranes sweeping over his largish corneas, and spoke. "Hhhew . . . Princssse? Imperriall Princsse? Hhew honor me. May I hhave your blood-organn?"

(*Easy,*) Jackie soothed her tight-faced partner. She spoke, snagging the alien's attention. "Per the Articles of War governing *Terran* use of *psychic* interrogation techniques, I do not have to ask a known enemy soldier permission to scan your uppermost thoughts. However . . . what I seek is not in your uppermost thoughts. The rules of being a *psychic* therefore require that I ask the following question: Will you agree to cooperate in teaching me your language?"

He blinked twice, eyes swiveling. Broad mouth opening, he

hesitated, then said, "Hhew wishh to learnnn Sssalhashh? Fromm me?"

"Yes. Do you agree to cooperate?" she asked.

He smacked his lips in an odd *pwok pwok pwok* sound that had Li'eth and the quartet of Solarican guards in the room stiffening, then bared his teeth in something that was definitely not a smile. Not with that many sharp, pointed, flesh-tearing incisors. "Yesss . . ."

(*He thinks this will take weeks and months, and waste our time with this pointless interrogation,*) Darian stated. (*To speed things up, I suggest we do this jointly, as if we were doing a teaching session on language transfer. But not actually teach anyone.*)

(*Li'eth, are you comfortable with Darian and I sharing thoughts that closely?*) Jackie asked her partner.

(*I am . . . and I appreciate the courtesy of your asking,*) he added.

(*A nonentangled Gestalt of two minds will be more intimate than one made up of many,*) she explained. (*It might upset you.*)

(*I think you'll find that what you're about to learn from the enemy will be more disturbing,*) he countered.

". . . Welll?" the Salik prisoner asked. "What wordss do hhew wish to lllearn firsst?"

Rising from their seats, Jackie and Darian each lifted those chairs and carried them down one side of the rectangular table. There, they set the chairs down, each one facing the backwards-sitting alien. Sharing a bracing look, they sat and linked one pair of hands behind the alien's head, merging shields and entwining minds.

Jackie, being the stronger and more experienced linguist, took the dominant position. Darian, being less likely to dive deeply into the alien's mind, took on the position of brakeman, ready to haul her back if things went wrong.

"I need you to think about your education days," Jackie stated, while the Salik looked at her, at the guards, and at Li'eth still seated at the far end of the table.

"Educasshtionn?" the Salik asked, eyestalks swiveling to stare at each of their faces.

"Yes. Think of a day when you were being schooled in how to add and subtract simple numbers," Jackie directed.

She felt him hesitate, then shrug and focus. Together, she and Darian touched their free hands to the alien's head, away from those sharp teeth. For a moment, they received feedback sensations of awful stick-flesh touching his cheeks, then Jackie forcefully pushed on the alien's mind, making him remember numbers, classroom, teaching, mathematics, twelve plus twelve equaling twenty-four, five minus three making two.

His mind bucked under theirs, trying to escape the compulsions to think, but together, they were stronger. Together, they chased down all words for numbers, for writing stylus, for computer and desk and chair, classmates. Learning from an alien mind, they had decided privately, was best done with concrete things that were relatable to every sentient species, and that started with an education in math, in the purest and least emotionally clouded of the sciences, the most easily relatable and translatable of subjects.

Abstract things like numbers and concrete things like physical objects were the easiest. Adjectives were a little awkward, because Salik eyes did not perceive colors and depths the same way as Human ones. Both psis shied away from exchanging tastes and flavors, from examining mealtimes too closely though they had to learn such things, had to know for being able to decode *prisoner* plans and manifests. Three times as the minutes stretched into hours, they both broke off to gag, swallow, breathe, and steel themselves to go back in again. To try to learn the Salik language and the Salik mind-set, so that they could pick out orders and translate them into V'Dan, or Terranglo, whatever it took.

The only advantages were that they had each other to lean upon. To band together their strength. To suffer alongside and thus bolster each other's flagging determination with silent, deep sympathy and horrified empathy. Salik did *not* think like Humans, deep down inside. Not normal ones. Darian had it easier than Jackie, however. He had served as a judicial psi before going into the military. He had touched the minds of sociopaths, even psychopaths . . . and this Salik definitely qualified.

Everyone was either a potential predator or potential prey.

There were plenty of alliances, but few actual friendships. Even their own kind could be viewed as someone to be eaten if given a chance. They had *rules* about such things, only allowed in certain circumstances, under certain conditions— on else they would never have evolved far enough to actually get the technologies needed to reach interstellar space—but ingrained in their psyches was the rather blunt, rather brutal *eat or be eaten, hunt or be hunted* that lay at the foundation of how they viewed life, the universe, and everything.

It was not a pleasant experience.

At the end of the hours-long interrogation, after at least three pauses to try to control the urge to vomit over some of the things the two learned, at the end of an increasingly grueling five hours of hard effort . . . it finally ended. They could not *speak* almost half of the language, but both Terrans *knew* Sallhash. Could listen to it, understand it, read it, write it . . . and thus translate it.

Darian tipped the alien's mind into sleep, parted his mind from Jackie's, and slumped back in his seat. Jackie could not relax. Grey minds were more *alien* than this Salik's mind had been, with far fewer reference points she could grasp. Particularly when it had been done in a hurry at a distance with a race whose mind screamed in pain the few times she had tried. But the Salik's mind . . .

Brutal.

An intercom snapped to life, bringing with it the voice of War Prince Naguarr. *"Is it donne? Orr are you illl againn?"*

"It is done," Jackie replied in Solarican. She *had* to do it in Solarican. The felinoid language had been far gentler to learn, and at the moment was *not* associated with all the subcontexts that had come across with Sallhash. Subcontexts that had been attached to her native Terranglo as her base reference point. *"We have the language, now."*

He switched to his native tongue. *"You said this llanguage trrransfer would teach the subject your tongue. Terrranglo. Does he knnow it nnow?"*

"He does," Jackie said, too tired, too mind-weary to think about her confirmation.

"Serrrgeant Parr Teing. Execute the prrrisoner."

A white-and-cream-furred Solarican soldier stepped forward, drew a pistol, and placed it against the top of the Salik's head, near the base of an eyestalk. Too late, her eyes snapped wide. The warrior pulled the trigger; a flare of light and smoke sizzled up from the prisoner's head. She yelped, hands clapping over her mouth in her shock, heart pounding. The stench of burned organics reached her nose, fat and meat and bone. Gagging, Jackie shoved out of her chair and moved quickly away, not wanting to look at the alien that had been slain in cold blood.

"You arrre a diplomat, Grrrand High Ambassadorr," the War Prince stated from the other side of the comm unit. *"You are genntle in naturrre. This is good. We need gentlenness to advannce as civilized beinngs. But the rrrisk of his escaping and teaching others this . . . code-talk of yourrrs is too high."*

"I know that!" she asserted in V'Dan, dropping her hands from her mouth and fisting them at her sides. "I *know* that. I *am* a soldier. But it is still one thing to kill in the heat of battle, in the immediate and *clear* need for self-defense. It is another thing entirely to *execute* someone!"

"This is my burrden, nnot yours," he reminded her, switching languages as well. *"You knnnow it is necessarrry."*

"I know. I don't like it, but I *do* know." Reluctantly, she forced herself away from the wall, to look back at the prisoner. At the body slumped in its chair. Darian had moved away as well, closer to the side with the charred, still-slightly-smoking hole in that lump of a skull. Trying not to breathe too deeply, Jackie firmed her mind once more, this time against a horror not created by an enemy race. "Darian and I will need to rest and sleep . . . if we can . . . before we will be able to interrogate the remaining sixteen."

"You have beenn invited to stay in ourr officerr suites," the War Prince stated through the intercom. *"Sergeant Naurren. Please show ourr guests everrry courtesy available."*

Nodding, one of the other three Solarican guards moved toward the door, opening it for the three Humans to exit. Grateful the War Prince had not picked the Salik's executioner to be their guide, Jackie left the interrogation room. The stench and the memories were not pleasant, and all she wanted was the sweet oblivion of sleep. If her mind would let her. Nightmares were a real possibility, while her brain tried to sort through everything it had just experienced.

CHAPTER 10

OCTOBER 24, 2287 C.E.
JUNA 15, 9508 V.D.S.

"*. . . And now that everyone is at their presumed thinnest and weakest in defensive coverage across all systems, the Salik are finally ready to invade in full force,*" Jackie translated, speaking in Terranglo. She had her eyes closed, couldn't see the interrogation room around her. A different room, physically, though it looked pretty much the same as the last save for the mirrored window being on the other side. "*Darian says Au'aurrran is part of a concerted effort to take over the Solarican worlds first. They want Solarican knowledge of other parts of the galaxy, other forms of technology, and are hoping that their—your—Queen will cut off this pocket of her empire, writing it off as a loss rather than attempt to regain control of it.*

"*It is acknowledged by the Salik High Command as a gamble since the Solaricans have unknown numbers of ships they could bring in from other colonial pockets. However, the Salik believe the* lack *of visits, the lack of sharing of other technologies with the local pocket of the known galaxy, is an indication that they are* weak *overall. That the Solaricans do not have enough resources to be shifted around.*

"*The Salik also know that the journey from colony to homeworld, just one way, is exceptionally long and difficult, exceptionally costly, and the Salik High Command therefore believes they will have enough time to find datafiles on nonlo-*

cal technologies and escape with advantages to combat the influx of oddities we Terrans have brought to the war. If they are attacked by extra Solarican forces, they will wage a war of attrition, allowing those colonies to be retaken but at such a cost that the Queen would be reluctant to add her remaining forces to the aid of the rest of the Alliance."

Jackie spoke in Terranglo to keep the Salik High General from understanding what Darian extracted from his mind. She also spoke in Terranglo because recordings of this session were being broadcast up to the *Embassy 1* in orbit, which had survived the other day's orbital invasion with minimal damage. No one wanted any of it broadcast in V'Dan, not even on the military channels, for fear of any Salik catching the signal and decoding it.

In the observation lounge to the right of the interrogation room, she knew Li'eth translated everything she said into V'Dan for the War Prince, the V'Dan General assigned to coordinate his people's forces with the Solarican government, and other observers. He spoke now into his side of the intercom, also using Terranglo. *"Do they know about Terran communications systems?"*

Jackie relayed that to Darian, who had tranced deeply to be able to read the High General's mind. They were taking turns going deep into the alien's memories, so that neither had to endure the ice-brutal thoughts of the high-ranked officer for ungodly long stretches.

(*. . . Yes. They know of it by now at the highest levels of command and are exceptionally frustrated that they cannot even approach one of the comm satellites without their ships' being damaged beyond repair, if not outright destroyed by the force of the blasts. They* want *our munitions technology with a hunger that is making me ill.*)

(*Five more minutes,*) she promised, checking the watch on her wrist unit. (*Then it'll be my turn to take over.*) Switching to speaking verbally, she relayed what he told her, adding in more as he picked them out of the High General's slimy, frustrated mind. Hearing Darian breathe in sharply, she asked, (*Does he know what we're doing to him?*)

(*I think he's beginning to get a clue,*) Darian stated. (*He certainly is frustrated that he's* thinking *about all of his people's plans. I'm having a harder time keeping him on topic. I should be able to get four more minutes though this may be my last round. You're the stronger xenopath by far.)*

(You're stronger at tolerating what you read,) she replied. *(We each have our strengths and weaknesses.)*

One of the Solaricans had politely cleaned up the floor-spattered mess of her weakness earlier. The ventilation system had kindly cleared the smell from the room half an hour ago.

"And you're sure the timetable schedule you listed is accurate?" Li'eth asked through the intercom. He could have communicated directly with her mind, but for politeness' sake chose to speak verbally, so that everyone knew which questions were being asked and how they were being asked, to give her and Darian's answers their full context.

She relayed that to Darian, too deep in the Salik's mind to hear anything physically.

(Pretty sure. And . . . yeah, he knows we're behind his thought somehow. He just tried to shift the schedule he memorized to try to cast doubt on it. He's fighting me hard, now. It's only a matter of time before he starts throwing offensive thoughts at me. Images of him eating sentients, gore and death on a hunt . . . or even just annoying advertising jingles,) Darian added, struggling to inject a touch of levity into their grim task.

Out loud, she said, *"We're quite sure the original information is correct . . . but the subject is now aware of our telepathic efforts. He is fighting the interrogation and trying to construct false thoughts."*

Silence reigned for a long moment before Li'eth spoke again. *"Are you willing to interrogate in equal depth a second, lesser-ranked subject? I cannot fault our allies for wanting confirmation of these timetables."*

Relaying that to Darian, Jackie consulted in subthoughts on each of their energy levels, then nodded. *". . . So long as it's more focused on timetables and such, we should have enough energy to complete that task. At least one more prisoner today, possibly two, and at least two tomorrow. These Salik . . . they have zero mental walls, zero capacity that I've seen to create a psychic shield. They cannot block us out, cannot force us to expend energy just to get at their minds, and don't seem to realize we are invading their thoughts and prodding their memories for the first hour or so. So long as they are kept isolated from each other, that is."*

". . . His Highness indicates his soldiers are working under pain of a full-body shaving if they so much as hint to any of the prisoners what is actually going on," Li'eth relayed, humor leavening his tone just a little. *"Apparently such a thing is maddeningly itchy when the fur starts growing back, and a very strong yet nondamaging punishment for any failure. He states the prisoners are not being housed even within shouting distance of each other."*

"That is a relief to hear," she acknowledged. *"Are we done with this prisoner?"*

". . . You said they think the various nations are sufficiently weak. Do they know about the V'Dan ships tied up with transporting Terran troops?"

She relayed that to the other xenopath. Gritting his mental teeth in disgust at having to continue one more time, Darian managed to prod out the truth on that question. (*. . . No. They honestly think the V'Dan are down three dozen of their biggest warships, probably taken out by Salik warships that just haven't reported back in yet. He believes it because the V'Dan have called upon their Alliance friends and merchant reserve vessels to fill in the gaps, and filled in the corners with 'those annoying silver sting-flyers' which are his mental-image-nickname for our OTL ships . . . though he now feels some doubt about that simply because I've made him think about it. If I weren't ethical, I could seriously turn him paranoid at this point.*)

(*Good thing you are, because we are both due for an ethics review this month.*) She relayed back to Li'eth the parts about the Salik ignorance of those missing warships.

Another pause, then, *"Thank you. And yes. War Prince Naguarr confirms we are done."*

(*Thank God,*) Darian muttered as soon as she relayed that, easing his way back out of the Salik's mind. (*I need to go bleach my brain now.*)

(*You and me both. We'll have another one to interrogate*

after a break, though.) Switching to V'Dan, she addressed the blinking, shuddering High General, released from her and Darian's mental control. "Thank you, High General, for your cooperation. Sergeants, we are finished with him. You may take the prisoner back to his holding cell now."

Rising, she and Darian moved themselves and their chairs away from the Salik, letting the Solarican soldiers handle the alien's heavy shackles and chains.

"The War Prince would like to know how much of a break you need," Li'eth relayed, still speaking in Terranglo.

"At least two hours," Darian replied, rubbing at his brow. *"And I will need a cold compress, and some of the special antimigraine tea we brought with us on the* Embassy *ships."*

"I remembered to pack a large tin in my personal bags," Jackie reassured him. *"We'll share a cup in the officers' lounge."*

"War Prince Naguarr wishes to commend both of you for your efforts," Li'eth added, still speaking Terranglo. *"He has ordered a feast in the V'Dan style for this evening . . . if your stomachs can handle it. Gentle foods, he promises, nothing too spicy and almost entirely vegetables, with some imported V'Dan fish for meat."*

Darian switched to Solarican, bowing toward the mirrored window with his hands pressed together, one inverted over the other with the fingertips curled together, in the formal Solarican style learned from their protocol lessons all the way back in quarantine many months before. *"Your Highness has more courtesy in your tail-tip than most people have in their whole leg. Thank you for those menu choices."*

He even managed to roll the Rs properly, using the back of his tongue rather than trilling with the tip.

"Your accent is delightful, meioa, for a non-Solarican," the War Prince stated through the intercom.

"It is one of our tasks as translators to speak as clearly as we can, if we can speak in that language," Darian demurred. *"I'd be just as careful in K'Kattan if I could."*

"They find this world a little too cold for their joints, but they will appreciate the courtesy of it on other worlds," Naguarr replied. *"Enjoy your meal, meioas."*

NOVEMBER 1, 2287 C.E.
JUNA 23, 9508 V.D.S.
SAFEST BREATH STATION
BEAUTIFUL-BLUE ORBIT, SUGAI SYSTEM

To reassure the colormood sensitivities of their hosts, Li'eth
wore his most formal uniform, shipped with V'kol specifically
for this occasion. Cloth of gold and cream predominated,
edged with the bare minimum of scarlet. It looked good with
his blond-and-burgundy hair braided back from his face, bar-
ing the lightning-jagged streaks of his *jungen* angling down
across his eye and cheek from his hairline.

This uniform did not bear the solid brass squares of a
Grand Captain, however; instead, the shoulders of the fitted
coat bore the golden swords with tiny crimson rubies of the
War Prince. It came with a matching coronet, mostly solid
gold—and thus heavy on his brow, though thankfully padded
along the inner edge for a modicum of comfort. Four rubies
sat along the ornate quillons of the swords forming each half
of the circlet, and a ruby half the size of his mother's formed
the conjoined pommel-nut at the center in front.

V'kol—now officially elevated to the rank of Captain Kos'q—
and three others representing the V'Dan military were clad in
cream versions of his cloth-of-gold uniform. All three V'Dan
bore frogging in gold across their fronts; two had the ornate
knotwork of Admirals of the Fleet, and the last wore the
plainer stripes and loops of a General of planet-bound troops.

(*I have no idea how Mother can bear the weight of her
version of this circlet,*) Li'eth complained silently, stifling a
sigh. (*I've only had this thing on for half an hour, and it's already threatening to give me a headache.*)

(*Use a tiny touch of telekinesis?*) Jackie suggested, reflexively checking the buttons of her Special Forces Dress Grays.
She looked over at her fellow Terrans, two of whom had been
shipped to Beautiful-Blue specifically for this meeting. The
newest of those two, Major Dewi Tang-Smith, stood near the
water dispenser provided for their comfort in her Army Dress
Greens, her formal hijab tucked under her uniform cap, chatting with the other two Terrans in the room: Admiral Nayak

in his Navy Dress Blues and Lieutenant Paea in Marine Corps Dress Browns respectively. They responded to her conversation quietly. Between the four of them, including Jackie, each officer represented one of the four Branches in color though both Jackie and Admiral Nayak had multiple colors striping their uniform sleeves and pant legs.

Their most formal uniforms, their Dress Blacks, would not be used while they were here as guests of the Gatsugi Collective. While the Terrans had the phrase "wearing your heart on your sleeve" to indicate blatant displays of emotional words and actions, the Gatsugi had the saying "wearing your heart on your hide," meaning that their emotions literally changed the color of their skin. Blues, greens, browns, and grays were reasonably acceptable colors.

Black, alas, was the color a Gatsugi's skin turned when they died. Black was the color for death. Perhaps another day they could wear their most formal uniforms, once the Gatsugi got used to the Terrans, but for now, it had been deemed culturally insensitive to wear black.

Admittedly, this was primarily a meeting of the heads of the various Alliance military forces more than their government leadership, but still, it would not do to be a figurehead of death among allies. Among *potential* allies, rather. The Terrans had managed to negotiate a number of treaties with the V'Dan, even winning a huge set of concessions from the Eternal Empress.

Unfortunately, while many *individuals* of the various other races and their governments were getting along mostly fine with Terran Humans, their governments officially did not yet consider the Terrans full members of this Alliance. They welcomed Terran assistance in their war efforts with open limbs, but seemed rather reluctant about ratifying the Terran charter. Ostensibly, this meeting was taking place on board the main military space station in orbit around the Gatsugi Motherworld so that they wouldn't have to slow everything down with a more formal greeting ceremony, the rituals for which could last up to two weeks down on the planet's surface. Then again, if they did that, they'd probably have to acknowledge the Terrans as a member nation.

Jackie knew instinctively that the Gatsugi and the rest of the Alliance were stalling on accepting the Terrans as a non-military, nonwartime power among them. One of Jackie's duties as the Ambassador while here would be to try to clear that up. She didn't know how to do that in the bare handful of days they would be here, but at least there were high-ranked government representatives in attendance as well as high-ranked military leaders.

(*I don't know why I'm fussing with my buttons,*) she sent, sighing in frustration. (*When I started all of this, nearly a year ago, I had put on pounds from civilian life. I couldn't breathe deeply in my original old uniform, before the new ones back then were issued. Now, I'm not only two dress sizes smaller, I'm almost a third size smaller. I'm burning through more calories psychically than I've been able to eat.*)

(*The only reason why this coat fits me at all is because it was tailored off the measurements taken just five days before my sister flung me off-world,*) he reminded her. (*And even then, it's starting to get loose. I blame the military food we've been eating. Between the relatively bland fare on board the* V'Goro *and your overseasoned zero-gravity food packs, it hasn't been the same as a real meal served up back home.*)

She started to reply, but the door to their waiting room opened, and the last member of the V'Dan delegation entered. Lifting her gaze to his face to identify him, Jackie offered a polite smile. "Grand General Ma'touk."

"Grand High Ambassador," he replied politely. They had started out a bit rocky with the *jungen* culture between them, but the V'Dan officer with the burgundy rosettes had success-fully adjusted his thinking early on and treated his markless allies with respect. And with courtesy, for he politely asked, "How is Lieutenant Commander Buraq faring? Were the doc-tors on the *V'Goro* able to successfully begin cloning her arm?"

"They already have the bones growing," Jackie admitted. "We'll see how it goes from there, whether or not her body will reject a V'Dan-grown version. She's on her second bionic arm in the meantime."

"Her second?" he asked, brows rising. He gave a nod to Admiral Nayak, who had drifted their way. "What was wrong with the first? . . . Admiral."

"Grand General," Nayak replied smoothly.

"Her first one had male ligature instead of female," Li'eth explained. "We've had a lot of meioa-es losing arms in the last few fights, so there weren't any appropriate spares. The wrong prosthetic ended up putting too much stress on the tissues of Buraq's shoulder and upper torso, so she's had to do without until late yesterday."

"Thankfully, the workshops on the *V'Goro* have retooled a spare so that it bends in the right way for her physiology," Jackie said. "We were told that subtle but wrongful stresses on the flesh as it heals can throw off a limb graft and wreck a patient's recovery."

"I have been lucky never to have lost a limb," Ma'touk murmured. "She has my sympathies, though."

"The Ambassador and I will pass them along," Admiral Nayak stated. "I was hoping to have a moment of your time after the meeting to discuss sending more V'Dan instructors to Earth to help train our soldiers for handling your style of spacecraft."

The door opened again before Ma'Touk could answer. A yellow-tufted Gatsugi soldier in a gray uniform beckoned them forward with his—her?—two left arms.

"Gentles/Meioas/Most Honored Guests," the alien stated. "Please/Please come with/accompany me. It is time/You are summoned/requested/required in/at the Stern Gray Battle Room/Planning Chamber."

Jackie gestured with one of her hands in a way that indicated her willingness to comply. He flushed blue in pleasure and replied with one of his three-fingered hands, thumb swirling in a gesture of gratitude. It amused her, linguistically. (*Their multiple layerings of meaning is awkward when spoken, but it does soothe them when we communicate gesturally as well as verbally.*)

(*You do realize I don't speak Gatsugi, right?*) Li'eth retorted. He adjusted his coronet one last time, following her out of the room.

(*You don't . . . ? Oh. Li'eth, I'm sorry; I apologize,*) she sent back. (*We live in the backs of each other's minds so much, unless we're actively walling each other out, I assumed you knew it, too.*)

(*You automatically wall me out when you're doing a language transfer,*) he told her. (*Completely. Which is actually fine because I don't know how to separate out personalities from information gathering to the extent that you do. I'd rather get the language from* you *after it's been properly filtered.*)

(*I'll schedule some days where I can give you Solarican, Tlassian, Gatsugi, and Choya,*) she promised. (*If you want K'Katta, you'll have to schedule it with Darian. I'm beginning to* like *them as individuals . . . but as a species, they still unnerve me. I got K'Katta secondhand from Aixa, but Darian can do it as well.*

(*. . . That is to say, I* still *have a problem with their appearance,*) Jackie explained herself firmly; he could still feel her unease, but her subthoughts swirled with determination to overcome it someday. (They *have nothing to do with* my *phobias. I will not blame them when the flaw is mine alone.*)

He clasped her hand, fingers lacing together with hers. (*That is one of the many reasons why I love you, your kindness and courtesy coupled to your willpower. I think you make me want to be a far better man than Imperial culture would ever encourage . . . and no being smug over your cultural "superiority."*)

(*Sorry. I do try to keep in mind your people have every right to be different.*)

(*I know. And mostly, you respect that, and that is deeply appreciated,*) he admitted. (*We are still new in many ways to each other, despite our link. We are still learning.*)

They didn't have to walk very far. Just as he finished sharing that, the four-armed alien gestured for them to enter a large room. Rather than a single table that would be shared, there were instead tables and seats for every oxygen-breathing, carbon-based life-form in the room, all arranged so that they faced each other and a dark-glazed window set in the wall.

Around the perimeter, Gatsugi soldiers stood, each clad in a sober gray uniform decorated with silver insignia. Each cluster of occupied tables held a delegation: the Gatsugi delegation, Solaricans, Tlassians, Choya, and the K'Katta. Barely visible through the smoky glass of the window, the Chinsoiy lounged on strange, slanted boards. The two curved tables that were *not* occupied had been pushed together, with seating for everyone crowded behind the pair.

Li'eth and Jackie both slowed at the odd sight, which meant the men and women following them also slowed. (*I think we have a problem,*) he sent to her. (*Each group should be separate, to indicate separate governments. For that matter, we technically should not have been left in the same room while we waited for everyone to arrive and assemble.*)

(*I thought it was a courtesy to our Gestalt, not separating us in the waiting area . . . but I do believe you are right.*) Switching to V'Dan, she stated aloud, "Captain Paea, please separate out one of those two tables for the Terran delegation."

(*Agreed,*) Li'eth confirmed. "Captain Kos'q, please assist him in separating a table for the V'Dan delegation."

Both males moved to do so, one muscular and tanned, his black hair short-cropped in the style of the Marines Space Force. The other, with his lighter skin streaked in hot-pink spirals, his light brown hair braided back from his face and shoulders. The tables scraped across the floor, and a flustered Gatsugi staff member hurried forward, all four arms fluttering in negation gestures.

"Please/Please/Please don't move/adjust the tables/seating. Keep/Keep them/the furnishings/groupings together/associated, meioas!" the blue-tufted alien protested. "Delegates/ Representatives must/need stay/remain together/together!"

(*I don't think so,*) Li'eth snorted mentally, aware of the undertones of pride in his statement. Out loud, he said, "We are separate/distinctly different governments, meioa. We will/ will/will sit apart."

"We are agreed/in concurrence," Jackie added, gesturing with both hands, one in a mix of polite if mild apology, the other in firm assertion. "We are most happy/blue when we are distinct/separate."

"This/You cannot/mustn't do that!" the Gatsugi fussed, hurrying forward to tug at each table, trying to haul them back together even as Simon and V'kol removed the innermost two chairs from the gap between. The alien flushed what had to be a frustrated muddy red. "V'Dan/Terran are/must be one/the same!"

Jackie and Li'eth glanced at each other, then looked at their highest-ranked officers to gauge their reactions. Grand General Ma'touk—one of the generals Jackie had met with frequently during her time on the V'Dan homeworld—cleared his throat, stepped forward, and *pulled* the V'Dan side table away from the Terran table with a loud, firm scrape. Admiral Nayak, barely missing a beat, moved forward and did the exact same just a moment behind him.

The Gatsugi turned a mottled brownish yellow, all four hands fluttering in distress signs, muttering and mumbling in some dialect Jackie did not know. On the bright side, the fuss over the tables was more annoying than her discomfort over the appearance of the K'Katta moving in the room.

One of the figures beyond the dark window stirred, and a voice came through the intercom. *"Energy waste equals adjusting tables. Needed is unity. Success requires unity. Why separating you do this?"*

A quick mental check between Li'eth and Jackie had him deferring the answer to her. He did so visually, releasing her fingers and gesturing toward her. Nodding, Jackie stepped up to the center of the right-hand table. Her lessons in the protocols for speaking to the Chinsoiy included the advice to keep her sentences short to avoid ambiguity. "We separate our two governments because we *are* separate, meioa. To push us together will not work. V'Dan are not Terrans. The Terrans are not the V'Dan. They do not speak for us. We do not speak for them. They do not control us. We do not control them. We are separate."

"You same species are. Unity is peace."

"If that were truth, meioa," Li'eth stated, "then the V'Dan Empire would rule everyone. Or the Solarican Empire would rule everyone. Or the Gatsugi Collective. But the Gatsugi do not rule over the V'Dan, and they do not rule over you. You do not rule over us, and you do not rule over the K'Katta."

"You same species are," the Chinsoiy insisted. *"Same species is unity."*

"No. It isn't," Jackie countered.

One of the K'Katta delegates, swathed in brown sashes a few shades lighter than his dark not-fur, chittered. His translator box went to work, using a pleasant neutral-male voice to recite his meaning in V'Dan. "I believe what Fearsome Leader Siirrlak is trying to explain is that when the Salik first reached into space, they *competed* themselves into space and attempted to solicit aid from the Alliance races to fight with them against each of their factions. Such behavior is appalling. We rightfully insisted that they settle their grievances with each other and unite under a single government system."

"I think it is fairrrlly obviousss the Ssallik willl always fight," one of the Tlassian delegates stated, the one with the reddest-scaled hide and a more practical, more uniform-like cut to his garments. "Ourr fllaw was inssisting they unite among themsellvesss. Thisss freed them to focus theirr innate aggrrressionss on the resst of usss insstead of each other."

"We/The Alliance cannot/cannot/cannot afford internecine/civil war/infighting among/with its selves/governments," one of the Gatsugi leaders asserted. The fussy gray-clad Gatsugi nodded—a common Human and Gatsugi gesture—and started dragging the tables back together again.

Li'eth lifted his hand and spread his fingers. The tables scraped apart under the force of his telekinesis, making the fussy alien skip back and blink his big black eyes at the furniture. "You assume, gentlemeioas, that the Terrans and the V'Dan *will* fight each other."

"You nearrrrly came to blows," a Solarican with sleek white fur and golden eyes pointed out. "Terrrrans cut off theirr communications offerrrings."

"That is not the same thing as actually fighting, meioas," Jackie replied. The fussy Gatsugi moved as if to try to drag the tables together again. She quickly twisted, sliding her hip onto the table, then hitched herself up onto it, swung around to face the others, and crossed her legs. Claiming the table's territory in such a way that it would be a physical affront to try to move it.

(*You insist upon making me wrinkle the dignity of the Empire, don't you?*) Li'eth muttered, though his underthoughts swirled with humor. Just a beat or two behind her—like Nayak had been behind Ma'touk—he did the same thing, hitching up onto the table, swiveling around, and folding his legs in the same crossed way as her. (*Cloth of gold* does *wrinkle, you know.*)

(*Telekinesis,*) she retorted helpfully. The Gatsugi flushed uncertain tangerine and retreated. It was one thing to fuss over inanimate objects; it was another, protocol-wise, to literally try to move two high-ranking dignitaries. She wanted to seize on that but wasn't sure how. (*I think they need an analogy to explain why we cannot be lumped together. You got anything?*)

(*I think so. Something I heard some of my fellow officers discussing when I was on a ship prior to the* G'Deth.) Out loud, he stated, "Allow me to explain to you in a metaphor what you are asking. You are trying to demand that an engineer who builds structures, an architect, build instead a ground vehicle. It is possible for them to make something that will work, but it will not work well and will not necessarily be safe, effective, or efficient.

"At the same time, meioas, you are asking an engineer who builds ground vehicles to create a building. They might be able to make one, but it will not be truly functional, it will not be truly strong and stable, and like the ground car, will probably wind up missing many important features. Yes, our two nations are the same species, they are both engineers, but the *kinds* of things we do are two separate things."

"We acknowledge this without rancor or animosity. We do not hate each other's differences. We are *not* the Salik—and I say this after having walked in the minds of twelve of them," Jackie added firmly. "We do not *need* something to hunt in our lives. We are not the Salik, and we *can* get along as structural engineers and vehicular engineers, without having to build the exact same objects. Let the V'Dan build their temples and palaces and bridges. They are good at what they do. Do not demand them to build metaphorical starships when that is not their specialty."

"Let the Terrans build their small but fast starships and communications networks," Li'eth agreed firmly. "Do not demand that they stop building such things just because you think they should instead design and erect domes for colonizing airless planets. That is not their specialization."

"It would make as much sense as demanding the K'Katta,

who in this metaphor could be the masters of agriculture, to give up farming foods and start erecting buildings instead," Admiral Nayak stated.

"Or to ask the Chinsoiy to spin and weave clothing for the Tlassians, when they do not have much in the way of clothing needs," Grand General Ma'touk agreed. "We may be the same species, but we are not the same people . . . and as much as I had to learn how to respect the Terrans as mature people, I have always respected them as a separate government."

"We have no desire to actively fight each other," Li'eth told the others.

"We have no desire to fight *anyone* if we do not have to," Jackie agreed. "But that is no different than the K'Katta not wishing to fight anyone else. Fighting is counterproductive."

The K'Katta delegate from before chittered again, his words chiding. "Yet you, Grand High Ambassador, threatened to go to war with the V'Dan when you closed your embassy among them."

"*Did* they go to war with V'Dan?" Li'eth asked pointedly before Jackie could answer. "*Did* they attack my people, Commander-of-Millions Tlik-tlak?"

"No, but they still threatened to do so," the alien pointed out, gesturing with a dark-furred limb.

"We admit we are not as gentle as the K'Katta race," Jackie stated, looking at the other races so she wouldn't flinch in looking at the K'Katta when he moved his multijointed limbs. "But that does not make us the same as the Salik. My statement was a warning of a defensive reaction to an inappropriate action. It was a warning against the former Imperial Heir acting rashly, without careful advance thought. We did not at any time go to war . . . because the V'Dan did not act rashly and without careful forethought once they received that warning."

"*Unity for Alliance membership is required,*" the Chinsoiy Fearsome Leader stated. "*One species, one government.*"

"Why?" Jackie asked, gesturing at the figure beyond the extrathick, radiation-dampening window. She twisted to look at the other tables, the Solaricans and Tlassians to her left, the Choya and K'Katta to her right. "Why *must* we become one government, when *your* governments do not have to become one with each other? There is no one government ruling over the K'Katta and the Choya and the V'Dan and the Solaricans and the Tlassians *and* the Chinsoiy—and jointly settled colonyworlds do not count for this discussion."

"Unity isss . . ." one of the other Tlassians began, before faltering. The sides of her green-scaled neck flexed outward, broadening for a moment by a thumbwidth at most. The red-scaled Tlassian who had spoken first briefly bared his teeth at her, and she subsided quickly, thinning the width of her neck.

A beige female among the K'Katta spoke up, her translator box putting inflections behind her words. "We must discuss the jointly settled colonyworlds because they are not jointly *held*. One government rules them. You recently came from Au'aurrran with the information we will soon discuss," she pointed out. "It is ruled by the Solaricans. They agree by the rules of the Alliance that they will allow certain physiological differences to be acknowledged and accommodated, and that within pocket communities, familiar laws may be upheld, but only among their own kind inherently.

"Any interactions with any other race fall under the parental government in charge of that world, in this case the V'Dan bowing to the laws of the Solaricans, even if they're just trading with our kind, the K'Katta, and not with the Solaricans. On Au'aurrran, Solarican laws rule," she stated, her chittering ending a few moments before her translator box finished speaking.

"Guardian-of-Millllionss is correct," the green-scaled Tlassian female stated, pushing her scaled version of a hand out toward the K'Katta. "She ssspeaksss with a clarrrity I could not sssummon. Thisss unity musst be observed, so that all are given the sssame laws for theirr kind."

Li'eth, sensing Jackie's confusion, offered, "I believe the meioa is discussing uniformity in those physiological allowances, and with it, entangled cultural allowances."

"Yess, but nothinng sso dry," the Tlassian female agreed, and looked briefly at her companions. "Our people arrre three within one. Mannny workerrss, some warriorss, a few priesssts, yet we arre one, clossser than you two are."

"Thisss great split between you iss . . . uncommfortable," the red-hided male stated.

"Yes/Yes/Yes!" the fussy Gatsugi with the blue not-hair agreed, flushing bright green in what had to be a touch of excitement with patches of blue pleasure. "The rift/gap/discord must/needs to be patched/united/healed! Please/Kindly unseat/descend from the surface/table. The tables/desks will/need to be pushed/returned together/unified! You/Your species must/needs to be unified for clarity/communication/peace!"

"If you ffffight, it could tearrr the Alliance aparrt," the Solarican with the white fur stated. She lifted her half-furred hand, palm turned toward herself in a V'Dan style of gesture. "We will nnnot tolerrate a ssecond aggrrressive race."

"I agree, you shouldn't have to suffer that," Jackie agreed. "But I am still not convinced either nation should abandon our thousands of years of history, our governments, and be forced to join with the other, nor be forced both to abandon our different ways of life to try to form a third version. My father's father had a saying, and that saying is, if it is not broken, do not try to fix it. The prince's system works fine for his people. My people's system works fine for us."

"Neither nation is broken, so there is no need to join them together," Li'eth agreed. "There is nothing broken that needs to be fixed."

"Our concerns are justified!" the dark-furred K'Katta insisted, curling two forelegs into his thorax-analog and thumping it as he chitter-whistled. "You get along *now*, yes, but there is no guarantee you will get along five years from now! Or fifty, or five *hundred*."

Li'eth raised his hand, palm toward himself. "Actually, we *know* what happens five hundred years from now, thanks to the words of the Immortal."

"Immortal is a prophecy-glider," one of the other Chinsoiy inside their contained preferred environment stated. They moved up to the window and pressed the leading edges of their extra-long outer fingers against it. *"Turbulent the airs of futures promised."*

"These prophecies have been accurate so far," Li'eth stated, gesturing toward Jackie. "I would not be alive if it weren't for those prophecies the Immortal brought through time, *and* the far-flying minds of the Ambassador's people. *She* would not have been in a position to rescue my surviving crew as well as her own if it weren't for such things.

"More than that, meioas, the Immortal predicted across *millennia* not only the existence of two Human Empires, but of a *third* Human Empire arising four or five hundred years from now. And in *all* of those prophecies, not a single war between any of the three nations has been predicted. Not one."

Jackie saw the doubt on the few faces she could read among the other races—mostly the Gatsugi—and noticed it in their auras. "Would you like an addendum clause appended to our joint nonaggression treaty?" she asked dryly. "Perhaps a double-indemnity clause of *both* governments having to pay high-fee penalties to every other government if we go to war with each other?"

"You sssay," one of the until-now-silent Choya delegates stated, two of her three crests rising a little, the other one flattening, "that you do nnnot wish to lose autonomy. How will you rrrule coloniess you both sssettle?"

"We're still working on that," Li'eth stated dryly. "For now, Terran soldiers understand that they are to be ruled under Terran military law, with the understanding that if they break any V'Dan civilian laws, it will be judged on a case-by-case basis, starting with a comparison to similar Terran laws, and ending with a double indemnity of suffering both civilian and military penalties. These rulings do not, however, include Terran civilians as at this point in time, the only Terrans who are not in the military are members of the Terran embassy and are protected instead by the common-held Alliance laws for such things."

"The most recent round of talks have included enclave laws similar to what the other representatives have described here," Jackie added. "We have also considered joint responsibility for supplies, medical services, military protection, and so forth, and options for declaring dual or single citizenship. Such negotiations take time, however. In the meantime, we do have a war to fight, gentlebeings. I would like to move on to that part of this meeting, rather than wasting time arguing over something—several somethings—that are not going to happen, and do not *need* to happen here and now, even if they could. Let us not waste our energy on a discussion that *can* be deferred to another time."

"V'Dan is certainly not going to submit themselves to Terran governance," Li'eth stated in agreement, uncurling his legs and slipping off the table. He tugged at his cloth-of-gold garments to straighten the heavy fabric. "Terrans are not going to swear loyalty to the Eternal Empress and start tattooing their faces with artificial *jungen* marks. Knowing what I know of both nations, from where I stand, the view I have, the only reason why we *would* go to war is if outsiders tried to use force to shove our two nations into becoming one entity, against our will."

Dismounting as well, Jackie dusted off her own wrinkles. "I suspect, Your Highness, if that were the case, my government *would* unite with yours . . . *just* long enough for us to mutually pound the idiocy out of anyone who thought that would be a good idea."

"I would have to concur, Grand High Ambassador. I am quite certain Her Eternity would willingly direct the Imperial Army to join forces with your Space Force in teaching any such aggressors an appropriate lesson," he agreed, clasping his hands lightly in front of him since he was done with fussing over his own uniform.

A strange, undulating whistle escaped one of the K'Katta who had not spoken, a smallish dark-furred male draped in red-and-purple sashes. It emerged from the modest machine he carried as a warm, open laugh, before he said something actually translatable into V'Dan. ". . . It is strange, but I find myself *reassured* by that assertion, meioas. You are like nestmates. Siblings. You each have your own life to lead, your own direction to take, and refuse to be forced to climb the other's exact path.

"You each claim a distinct and separate tree . . . but when your forest is threatened, you will defend each other firmly against all out-dwellers. A very nestmated thing. I shall accept your assertions as fact," the arthropoid stated, his translated tone warm with amusement.

"President Marbleheart, that is insufficient data for reaching that conclusion," the Commander-of-Millions, the other male, countered in a chittering, not-quite-scold. His civilian superior apparently had one of those names too difficult for a non-K'Katta to pronounce, so the underlying meaning of their leader's name had been translated and used. "Is it wise to base policy decisions on such things?"

"V'Dan minds are similar to our minds, Commander-of-Millions Tlik-tlak," the K'Katta leader stated, raising a foreleg as he made his point. "Independence for the individual, coupled with unity among kin when faced with an external danger, is a trait our own people shared before developing the writing skills to describe and record it."

"Innn other worrrds, you trrust them because you know it is sssomething you woulld do, with your simmmilar minds?" the white-furred Solarican asked. "That is nnot a trait restricted to your ownn kinds."

"It isss endemic to a wide variety of sspecies," the Tlassian red-scale stated. "We are nnnot entirely convinced of these assurances, but . . . we arrre willling to delay that dissscussion for llater."

"Thank you, meioa. Are there any other objections that *must* be discussed right now?" Li'eth asked the group. "Or can we begin discussing the real reason we have gathered here? The time schedule of Salik attacks over the next few weeks gives us a narrow window of opportunity for hunting them, before they realize what we know and drastically change their battle plans."

". . . *Are* there any objections on the subject of the V'Dan and Terran Empires remaining separate?" Jackie repeated after a few seconds of no one speaking. "No more? Then I thank you for expressing your concern. Please accept our reassurances that at this time, they are not necessary. I, for one, am ready to sit down and begin the real work of the day," she continued, seating herself at the center of her curved bit of table. Her fellow Terrans followed suit. "Do you have any further concerns on the subject of our separate sovereignties, Your Highness?"

"We see no need to say anything more on that subject at this time," Li'eth stated, taking the center seat at his own table. His delegation seated themselves around him while he looked to the leader of the whole Gatsugi Collective, President Anoddra Light-Hopes-Many-Shadows. "President Anoddra, you have our apologies for the disruption of your people's schedule for these events. Please, begin this meeting whenever you are ready."

As the War Prince, he tried to look unruffled by the Alliance's assumptions and assertions, though his subthoughts tangled around Jackie's in a mix of indignation, assertion, amusement, arrogance, and just plain relief they weren't going to have to fight any further through the idea of "Human Unity" just to get some *real* war work done today. She agreed on many levels, but using the patience of a lifelong civil servant, resigned herself to waiting until they did get to the heart of the reasons they were here.

The introductions, as usual when done in the Gatsugi style, took about three times as long as they would have taken when performed by any of the other races. With the general location of Terran space now known by the various leaderships, that meant the Collective was still close to the center of known space, and made them the default hosts. They knew that the other races would speak plainly and bluntly by comparison and could tolerate it for expediency's sake but preferred "true" communicative elegance for those portions of the meeting that showcased their hospitality.

(*I think he's drawing to an end,*) Li'eth warned Jackie after a while. (*You're up next.*)

(*I know. Once you get used to the speech patterns, and the way they look at the universe, they use rhythms similar to those of many statesmen back home.*)

". . . will/shall now/at this time explain/expand/expound upon their findings/revelations/information. Meioa Ambassador, please/kindly speak/enlighten us."

"Thank you, Meioa President," Jackie replied. "As you will remember from the briefings we sent, transmitted in Terranglo to your hierarchy's assigned code-talkers, Darian Johnston and I used our alien-oriented thought-sensing abilities to learn the language Sallhash. This has come at a cost of many nightmares and sleepless nights," she added, "but we have managed to use that familiarity with their language to prod out of the minds of several captured high-ranking officers the scheduled plans of attack for the next few months.

"This information took days to confirm, and has to our

deep regret cost the fall of the Tlassian colony of Glau, which happened just two days ago," she admitted grimly. "Glau was too far away from any significantly sized Alliance force to thwart the Salik full invasion fleet . . . but had we acted instantly, there was a chance a modest fleet could have been sent in time to reduce the full brunt of their forces landing upon and ravaging Glau.

"My government expresses our grief, regrets, and condolences, War Leader, and I carry to you the personal assurance of the Council that the Terran Space Force *will* retake that world at your side, to rescue those who may yet survive and avenge those who did not."

"We werrre apprised quickly enough," Warlord Tennssach stated. His neck-hood twitched a little, but only by a tiny bit. "It wasss our descisionn not to pursue a ffight immediately after they lllannded. It is our shame that our choicess for strrategy enndangerred our people. Sometimes, prrey must falll, to put the predator off their guarrd. The guilt is sshared."

Admiral Daksha Nayak, next to her, activated his V'Dan datapad. The information appeared on the monitors embedded in every table, and along each of the walls, a map in the Alliance style, showing colored blobs in a slowly rotating two-dimensional image that conveyed three dimensions without straining the eyesight of some of the member species. "All along, the Salik have been waging a war of attrition. They have been whittling away at every system with random strikes designed to take out as many of your ships as possible, in order to leave your worlds pared down to the minimal defenses against certain sizes of fleets.

"Our analyses indicate that each world is now exceptionally vulnerable to a hard, heavy push. Before we Terrans came along, it was a brilliant setup," Nayak continued, his face pale under its natural tan, his expression grim. "And even *with* our help, only the motherworld systems will be able to hold off an armada the size of the force we faced at Au'aurrran at this point. In order to defend each system slated for attack, we will have to strip away the ships in orbit, leaving *other* worlds defenseless."

World names started flaring on the images, along with

Alliance Standard dates on when each indicated colonyworld would be captured.

"Chronologically," Jackie pointed out, "even if we do start moving around fleets like that, they *are* going to be able to hit two, maybe three more worlds, taking them over before we can assemble a large enough task force to take out their main fleets. And I do mean fleets, plural. Even with the invasion of Au'aurrran thwarted, they still have six more major groups.

"Without our communications technology—and I do not say this as a threat," she quickly cautioned, "just a statement of how things stood before we came into the war—the Salik will be picking off your planets one at a time."

"The expression you want is 'gathering up,'" Li'eth corrected, automatically sliding into the habit of being her cultural liaison. "Not 'picking off.'"

"Thank you, Your Highness," she replied smoothly. "They will gather up your worlds one at a time. But those six fleets are not the only concern."

"They arrre not?" Warlord Tennssach asked, chin lifting up a little in surprise.

"What new problems await us, in your estimation?" the K'Katta Commander-of-Millions asked.

"Right now, this very moment, we have an advantage of knowledge," Admiral Nayak stated, gesturing at the screens. "But this opportunity only works for a few weeks, maybe a V'Dan month at most. As soon as word gets back to the Salik that their schedule has been compromised, they will change how they operate. We do still have that communications lag on our side, but eventually, they will change everything.

"We *must* take advantage of this gap in their communications ability," he emphasized, thumping the white tabletop with a tanned finger. "I can imagine that most of you are looking at that schedule and thinking defensively, reactively, about how to stop that incoming fleet. But we must *also* take the fight *to* the Salik. To act offensively, actively engaging them where they least expect it."

"Do you have a plannn?" the white-furred Solarican, War Princess Pallan, asked. She blinked her golden eyes, tilting her head, earrings and chains swinging a little. "If you have a plann, sharrre, please."

Jackie exchanged a brief look with Nayak, who tipped his head slightly, silently deferring the responsibility to her. Drawing in a breath, she let it out. ". . . As we Terrans are a sovereign and separate nation, we have chosen to act independently in advance of this meeting. The timing of everything demanded it. Every ship we can spare has been recalled to Earth. Those who get there first will load their cargo bays with hydrobombs and communications satellites, and deliver them to supply depots.

"Every ship that can get to those depots will load those bombs to maximum capacity as soon as they can. This part of the plan is already in motion," she explained. "We have two more days before *where* we take those bombs becomes critical. We have two possibilities in mind on where they could go."

Li'eth spoke on the heels of her words, adding smoothly, "By my right as War Prince of the Empire, I have commandeered several vessels, both civilian and of the Imperial Fleet, for similar transporting needs. We will be able to transport thousands of these bombs within the week, either directly or in relays of ships. But again, we need to know where to take them."

"The question, meioas," Admiral Nayak stated bluntly, "is do we seed the orbits of the worlds that are going to be invaded in the next few weeks, and take the fleets that we can to those worlds that are entirely Salik? Or do we send our fleets after their ships . . . and seed the Salik colonies with our hydrobomb technology?

"As an Admiral of the Space Force, my preference would be to send fleets after fleets for the sheer mobility permitted. Those bombs, once placed, will not be able to give chase as a ship could, and can be detonated and destroyed at a distance. I would rather drop our bombs onto Salik colonyworlds in a series of increasingly destructive but swift attacks that will destroy their infrastructure, their ability to support their current fleets, their current war machinery, and remove their ability to create even more."

All five K'Katta chittered, in a sound that had no translation for a few seconds, then their leader click-whistled, and the others fell silent. "What you are suggesting," his translator box stated, "sounds like xenocide. Our people will fight the guardians of the enemy when they make an attack, but we will *not* permit the slaughter of their civilians!"

Two things happened simultaneously; the neck-hood of the Tlassian warlord snapped wide, and the Solarican War Princess hissed. Both bared their teeth, and *not* in anything resembling a friendly Human smile.

Before either could speak, Li'eth spoke, his voice snapping cold and hard. "*Tell that* to the citizens of Au'aurrran and Glau!"

"Gentlebeings! What I *believe* we are trying to say," Jackie offered with a tiny bit more diplomacy, her voice cutting off the rising protests, "is that the Salik do not distinguish between civilian and military targets. Not only for their targets, but for *themselves*. From what I have learned, having searched the minds of dozens of their kind . . . they do not *have* civilians. Their leadership consider *every* Salik citizen a member of their military structure. Even the females who are raising their children are considered to be training future soldiers.

"They know that the fighting on land will be harder than the fighting in the skies, they *expect* to have to fight soldier to soldier, citizen to citizen, on the ground, and they are prepared to spend *decades* subduing your worlds once they have destroyed *your* infrastructure and *your* ability to travel from world to world."

"You do not *know* that all of their citizens are actively supporting their government!" the Commander-of-Millions retorted, gesturing with two forelegs in his agitation. "You cannot crater whole cities!"

"Our *plan*, gentlebeings," Admiral Nayak asserted, his hard tone cutting through the rising chitterings of the upset aliens, "is to target their *military* infrastructure first. Primary targets will be industrial complexes that cater to the needs of their military and their transport systems. Spacedocks and shipyards, fueling depots, supply depots, munitions caches and manufactories, and spaceports that cater in the main to military vessels.

"When they try to retreat from the Alliance fleets to get

their repairs, when the people back home try to build new ships to replace those lost, they will have *nothing* to fall back upon," he asserted. "Let *them* be pushed to the brink of collapse, as they are pushing *you*."

"I will remind you that this is just what we can do with the Terran and V'Dan fleets," Jackie stated in the contemplated quiet following his words. "When we realized the only mass munitions your people have on a scale compatible to ours were based on the old radioactive fission bombs, we increased our military and communication productions dramatically. If we can arrange for more vessels to pick up our equipment and the Terran technicians to handle them, we can have every colony-world seeded with orbital explosives."

"Nonradioactive, these explosions?" one of the Chinsoiy asked.

"That is correct," Admiral Nayak confirmed. "We are not like your race. Our bodies and our environment cannot tolerate radioactive explosions."

"Powerful they seem as the life-bombs of our kind," another Chinsoiy stated through the intercom. *"Scaled as such, devastation comparable would be to radiative means."*

"They are indeed comparable to thermonuclear devices in their size of impact," Nayak confirmed, a little wary now on where the subject was headed. "They will cause a great deal of devastation. But unlike those devices, we can calibrate the effects by reducing the fuel to be catalyzed before launch, or even midlaunch, provided we have a *mi-nah* of advanced warning."

"We do not *want* to bomb the Salik," Jackie stated firmly. "But we do not *want* to go to war, either. Yet here we are at war, and we must act to survive. These are weapons that we can use, and feel we must use, in order to end this war quickly, with the least loss of lives. I may prefer peace, meioas, and I am *not* advocating the wholesale slaughter of the Salik race . . . but even I know that wars are very rarely won by purely *defensive* actions."

The K'Katta were not pacified; the lighter-furred female waved a foreleg in negation. "No! That is unacceptable! Bombs of a size comparable to radioactive nuclear fission are too destructive. Massive weapons of such a scale are forbidden by the Alliance Charters."

"Gentlemeioas," Lieutenant Paea stated, speaking up for the first time. His face still had pink spots where his flesh was still healing from the harsh peppering of glass fragments from that broken window back on Au'aurrran, but his hearing had been restored by V'Dan microsurgery, a much faster repair than his superior's removed arm. "I understand your concern . . . but *you* thought you knew how big the Salik fleet really was. You have made your estimations based on what you thought you knew of Salik manufacturing rates.

"The Salik colonists on Au'aurrran were able to either smuggle in or directly manufacture for themselves the parts for a mechsuited *army* . . . and from what War Prince Naguarr reported to the Ambassador in the aftermath of the invasion attempt, his people did not notice anything of the sort in the eight years of records they hold for all imports to that planet *prior* to the start of your war. This means they might very well have spent the last few years manufacturing those suits on-site . . . *or* that they have been stockpiling weapons and ships for a *lot* longer than you think.

"There are a *lot* of stars out there," the lieutenant reminded everyone. Like Jackie's Hawai'ian accent, his Samoan accent handled the glottals of Imperial High V'Dan even as it forced his listeners to concentrate on the rest of his pronunciation. "Gas giants where they could siphon methane and other gases to process into starship fuel. Asteroids and such that could be rich in metals and churned into raw materials and basic components for shipbuilding—I'll remind you, all of their ships are very uniform in shape and size, from class to class. The hulls could have been made decades or even *centuries* ago, and simply retrofitted with the latest technology.

"Until we capture more members of the Salik High Command, until we can interrogate them telepathically, *we do not know* how big their stockpile of war machines is. Given how *our* ships are mass-manufactured," Paea continued, "we can swap out parts very quickly and retrofit the latest and greatest gizmos in a matter of hours. *But* those latest and greatest most likely will come from major industrial centers on major planets, where they have the best access to a lot of raw materials. And those centers *must* be destroyed.

"To do anything *less* is to waste our time arguing about how dangerous the weapons in their grip might be while completely ignoring the weapons sheathed and holstered on their bodies and stockpiled all around them. And that is not only negligent, that is *aiding* the enemy, by permitting them to continue to have the resources to attack, and attack, and *attack*," he continued, thumping the table with his finger, much as Admiral Nayak had done. "*That* is why we must strike now, strike hard, and *stop* them.

"*I* don't want anyone else to be captured or killed during another Au'aurrran, or another Glau. Do *you*? Can you sit there and look into the eyes of these Tlassians, these Solaricans, and tell them you *don't* want to stop another Au'aurrran invasion? Or another Glau?" Lieutenant Paea challenged the K'Katta.

The beige-furred female wasn't the only one of the arthropoids to curl in her foremost pair of legs. So did the two dark-furred males. None of them said a word to their counterparts on the other side of the circle.

"Nnnone of usss are strong enough to withsssstand the SSalik assaullt unnnopposed," the Choya war leader stated in the quiet following his words. "Therrefore, we *mussst* oppose it. We musst fight. I agree to dessstroy their infrasstructure, and demorrallize their citizenss with these nnnonradioactive weaponnns."

"The Terrans have a similar preference," Nayak agreed. "Precise bombing of Salik targets, while the fleets fight and give chase."

"The Collective/People will/will oppose/thwart/fight the Salik/enemy in any viable/successful method/way our militaries/allies/analyses deem/determine/prove are most/most effective," the leader of the Gatsugi race stated, his skin flushing a determined shade of reddish violet. "Mobility/Movement is vital/imperative for victory/success. Fleet against/at Fleet, yes/agreed, but infrastructure/war machinery must/must/must fall next/soonest as well."

That gave them three votes for the plan. The Grand General, glancing at Li'eth and receiving a nod of confirmation, spoke next. "The V'Dan military believes that victory lies best in mobility and swift, decisive action. We also vote to use the Terran bombs on their infrastructure, and the Imperial Fleet against their ships."

He looked to the Solarican delegates at the next table.

The Solarican War Princess of their foremost colonyworld flicked her ears, sending her rank-jewelry swaying. "The Sollarrican Empire wishes for this warr to ennd. It must ennd swiftly. We have an advanntage we cannot affforrd to waste. We know as hunnterrs that mobility is vital for success. We will chase fleets with flleets."

". . . And the bombing?" Admiral Nayak pressed. "What is your choice in that matter?"

Those golden, alien eyes closed and opened. Her ears remained up, her whiskers level, but her tail-tip flicked visibly. "Countess Prrang has a Sallik warrrship that lllanded upside down over part of the city of Gonn Staa because of colonnists she trrusted. That ship alllmost destrroyed parrt of the city when it crrashed. I will perrrmit the use of these weaponns on purrre Salik worllds, but *nnnot* on the jointly held onnes."

"That would be our preference as well," Nayak agreed.

"That is *nnot* a confirrrmation," War Princess Pallan not quite growled. Her tail stilled, but her ears dipped down and back.

"If there is a viable target that is clear of non-Salik personnel, we will take it," Nayak countered, holding her gaze.

"Thank you, Admiral, for clarifying what we *could* do," Jackie chided. "But the final decision will be made by the Admiral-General, by the Ambassador to non-Terran worlds— which would be me—and by the Premiere, as your superiors in the Terran chain of command."

One of Pallan's ears flicked up. "That stilll does not clarrify yourrr position in this matterr."

"Admiral Nayak is correct in that it is a viable option *if* there are no non-Salik personnel known in that area," Jackie repeated, expanding on her answer. She didn't *like* the answer she had to give, as a civilian, but knew it was the only one she could give, as a representative of their military's highest leadership. "But the Terran government would prefer to stick to purely Salik worlds and space installations. We cannot and will not make any decisions more clear than that because we do not believe in tying one limb behind our backs.

"I don't *like* it," she confessed, wrinkling her nose in distaste, "and we will use those weapons first and foremost with the highest preference on clear military targets. But we will *hope* that they decide our resolve to bomb them into worldwide rubble is strong enough that they will choose to surrender, rather than keep fighting, and keep being destroyed site by site, world by world."

That tail twitched again, but Pallan's other ear relaxed back to neutral. "Then we willl have to be satisfied with that."

She turned to look at the Tlassians. The Worker Caste representative, her scales olive green and yellow, spoke. Not the head of their Warrior Caste. Her accent was nearly flawless. "We will agree that fleet must chasse fleet, and infrastructure must be reduced . . . though we regret the losss of lives nonwarrior. Yet this brings a very important quesstion to our minds. We mussst therefore ask it.

"How do we *contain* the Salik?" she asked, lifting her saurian hands into view, touching the short, blunt claw-tips together in a cage shape. "How do we ensure they do not attack again in jussst a few years, once they have rrrebuilt?"

"Slice their wingskins," the Chinsoiy Fearsome Leader asserted. *"Their ships remove, restricting them to slowness of insystem speeds. No unassisted travel between skies."*

"That will be tough to do without bombing their infrastructure as well as their fleets," Nayak stated, looking over at the K'Katta. A rapid clicking sound emerged from two of them, but no translator box activated. He looked over to the Tlassians. "I don't like the idea of bombing civilians. It goes against my beliefs as a warrior, that fighting should be restricted to those who are trained. That fighting should be done away from cities and settlements so that the innocent and the helpless do not suffer.

"But I cannot even look at your people without remembering that we could not do anything to stop that fleet from heading to Glau," he told her. "We *might* have been able to meet it, maybe damaged it at a great cost of many ships lost on our side, if not all of them. But we could not stop it *before* it was launched. We can, however, stop future fleets before they are built. *That*, I will fight to prevent. It must not happen again."

His attaché, Major Tang-Smith, spoke. "One of our greatest military minds of our ancient days, Sun Tzu, wrote that it is good to stop a war by winning all the battles, but that it is better to stop it with the fewest number of battles, and best to stop future battles with armies long before they can even begin to gather their supplies. We must stop the next Salik ships, the next Salik armored suits, the next Salik plans from being made."

The Tlassian Work Leader stared back a long moment, then dipped her head to the side. ". . . We will support the choissce of our Terran allies."

She looked at the red-scaled male to her right. Warlord Tennssach eyed the Terrans and tipped his head as well. "We have the perrrmisssion of the Workerss. The Warriorrs have the willl to fight. We willl battle flleet to flleet and misssiles to mannnufactorries."

"Our Priesssts will turn ourrr inner eyess to sseeking suit-ablle tarrgetss," the third member of their triumvirate promised. "But will the Terrrran priessts do the ssssame, Ambasssadorr?"

"Precognition is the hardest gift to master, meioa," Jackie reminded him. "We have always known that. The future is fluid, and subject to many shapes and many changes. It is like water, in that it is too difficult to grasp in more than briefly snatched handfuls. But we *are* paying close attention these days, working with the military and the government—with our own warriors and workers—and will share anything we can make sense of whenever we can. We will try to have clair-voyants and xenopaths available for spying on the lands and scrying the minds of the enemy."

"Then the Priesssts will agrree to yourrr plann."

All three clasped their hands in front of their chests, and the Warlord spoke formally, almost ritually. "All arrrre in agreemennt in thisss. It willl be donne."

"See we clear-eyed this path. Rough but flightworthy," the Fearsome Leader on the other side of the darkened glass stated. *"Ships of the void we lend to the fleet. Nothing else can*

we give in safety of carbon-based life. Yet of the manufactured weapons, such weapons are of sameness. Such elements we can detect. We lend our ships for the scouting flight, fast-soaring, fast-seeing. Great is the risk.

"*We do not like bombs striking worlds. This a tactic is of the Salik,*" the alien added, resting his hands against the window, long outer fingers pressing down to their tips. "*No use to them is Chinsoiy life. No feeding of biology. Destruction strikes our skies in repetition. You will have teachings given of wrongfulness this act, lessons of harshness. Children struck is wrong, yet some children only feel, cannot reason. They taught must be by feeling/feeling/feeling of pain, of negative conditioning. They taught must be in swiftest flight, to end all destruction soonest and best.*

"*We commit our leaps to these regretful clouds, these sad-dened peaks, these harmful skies.*"

(*Well said, even if the grammar mangles High Imperial V'Dan,*) Jackie breathed in the back of Li'eth's mind. (*And here I thought the* Gatsugi *could be poetic . . .*)

(*You do realize they used a Gatsugi emphasis,*) he murmured back, though his own underthoughts agreed with hers.

"Well?" Grand General Ma'touk asked, his attention on the remaining delegation. "Do you agree to our course of action, President Marbleheart? Or do you and your people abstain?"

Again, that rapid, high chitter-clicking that had no transla-tion. Not just from the dark-furred leader of the K'Katta nation but from the others in his delegation. They even rocked a little on their elevated stools, looking too agitated to sit still.

Jackie squinted a little, invoking her—Li'eth's—awareness of auras. The colors that swirled around the arthropoid aliens were all colors of ambivalence and distress, striated and muddy-bright. Turbulent. But as she watched, the aura of their leader slowed and solidified into a rather odd shade of grayish violet. A grimly determined shade, Li'eth's awareness in-formed her, seeping through their bond. Marbleheart reached out with secondary forelegs, touching and stroking the nearer limbs of his companions. Soothing them.

When he spoke, the well-programmed translator box con-veyed his words with quiet finality. ". . . We will fight. We will not permit another Glau. Not now, and not in the future. But neither will we *allow* Sallha to become another Glau. Your acceptance into the Alliance requires confirmation by *all* members . . . and the K'Katta will watch how you treat your enemies, to know some of how you will treat your friends," he warned Jackie, Nayak, and their two junior officers. "We will be watching you. Climb carefully, in the days ahead."

Jackie could not fault him for that, given what she knew of K'Katta psychology so far. But she lifted her fingers off the table surface when Nayak drew in a breath to speak, silencing him. This was her purview, not his. "Do not let your species-wide distaste for conflict prejudice you against our efforts, Meioa President. We do try to act with honor and compassion . . . but neither will we cut off a limb just to keep it from attacking someone that has proved to be a relentless foe.

"*Nor* will we allow anyone *else* to cut off one of our limbs," she added, sitting forward, her gaze fixed on the brown-furred leader, for once able to look past his appearance to the mind inside that multieyed head. "Do not let your prejudices blind your seeing to our actions. Do not let your preferences close your hearing to our words.

"The Chinsoiy are right. We must consider what to do *after* we have won . . . *when* the Salik are beaten, but *still alive*. We do not have enough bombs to destroy the Salik homeworld," she finished.

Nayak cleared his throat. "Apologies, Ambassador . . . but technically, we do. The lack of radiation would not be a concern . . . but nuclear winter would, with enough carbon blasted into the stratosphere from ground-contact explosions. The Salik are more susceptible to temperature fluctuations than Humans, Solaricans, and the K'Katta."

She looked over at him, grateful for his honesty, even as it gave her a moment of embarrassment in front of others. Saving face, she clarified dryly, "That we would *use*, Admiral. We have enough in orbit around Earth to destroy it five times via nuclear winter, but we will be facing *several* Salik-only colonyworlds, each with a military-industrial complex capable of cranking out extra problems for our fleets. They must be dealt with, and so we do not have enough to destroy *all* of the Salik worlds. *Nor* would the Council allow that!"

"My apologies, Ambassador. I did not realize you were fully

informed of our capacities," Nayak murmured. "I do think it is still an option as a *threat*, Ambassador. An option our allies should know about."

It felt a tiny bit awkward, accepting an apology over a military matter from a man who, in the military, was technically her superior. Yet in that moment, in that role, she was *his* superior, as a duly appointed representative of their representational government, and the personally appointed proxy to the Premiere, their commander-in-chief. "Admiral Nayak. Please remember in the future that there is an ethical difference between discretion and lying.

"I do not lie to my allies, and am not allowed to lie outright to any enemies unless it is to save lives. But while I must not lie to these people, I *am* allowed to be discreet, Admiral. That includes choosing not to mention we *can* turn the Salik Motherworld, if only that one world, to rubble. That ability, Admiral, for all we hold it," she stressed, "is *not* the choice of the Council."

He lowered his gaze. ". . . Yes, Ambassador. My apologies, Ambassador. The Space Force will abide by the choices of the Terran Council."

"Apology accepted." Jackie knew the others were giving her and her chief military advisor curious looks, seeing a side to Terran politics versus Terran expediency and capability that was not normally publicly aired. A deliberately aired side, in this case. She raised her voice back to normal discussion levels and returned to the topic with barely any acknowledgment. ". . . With all of that settled, we will need to focus now on troop and supply movements. We have the schedules and timetables for the Salik attacks.

"Those by their very nature will dictate *our* movements," Jackie continued. "We need only decide which ships to move to which location to counter them. The choice of which infrastructure elements to take out and in which order on which world must also be decided at this meeting."

"We/Each of us must/will send for/fetch the latest/freshest reports/scans/information for that/the targets," President Anoddra asserted. "Such/That may/will take/require time. Send/Send/Send for/fetch the reports/information, and/then fill/use/work in the time/waiting period to discuss/coordinate fleet/ship movements/choices. A break/moment to rest/stretch/de-stress can/should be used/utilized now/at this time."

"That would be a good use of our limited time, President Light-Hopes-Many-Shadows," Li'eth praised their host. "Remember, meioas, to use your Terran codes and Terranglo code-talkers when ordering reports to be sent here over the hyperrelays. We may have Terran satellites at every inhabited planet in this system, but there is still quite a lot of empty space within this system for the enemy to sit unnoticed while they eavesdrop. Those satellites must be reached by lightwave communications, which can be cracked if we use the more normal Alliance means to communicate through them."

"We should allso consider dividinng each fleet attack by who cannn reach it besst," the Choya military representative stated. "One of thessse worlds is nnear my home colllony, but allso near the K'Katta."

"Agreed," the Commander-of-Millions concurred.

"We will/Let us break for sixteen *khanas*," the Gatsugi President stated, and changed the image of the known galaxy on the screens to one of a timer counting down in V'Dan numerals.

Jackie rose to stretch her legs a little, always a good idea when stuck in a seated job for any length of time. President Marbleheart climbed down from his stool perch and moved over behind the Gatsugi and Choya delegations, approaching her. (*Great. His aura looks like he wants a confrontation, and now I'm back to feeling creepy creepy creepy-ness.*)

(*You can do this. He won't yell at you,*) Li'eth added in silent, encouraging support. (*You will be fine.*)

"Meioa Ambassador. I have an important question for your people," Marbleheart chittered through his translator. "If you have enough of these hydrobombs to destroy your species' Motherworld five times over, how do you plan to dispose of any unused weapons?"

The question was such a non sequitur, and a nonissue, that it took her aback. Blinking, she replied, "Once their water tanks are drained, they are harmless, meioa. They will not explode. Nor *can* they explode even when hit, unless and until the catalytic process of converting water back to hydrogen and oxygen has been activated."

"Yes, but the *catalyst* is dangerous," Marbleheart insisted, only to pause when she shook her head, still bemused.

"Sorry, but *no*, Meioa President. The catalyst by itself is also fairly harmless. Even if you dropped the catalyst directly into an ocean, it would only be able to convert a small amount of water to base gases before those gases would become dissolved into the rest of the water. It is the entire *process* of the engine, not just the catalyst, that causes the explosion to be, well, *explosive*."

"But the catalyst is still a danger. You will disassemble these bombs, yes?" he pressed, lifting a foreleg to touch her sleeve.

For a moment, it was all Jackie could do not to leap back with her body and shove away with her mind. Swallowing, she clamped down on her arachnophobia, breathing deep, staring *through* the alien so that she could not focus on any one feature, but not looking away and letting the corners of her eyes play tricks on her, either.

(*You can do this,*) Li'eth soothed her. (*He will not harm you, trust me on this.*)

(*I know, I know . . . creepy creepy* booting modo creepy . . .) Breathing deep again, she managed a reply. "The water, as I said, will be drained from the tanks. The catalyst and suitable engine components will be reused in communications satellites wherever possible since the bombs are literally satellites without hyperarrays and communications circuitry. If there is excess beyond what we need, then the catalyst will be recycled back into more normal hydrogenerator engines for use in vehicles, starships, and so forth. It is, after all, a catalyst. It can and will be reused tens of thousands of times before it even begins to degrade past usability."

The alien stared up at her a long moment, then bobbed slightly, legs flexing. "Good," he whistled. "I will hold you to your statement that you do not lie. Please excuse me. I must discuss other matters with the War Princess, next."

Relieved he moved on, Jackie tried not to let her flesh crawl too much at the thought of the giant-spider-style alien being somewhere behind her back for a few moments. (*I will be grateful when we're finally at a point where I can have someone* else *deal with the K'Katta in all things, in my stead.*)

(*You did very well in dealing with them, mid-debate,*) he reminded her.

She closed her eyes, nodding subtly on the outside, more strongly on the inside. (*I was mad enough, I could look past his physical shape to who he is on the inside . . . I will try to remember that feeling so I can continue to successfully deal with his kind.*)

(*A pity they're not very argumentative, or it would be easier each time,*) he tried teasing lightly.

A soft, brief laugh escaped her. Shaking her head, Jackie opened her eyes to find each of the Choya studying her. Not in suspicion, just eyeing her in curiosity, from the looks of the delegates' auras. Finally, one of them spoke.

"Meioa Ambassadorr. You make movemment with your facess when you ssspeak mind to mmind," one of the junior delegates stated. "We have nno such thing among our kinnd, thisss mind-to-minnd. I would innquire, what iss that feelling?"

(*. . . And a diplomat's work is never done, since I must now represent the Psi League and all the psychic sects of the Witan Orders.*) Breathing deep to clear her mind and body one last time of the lingering aftereffects of her arachnophobia, Jackie readied herself to explain to a nontelepath what telepathy was like. "Imagine someone speaking just behind your ear, your hearing organ. Not very loudly, but definitely closer than anyone else normally speaks. Next, imagine that this sound is sensed *inside* your body, and not coming from outside it, and not in the voice you use when thinking your thoughts . . ."

CHAPTER 11

Almost an hour later, with every available screen displaying a different star system from the rest, General Ma'touk sighed and rubbed at the bridge of his nose, just below a *jungen* mark. "This still isn't going to work. Not quickly enough. Not *decisively* enough."

Jackie knew how he felt. Her own fingertips had massaged

her temples a few moments before, but it hadn't helped. The military and civilian leaderships present in the conference room had hashed out most of the plans they could, dividing forces, assigning fleets . . . but even with the Terrans' help, they just did not have enough ships, enough resources. "We're building ships as fast as we can, meioa, and our shipyards are not under any threat by Salik forces, so we can keep building them and sending them out. But we can only build them so fast, and we can only train our pilots so fast."

"It woulld worrk betterr if we had enough bommbs," War Princess Pallan muttered. She quickly held up her arm, palm and claws toward herself, to forestall protests from the K'Katta. "Nnot to *use*, but to *thrrreaten* them into submissionn."

Nayak sighed, forearms resting on the curved table edge, head drooped a little in exhaustion. Somehow, his Dress Cap remained in place, the only one of the four Terrans to still be wearing one. Like Jackie and Paea, Tang-Smith had removed her uniform cap from her matching dull green headscarf, and had even unbuttoned her jacket, revealing the white shirt underneath as she slumped back in her chair. But it was Simon Paea, sitting up sharply from his own slouch, that caught their attention. Specifically, with a single word.

"Nagasaki."

". . . Lieutenant?" Jackie asked, distracted by his non sequitur. Beside her, Nayak lifted his head, peering past her at their juniormost officer.

"Hiroshima and Nagasaki, the two cities in Japan destroyed by the first atomic bombs," Simon stated. "The first two atomic bombs. The *only* two atomic bombs of their day."

"Your point, soldier?" Nayak asked dryly.

"What did the Americans tell the Japanese they would do to the *rest* of their cities that got them to surrender?" Simon prompted them.

Jackie's eyes widened. *"Oh!* Oh, yes, it's perfect . . ."

Major Tang-Smith sat up, her brown eyes widening just as much. "It's not just perfect, it's *brilliant*, Lieutenant. It's been done before, but even an old trick can still be a perfectly good trick . . ."

President Marbleheart chirped, tapping a foreleg on the surface of his own bit of curved table to get their attention.

"Meioa Terrans. Would you please explain what esoteric thing you are discussing? You seem to be placing great emphasis on it, as if it is our salvation, but it lacks any meaningful context for the rest of us."

"Meioas of the Alliance," Jackie stated carefully, looking at the K'Katta delegates. "Do you have any problems with us *threatening* to bomb the Salik into oblivion? I am *not* talking about actually doing so. I am *only* talking about verbally threatening and intimidating them."

"I would threaten to eat my own mother in front of them if I thought it would back them down," Marbleheart retorted. "Save that such a thought of *doing* it evokes nothing but feelings of regurgitation and vows of starvation in me. Particularly because they would insist that I start chewing off half of her limbs before they'd believe me."

Tlik-tlak, the Commander-of-Millions, spoke up, ignoring his leader's indelicate sardonicism. "What is this threat that you imply is not an *actual* act of violence?"

"It is a trick that is dependent upon one thing," Nayak cautioned everyone in the room. "Gentlebeings. Is your scanning technology still having difficulty penetrating our ceristeel hull plating?"

"Of courrrse it is."

"Annoyingly sssso."

"Such is halfway blocked in our scannings. Data discernment is difficult. Technology of our nature the Salik do not possess."

"Your point with that question?" Li'eth asked, though Jackie knew he did have a glimmer of an idea, thanks to their Gestalt.

"The manufacture of our interstellar ships takes a great deal of time and effort because of the complexity of their interior workings," Tang-Smith explained, rebuttoning her Dress jacket as she sat up neatly, "as does the manufacture of the exact mechanisms that make a hydrogenerator capable of working, plus the modifications necessary to make it an even more powerful bomb . . . These things all take time and have to be planned in advance. We have also stated that we tend to use assembly-line manufacturing processes to speed up the mass production of our military systems.

"The bottom line of this equation, gentlebeings," the major stressed, "is that we may only have so many ships and functional satellites and bombs . . . but we have tens of thousands of *casings* already manufactured. Most of them are already fitted with basic propulsion systems. Our insystem-thruster technology has been around for many years and has been maximized for swift and cheap production.

"Because we build in modular stages," Tang-Smith continued, "they already have a tiny hydrogeneration system installed to operate those thruster fields. It's not capable of exploding," she added quickly in reassurance, looking toward the K'Katta, "because it's not configured to explode. In fact, that engine has the exact same fail-safes that all of our vehicular transports have, to ensure they *cannot* be turned into a bomb. That's the difficult part, creating an engine that *can* become an explosive. We did it that way because it makes industrial sense to get all of the quickest things handled and assembled first, and we kept the propulsion separate from everything else, so that it can be moved in a hurry if a critical cascade is accidentally triggered in the greater hydroengine."

Nayak nodded, confirming her words. "We were mass-producing them that way even before the precognitives were beginning to catch glimpses of the *Aloha 9* meeting up with the Salik and His Highness. We started building them in large quantities in the first place because we knew we wanted to seed all the star systems within a hundred light-years of Earth with multiple relays placed throughout each system for astronomical, astronavigational, and exploration-based purposes—every single one of our *Aloha* mission vessels deployed two to three satellites per new system it visited, visiting five and six systems at a time, before they were repurposed for the war effort."

"The only thing slowing us down is that the catalyst that allows us to turn plain water into energy-generating fuel can only be produced at a certain rate under current manufacturing methods," Jackie explained, filling in the rest of the blanks. "We're attempting to expand that infrastructure, though it will take time. But in the meantime, we built all the bombs and the hyperrelay satellites to be interchangeable in the shape of their outermost ceristeel casings because we didn't want the Greys getting their hands on our hyperrelay technology."

"As in all things that are mass manufactured," Paea told their listeners, "large production runs are cheaper. Additionally, ceristeel is tough enough, it can sit around for at least a hundred years in the burning heat and icy cold of outer space without losing any of its quality or structural integrity beyond a little bit of scuffing and pitting from micrometeors. They even already come with an aerodynamic shape because that production shape was already in existence for delivery drones, the kinds of remote-piloted drones that deliver packages from door to door, or send medical equipment out in an emergency."

Jackie nodded. "I even voted on the budget for the half-built casings, as the Councilor for Oceania. It was one of my first voting sessions as a Councilor years ago."

"All of this means, meioas, that if the non-Chinsoiy scanners still cannot penetrate our ceristeel plating," Nayak stated, "then the odds are very high that the Salik cannot, either. That means we could easily bring ten thousand fake bombs to each world, *if* we have the means to transport them. A systematic saturation of their military infrastructure with the real bombs, plus the threat of ten times as many more supposed weapons lurking in orbit, *should* be enough of a threat to get them to surrender. A threat made of casings they cannot scan for veracity *should* be enough to convince them, yes?"

By his physiology, President Marbleheart could not blink in shock like a Human. But he did dangle his first four limbs in a limp droop that conveyed it rather well all the same. And when he whistle-chirped, the word came out in a breathy V'Dan male voice. ". . . *Brilliant.* I am *blinded* by the brilliance of your idea. All my eyes are stunned by the cunning you shine upon us."

"I belllieve it willll work," the top Choya military advisor stated. His title translated something like *Madouk*-of-Cho, some sort of odd amphibious weapon, either like a trident or some sort of polearm, spring-loaded and dangerous. "The Ssalik are innntimidated only by deeplly ssstrronger opponenntss. They unndersstand xennocide as a vallid attack method."

"Then we will delay the next delivery of infantry troops in favor of instead packing those transport ships with fake bombs. Along with the real ones, of course," Jackie decided. "Those troops can be picked up later and can be trained for handling the gathering and transporting of Salik prisoners."

"Trranssporting?" Pallan asked her.

Li'eth answered for Jackie. "War Prince Naguarr of Au'aurrran gave us the impression that he wished to remove all Salik colonists from his world, to ensure it could never be attacked again from within by subterfuge and misplaced trust. The Eternal throne agrees with this policy. The Salik have lost the privilege of being a trusted ally, and with it all the rights of being a trusted neighbor. If they wish to attack and eat fellow sentients, they should be confined to their own worlds and have access only to their own kind."

That same undulating chittering escaped from the K'Katta, but it was milder. President Marbleheart silenced his companions after only a moment. "It is repulsive as an idea . . . but under the sting of the irony insect, it *would* be culturally appropriate. If they insist upon inflicting such sorrows upon anyone sentient, it should be kept strictly to their own kind. Just because one race's stimulant is another race's hallucinogen is no reason to deprive the first race of its morning *caffen*."

(*See? Even the K'Katta prefer our V'Dan kind,*) Li'eth half teased.

Jackie tried not to let her lips twitch. (*Oh, hush, you know that's not exactly what he meant. Behave. Or I'll make you drink more Terran coffee.*)

He grinned in the back of her mind, warming the undercurrents of awareness that lurked between them.

NOVEMBER 16, 2287 C.E.
JUL 8, 9508 V.D.S.
V'GORO J'STA, INBOUND TO LLGHK-PWOK
BZ-TLD 7661 SYSTEM, TERRAN STANDARD
T'UN SHIEN-SWISH 1271 SYSTEM, SALIK STANDARD

The bitter-rich aroma of arabica beans wafted Jackie's way, mixing with the scent of her scrambled eggs and tangy V'Dan cheese breakfast.

Ayinda, the source of the scent, set her cup and her meal tray down with the little slide that hitched the clips at their bases into one of the slightly raised metal strips crossing the table. Having traveled on the *V'Goro* for a few weeks by now, they were all used to these necessary little steps to secure items against being flung around accidentally during maneuvers, and the dark-skinned woman didn't miss a beat in her conversation with Anjel.

"*. . . but I don't understand why I have to memorize Salik system designations,*" the navigator complained in Mandarin. "*I mean, I do understand that's how the Alliance encodes all the settled systems within a particular nation's borders. The first of the settlers get to name the stars and the planets. But they're the enemy! They're about to be bombed into oblivion, if not already, since the other ships were supposed to arrive ahead of us and get started on that—Jackie, they have arrived already, right?*"

Jackie looked up from her display tablet and nodded. She framed her reply in V'Dan, however. She could understand Ayinda's discretion in complaining about semiarbitrary rules for naming star systems across the Alliance in a language no one in the Empire would understand for a few more years, but her reply to that particular question was not quite so indelicate, it couldn't be aired in the local tongue. "They have started the battle, yes. The outermost airlock assigned to it is open and the hyperrelay is transmitting ship to ship with the fleet vessels currently engaging the system defenses. We still have another fifty-plus minutes before we'll be in combat range."

"You sound rather *blasé* about that battle, *amiga*," Anjel observed. She lifted her chin at the Terran-style tablet in Jackie's hand, clipping her own dishes to the table in the officer's mess the Terran crew had been given for their personal use. "What's got your attention?"

"Mail from V'Dan. I've already gone through the stuff from home. My niece broke a bone in her foot a while back, and they finally let her out of the walking boot." Jackie smiled wistfully. "Lani thinks her mother—my sister—is being mean because Hyacinth won't even let her use a bodyboard for two more months, let alone a surfboard."

"Poor kid, that does sound a bit mean," Anjel sympathized, digging into her meal. "I don't surf, but I have gone bodyboarding on one of the rivers back home, in the waves at the base of some rapids. How did she hurt her foot?"

"She pearled her *he'e nalu*—drove the nose of it under the wave accidentally—and smacked her foot into the board when she wiped," Jackie explained. "I think Hyacinth's right to be a little paranoid at the moment, though *I'd* only restrict her from surfing for a month."

"I don't know, I'm going to have to side with the mother," Jasmine said, joining them. She, too, had a tray of food, which she balanced in her good arm, carefully slotting it into place. She lifted her other arm, wiggling the artificial fingers awkwardly. The skin tone looked palpably more golden tan than her natural warm brown, and someone had streaked it with pink fake-*jungen* marks. "I've been getting the physical therapy lectures for V'Dan-style limb replacement. If that charming little girl just got her walking cast off, then she's got tight fascia covering atrophied muscles, all of it attached to tightened tendons."

"Ah, the three-days-in-bed syndrome," Anjel agreed, nodding sagely as she dug into her food.

"Come again?" Ayinda asked.

"Yeah, what?" Jackie added, confused.

"It's an old physical-fitness study from a few centuries back," the pilot and gunner explained. "My regimen trainer talked about it at the Academy. Apparently, some scientists took Olympic-level athletes at the peak of their training performance and tested their performance abilities. Then the scientists had them lie in bed for three days straight, virtually no movement, no walking, other than, I presume, short trips to the bathroom."

She paused to take a bite of her food, making Jackie antsy to hear what happened next. While Anjel chewed, Li'eth came in and moved over to the galley window, requesting his own breakfast from the V'Dan-staffed kitchen crew. (*Good morning. Again.*)

(*Good morning, and shh. Anjel's telling a story, something new,*) she replied. She quickly fell silent as the pilot cleared her mouth and spoke again.

". . . Anyway, at the end of the three days, the researchers started testing the athletes' performances as they resumed their training. They discovered that it took each athlete about *two weeks* to get back into top physical shape after lying in bed for just those three days," Anjel told Ayinda and Jackie. "It's absolutely crazy how long it takes to get back into shape after just a few days off."

"Now that I think about it, I can totally believe it," Ayinda told her, and lifted the mug of Terran coffee out of its clip line. "Every time I've been laid out flat with a bad cold for just a few days, I've felt as weak as a new kitten, and it takes me a week or more to get back on my feet. And that's *with* being free to move around and not literally spending every hour in bed save for toilet breaks. Certainly, I can't lie around all day even if I wanted to because I have too many responsibilities."

"Agreed," Anjel asserted, lifting her mug to clink it lightly against the other woman's. "Whoops, sorry, didn't mean to smack your knuckles, there . . ."

"No damage done," Ayinda reassured her.

A moment later, Li'eth moved over to their table, speaking aloud with the Terran manners he had learned. In V'Dan military matters, any higher-ranking officer could join any table and sit, as a privilege of their higher rank in the Tiers, but there wasn't a similar privilege for the Terrans. So he asked, rather than assumed. "May I join you meioa-es?"

Anjel slanted a look up at him, then eyed Ayinda and Jackie. She grinned, and quipped slyly, "I don't know, it might ruin our little Bechdel Test moment, here . . ."

Ayinda choked on her coffee as she laughed, and had to scramble for the napkin holder to mop up the spluttered mess.

"Anjel!" Jackie protested, though she couldn't stop herself completely from smiling in amusement. "That is *not* appropriate . . . *Yes*, Li'eth, you can join us. Please, sit down and ignore our laughter; it's honestly no insult toward you."

"I'm sure I'd probably find it equally funny if I knew the cultural background behind it," he murmured, mouth quirked up on one side.

"The Bechdel Test is an old . . . umm . . ." Anjel tried to figure out how to explain it. "Basically, it's a way to gauge sexism in entertainment shows, back when women were being portrayed as warping their whole lives around how they related to men, as if men were somehow the center of all existence."

"Men are important," Jackie reassured Li'eth, catching his

puzzled subthoughts as well as his puzzled smile. "But for a very, very long while, most cultures back on Earth suffered from toxic patriarchy. The Bechdel Test was proposed a few centuries back as just one of many ways to measure how well each culture allowed women back then to have and display their own story arcs, *separate* arcs, rather than their existence in the story being centered around or dependent upon some man in the script."

"This isn't scripted," he pointed out. "And it isn't an entertainment show. It's breakfast on a battleship. The only thing we're supposed to be centering our lives around is surviving a successful fight against our enemies."

"No, it's not scripted," Ayinda rasped, coughing again to try to clear her throat. "But it *was* funny, even if I half drowned, there."

"I do apologize if the cultural quip caused offense, Highness," Anjel offered formally. Mostly seriously, too, though the corner of her mouth kept quirking upward.

"I accept the apology, though it didn't cause any offense, just some confusion. Speaking of which," Li'eth added, frowning thoughtfully at the quartet of women sharing their table with him. "Last night, Robert showed that movie about *zombies* . . . What *is* your people's fascination with the gruesome idea of supposedly dead bodies that somehow get back up and start attacking people? V'kol said he checked the database and found *thousands* of cultural entertainment methods referencing these horrible things."

All four women raised their brows, opened their mouths . . . and ended up eyeing each other in helplessness. Finally, Jackie just shrugged, and said ". . . To be honest? We don't know. We honestly do not know. It's just . . . something we do, culturally."

Ayinda shrugged. "Historically, the actual, original zombies were simply Humans living in one particular archipelago of islands whose minds and bodies were drugged by a local plant life into a very lethargic yet highly suggestive state. While in this near-mindless, drugged state, they were used as slave labor by the people who drugged them.

"I don't think anybody here with us knows *how* it changed from that," the navigator confessed, continuing. "There's probably been doctoral dissertations on it at several universities back home by now, since it's been centuries. But all I know is that somehow, it evolved from shuffling drugged slave labor to necromantically raised dead brought out of the grave as mobile, shambling corpses, then as faster shambling horrors caused by strange viral infections. In the centuries since the idea of zombies entered popular culture, there have been a hundred different varieties from that, each one more frightening than the last."

"Hang on, Ayinda. That's rather biased. There *have* been some rather funny zombie movies, *and* some romantic zombie stories," Anjel interjected. "And even a couple romantic zombie comedies. Not all of them have been horror stories."

Anjel rolled her eyes, clearing her throat so she could mutter, ". . . And the moment we mentioned romance, we *definitely* failed the Bechdel Test."

"We did not," Anjel argued. "We haven't mentioned any men, yet. There were at least two perfectly good lesbian-zombie romantic comedies made. Well, not *perfectly* good," their backup pilot amended, briefly waving her hand in the air to negate any misunderstanding. "More like campy good for at least one of them, and fairly decent but still not perfect for the other. But that could be said for pretty much most of them. Zombie stories are not exactly the highest form on the art-and-culture scales."

"*You've* watched lesbian romantic comedy zombie movies?" Ayinda asked, brows rising. "When, exactly, were you going to share these hidden cultural depths with the rest of us, Anjel?"

Li'eth sighed and spoke telepathically to Jackie, ignoring the two women as they continued their teasing cultural conversation unaided by the other two. (*I think that even after thirty more years of being exposed to your people's plethora of cultures, I will still not completely understand them by the time I turn old and gray. Any of them.*)

(*Fair's fair,*) she pointed out, meaning her own occasional confusion over certain V'Dan customs and preferences. (*All the nuances of Imperial culture are going to mystify me from time to time, too, even when I'm old and gray. Are you ready for the coming battle?*)

(*So long as we're the mop-up crew when it comes to the orbital and insystem defenses,*) he agreed, digging into his breakfast. (*I'm tempted to put on an emergency suit before we get there, in case of a hull breach. I don't ever want to feel as near helpless as I did while on board that shuttlecraft.*)

(*So says the man who blasted pure pyrokinetic power through a* capital *ship,*) she reminded him, finishing up her own breakfast. They had slept in the same cabin, but she had been awakened early to answer the communications files shipped to them as soon as the *V'Goro* came out of faster-than-light speeds. (*We may have been in a multimember Gestalt, but that* had *to have taken at least a Rank 14 effort, purely on your own power, before compounding in my efforts as your Gestalt partner, then the others' help, like frosting on the cake top. Possibly even a Rank 16, though we won't know for sure until we can get back to some place with a KI machine.*)

He started to reply but caught her distraction when a new message came through, broadcast from the hyperrelay located a few decks away to her Terran-style datapad. (*New message?*)

(. . . *Coded message from the Premiere.*)

(*I'll back out of your thoughts,*) he promised, scooping up a sporkful of fruit, (*and focus on eating my breakfast instead.*)

(*Thank you . . . and I do appreciate your discretion every time,*) she added, erecting her innermost shields between them. It didn't take long for her to read through the message in full. When she did, she relaxed the wall screening out stray underthoughts. (*Nothing too sensitive. He's just reminding us that when we take prisoners, Darian and I are to xenopathically scan them for the exact locations of the Salik war-matériel industries for their eradication.*

(*There will be more xenopaths arriving to help assist with that task—so I'm to help them learn Sallhash, oh joy—and he closes with a fervent wish that we all survive with minimal casualties, and none to the two of us. He sends greetings and hope of your good health, by the way,*) she added.

(*Please write back and let him know I'm doing well, thank you,*) Li'eth returned. (*I suppose he didn't know exactly when we'd drop out of faster-than-light speeds, and it doesn't sound like he needs a reply to anything, so a letter sent via the matrix is more practical than trying to align a vidcall.)*

She smiled at that. (*You've been in and out of my mind for three-quarters of a year now, and you still call it 'the matrices' and not 'the net' for the Terran version.)*

(*I am a marks-on-the-skin V'Dan,*) he reminded her. Then winced. (*Sorry, that was rather* jungen-*ist and ageist of me, wasn't it?)*

Her smile widened into a grin. (*My turn to give* you *the correct phrase to use. We say "dyed-in-the-wool."*)

(*That's an odd turn of phrase. Where does it come from?*) Li'eth asked her.

Blinking, Jackie eyed him. (*You know, I haven't a clue. If we weren't hundreds of light-years from Earth, and seconds of lag time on messages, I'd search our* nets,) she teased, (*for the background information on where that phrasing originated.)*

(*I'll try to make a note of it for later. Our host, Admiral A'quon, wants us on the bridge for the battle,*) he reminded her. (*I know Buraq would rather have us on the* Embassy 1, *ready to launch, but the bridge is the most heavily shielded and sturdiest location on the ship. We'll have a higher chance of survival than in your tiny little ship, even behind airlock doors.)*

(*I'm willing to be there if they're willing to let us use the comms to demand the planet's surrender.)*

(*That's the other reason she invited us,*) he agreed. (*It'll look much more imposing and impressive to have a familiar V'Dan Imperial Warship bridge for your background when demanding their surrender. Your tiny Terran cockpits aren't very impressive, I'm afraid. Kind of like being asked to surrender by someone sitting in the cockpit of a fighter craft.)*

(*I'd claim that was an insulting comparison if you weren't so very close to being right,*) she allowed, amused by the truthful analogy. (*One day, we'll have faster-than-light ships of our own, ones with working gravity, and can make our bridges look properly imposing, too. Now, if you'll excuse me, since my breakfast is finished, I need to go make my daily recording of my Oath of Service, then dress up in a more formal*

*uniform so I can look imposing enough to belong on a V'Dan
warship's bridge.*)

———————

Admiral A'quon looked just as imposing as her bridge; even
seated, her back was straight, her shoulders square, her jaw
and gaze level. Jackie had seen her several times before, of
course, but each time, that first-glance impression threw the
Terran. A'quon's *jungen* marks, colored a rich dark brown,
streaked her face rather dramatically with jagged lightning
strikes from her upper-right brow to her lower-left jawline, and
even down onto her throat. Given that her hair grew in shades
of a similar dark brown streaked with thin strands of gray, it
almost looked on first glance like she had lumpy, straggled,
extra-long bangs angling down across her golden tanned face.

"The War Prince sees you," she warned her bridge crew,
her contralto voice quiet and steady. The red-uniformed men
and women seated at the banks of workstation controls and
monitoring screens sat up a little straighter but did not take
their eyes off those screens. Particularly when she added,
"Give him your discipline."

When the crimson-uniformed woman turned in profile to
listen to the murmurs of a bridge officer, the truth of her *jungen* showed. All of her hair had been pulled back firmly into
a complex braid tucked up into itself, forming a sort of flat,
plaited bun. Enlisted men and women of the Fifth Tier had to
keep their hair regulation short because they were the ones
most often headed into combat, but Fourth Tier noncoms and
higher were all allowed more leeway in the length of their
locks.

This wasn't Jackie's first trip to the bridge, but each time,
she found it impressive. Most everything had been painted or
manufactured in neutral shades of gray, even down to the seat
cushions. Crew uniforms provided some spots of color; banks
of control panels and curves of monitors provided the rest.
This time, she wasn't being shown right away to a particular
seat, so she strolled over to the door at the back of the room,
on the highest tier but off to one side of the command station.
Her goal was a creamy plaque marked with dark lettering

In a tradition oddly and inadvertently shared with Terran

warships, someone had crafted a nameplate display for the bridge bulkhead. Not out of bronze, but out of some sort of carved stone, alabaster perhaps. Jackie wasn't familiar with all that many stone types. She was, however, familiar with the foreign lettering, incised and inlaid in polished, blue-toned steel.

The plaque displayed the official name and numerical designation of the ship, its date of construction, its launch date, and basic information about length, width, height, number of decks, number of life-support bays, number of shuttle bays, minimum crew capacity, and maximum recommended personnel capacity. Which, for a ship of this class, they had already overburdened on other vessels with Terran soldiers by a third again. On this ship, on this trip, they did carry Terrans above and beyond the crews of the *Embassy 1* and *14*, but only enough to serve as translators and hydrobomb operators. Not thousands meant to land on a planet's surface and hold it against the enemy.

"This way, Grand High Ambassador," someone stated. The polite young man, wearing a solid brass parallelogram for his rank insignia—a Warden Superior, member of the Third Tier of demiofficers—gestured toward a station one level down from the Admiral's seat. Two extra seats flanked the chair centered in front of its screens. "You will be taking my seat for the broadcast though I will, of course, still be operating the controls. I will endeavor to stay out of the projection range."

"Thank you, Warden Superior . . . Taq'enez?" she added, glancing at the nameplate stitched onto his uniform and giving it an emphasis on the first syllable.

"Tok *en*-ez," he clarified, giving her a brief but warm smile to take the sting out of his correction on her pronunciation. Unlike the Admiral's, his *jungen* marks were small, almost discreet, lavender that decorated his throat just under his jawline in three small dots down each side. "My bloodline is from the Polar Isles on V'Dan. We were a bit isolated for around two thousand years, so . . . well, we still pronounce things differently."

"Half of my family line comes from a set of tropical isles in the middle of an ocean that covers one-third of our home planet," she replied, smiling back. "I understand about isolation influencing the people of an area. Including many centuries *after* mass transportation gets developed."

He grinned and walked with her to his duty station. "Normally, I manage isolated or special operations activities . . . which sounds much more impressive than it actually is. I'm responsible for scheduling nonvital maintenance work such as painting bulkheads, repairing furniture, the things that can be handled in transit from one system to the next. When we arrive and drop below lightspeed, I spend most of my time analyzing lightwave readings as a backup to the navigation and communications teams. We're a large enough ship, we run a lot of backups, because we're responsible for a lot of lives."

"I can understand and appreciate that," she murmured. Picking the right-hand seat, she settled into it, letting him take the center seat. Li'eth stayed up by the Admiral, murmuring with her about what they'd analyzed so far of the battle taking place around the Salik colony, which most people in the Alliance simply called Pwok for the fact it was the one part of the alien name that most everyone could pronounce without needing either a translator unit or to actually be a Salik. "Estimated arrival?"

"Ten more minutes. You can see the countdown there," he added, pointing at the lower-left corner of one of the screens. "We have about two seconds of lightwave lag. That set of readings there indicates that everything appears calm, according to our tactical officers' assessment of the battle's aftermath."

"We still have another forty minutes estimated before the first ships from farther out in the system could arrive, summoned by lightwave broadcasts of our attack," the woman seated at the station to Jackie's right warned them.

Her insignia was also a slanted rectangle, but it displayed a hollow outline bisected by a straight bar, making her a High Warden in rank, one step higher up the ladder from Taq'enez. Jackie couldn't see her nameplate easily.

"We will have a thirty-*mi-nah* window of opportunity to launch and demonstrate our firepower—in fact, they're already being launched. It's rather tight," the high warden muttered. She glanced at Jackie, her brown eyes clipped on one side by a bit of mint-green crescent. On her brown skin, that green mark made Jackie think of a sort of reversed mint-chocolate-chip ice-cream effect. "I hope the Admiral can convince them . . . or if not, that you can."

"So do I, meioa," Jackie agreed, eyeing the magnified view of the cloud-and-water-marbled planet they approached.

Li'eth came over, taking his seat on the other side of the warden superior. He wasn't supposed to show on the screen at all; if the Salik in the system knew that the War Prince was there personally, in a seemingly undermanned fleet of mostly battle-damaged ships, they just might launch everything they had. They understood the value of a V'Dan War Prince, having lived in the Alliance for many years.

They did not yet understand the value of a Grand High Ambassador who looked like a juvenile V'Dan. Jackie hoped they would surrender quickly rather than need to learn. As Empress Hana'ka herself had once said, however, there was no point in holding one's breath.

Bridge chatter, some of it familiar from Terran similarities, other parts foreign, flowed around her in quiet ripples of conversation, monitor noises, and personnel movements. Most of the intership chatter with the eight surviving K'Katta, three Tlassian, three Solarican, and four V'Dan warships in orbit revealed that the Terran personnel accompanying the battle on some of those ships had managed to do most of the damage to the enemy vessels.

Some of that comm-system chatter came from the Salik government, requesting permission to send small insystem-capable ships to rescue any survivors. Others were requests to send out the orbital sweepers, ubiquitous little machines that shared a common, simple design across the Alliance, and even had counterparts among the Terrans, built with great mesh sails charged with static energies meant to attract and trap even the tiniest particles whipping around a planet at orbital distances and speeds. So far, Admiral A'quon had denied both requests. Even the K'Katta, compassionate to a fault, knew better than to offer to pick up Salik survivors without a formally broadcast surrender and a lot of backup.

One of the communications officers spoke up, a fellow with a chartreuse streak down the back of his dark blond head, woven awkwardly through his short braid. "Admiral, the Grand High Governor of Pwok has finally agreed to discuss terms of surrender with the lead Alliance vessel."

"Does the Commander-of-Tens-of-Thousands still agree to let us handle the matter?" A'quon double-checked, naming the highest-ranked K'Katta Guardian in the system. As the fleet with the greatest number of surviving ships and thus the greatest amount of resources at hand, this battlefield was technically their cleanup to manage, according to Alliance combat rules.

Another fellow answered, shorter-haired with a hand-sized blotch of burgundy among his dark curls. ". . . Confirmed, Admiral; Commander-of-Tens-of-Thousands Kana-k'ka confirms this a Terran and V'Dan battle. He wishes you a harder exoskeleton."

(*That means he wishes her good luck,*) Li'eth translated absently, (*one combatant to another.*)

"Please let him know I . . . we . . . shall beat them until softened and surrendered," A'quon stated. "Grand High Ambassador, are you ready?"

"Warden Superior Taq'enez, are we being recorded by the Terran comm systems?" Jackie asked.

"Yes . . . we are recording, meioa," he stated, and unbuckled his safety harness so that he could switch seats. "Please take my place."

Swapping places so that she sat between him and Li'eth, Jackie buckled the lower belt but did not bother with the upper straps. A brief query to Li'eth had him reassuring her that she looked good, her hair pinned at the nape of her head, no strands out of place. He did use a pinch of telekinesis to pick off a pale bit of fluff from her Dress Blacks, then gave her his silent approval.

Nodding, she looked into the pickups buried in the monitor screen, and stated, "I am Grand High Ambassador Jacaranda MacKenzie of the Terran United Planets, Colonel and Vice-Commodore of the four Branches of the Terran United Planets Space Force. I am aware in advance of the nature of the various orders I am and may be about to give, and I accept the possible consequences to myself, to the United Planets, and to the various member nations of the Alliance. I accept also that there will be consequences to the Salik nation, with whom we are at war."

Sensing Taq'enez leaning forward slightly, twisting his head to peer at her face, she glanced his way and arched a brow.

". . . Yes?"

"Do *all* of your military officers make such statements before going into battle?"

"Warden Superior . . ." Admiral A'quon chided softly.

Jackie couldn't see the older woman's face, but she could hear an implied eye roll in A'quon's tone. Permitting herself a brief, amused smile, she shook her head. "No, Warden Superior—and that was a valid question to ask. I have to make that statement wherever possible because I am a *civilian* authority. A very-high-ranking civilian. When *I* speak, meioa, when I make decisions that involve great changes in a situation, and particularly a situation requiring force or violence . . . my decisions can literally decide the lives and deaths of millions, if not billions.

"Your question *is* quite valid. Since your people do not know mine all that well just yet, you have every right to ask about the steps my people take. Just as my recitation that I am indeed aware of many possible consequences from the choices I make today is equally valid, and even more necessary."

He blinked a little, and nodded. "Thank you for enlightening me, Grand High Ambassador. I will strive to enlighten others should they ever be puzzled by it."

"That would be appreciated. Admiral A'quon, I am ready to assist you in calling for the colonists of Pwok to surrender, and hopefully the rest of the system as well," she finished. "Thank you for your patience with our legal customs."

"I hope the legal repercussions will not be severe, should things go wrong," the Admiral replied.

"Well, usually it sounds more serious than it actually is, when things go wrong," Jackie allowed.

". . . Admiral, the Grand High Governor of Pwok is requesting again to speak with the leader of the Alliance forces," the tech with the chartreuse streak of hair repeated.

"How goes the dispersion of the Terran devices?" she asked. "And do we have Salik prisoners on their way to divulge the location of their important bases?"

"There are prisoners, yes," one of the officers off to the starboard of the bridge stated. "The Solaricans managed to capture a bridge crew intact." She nodded at her screen. "Leftenant Jons-tun is on board Shuttle 312-6, and will reach their ship in less than ten *mi-nah*."

"Eighty-five percent of the *BM*-class devices have been launched, Admiral, but only sixty-three percent of the *MT*-class are still on board. The rest are in the queue for launch," another added. "The gunnery teams estimate the last of them will be released in the next three *mi-nah*, and will be sufficiently spread out after another twenty."

"Excellent. You may now open the link, full video," A'quon directed.

Taq'enez shifted, stretching out his arms while holding himself back and to the right, touching the controls so that the center screen displayed a greenish-blue figure with bulbous bright yellow eyes. Once again, the view was from above, showing a good portion of the alien's torso. This Salik, however, wore fitted garments in a russet red a bit too brown to be Imperial scarlets but which went rather well with his skin tones.

At least, to her Human eyes. For a bizarre moment, Jackie wondered if the Salik cultural mind-set believed in certain body parts being accented for attractiveness. Back on Earth several centuries back, male Humans had worn false padding inside their stockings to make their calves look more shapely, in the name of fashion. Low-cut gowns for women had come and gone in fashion. There had even been a fad for highly toned arms at one point, back before the AI War. She had no idea what Salik physiology would be considered attractive, however.

"Who sspeaksh for the Alliancsse?" the alien requested, dark pupil slits narrowing slightly as he focused on images being displayed on his side of the connection. "A V'Dan? A . . . juffenile?"

Without prompting—Jackie knew she had not projected telepathically—Taq'enez did something to the controls that projected an image of Jackie herself on the monitor to the right of the main one, and an image of A'quon on the screen to the left, leaving the Salik in the center. He nodded subtly in silent satisfaction and sat back, waiting for the next moment he might be needed.

"I am Admiral A'quon of the V'Dan Empire, aboard the Imperial Warship *The Hard-Handed Judgment*. I speak for the Alliance fleet in this system. I am assisted in the command of this battlefield by Grand High Ambassador Maq'en-zi of the Terran government," she added.

Jackie had given her a telepathic translation session on the very first day she had boarded the *V'Goro J'sta*, but the soft, relaxed *kuh* of her family name was not nearly the same as the more shaped *kooh* of the glottally shaped q the V'Dan were used to using.

"I am Grand Hhhigh Governor Shhnaq-wzz-Tiell," the Salik replied. His accent when speaking V'Dan came across a bit differently than the other Salik Jackie had met. Not that she'd heard all that many speak so far, of course. "Your forcesh are sstrong. You hhave acquired ffictorry hhere." A pause, and the governor of Pwok bared his teeth in a challenging smile. "I wonderr how many other placesh your people have losht because you are hherre annd not therrre."

A'quon did not rise to the bait. "You have lost your orbital defenses, Governor Sh'naq-wuzz-Tiell. You have insufficient ships in this system to defend your territory. Your military bases are going to be identified and destroyed. Once they are rubble, the rest of Pwok will be destroyed, piece by piece, until you surrender."

Jackie watched the Salik's expressions. She had walked inside their minds, learned how they viewed the world. She couldn't *see* the exact same colors a Salik saw, so she was missing a few social cues from subtle shifts in skin tone, missing some of the near-infrared wavelengths Human eyes just couldn't pick up, but she did notice a subtle dimpling in the skin of the skull between the eyes and nostril-flaps. (*He's worried.*)

(*Good. Let him and his people suffer.*)

She sighed roughly in her mind, ignoring the response the governor gave the Admiral. (*I don't like them either, Li'eth, but—*)

(*—Jackie, there were rumors that this world had a primitive sentient race developing on it when the Salik first settled* *here a hundred years ago.*) He stared at her. (*The Salik claimed they were nothing more than dumb herd animals . . . which they ate alive. "Animals" that used tools. I've seen some smuggled vid of it. Don't you Terrans classify tool-using animals as the nine-tenths? And give them extra protections, the great apes, the cetaceans?*)

(*Then we should be even more careful in attacking them.*)

(*The Salik have only been on this world for a hundred years,*) he told her. (*That "herd animal" hasn't been seen by any V'Dan for over five years. They ate them all. Hundreds of thousands of the beings eaten alive, as their people flocked to that world to go on vacation, hunting and eating those beings. They even* advertised *the species as going extinct, ". . . so get a last bite while you can!" And while there might be a few left somewhere, I doubt it.*

(*Just before the war started, I was told Pwok's internal tourism had tapered off in the last five years,*) he added grimly. (*I don't think they ever quite learned how to successfully breed those beings. They* do *know how* we *breed.*)

That statement came with an unpleasant underthought packet of V'Dan and Humans penned in cages, naked and prodded into producing more "herd animals." Her stomach churned when she realized those subthoughts were what the V'Dan Empire believed was happening to their captured colonists, not just what Li'eth believed personally.

". . . and I do not undershtannnd why you show me a jufenille the same shcreen as you. Is thish shupposed to be inntimidatinng?" the governor asked, redrawing her attention to the screen.

Only to have it distracted again by V'Dan lettering scrolling along the edge of her screen, warning her that the first of the Terran bombs were within range of the first known target, estimated time of impact ten V'Dan *mi-nah*. Along with it came the information that two of the K'Katta carrier ships still had fighters out there and were able and willing to provide escort for covering fire.

Shifting her hands to the keys, she typed in her orders, accustomed after all these months to using V'Dan equipment with V'Dan lettering and V'Dan command codes. Beside her, Taq'enez shifted a little in his seat, no doubt to either caution her or warn her or offer to do it himself, but he didn't say anything aloud since that could send his voice to the alien governor. Watching her work, he subsided again, apparently content that she did seem to know what she was doing.

As she typed, she spoke. "Governor Sh'naq, allow me to enlighten your ignorance. I am a *Terran*. Not a V'Dan. Please do not make the mistake of thinking that because we look alike, we are not different. My people are allied with, but not actual members of, the V'Dan Empire. We do not think like them, and we do not take orders from them.

"We are, however, giving you a joint ultimatum from the V'Dan Empire and the Terran United Planets, as well as from the other Alliance races. I am giving you a decent chance, Governor, to surrender immediately and completely, if you wish for your citizens to survive. When you do, you will be treated fairly under the terms we will impose upon your people. In the meantime, you have ten *mi-nah* to evacuate all personnel from your military bases. I suggest whoever is monitoring this broadcast send the evacuation signal immediately if you wish to save their lives."

The alien blinked his eye membranes as he looked up at her. "Hhyou think to order—"

"—This is not a negotiation, Governor," Jackie stated, her expression implacable as she sent the final command. "Those bases *will* be destroyed. Pwok is the first Salik colonyworld to fall under the hammer of Terran assistance. We acknowledge that you lack the interstellar communications we possess. We acknowledge that this means this scene will have to be repeated multiple times on multiple worlds because we acknowledge each world's governor will not believe what we are capable of doing to enemies who insist upon fighting us.

"But we are not unduly cruel. We hope to use the recordings of what is about to happen to your world to warn your fellow citizens how it is much better to surrender fully and swiftly, rather than be annihilated one city at a time."

"You will nnnot deshtroy our citiess," the governor scorned. "The K'Katta will nnot allow it."

"On the contrary, Governor. Your people have finally pushed the Alliance too far. Even the K'Katta have agreed to annihilate you if you do not surrender," she stated. "Let me explain to you something about the Terran mind-set, Governor. My grandfather, who was a major government figure, taught me as a child to be nice. To always be nice first, wherever and whenever possible."

From the way those nostril-flaps flexed, the Salik was not impressed. Jackie continued, gaze flicking occasionally to the secondary screens showing some of the *BM*-class casings headed into the atmosphere at different locations, K'katta fighter craft providing covering fire against what appeared to be defensive laser and missile strikes being launched from the surface. To her satisfaction, those lasers didn't even dent the ceristeel casings.

"My grandfather explained that if we started out being mean, no one would ever believe it when we tried being nice later on. He *also* explained that if you pretend to be nice in order to hide the fact that you fully intend to be mean, then that isn't actually, honestly nice," she stressed, looking at the alien again. "V'Dan, Solarican, and K'Katta military-intelligence reports all confirm that since this war started, you have stated you joined the Alliance under the pretense of being 'nice' only so that you could lull everyone into a false sense of friendship.

"You pretended to be nice in order to gain access to and improve upon everyone else's advanced technologies, and to await the time when you could build up your forces large enough, supplemented by those technologies, to go to war against everyone else. With the expressed purpose of eating fellow sentient beings while they are still alive," she added, looking at Sh'naq-wzz-Tiell. "*That* qualifies very solidly as 'not nice' in the Terran perspective.

"It is *also* important, my grandfather instructed me, to punish those who are not nice in a way that is appropriate to the current circumstances. Sometimes, it is simply telling them what went wrong, trying to elicit empathy and sympathy for those they have harmed emotionally or physically, perhaps even requiring them to make amends, take lessons in anger management, pay for medical treatments, and so forth. Sometimes it requires economic sanctions against those who create economic havoc. But in war, Governor . . . you are trying to destroy us on the most fundamental level. You are trying to slaughter my species and the other sentient races in the Alliance.

"Your people are 'not nice,' Governor. Your government is 'not nice.' You are 'not nice' in the worst of ways. So we must punish you until you agree to *be* nice . . . at which point, when you show you can be nice, we will resume being nice to you. Five *mi-nah* to finish your evacuations. If your people hurry, they should be out of the worst of the blast radius."

The governor made a sort of snorting, whistling sound, blinking twice. It was, Jackie knew from her language translation, a Salik statement cursing ancient troublesome water spirits. He switched back to V'Dan. "Your weaponsh are tiny. We are not impresshed."

"They are capable of being huge," she corrected. "As we speak, each one is being calibrated to the exact acreage of each targeted military base. The known bases, that is. But we are not worried. We will soon have knowledge of the *hidden* bases as well."

Those pupils widened slightly, one stubby eye rotating to look off to the side at some other screen. "They arerr radioactif? You break Allianshe law by using radioactif weaponsh?"

"They are not radioactive, Governor. We have no interest in poisoning your biosphere." She paused, then allowed, "Of course, you'll still have massive sonic shock waves to contend with, and probably some firestorms at the epicenters. But no nuclear fallout sickening the terrain for generations."

"You do not haff to deshtroy ush," Governor Sh'naq said.

"Do you surrender completely?" Jackie asked, fingers poised over the keys.

"We demand timmme to discussh this with our citizens," he prevaricated. "Call off your bombsh."

"No." She spoke flatly, holding his gaze. Reluctant though she was to *think* like a Salik, she still tried. "This is your deep warning, Governor. The destruction of your military infrastructure has been mandated by the entire Alliance. The Terrans, my people, have agreed to carry it out. Your facilities that manufacture and maintain your starships, weapons, troop transports, and all similar support mechanisms for your military efforts *will* be destroyed, regardless of how fast or slow you surrender.

"The only thing your surrender gains is a little bit more of the time needed to evacuate your personnel from those facilities. However, as we are aware that could be taken to mean giving you plenty of time to evacuate weapons and war machines . . . we will only give you just enough time to evacuate your fellow sentients, even if you do surrender. Terran warriors are not juveniles, Governor, for all we do appear to be unmarked V'Dan," she finished. "When it comes to war, we do not play games."

"We are broadcasting this warning in all lightwave frequencies to any and all ships coming in from the outer edges of this system," Admiral A'quon added. "If you attack this fleet, you, too, will be considered a part of the Salik military structure, and you will be destroyed."

(*I should probably be absolutely clear in communicating our intent, shouldn't I?*) Jackie asked Li'eth.

(*Yes, you should,*) he agreed. (*Hopefully, it will make them realize they should surrender while they can.*)

Nodding, she shaped her lips around what syllables, consonants, and sounds she could make, but actually spoke using the sonokinetic portion of her holokinetic gift. *"Ssnnash-gwish-plich guwash a-shaa svik twee-plish-znng . . ."*

The Governor's eyes widened, pupils dilating. He interrupted her, nostril-flaps whistling in his astonishment. *"You speak Sallhash! You speak it without the biology to speak it!"*

". . . Terrans are not V'Dan, Governor. I am a specialist in languages, as well as a high-ranked official for both my government and our military forces," she explained, replying in the same tongue. Or rather, as the Salik said in their own language, replying with the same nostrils, even if hers were nothing like a Salik's. *"As I was saying, we are going to destroy your military infrastructure, whether or not you surrender. If you do not surrender, we will finish destroying your military bases, supply depots, manufacturing plants and so forth, and move on to targets that provide support services to your military.*

"We are aware that this includes civilian targets. We are aware we will be destroying shops, houses, farmlands, and

crèche-ponds. As you may have noticed," she added, replicating just the right whistle-flap smack to indicate the Salik equivalent of sardonic dryness in one's tone, *"we brought enough bombs with us to ruin every major settlement, above and beyond your military sites."*

He stared up at her with one eye, the same eye as before glancing off to the side. *"Five V'Dan mi-nah have passed, Juvenile,"* Sh'naq-wzz-Tiell retorted. *"Your warnings are toothless."*

"My deep warnings were planned to give your people a gap of time to get evacuated off base," she told him. *"We've thrown in a few extra after that window closes to allow your people a chance to escape the shock-wave radius of the blast, too. Of course, we have never detonated one of these bombs in your particular atmosphere. Hopefully, we haven't underestimated that radius."*

"You speak as though you care about us," he scorned. *"Yet you move to destroy us."*

"Terrans, Governor, prefer peace and cooperation. However, unlike the K'Katta, we can become quite ruthless when roused to fight. Particularly when taking the steps necessary to end all fighting." She lifted her chin up, knowing that in Salik gestural language, looking at him out of the bottoms of her eyes in the Salik blind spot meant she didn't consider him much of a threat. *"The Alliance has decided to end this war swiftly, to save the lives of its member species. We are willing to give you a chance to survive, but since you are no longer a part of the Alliance, you are no longer on the list of those who need to survive."*

V'Dan text scrolled down the side of her monitors, informing her that the first bombs had been detonated. On the other side of the commlink, it took a few more seconds for the results to appear. Two sharp pulses of light flared down on either side of Sh'naq's face. The Salik colonial leader swiveled both of his eyes sharply to one side, then snapped them to the other, checking his own secondary screens.

"Decide quickly, Governor. If you do decide to surrender, we will give you an extra fifteen mi-nah *to evacuate your people."*

Two more bright flashes came in from either side. A fifth

flash. Three more. The K'Katta had already streaked away from the blast sites, their escort duties done. On her own monitors, she had many more sites to watch, all of them viewed from orbit; that made them look like tiny blips of light, followed by dark-boiling clouds of smoke, compared to whatever closer images the colonial leader saw.

"You destroyed a suburb with that hit!" Sh'naq protested, nostril-flaps fluttering in his agitation, his pupils widening. *"You destroyed civilians!"*

She didn't know which site he referred to, but knew from the briefings the other Alliance members had given them that some of the bases on Pwok wrapped around the towns providing support services to the technicians and troops. *"It is regrettable, but explosions of this size are difficult to shape in a way that protects a specific wedge tucked into the sphere of its destruction. Particularly a wedge that supports the functioning of your military aggressions."*

"You cannot do this! You are members of the Alliance!" he protested, glaring at her with pupils so wide, she knew from her language transfer that he was on the border between hunter-mode and prey-mode.

"Our charter, Governor, has not yet been accepted by the Alliance states," Jackie clarified.

That, oddly enough, was a legal point that the K'Katta had stressed as an advantage. Whatever the Terrans did *before* formally joining the Alliance could not reflect upon the Alliance rules, because the Terrans might be allies but were not a part of that system. Yet. By the same token, the K'Katta had made a request that made Jackie's own conscience in these rather brutal steps easier to bear. A request easy enough to accept. After all, it was the *objects* of war they were trying to destroy, not the Salik people.

"The Alliance has authorized the use of full force specifically against your military industry. They want everything that allows you to wage war against them to be destroyed. We Terrans have the capacity to ensure that destruction, and the will to ensure it. Your people, Governor Sh'naq-wzz-Tiell, made the mistake of whittling down the Alliance forces to the point where they have to rely upon Terran technology and determination to win this fight. Your people have also

made the mistake of refusing to distinguish between Terrans and V'Dan . . . which makes it necessary *for us to win this fight."*

"You're not a very moral species if you're willing to kill civilians," he told her. From the way his cheeks and brow dimpled, it was meant as a compliment. *"You are a worthy opponent. Bring your troops down here and fight us grip to grip!"*

She had seen the devastation the Salik ground forces could wreak in open terrain; even if shot midair, a dying Salik soldier could literally fall upon an enemy with damaging force, and they could leap unnervingly prodigious distances. Her answer held that threat firmly in mind.

"No. We are not actually here to fight you, Governor," Jackie added, while yet more targeted areas flared with light and blackened with ash. *"We Terrans are here to destroy your capacity to wage war. Your spaceships, your weapons, your troop transports, your support structures, the objects you use to fight the rest of the Alliance. That is it. That is all we are here to do. It is the only reason we are launching these bombs. Our priority targets are your spaceports, munitions depots, weapons and war-machine caches, your military bases, and the industries that create and repair those things.*

"If, after those things have been destroyed, you continue to insist on fighting with empty grips, then we will begin targeting major population centers . . . because those are where your soldiers are created, and therefore are to be considered part of your ongoing war industry. If you refuse to surrender before then," she cautioned mildly. *"That choice is yours, but it does have a time limit. Our bombs are not radioactive, but they will cause problems with the weather and the atmosphere on your colonyworld. Of course, the Terran government assumes no liability or responsibility for fixing the damage wrought to Llghk Pwok or any other Salik-held world because of your refusal to surrender immediately. We have no interest in settling on your planets, so we will not be affected by any damage."*

An especially large flare made the governor wince, slit pupils narrowing against the brightness of whatever view that might be. His eyestalks swiveled back to peer up at her, his skin quite dimpled with tension. *". . . You have bested me. The government of Pwok surrenders to the might of the Tehranz."*

"Do you surrender completely, agreeing to follow all of our commands?" Jackie asked. More explosions. They were getting close to the halfway point on how many *BM* bombs could be spared to attack Pwok. The planet had hundreds of *MT*-class casings orbiting it, but only so many that could actually explode. *"Please answer in V'Dan on a wide-band broadcast so that the members of the Alliance understand your compliance,* or *lack thereof."*

Two more explosions. The Salik flinched, cheeks relaxing, but that patch of skin between nose and stalks rippling subtly again. *"Yes!* Yes, Pwok surrendersh completelllly! *All soldiers, cease your huntings!"* he added in his native tongue. *"Pwok must surrender to survive through these harsh currents and starvation times."*

She typed in a command and spoke in V'Dan. "Thank you for your cooperation. You have a fifteen-*mi-nah* reprieve to evacuate the remaining sites . . . that is, once the current round of bombs finish dropping. Some of them are now too close to be stopped."

"That ish nnnot enough timme!" he protested. "We nneed more time to effacuate!"

"You have had plenty of time," she countered patiently. "The original fleet of ships attacking you warned you immediately upon their arrival that your military complexes would be destroyed. We confirmed this warning was given on our way inward via lightwave samplings."

"We did nnnot belieffe you!" he insisted.

That phrasing pleased her. What she had learned of Salik xenopsychology, of Salik ruthlessness, allowed her to state calmly in his own language, *"Your belief in our resolve is immaterial. Your resistance is immateral. And your admiration is immaterial,"* she stated, knowing that her words would be a psychological blow to a species with a culture that greatly admired prey that fought back. Refusing to acknowledge Salik valiance, bravery, cunning . . . it was an insult to ignore them. *"We are here, Governor, to destroy your capacity to fight.*

"It is a simple enough job, but one that we will complete," Jackie told him, still speaking sonokinetically. The Salik con-

sidered Imperial High V'Dan to be a simple language, matched to a simple, softhearted, more-prey-than-predator species. *"You may leave your people in the same locations as your military materiél, or you may evacuate them to shelters or places beyond the blast radius. It does not matter to us how many survive or not, so long as you are unable to fight back effectively with more than just your empty grip by the time we are through."*

Another curse escaped him, this time something about sucking mud and begetting yet more vegetarians.

"I do enjoy eating vegetables, yes, thank you for asking about my healthy dietary habits," she quipped in Sallhash. *"And no, I don't need to know about yours."*

That startled an odd nostril-whistle out of the Governor. An actual laugh, for his species.

Switching back to V'Dan, she stated for the record, "The Governor of Llghk-Pwok has agreed to a complete and unconditional surrender, with the understanding that any resistance at this point will be met with lethal retaliation. We will also continue to target military infrastructure, both known right now and as discovered in the future. It is hoped that the Salik in this star system will be wise about surrendering and evacuating all such targets."

She twisted to look up and behind her at the Admiral. A'quon nodded and addressed the ships that might be listening. "If any inbound Salik vessels wish to alter course and head toward your sibling colonies to warn them, you are free to do so. In fact, it might be wise. You will want to evacuate those planets' military targets as well. That is, if you care about saving your people's lives."

She paused, then smiled with bared teeth. Hers were not the predatory, flesh-tearing kind of a Salik; hers were flat incisors, save only for her pointed canines. But that smile, delivered in that way, conveyed the same sort of threat found in the Human version as it would be interpreted by most of the other aliens.

"You have indeed pushed us past the point where we have stopped caring about your lives. Thank you for your cooperation, Governor. We will now transfer you to the K'Kattan Councilor for Surrender and Capitulation Protocols. Please continue to cooperate, and urge your people to cooperate. We do have your position triangulated."

Another mutter in Sallhash, this time about farts underwater. The image on the screen shifted to the crossed and curved lines of the Eternal Empire, red and gold on white. Jackie blinked a couple of times before being quietly urged by Warden Superior Taq'enez to relinquish his seat so he could package up the conversation with the Governor of Pwok, and all the destruction that had ensued. That was still ensuing, albeit given a brief reprieve of just a little more time for an evacuation.

(*Something's disturbing you,*) Li'eth murmured, joining her in rising. (*What's wrong?*)

(*I just had the disconcerting realization that I find Salik epithets actually amusing,*) Jackie replied, blinking a few more times. (*Did you know what Llgkh-Pwok actually translates as?*)

(*Yes, the closest comparison would be your Terran "Come and Get It" thing that your family called out when the roast pork was ready at the lu'au you held,*) he replied, touching her back not so much to guide her out of the bridge, but because it was simply necessary to connect with each other.

She leaned back into his arm, matching her stride with his so they could walk comfortably side by side. (*Yes, but it just occurred to me that they just "came and got it," in terms of harvesting what you plant. The Governor's last curse in Sallhash was all about those who eat flatulence-causing foods having no right to complain about farts flavoring the lake water.*)

(*That* is *actually a little bit funny,*) he allowed. (*Gross, but funny. I'll have to remember to share that with V'kol. He enjoys a good flatulence joke. I certainly can't share it with anyone else, as a member of the Imperial Tier.*)

(*Share it with my nephew Ahe,*) Jackie offered. (*He's still at that age where flatulence jokes are considered hilarious.*)

(*Good point. As soon as we can figure out what time it is back there, we can give them a call, maybe find out how Lani's foot is doing.*)

(*I love you for being concerned about her,*) Jackie told him, nudging him with her arm. Just a little bump, to let him know she meant it wholeheartedly.

In turn, he squeezed her subtly, arm slipping a little more around her ribs. At least until they had to part to get around one of the crewmen in the corridor outside the bridge. Their next task was to go help the V'Dan version of a councilor for managing surrenders and capitulations, to work as an adjunct and a watchdog over the proceedings.

(*You've told me how important* ohana *is. It's family,*) he reminded her. (*Family is important even to my people.*)

That wrinkled her nose. (*That reminds me. How is your eldest sister doing?*)

(*Vi'alla? Last I heard was the same that you heard. If she keeps giving the Empress headaches, however, she just might find herself shipped off to a remote monastery.*)

(*Make sure it's not the one with that one priest from the Winter Temple in it, the fellow who kept trying to push his way into royal minds,*) Jackie cautioned him.

(*Agreed. That would be bad. Maybe we'll just get her shipped off to a colonyworld . . . except there will be a lot of Terrans escaping Earth and spreading out across the Empire, trying to find enclaves to settle in. At least, until we can get you your own colonyworlds.*)

(*Let's open up some of the newest ones for settlement that the V'Dan have already started to colonize,*) she compromised. (*We're almost done refining the rules for who governs what, for those.*)

(*We'll still have a few years, while most of your people get filtered into the Alliance via military service,*) he reminded her. (*Once we get all of the Salik to surrender, and evacuated from any joint colonyworlds, then we'll have to keep them blockaded, and that means a huge military force will constantly have to cycle through each Salik-held system. It'll be a full-time job, watching for escaping ships, potential rebuilding of military infrastructures, and the insane members of each race that think smuggling in goods for black-market profits are worth the risk of being eaten alive by their clients.*)

(*Nobody ever said it had to be easy,*) she pointed out. (*Which deck are we going to, again? This ship is too big.*)

(*Two down, two corridors over, third door on the left.*) He added a mental kiss to her brow. (*And this ship is not too big. Your ships are just too small.*)

(*We know, we know . . .*)

CHAPTER 12

NOVEMBER 24, 2287 C.E.
JUL 15, 9508 V.D.S.
GLIGIELGKH
SWISH-SWISH-PLIK 344 SYSTEM

"So it is working?" Augustus Callan asked. "These star systems are surrendering?"

"Yes, Premiere," Li'eth answered him. "The plan is succeeding."

Jackie was supposed to be here, but she had been called away to consult with Darian on some of the information the xenotelepath had retrieved in this system. Li'eth knew everything she did, more than enough to make this report to the various leaderships, military and civilian of the Alliance. The *V'Goro*'s communications system had been hardwired into the Terran hyperrelay poking out one of its airlocks, and since the hyperrelay system used highly focused beams to broadcast through the pinhole aperture created by the devices, there was no chance of the Salik overhearing anything.

It was an elegant way to communicate. Plans were already being drawn up to convert a minor section of this ship into the vacuum-pressured bay it needed for communication—Terrans had already tested the system to see if it could be used in its tiniest setting directly on one of their other planets, Mars, and had discovered that they could do so *if* it was done in a vacuum. Nothing bigger than a pinhole for streaming data, however; the gravity well of a planet could warp the opening into collapsing above a certain aperture size just as surely as a stream of atmospheric particles could.

He looked at the other leaders projected onto the conference cabin's screens, making sure they were digesting the good news. "The ships sent to the Kagliej-Nokh System are reporting the same level of success that we're having here at Gligielgkh. We broadcast the battle, destruction, and surrender of Pwok, along with the warning to evacuate their military centers.

"They didn't believe us at first, and that has led to an estimated tens of thousands of lives lost to the bombings, but with the *BM-* and *MT*-class missiles striking their surfaces at different intensities calibrated to do the minimal amount of effective impact and explosion damage, we have convinced them we are sincere in our targets and our resolve," Li'eth stated. "This system surrendered half an hour ago. We gave them the minimum amount of time to evacuate to limit how much war materiél they could evacuate with their personnel, and the bombardments have since resumed, removing their ability to create any more war machines," he told them. "Surprisingly, the *MT*-class weapons are turning out to be far more efficient at that task than the *BM*s have been, for anything but the larger military bases."

The Gatsugi President flushed a bright bluish green in surprise. "They are/are? How/Why is this so/happening?"

Touching the controls on his console, Li'eth sent them prepared files of surveillance footage. The craters displayed were devastating, but only on a scale of tens of *mitas*, instead of hundreds of *mitas* wide. "One of our technicians on board the *V'Goro* pointed out that since they're aerodynamic and have their own thrust systems, they could be used as kinetic-impact weapons. Their mass is known, and we have access to atmospheric pressure information for all sites.

"After that, it's just a matter of calculating how much additional thrust to add on top of the local terminal velocity to create an impact of sufficient strength to obliterate a target," he stated, and smiled slightly. With closed lips, of course; this was an amused smile, not a fierce one. "The mathematicians aboard the *V'Goro* have been amusing themselves with trying to calculate the exact kinetic impact required for each strike off the tops of their heads, then guessing an estimation of the damage spread."

"Meioa War Prince," President Marbleheart chittered through his translator box, "please remind these mathematicians that this is not a matter for jesting and betting. Lives have been lost with these impacts."

". . . Of course, Meioa President. I will chastise them," Li'eth replied quickly. To a V'Dan—to a Human—sometimes a member of his species just needed to jest and joke in the face of horrible things, to alleviate the strain. But he understood the solemnity of the moment. "We *are* aware of the seriousness of these strikes. The stress of it has led to inappropriate levity."

Marbleheart flexed the fingerclaws of one of his forelegs. "We understand that pressure and strain can trigger inappropriateness. We appreciate more effort on your part in mindfulness and awareness to prevent it from happening again."

"Arrre you still on schedulle for arriving at the next system?" the War Princess asked them, returning to the topic at hand. "The trrransports we loanned are slightly ahead of schedulle."

Li'eth nodded. Before he could actually speak, however, the conference-room door slid open, and Jackie entered. Holding up a hand to stave off questions, he said, "Please wait. The Grand High Ambassador has arrived."

"And I will be glad when I am not wearing three hats at once," Jackie said, slipping into the seat next to Li'eth's. He quickly shifted the focus of the cameras so that they recorded her image as well as his.

"Thrrree hats?" the Choya military leader asked.

"Ambassador, military supervisor, and chief of psychic operations. We have a slight-but-serious problem, meioas," Jackie stated, staring straight into the pickups, her expression sober and somewhat exhausted-looking. "The plan to extract locations of hidden military industry is working at a far higher cost than anticipated."

"What cost is that, Grand High Ambassador?" Empress Hana'ka asked her.

"The minds of the Salik are very different from ours. Accessing them creates a sort of dissonance distress in the xenopath doing so—it is not dissimilar, I think," Jackie added, "from the distress a K'Katta would feel when tapping into the mind-set of a natural predator."

"Natural predators the Salik are," Fearsome Leader Siirrlak stated. Since this was a conference call and not a conference meeting, the Chinsoiy delegation did not need to be relegated to a zeolite-lined suite of rooms connected only by a thick window and a comm unit. They were all connected via comm units right now. "How enduring are the mind-walkings?

"The higher the rank, the more we can endure," Jackie admitted, "but while Lieutenant Johnston is quite strong, he is nearing his limits. I have placed him on official rest for the next two weeks, in the hopes he will be able to recover. I will do what I can to pick out a few more targets, but I, too, am beginning to exhaust my reserves in dealing with the dissonances of trying to comprehend their minds."

"The Seer always sufferrrs from what she sees," War Princess Pallan sympathized.

"How much cann you get donnne beforrre you mmust ceassse and deparrrt for the next colony?" the Tlassian war leader asked next.

"Not as much as I'd like, and not nearly as much as you'd need, to keep up the current pace," Jackie told him. "The problem for myself and my fellow *xenopaths* is a strong one, but with the majority of the war machines of the enemy being destroyed, each fleet of Alliance ships and Terran munitions left in place to monitor each of these worlds should be able to hold them in check until more xenopaths can be brought in to start scanning minds. So while the problem is quite serious for me and my fellow mind readers, it is not actually a true hardship for the Alliance. At least, not just yet.

"Now, can any of you tell me if you've worked out a solution for the conflicting problems of getting all Salik everywhere to grasp the fact that their people have indeed surrendered, without allowing any Salik ships to escape and regroup into a fleet?" she asked.

War Princess Pallan answered that question. "The pllan is to strrap a communications satellite to their hulls, and set it to detonate if it does nnnot receive a confirmation signal within a certain time frrame from ships within the correct system."

"I like it," Li'eth stated. "It's straightforward and to the point."

"It is a horrible idea, very unethical," President Marbleheart chirped, translator box conveying V'Dan-style emotive tones of a male disturbed by the very idea . . . followed by palpable reluctance in admitting, ". . . but it is the best idea we can come up with. They are prisoners, and sometimes prisoners are just too dangerous to be allowed to escape."

Empress Hana'ka nodded. "General I'osha learned that lesson when a moment of carelessness in guarding the captured Salik on Ton Bei allowed them to escape. Over two hundred citizens and soldiers died, Terran and V'Dan, before the prisoners were reclaimed or killed. As soon as the Salik High Command has surrendered, I want them shipped off our sovereign colonies and dumped onto their own worlds."

"You will have no objectionns from my goverrrnment to that," Pallan agreed, earrings swaying with an annoyed flick of her ears. "Au'aurrran is sufferring similar prroblems."

"Morning winds come soon, gentle glidings to a safe landing for all," the Chinsoiy stated. "Long has been this night flight. Glad to see an end to all bombardings will we be."

"It's not our preferred choice of dealing with people, no," Premiere Callan agreed. "But it is saving lives on our side, and our ceristeel casings are thwarting the attempts to destroy them by their defense lasers. Particularly when they try to target the *MT* bombs, only to find them empty of all munitions."

Li'eth blinked. They were all speaking in V'Dan, but he finally *got* the designation. *MT . . . is short for Empty. How clever . . . (Jackie, if MT stands for "empty," what does BM stand for?)*

(The onomatopoeia in Terranglo for the sound of an explosion. "Boom.") She sounded—and felt—tired. Emotionally, not psychically, he knew. Some tasks wore down one's endurance, but others . . . others eroded a person's soul. Dealing with the Salik mind-set had to be like bathing in acid. As much as he didn't want to touch their minds himself . . .

(Is there any way I could take over some of your Salik mind-scanning duties?) he found himself asking. He did not like the idea of touching Salik minds, but . . . he didn't like the strain she was under, either.

(*I think I will have to take you up on that offer. The first dozen sessions, we'll have to do together. After that, yes. For a little while. But their thoughts are* vicious,) she warned her Gestalt partner.

(*I know. I can feel the strain you're under. You've also been suffering nightmares as we sleep these last few weeks,*) he added.

(*I know. We'll discuss it later; we need to pay attention,*) she reminded him. The others had moved on to talk about how to receive the formal offer of surrender from the Salik leadership on their Motherworld without the Salik somehow ambushing the surrender site, whether that was in space or on the planet.

"Gentlebeings," Hana'ka stated, "it has occurred to me that the Salik have planned in advance for every contingency. Even as arrogant as they are, surely the Salik have arranged some sort of command code to confirm an authentic full surrender? Perhaps the *xenopaths* among the Terrans can pluck it from their minds? That, more than any location for hidden military equipment, is vital for bringing this war to an end. Once they *stop* fighting, we will have the leisure to uncover such things at a more comfortabie pace."

". . . That is correct," Jackie agreed. "That, we could save our strength to do. I agree that it holds a higher priority if they do have anything like that prepared in advance."

"They have to," President Marbleheart stated. "They have never had instantaneous interstellar communications. Everything they do must be planned in advance or conducted independently . . . and a full, nationwide surrender must be something considered in advance."

"Not/Not necessarily/possibly, given/understanding their/the Salik natural/inherent arrogance/pride/blindness . . ." President Anoddra hedged, turning an upper hand palm up in silent philosophical commentary, his skin flushing a mixture of annoyance, grimness, and a few other nuances Li'eth wasn't experienced enough to discern in his colormoods.

Listening to the debate as it continued, circling around whether or not the Salik could and would plan for such a thing, Li'eth could feel Jackie's subthoughts swirling and churning with a seed of an idea. Sampling it, he turned it over a few times in his own mind, then asked, (*Do you really think we could do that?*)

(*We'd be fully rested, no spontaneous teleports draining away most of our strength, and our needs would only cover a very small area,*) she reminded him. (*Put enough layers on, make them flexible enough . . .*)

"Gentlemeioas," Li'eth interjected as soon as there was a break in the flow of conversation, "the Grand High Ambassador and I have an idea that just might convince the Salik that we are even more ruthless and powerful—or at least that our new allies are far more ruthless and powerful—than anything they have ever dealt with before. It is an idea I think might just be the psychological deathblow to the conquest ambitions of our mutual foe, *if* we are on Sallha when we accept their full surrender."

President Marbleheart lifted a foreleg. "Your offer intrigues me. We will listen."

JANUARY 4, 2288 C.E.
AUT 25, 9508 V.D.S.
CITY OF BUBBLINGS, SALLHA
SALLKHAG'GNITH SYSTEM

"Water, water, everywhere," Jackie murmured in Terranglo, mangling the original quote. *"And so beautiful I could hardly blink."*

"It is spectacular, isn't it?" Li'eth murmured back, equally impressed by their surroundings. Over their heads, a quartet of cameras hovered, remotely piloted and staying close, dutifully recording and broadcasting this momentous meeting.

Both their eyes darted here and there, taking in the liquid coursing over sculptures and flowing through pipes that ranged from opaque to transparent, so clear that the water almost looked unsupported as it flowed from one place to the next. Spheres predominated in the architecture, most transparent, some translucent, spun from metal, blown in glass, carved from stone, and crafted in dozens of exotic materials.

A hint of sulfur perfumed the warm, moist air, a rotten-egg scent that spoke of the many mineral springs permeating the

local landscape. Waterfalls cascaded down the sides of buildings, rippled along windows, washed in shallow rivulets over
the pathways. Behind them, the bulk of the *Embassy 1*
thrummed and lifted off again, kicking up a small amount of
spray from a nearby reflecting pool. Within moments, their
group was alone in a city with hostile aliens lining the windows of the ornate office buildings around them.

War Prince Naguarr had requested the right to represent
Solarican interests. His cream robes, brocaded in tiny, plant-
like designs, echoed the cream robes of the Warrior Caste
representative who towered over him by several centimeters.
First Star Admiral Hainann was not nearly as highly ranked
as the two War Princes, one V'Dan, and one Solarican in their
midst, but she was the Tlassian who had managed to wrest
control of the orbital skies around this world, leading a full
fifty Tlassian warships stripped from every colony and even
their own Motherworld, just to join the battle to annihilate
Sallha's insystem defenses.

Beside them, Commander-of-Millions Tlik-tlak moved
with a machine-smooth grace that could only come from a
creature used to marching formally with more than two loco-
motive limbs. Li'eth walked on that side of the group, so that
Jackie did not have to be near the object of her phobia. To her
right marched the Left Palm of Cho, third-highest-ranked
leader of the Choyan military. Her four crests stood stiffly upright, a combination of bravery and anger mixed with a touch
of fear, Jackie had learned in the months since reaching
V'Dan.

Beyond her strode a Gatsugi general whose name translated as Stormblade. They stalked with a strange grace that
was both more fluid than not yet as exactly precise as the
K'Katta on the other end. The Chinsoiy did not, and could not,
attend, but they had indicated their willingness to abide by the
choices and outcomes determined by the others. Surrounding
them in the mottled grays of urban camouflage strode Lieutenant Commander Buraq—her limb replacement deferred
until this moment was over—Lieutenant Paea, and six other
Terran Marines detailed to be their escort.

Everyone in this acceptance delegation was a fully informed volunteer. If the Terran plan did not work . . . only

fifteen souls would be sacrificed. Jackie had confidence it would. Each of her Marines wore their weapons holstered, for each one carried a pair of stunner-disrupting grenades, pulsing in staggered patterns at a rate of several per second. They did so in faint flashes almost completely lost under the bright local sunlight. That was their first layer of defense. Their second lay in keeping the others all within a tight radius of ten meters, in order for their third layer of defense to work properly.

Their target lay at the far end of the great plaza they had used as a drop-off site, a low stone platform ringed by a shallow moat crossed by five bridges. Most of the plaza was empty, save for a cluster of formally uniformed Salik officers awaiting them on that stone circle. Naguarr flicked his ear and looked at Li'eth and Jackie.

"Can you rrread their minnds from here, Ambassadorr?" he asked in Terranglo. Everyone in this delegation spoke it, allowing them to speak freely to each other.

"They have indeed prepared a massive ambush, as we figured. This entire plaza is filled with trapdoors, and I can sense well over a thousand aliens ready and waiting to emerge. They are not aware of our anti-stunner technology," she added, mind reaching out and down, sampling the thoughts of dozens of Salik soldiers lurking within a dozen meters.

They were still at war with the Salik, and the rules for telepathy during war were a little bit different. Her scrying would have been immoral and unethical in peacetime, in a peaceful situation, but telepaths were not hobbled by the rules when it came to surviving a battle. She was still forbidden from *attacking* any minds telepathically if there was some other method she could use with an equal or greater chance of success—which was why telepaths were so valuable against the Greys and their extremely advanced technology—but she was allowed by the rules of warfare for psychic conduct to sample surface thoughts to get an idea of exactly what danger level awaited her.

"They are a little disappointed there are so few of us," she added, leaning on Li'eth's presence to shelter her mind from the almost feral hunger she sensed in those brutal, icy-hot

thoughts beneath the plaza street. *"They are willing to fight each other to get a single bite of alien meat."*

"Are you holding fast in your mind-health's grip, Seer? Or are the visions clawing into you?" Naguarr inquired softly.

"I have my mate to support my mental state. I will be fine."

"I am glllad. Seerrs are a rare and prrecious gift," he told her. *"Especially ones of your powerr."*

Li'eth arched a brow at that and let his lips curve up in a smile, something he knew the Solarican would interpret correctly. *"Are you flirting with my mate?"*

"I am a War Prrrince. I merrely flirrt with dannger."

Jackie tightened her gut against the urge to laugh at that quip. Confining her reaction to a closed-mouth smile, she poured her energy into her shields instead.

They reached the low, curved bridge; at its apex, they saw clearly the famous mosaics decorating the huge, circular platform. Some artist had shaded the surface in large swaths of tiny pentagonal and star-shaped tiles, forming a macroscopic image of boiling water. According to old tourist brochures for this city, the Bubbling Mosaics were over eight hundred years old, carefully maintained as a point of pride.

Delving further into the Empire's translated records of such things—out of curiosity and boredom on the faster-than-light trip to get here—Jackie had learned that the boiling waters in question were a tribute by the artist in reference to the hottest mineral spring, a deep pool used by the city's school for graduation hunts. The artist in question had been slated for slaughter along with four others upon graduation but had unexpectedly gone on to slaughter all twenty of his high-ranked graduating classmates, earning the right to live his life as he liked.

Despite their almost psychotic mind-set, art was prized among the Salik, particularly water-based art. It just had to be coupled with ferocity to survive. They respected fierceness, prized ruthlessness, honored remorseless strength. The Salik only bowed to those who proved themselves superior and scorned the rest.

The minds of the aliens in front of her were, one and all, the most ruthless, arrogant, and disciplined in—or under—the whole plaza. They were also as open to her light scans as any of the rest.

"Idennntitiess?" the Left Palm of Cho asked quietly. Her name was too difficult to pronounce in V'Dan, so she had requested the others simply refer to her as her title.

Jackie took a few moments to consult with Li'eth, then nodded. *"Confirmed. These are the Grand Generals, with the Grand High General of their military in their center."*

She did not add how the male salivated internally as he stared at her Gestalt partner, taking in that distinct burgundy jag of *jungen* marks angled across his right brow, eye, and cheek. A very-high-ranked prize he would soon eat, one screaming bite at a time, all of it recorded by the horrified operators of those hovering cameras.

"Sssuch a small delegationn," the Grand High General observed, eyestalks shifting to take in each member, mottled-beige skin smooth and relaxed. "I exsspected more of hhew to be hhere."

Li'eth, considered the highest in rank of the coalition of races present, and the one Alliance member who could reasonably speak for the non-Alliance Terrans, reached for Jackie for mental support. She gave it fully, knowing as he did that someone as canny as this high-ranked warrior would be proficient at reading Human facial expressions. While not technically an empath, she was his Gestalt partner, able to soothe much of the fear and loathing within him. Allowing him to speak without any external sign of his inner turmoil.

"We are all that is necessary to accept your full and unconditional surrender, Grand High General K'plish."

"Your accssent is atrociouss." His statement was nothing more than a little posturing, a little attempt at rattling the V'Dan Imperial War Prince.

"So is your attitude," Li'eth replied. "You will order your entire nation to surrender, fully and unconditionally. You will inform us of all bases, manufactories, and facilities capable of producing starships, fighter craft, weapons, armor, and other materiél designed to be used for waging war. Those locations will be destroyed, and you will construct nothing new along those lines, under penalty of those facilities also being destroyed with little to no warning.

"Your people from this point forward will live confined within the atmospheres or gravitational pulls of the planets and moons you currently occupy in the eight star systems designated as purely Salik territory," he continued. "All Salik colonists will be deported from all other locations and delivered to those designated colonies. You will be permitted no insystem travel and no interstellar travel without escort and authorization by a joint fleet of Alliance forces. In short, Grand High General K'plish, you and your people will be blockaded, confined, and limited to these eight systems, subject to frequent inspection to ensure you cannot and will not ever again rebuild your capacity for interstellar war.

"If you wish to hunt and fight and *eat* other sentient beings, Grand High General . . . you will do so from this day forward strictly upon the surface of your own worlds and strictly within your own species," Li'eth asserted. "Travel to and from each of your colonyworlds and your Motherworld will be strictly monitored, regulated, and, for the most part, interdicted."

"Forr hhhow lonng?" K'plish asked, stepping slowly forward. So did the two officers flanking the alien war leader.

Jackie let the trio cross their third line of defense.

"Ffor an Allliance yearrr?" the Grand High General inquired, curling up a tentacle-limb. "Fforr a decade?"

Li'eth did not back down. He stared into those greenish-gold eyes without flinching, trusting, *knowing* his partner could and would keep their delegation safe, and spoke the words written in his people's most ancient prophecies. "For as long as it takes you to learn how to get along with other races . . . or until your species destroys itself."

Eyestalks swiveled. Pupils widened. Tendril-limbs curled and uncurled. Jackie, skimming the muck of his uppermost thought-images, dropped to her knees and focused her powers. *"Code Mike Tango Zero One. I repeat, Code Mike Tango Zero One, authorization Alpha Juliett Mike. Twenty meters directly in front of me, on the far side of the plaza circle from my position."*

Grand High General K'plish looked her way for a moment, no doubt wondering what she had just muttered, but he did not speak Terranglo. Did not understand her command. That large mouth pursed and sucked in, echoing that mocking *pwok pwok pwok* sound the Salik loved to make toward their tasty prey. "That juffenile is weak, but . . . hhhew are all too tasssssty to wassste."

Hundreds of trapdoors all across the plaza snapped open. Soldiers sprang up and out, their leaps terrifyingly high, their flippered version of combat boots slapping hard enough on the cobblestones to make the ground shake with the smacking of so many impacts. Weapons lifted and aimed, they surrounded the platform, ready and willing to fire.

K'plish bared his sharp teeth slightly in a low-level warning. "Hhhew darrred come here to give usss ultimatummms. Warrr *Prrrincsse*," the Salik growled. "I will eat hhyour blood-orrrgan in frrront of yourrr warrr-motherr."

He curled two microtendrils on each side, and soldiers hop-jogged across the bridge in low bounds, moving into position to stun the delegates.

Calm inside and out, his trust in his Gestalt partner absolute, Li'eth responded not to the Salik, but to the non-Salik around him. "I suggest that *now* is a very good time to move low to the ground."

With that, he crossed his ankles and sank down onto the mosaic tiles, settling next to Jackie, who already rested on her knees and her heels. Naguarr dropped as well, physiologically capable of sitting cross-legged. The Gatsugi and Choya settled with their legs stretched out, the Tlassian crouched and knelt like the Terran Ambassador, and the K'Katta . . . tucked his limbs under his body.

"Hhew do not fffight? Hhew are almost *pity* meat." K'plish backed up to let the two soldiers have a clear field of fire with their black-and-beige stunner weapons. Two things happened simultaneously; the rifles failed to fire, and the Grand High General bumped into solidified air. His eyestalks swiveled backwards at the nothingness that kept him from retreating, then forward and out to either side, eyeing the soldiers trying to make their weapons work.

All eight Terran Marines, now kneeling just like their black-clad commander, smiled with bared teeth and lifted the pulsing grenades in their hands.

"Terran science, General, is protecting us from your forces . . . and protecting you and your two fellow officers from annihilation," Li'eth explained, smiling as well. Closed-lipped, because he wanted the Salik to know he was amused, not just angry.

"Annihhhilationn?" K'plish repeated.

"Yes. You agreed to a cease-fire. Specifically, you agreed that you would not attack or even threaten this delegation. Your soldiers were not supposed to be here. They were not supposed to use weapons on us. Your soldiers will be annihilated. Destroyed. Wiped out. Their lives have been forfeited."

The Grand High General snorted. "With what warrriors? Fffiffteen againnst fiiffteen hundrrred?"

"Grand High Ambassador MacKenzie, how much longer until these soldiers are destroyed?" Tlik-tlak asked bluntly.

"About twelve more *se-cah*. I suggest covering any hearing organs you possess," she added politely, and tucked her index fingers into her ears. "This might get a little loud."

Pallan swiftly clamped her hands atop her ears, smashing them flat. The others followed suit, the K'Katta curling midlimbs under his body so that the footclaws could cross-cover the special hairs at his knee joints that sensed sound vibrations. The Marines, still clinging to their grenade spheres, still grinning one and all, stuffed the tips of their forefingers into their ears. Paea even turned to smile at Jackie, confident in her abilities. Buraq, however, looked up.

So did Jackie. The tiny dot they both sought was rather difficult to spot . . . but the ring of clouds it had left in its wake high, high above, was not. That gave her a line of attack to focus upon—and she spotted it a split second before it slammed into the crowd behind the generals and admirals near the far edge of the platform circle. They vanished faster than a blink. As did the rest of the plaza and the city, reduced in an instant in a ground-shattering smear of gray dust and reddened mist.

The noise of the impact slammed up through their bones from the ground, which literally shifted back several centimeters. Shoved, but kept intact by the layers of spheres Jackie had laced *through* the plaza stones. Intact, and aloft, the partial remains of the Great Mosaic floated serenely in the midst of the chaos. Two of her outermost telekinetic shields had collapsed, but the inner three still held, sheltering them with flexible surfaces that had absorbed the deadly shock wave of the ceristeel casing's supersonic impact.

Dust finished billowing outward, revealing an awkwardly pitted crater. Some of it settled onto the surface of the otherwise invisible dome of force. A simple mental ripple shivered it off the walls, permitting them to look upon the wreckage more or less unobstructed.

K'plish swiveled his eyes all around, pupils dilated so wide, his eyestalks looked like they were topped with black orbs. His two officers, the two soldiers, also looked around them in wild-eyed shock. Unable to find the words in V'Dan, he fell back on his native tongue. *"How . . . ?"*

Unfolding her legs, Jackie rose to her feet. "Terrans, Grand High General, do not hesitate to bomb our own positions in order to win. That is because our Terran science is superior to all others. I have permitted you five to live because it was convenient," she added, as his eyestalks swiveled to face her. "You will order your people to surrender, and you will comply fully with our commands and restrictions. Or we will continue to bomb everyone and everything around us until *we* are the only ones left who can stand."

K'plish's eyes tilted outward, surveying the grim truth of her words. Enough of the debris cloud had billowed outward to begin showing the smears on the ground. Those areas that had concealed access corridors for underground troops to march into place and prepare an ambush, those formerly hidden passageways beneath all those trapdoors . . . were nothing more than corrugated rubble for fifty meters in every direction but directly behind the bubble-shield Jackie had held.

Two-thirds of the Great Mosaic had vanished, vaporized at the heart of the impact site. Around the edges of the crater, tumbled pieces of alien body parts lay scattered over the landscape, dismembered by the blast. Water, spilling from broken pipes, hissed and steamed wherever it came into contact with the kinetically heated materials near the epicenter.

"Do you and your people surrender fully and completely?" she asked. "Or shall my fellow Terrans drop more? The next strike will be a ring of bombs of a similar size and strength. They will collapse all the buildings around us. The one after that . . . just *one* bomb, but one that will be several orders of magnitude more powerful. That third strike will destroy this entire city, and devastate the countryside. These things, I tell you not as a threat but as a fact. I tell them to you to drive home the two choices in front of you, annihilation or compliance.

"Of course, *you* will still be safe . . . so long as I continue to contain you within my shields," she added dryly. "But you will have to watch your entire city be knocked down and dissolved in an instantaneous firestorm. The equivalent of a thermonuclear device detonated at a range close enough for a child to hit the epicenter with a flung stone."

Those eyestalks swung around the circle, then converged on her. "Hhhew . . . ssssuch powerrr . . . Perrrssonal shielld generatorrr?"

"No more delays, Grand High General. We Terrans are not V'Dan. We are the *Motherworld* of the V'Dan race, and we are not going to waste our time with petty maneuverings and pointless posturings," she told him, her tone flat and mild. *"Code Mike Tango Zero Two through Zero Seven, authorization Alpha Juliett Mike.*

"My government gives yours just two choices, Grand High General. Surrender, or annihilation. You have twenty *se-cah* to decide. Don't take any longer than that."

His arm lashed out—and smacked into a telekinetic wall he could only feel, not see. The blade in his suckered grip didn't fall free like it would have from a Human hand, or perhaps even a Solarican one. But he did blink, skin dimpling all over in distress.

". . . Sssurrenderr. Commplete and fffull ssurrender. The Ssalik nation sssurenders to the ssuperriorr might of the Terrrrans," K'plish said, uncurling his suckered limb from the blade.

Jackie didn't let it clatter to what little remained of the tile-covered platform. She picked it up telekinetically and swooped it through a small, brief hole in her layers upon layers of shields. Floating it horizontally, she offered it hilt first to Li'eth as he stood.

"Code Mike Tango, abort, I repeat, Mike Tango, abort," she stated in Terranglo, before switching back to V'Dan. "War

Prince Kah'raman, the Salik nation has been ordered by its highest authorities to surrender completely and fully. Do you accept their surrender?"

"We sssurrender to *hhew*," K'plish asserted. "Hhew are worthy! *They* arrrre nnot!"

Jackie looked him up and down, and—mindful of Salik-style psychology—told him, "*You* are not worthy of *our* time or attention. War Prince Kah'raman, the Terrans hand over the unconditional surrender of the Salik to the Alliance nations to manage. *Unconditional*, Grand High General, means you cannot impose any conditions whatsoever."

She had to stop for a second as six hydrobomb casings swooped past overhead, followed seconds later by a scattering of loud, sharp *cracks* from the sound-breaking speeds of the aborted missiles. Waiting until the noise faded, she resumed her speech, eyeing the Salik leader.

"That, Grand High General, includes whoever we delegate to manage the punishments and reparations for all the messes you've made."

Looking up into those wide-pupiled, gold-green eyes, she reached out telekinetically. She lifted pieces of the rubble, broken chunks of stone, alloyed metals, even body parts, swirling them around in rising helix spirals, making his eye-stalks sway back and forth between watching the macabre dance and keeping his attention warily upon her.

"Do not make me come back here again, General," she warned softly. "If I do, I *will* start taking your planet apart piece by piece with my Terran science. *If* you annoy me enough."

Everything dropped, chunks, pieces, and parts, sending up a fresh, faint, outward puff of dust. The clouds hit the edges of her outermost shields and curled upward before fading.

Behind her, Li'eth spoke calmly. "The Eternal Empire and its allies accept the management of the Salik Interdiction and Blockade. We will be ruthless in destroying all known and uncovered Salik military mechanisms. Cooperate fully, Grand High General, and we will allow your colonists to visit each other and this world, under supervised transport. Resist . . . and we will be ruthless."

"Hhew are ffictorious because of *them*," K'plish snapped, nostril-flaps flexing. "Hhew hhide behind their technology!"

"That fierce and powerful female is my *mate*, Grand High General," Li'eth corrected him. "*She* considers me worthy, and has been teaching me her Terran science. As she will teach others in the Eternal Empire. And in the Collective, and in all the *other* nations . . . all, except for yours. You are no longer worthy. Now, I do believe the terms of surrender include handing over all of your command codes. Including the security codes for confirming your surrender is authentic, so that all of your colonies and soldiers will know that Sallha has fallen to the Alliance."

That was Jackie's cue. It was also not what K'plish wanted to hear, for he bared his teeth fully, and hissed, "Ssssuck hhyour ownn eggss!"

Even as K'plish snarled, Jackie read his thoughts on the matter. She knew he would never say the words. Would never give out the authentic command codes. Would, in fact, only ever give out falsified codes. In that fraction of a moment, she knew she had a choice. A life-altering choice.

She chose. Ransacked the three officers' minds. Within seconds, she had what the Alliance needed, and nodded.

K'plish swiveled his gaze her way, but it was too late; she had already studied him visually. Wrapping her mind around the alien, she pinned him in place telekinetically so that he couldn't disrupt the lines of her illusion and merged a holokinetic doppleganger over his body. A moment later, the true command phrases emerged from "his" nostrils and lips in perfectly enunciated Sallhash. She waited five seconds, then released him from her grip, blending the fake image back into the reality.

The alien war leader stared at her, tendrils curled up into bulky, spiraled fists in his shock. The two soldiers and the two officers who had survived lowered themselves to the ground, their backwards-pointing knees folding, their tendril-fingers curling into the suckered equivalent of fists. Surrendering as commanded.

It was not ethical, what she had just done. What the leaders of the Alliance—and her own government—had asked her indirectly to do. She was going to get into trouble with the Psi League for doing it because it was a violation of his sovereign rights as an individual sentient. But at the same time, while it was not ethical from an individual standpoint, it *was* ethical from a saving-many-lives point of view. Not purely, or even more than halfway ethical, no . . . but it was expedient to end the war by faking his compliance.

Sometimes, Jackie knew, ethics had to bow to expediency. She just never thought she'd kill her career while standing in the cratered remnants of an alien city hundreds of light-years from home.

"Hhhow . . . ?" the Grand High General demanded, recovering from his shock.

"As I have said," she repeated, and smiled coldly at him, "in certain areas, our Terran science is light-years beyond anything you know. We can do things you will never be able to do. There is no shame in being defeated by a vastly superior foe. There is only shame in refusing to recognize it."

Nostrils flexing, the Grand High General lowered himself to his knees and rested his equivalent of buttocks on his backwards-facing heels. Defeated, not just surrendered.

(. . . *You just shakked away your political career, didn't you?*) Li'eth observed in the back of her mind. (*What we asked you to do in getting those codes, so that all of the Salik we broadcast this moment to will believe he actually surrendered his nation of his own free will . . . you destroyed your career.*)

(*Yep.*) A bittersweet moment. (*But I saved the Alliance decades more of loss and heartbreak, and untold millions of lives.*)

"Grrrand High Ammbassador," Naguaar stated, turning to her to say something. To make some request of her as the representative of her representation-based government.

Heart aching deep inside, Jackie managed to keep her expression mild, her voice calm. "Actually, War Prince Naguarr . . . at this point in time, I wish to formally announce my resignation in full from the position of Grand High Ambassador of the Terran United Planets to the V'Dan Empire and its allies, subject, of course, to the approval of the Premiere and the Terran United Planets Council.

"As my last act of office, I appoint Lieutenant Commander Jasmine Buraq to stand in for my position as temporary Ambassador during the cleaning up of this mess, until such time as Assistant Ambassador McCrary can consult and appoint a suitable replacement. With that said, I recuse myself from further participation in these discussions."

Jasmine blinked a few times but drew herself upright and saluted Jackie, who returned it. She was still a colonel, still a superior officer . . . and might actually have to face a military tribunal over this. But given the sheer number of lives she had just saved, Jackie could live with that kind of a payment.

"My government insists you retain a portion of your position as a cultural liaison at the very least, Meioa McKenzie," Li'eth stated. (*I'm not letting you completely flush your skills and standing down the sewage drains.*)

(*Thank you,*) she replied. Bowing her head, Jackie acknowledged aloud, "In the interest of maintaining good relations with the V'Dan and their allies, I will accept the role of temporary cultural liaison until my situation can be discussed by my government."

"And I will be *happy* to consult with my new cultural liaison," Buraq added, relief at having that option coloring her tone despite the solemnity permeating her words.

"Hheww giffe up your positionn? Hhyour power?" one of the two officers asked, finally speaking.

Commander-of-Millions Tlik-tlak chittered at him. "Terran culture is not V'Dan, it is not K'Kattan, and it is not Choyan. Be respectful to your superiors with your silence whenever you do not understand what is happening."

"Thank you, Commander-of-Millions," Jackie stated. "Acting Ambassador Buraq, if you will take my place, I will take yours as acting head of your security team."

In a strange way, just *saying* that gave Jackie an odd sense of relief. A lightening of a burden she hadn't realized she carried. She still felt anxiety twisting deep inside for losing her highest career but could not deny that this moment came with an odd sort of relief. *Which I'll have to think about later,* she thought, as Lieutenant Buraq replied.

"Colonel MacKenzie, you may certainly do so, sir," Jasmine agreed. Handing over her rifle as the two women crossed paths, she muttered under her breath in Mandarin, *"You are crazier than a donkey eating its own feces, woman . . . but I respect you for all the lives you just saved."*

"Don't forget to say that at my tribunal if I need any wit-

nesses in my defense," Jackie replied, moving to the left of their formation. *"But do phrase it more politely."* Checking the weapon to make sure she knew if it was loaded, she watched Jasmine take her place between Li'eth and the Palm of Cho.

Taking Buraq's position put her right next to the K'Katta war leader. Oddly enough, after walking for weeks through Salik minds and now cratering her political career, Jackie didn't feel nearly as creeped out about a two-meter-wide spider-person. K'Katta truly were gentle-hearted for the most part, or whatever passed for the emotive equivalent of their circulatory organ. *It is quite possible,* she thought privately, *that I'm now going to develop a phobia of frogs, ostriches, and octopuses . . . Octopi?*

Booting hell . . . I don't think anyone *has solved that linguistics dilemma in the last few centuries.*

At least it was something to keep her mind off what she had done.

EMBASSY 1, SALLHA ORBIT

"Are you feeling insane?" August Callan demanded in Portuguese, giving Jackie a dubious look through the comm system. *"Did you somehow sniff something hallucinogenic in the air on that alien world out there?"*

"Premiere, I had no choice but to resign immediately. I conducted myself in an unethical way and needed to remove myself immediately from my position of power," Jackie replied, and waited for the six-second delay between the Salik system and her homeworld.

The only other person in the cockpit was Robert, and he had on a pair of audio headphones, the chords and rhythms of country music filtering faintly through the bulky headset while he nodded along, keeping watch on their surroundings as they orbited the Salik Motherworld. Not that he spoke Portuguese, but he wanted to give her a chance for this conversation to be completely discreet since it couldn't be completely private, thanks to the need to have the cockpit manned at all times while in orbit around a hostile planet.

"You saved lives!" Callan protested, throwing his hands up in the air when her end of their conversation finally reached him. *"You saved millions, if not billions, of lives and resources and years of constant guerilla warfare as we tried to pacify and subdue all those planets—General I'osha on V'Ton-Be contacted me within one hour of rebroadcasting that surrender code to ask me to pass along her personal thanks to you. She said that because of that broadcast, all rebellious activity among her Salik prisoners had actually stopped! You saved the* Alliance, *young lady!"*

"I faked *his surrender!"* Jackie shot back, snapping the words in his native tongue. *"Yes, I saved countless lives, but I holokinetically* faked *him surrendering. I cannot go on to represent* any *group of people with that* on my conscience! *Who would trust me after I* faked *a major political deal?"*

Six seconds later, while he strained to listen to her words . . . Callan's shoulders slowly slumped. Rubbing at the bridge of his nose, he dragged in a deep breath. *". . . You're right. You are absolutely right . . . and a part of me is cursing you for* still *being a near-perfect civil servant, even in your abandonment of your career. I understand His Highness still wishes you to serve as his cultural liaison while he's doing this . . . War Prince thing. Is that correct?"*

Jackie nodded. *"We do still have an immense advantage in acting as cultural liaisons to each other. However, if you feel I should step down from that position, I am ready to do so,"* she added. Below the edge of the cockpit comm-station console, her hands curled into fists. It *hurt* to give up her career, to have deliberately chosen to lie to everyone . . . but it was good to know she *had* saved so many lives by conning the Salik into surrendering for real. *"I will abide by whatever the Council decides to do with me. The only thing I cannot agree to do is leave His Highness' side, as that would cause harm to the son of our closest ally in the Alliance."*

"No one back here would ask you to do that," he snorted six seconds later. *"Jackie . . . you were supposed to find the codes in their minds and say them yourself."*

"Their minds don't work that way. They'd never accept those codes from the lips . . . or nostrils . . . of an alien," Jackie told him. *"They had to see and hear it coming from*

their own leadership. I hoped it would end the war for good, and it did *end the war for good . . . so . . . it was worth it. Imploding my career* will *be worth it."*

". . . Yes, and if you keep saying that enough, you might one day believe it," he retorted wryly. *"As much as I want to throw a tantrum and protest that you cannot abandon your post, that you have to remain our Ambassador—because you* are *good at it—I can respect your professionalism . . . and the reason why you should not be trusted with that level of power ever again. However, I still intend to harness your skills and experience.*

"The Council will hold a closed session to discuss your actions today," he continued, *"at which time I will strongly recommend you be appointed official Terran Cultural Liaison to the V'Dan Empire, and encourage the V'Dan Empire to permit you and your Gestalt partner to travel to all the worlds where Terrans will be settling. You and your insights into both sides of the Human cultural divide will still be put to work helping to shape policy for integrating and respecting our two nations as we start settling worlds beyond the Sol System.*

"You won't be signing *any of those policies,"* Premiere Callan clarified, no doubt anticipating that question, since the lag time involved between their locations meant there was no way she could protest atop his words and actually interrupt him at the right moment. *"But you will be* shaping *them. If I have anything to say about it."*

"What about my military career?" Jackie asked. *"I did conduct myself unethically as an officer of the Space Force. I'm going to have to face a tribunal for my actions."*

"That's technically a much bigger gray area since subterfuge and deception are accepted and acceptable tactics," the Premiere reminded her. *"But from all the cheering I've heard among the Command Staff over the war ending so quickly with so few lost lives, I'd say it won't be anything more than a brief inquest at most, never mind a formal tribunal."*

"Then . . . as soon as the inquest is over, Commander-in-Chief," Jackie asked plaintively, rubbing at the bridge of her nose, *"could I please have your permission to retire my commission as an officer in the Space Force? I've been so many things on this mission over the last year plus a day, it'd be nice to be* one *thing, just for once."*

She waited for his answer. This *was* her career—what was left of it on the line—and yet the stresses Jackie had suffered over the last several months had been exacerbated by trying to be all things to all people: Ambassador, Councilor, Military Advisor, Cultural Liaison, Translator, Psychic Soldier . . .

Oddly, it was only after she had exploded her right to hold one of the highest positions of her people that Jackie realized she *had* been under a great deal of stress. She wanted *out* of the excessive layers and tangles of responsibilities in which she was still enmeshed. Or at least to have some of them reduced.

That, however, was up to her superiors. Once again, her career—the new direction of her career—lay in the Premiere's hands.

Callan rubbed his chin when her question reached him. He thought for several moments, then shrugged and nodded slowly. *"Yes, I do believe you have been wearing far too many hats of late . . . Now that we have a lot more Space Force troops out there, we're moving higher-ranked and better-trained officers in who can and should take your place. Plus, without a formal war needing a government representative to help authorize their activities, you won't have to personally direct them.*

"Of course, there is this whole interdiction of the Salik worlds we'll have to enforce. They believe *that they have officially surrendered, so that is an official end to the war . . . but everything we've learned so far about the Salik suggests that we will still have to deal with pockets of covert insurgency flaring up here and there."*

Jackie nodded. *"Yes, their minds are master manipulators of interpretation when they want to get their own way. Alliance policy prior to the war was to pin them down in reams of unambiguous, carefully defined contracts hundreds of pages long."*

"Well, they're under house . . . planet . . . arrest, so we won't have to deal with that. Of course, you'll *still need to be called upon to serve your share in the xenopathic rota, extracting locations of hidden bases and equipment stockpiles . . . which means you will probably have to suffer being a Colonel in the* Reserves *for a while,"* Premiere Callan added

pointedly. *"So don't stop your daily calisthenics just yet. But at least it'll be a partial retirement from the service."*

"Aughh! . . . *Can I at least swap my time in the rota in exchange for the mandatory weekends of training and duty-service shifts that the Reserves normally have to do?"* she asked. Begged, even. *"I agree with you completely, sir; I am wearing far too many hats, out here! We need to reduce it down to something manageable because we are getting more and more of our people out into the rest of the galaxy. You are the Commander-in-Chief, you know; you can authorize it."*

"Technically, the military falls back under the Secondaire's purview when war is over, so you'll have to get on Pong's sweet side," Callan countered dryly . . . and smiled, teasing her. *"Fine, I will see what I can do. As Cultural Liaison, you won't be able to get out of the translative side of your duties, so don't expect to hang up that career hat anytime soon. It's just that you'll be handling military secrets, so you need the military rank to be able to handle whatever information not only you yourself extract, but the civilian xenopaths who'll be contracted to the military, when it's your turn to supervise the rota."*

"I don't mind translating, because languages have always been my fallback job," she said. *"So I don't think that'll be a problem. Thank you for understanding why I did what I had to do, Augustus."*

He listened to her words as they reached him, then shook his head wryly. *"That's just it, I both do and don't understand why you did it. I understand your wanting to save lives because you're a compassionate person, and I understand you needing to step down, because you're quite ethical, too . . . but at the same time, you've been proud of your status as a high-ranked civil servant. There was no hint that you'd do this in the meetings leading up to today."*

She nodded slowly. *"It was very much a last-moment decision. If I had a chance to go back in time and do it all over again . . . I'd still do it this way. It's ruined me for politics—I wouldn't even trust myself as an Advisor—but yeah . . . I did save a lot of lives, today. I ended a war. I made that call,"* Jackie admitted, as much to herself as to her superior. *"There aren't very many people in all of existence who can honestly say that they personally ended a war. And that makes it worthwhile."*

"Yes, about that . . ." Callan drawled. He picked up a printout of something. *"Just before you contacted me, I got word from President Marbleheart on what he and his top advisors think about what you did, today. The K'Katta want to give you several 'Guardian honoraria,' to express their deep appreciation for your efforts knowing that you sacrificed your career in order to ensure peace for their people. From what I understand, it involves letting them get close enough to put sashes over your head and shoulders. Given what I know about your arachnophobia . . . how do you want me to reply to their request?"*

That was a fair question. *"I'm still a bit disturbed by their appearance,"* Jackie confessed. *"But compared to the scary things lurking inside a Salik's mind, I'd rather converse with a K'Katta any day. So . . . yeah, I could accept a few awards up close and personal if they think they should bestow any."*

"I'll let the other governments know you'll be willing to accept medal equivalents from them as well," Callan stated.

"Wait—what?" Jackie asked, but there were six seconds of lag between them, twelve of turnaround time, so she fell silent while he continued.

"The V'Goro J'sta should be headed back to the V'Dan homeworld in a few days. I'd like you and the Embassy 1 to be on board. Ambassador Ah'nan will finally be returning to her people to take up her position as the Imperial Heir. The Empress has expressed a desire to appoint her eldest son as a chief liaison for tasks similar to yours, explaining cultural differences, smoothing over misunderstandings, and . . . yes, you heard me right. His Highness would be well suited for the task of working at your side, helping our people establish enclave settlements on some of their worlds over the next few decades.

"I'm hoping to have all the details worked out by the time you do reach V'Dan, so that they can be presented at the welcoming-home ceremony. The two of you working together as a team for that need would suit both governments excep-

tionally well," Premiere Callan added. *"Particularly as an example to hold up to the other Alliance members of how we can remain separate and distinct, yet still get along just fine."*

"I was hoping she'd be amenable to that," Jackie admitted. *"Will McCrary remain Grand High Ambassador to V'Dan?"*

"Until we can train a successor for her, yes," he replied. *"By that point, we should be members of the Alliance—I'll have to get used to writing 'T.S.' after every year, for Terran Standard, instead of 'C.E.' for Common Era, but I expect it'll be no more annoying than remembering to write 2288 instead of 2287, now that we've passed the New Year back here."*

"Oh, that reminds me. Happy New Year," she told him.

"Happy New Year to you, too, Jackie," he replied, smiling wryly. *"You've had one heck of a year, too. Thank you for putting up with all of this. I'll bet it was nothing like what you'd imagined your life would be, back at the end of '86."*

Since that was the absolute truth, she could only nod to that. *"It's definitely different. I'll talk with you later, then. I need to go join His Highness in having a snack in the galley. I'd wait until we get back to the V'Goro, but it's off helping pull Salik prisoners out of starships for shipping back down to the planet, so the Alliance can scuttle what's left of their Fleet."*

"I'll be in touch."

───────────

"Eternal Empress," Li'eth greeted his mother as soon as the connection went through. He waited for her own response, knowing she'd speak as soon as the signal reached her end of things.

"War Prince," she acknowledged after eighteen seconds of round-trip lag time. Her voice trembled a little. "My son . . . I did not realize just how dangerous the proposed ploy would be. I thought it would just be like watching a hovercar crash. If I had *known* . . . I am deeply relieved you survived. I also wish you had vetoed volunteering for that."

"We were not in any real danger," Li'eth reassured her. "Given the other dangers we had already faced and survived, I had full confidence in the Ambassador's abilities to protect our group. We survived, and we are now at peace. The war with the Salik nation is over. They are, in fact, cooperating in being rounded up, from everything I've been told."

"Yes . . . about that. You are still the War Prince for a few days more," Hana'ka told her son. "But I will release you from your service to the military when you return home. You *will* return home as swiftly and safely as is reasonable."

"That is the plan, yes," he confirmed when she paused long enough for her words to reach him. "At the moment, the *V'Goro* is assisting the fleet in rounding up stray Salik ships. The Solaricans have agreed to take up the highest-ranked Salik officers as their prisoners, to separate and incarcerate them so that they will not be able to organize any rebellions. Because of this generosity, we do not need to linger and plan to leave in just a few days."

She nodded after nine seconds, listening to his words. "We shall make sure the Solaricans have our best assistance. Regarding the . . . your partner. Is there anything you can tell me about her declaration in the trail of the final moment of surrender?"

It was a delicate question, with a lot of subtext. Li'eth knew what his mother—his Empress—was fishing for. "I've had reassurances that Meioa McKenzie's government plans to appoint her as a cultural liaison to our people. Preferably, they would like me to be appointed to a similar post to their people, and then the two governments would employ us jointly to work on the integration of the Terrans into the known galaxy. They would like the two of us to focus on establishing settlements and enclaves on other worlds, and assisting them in building up a suitable fleet to join the rest of our forces on the coming blockade of Salik worlds."

"Yes, that would be ideal. You have a deft level of skill in bridging the gaps in cultural understandings. I will confirm your appointment as a nonmilitary cultural liaison once you return home," Hana'ka stated. "Speaking of which . . . it would be easiest if the *V'Goro J'sta* could detour to Earth to pick up Her Highness and her family.

"While you are there," the Empress continued before he could question the detour, "you will also need to pick up the extended family of your holy partner. I have extended them an invitation to come to the Summer Palace for a couple months.

The Governor of *Ohsee Anneeya* has approved his leftenant's vacation for that length of time. And when you get here . . . you will both be given an heroic welcome home. You both do deserve it, for fulfilling the ancient prophecies and bringing peace back to the Empire and the Alliance.

"Of course, there should be another set of ceremonies taking place, too, shortly after your arrival. It may be a bit quick for any other situation, but as the two of you have been together for about a year, and are confirmed holy partners . . . I was thinking it would be appropriate for the two of you to be formally betrothed, then married, in those two months while her family is visiting the Empire," she added lightly, and paused with a pointed look to let him react to her assertion.

Li'eth felt his face heating up, and held up a finger to let his mother know he was considering her offer for longer than the eighteen seconds of lag time between their positions. (*Jackie?*)

(*Yes? Did she tell you something upsetting?*)

(*Not upsetting, no. My mother wants us to swing by Earth, pick up your and my sister's families . . . and then see us formally betrothed and married within the two-month period of their visit, when we get back to the Summer Palace,*) he told her. (*Plus perform a ceremony celebrating our heroic return, which will require another parade in the plazas outside the Palace proper. And blessings ceremonies with the Sh'nai Faith, and probably a round of Trinitist blessings as well, as the second-largest faith . . . a lot of ceremonial stuff, now that we're no longer going to be suffering under the austerity of full, Empire-wide war. Even without the heroic accolades, Imperial marriages are a fairly big deal, especially when it involves someone of the Imperial Blood when they have the approval of the Eternal Throne.*)

(. . . *Okay. I can see all that happening. I don't know if Mother can be away from her governance duties for that long, though,*) she cautioned.

(*The Empress said it's been cleared with the Governor of Oceania, which is why we only have two months to get the majority of ceremonies done. Usually it takes closer to six. But she acknowledges we've been together for about a year, so it's clear we already know our minds about it, even if we weren't bound in a holy Gestalt. That is, if you want to get married.*)

(*Of course I do. So . . . okay, then. We'll get married. Just one word of caution: You'd better warn her that my family* will *expect to have a chance to surf the waters on an alien world,*) Jackie reminded him. (*And they'll want to try to coax your family into joining them. I don't even have to consult with my family to know that's what they'll want to do. It's what I still want to do. You owe me surfing time on V'Dan, and that includes surfing time* with *my family.*)

(*I know I do. Actually, I think Balei'in or Mah'nami might join us in trying that,*) he replied. (*Mah'nami in particular said it sounded intriguing, and she's normally so wrapped up with her research, it's hard to get her interested in physical activity. But I'm not sure Ah'nan or Mother will. And Vi'alla will probably flat-out refuse to come . . . not that I'd want her to show up. I still love her, but I can't yet forgive her . . . and your family does not deserve to have to deal with her.*)

(*One day, we can forgive her for what she did, when she realizes what she wanted was wrong for everyone,*) Jackie told him. Her underthoughts reminded him that they could afford to be generous toward his sister. (*But anyway, you're still talking with your mother. Let her know that I think that'll be fine. All of it, my family visiting, her generous hosting, the betrothal and marriage, everything she's asking—as far as I'm concerned, we're already married, mind to mind. The rest is just pleasing others with a bit of ceremony, and the various governments with a bit of paperwork.*)

(*That we are, and that it is,*) he agreed, and gave his patiently waiting mother a smile. "Jackie says she's willing to go through a betrothal and marriage V'Dan style."

(*You'll also get to go through one Terran style; my mother will insist,*) she added, listening in as he relayed her agreement. (*And yes, I'll stop paying attention to your thoughts, now.*)

Hana'ka gave him a relieved look even as Jackie raised a polite shield wall for privacy between them. "Good. I shall arrange everything on this end. We will not have complete peace, having to blockade the Salik from ever reaching out to the stars again . . . but we will have *some* peace. And I look forward to greeting Jackie as a Royal Consort—I shall give your sister Vi'alla the option to gracefully bow out of any of the ceremonies that would normally require her attendance.

Ah'nan's approval as the incipient Imperial Heir is all that is really needed, and I know she already likes your partner."

"Let Vi'alla know that I do love her, Mother," Li'eth said. "I won't let her harm my wife or my in-laws with any lingering prejudices, but I do still love her."

"I am certain she knows that. If she can bring herself to understand and accept that her flawed thinking is indeed flawed, then she will be welcomed back into the Palaces. Until then . . . even if Jacaranda MacKenzie is no longer the Grand High Ambassador, her people will still judge us by how we treat her as well as the rest of them," the Empress admitted. "I shall not allow our greatest hero in our greatest time of need to be disrespected. Not after all she and they have done to help us save the Empire and the Alliance."

"I hope Imperial Princess Vi'alla can learn to accept a proper touch of humility in her thoughts, Eternity," he agreed, resuming the formality her words required. "For myself, I shall do my best to continue to smooth over and strengthen the friendships that are growing between the Empire and the Terrans."

"Your sister won't be the last eldest-born to be set aside for the good of the Empire." His mother sighed. "I would claim I do not know where I went wrong with her, save that she *is* a fully grown adult. That attitude of hers is entirely on her hands, not mine. Well, enough of her," Hana'ka dismissed. "I would like to hear from you as the War Prince—even if you are one only for a little while longer—on what you think the Fleet and the Army need to do in the next few months to help expedite the dismantling of the Salik forces. The sooner we get that done, the sooner I can stop wearing the War Crown. The war may be over for you as soon as you return, but I am still responsible for cleaning up the aftermath."

"Of course, Eternity."

EPILOGUE

Floating on her *he'e nalu*—a new one decorated in black shark's teeth and blue jacaranda flower motifs, a gift from her family—and with her *kane* at her back, trusting her on gauging the waves riding in toward shore, Jacaranda MacKenzie peered back one last time at the distant ripples in the water, picked one to aim for, and started paddling.

With three moons orbiting this world, V'Neh, V'Yah, and U'Veh, the tides on V'Dan were complex compared to Earth's. However, the smaller moons of this world did not exert nearly as strong a pull on the rise and fall of the oceans as she would have thought. It had actually surprised Jackie to learn that the max average difference at high tide was only three extra meters, outside of storm surges. Even the height of eclipses only added two more.

Then again, the trio of local moons not only had different masses from Earth's larger Luna but also different distances than Luna's in their orbits. Thanks to the inverse-squared law of gravity, the tidal-force tugging of that outermost moon turned out to be a play on its rather apt name of "The Maybe"— V'Dan had more gravitational pull on it than it had on V'Dan. Still, a handful of extra meters was nothing to sneeze at, so they were trying this experiment on a relatively low wave-height day, with the moons spaced out around the planet and barely a meter and a half to the crests at the point where they started to curl over and froth into shore-drenching foam.

The beach here had a steeper slope than the ones at home, not exactly shallow. It lay covered in soft sand somewhere between pink and purple, like a beach she'd seen once in Bermuda. Like that island cove, the water here under the late-summer sun was warm, with enough salt for buoyancy and no inimical life-forms nearby.

Best of all, Li'eth and his family had taken an entire day off just to have a beachside party with Jackie and *her* family, all of them brought all the way from Earth at the Empress' insistence. In turn, as she'd expected, Jackie's family had insisted on bringing longish surfboards and silk-crafted *na lei* specifically so they could introduce the Imperial Family to the concept of a Hawai'ian beach party.

So far, it was a success. An exhausting success. They'd surfed a good dozen times so far, but she was out of practice stamina-wise after traveling through space for so long. The trees she aimed for, paddling harder and harder to try to get the longer board with its double load to move, looked nothing like palm trees, and only a few even somewhat resembled the Terran-native trees the V'Dan versions had originally sprouted from, but it was a shoreline; it had waves and sand and bushes and buildings in the distance.

It was just a little hard to get to that shore, hauling their way across the water with only her own arms paddling.

(*Aren't you going to help this time?*) she finally demanded. (*We'll get stuck bobbling in the flats instead of riding the waves if we can't get up to speed.*)

(*Bright Flower,*) Li'eth asked—drawled, really—in the back of her mind. (*We are both getting tired, but only physically. Why are you paddling with your* arms, *when you could be paddling with your* mind?)

She lost her rhythm for a few moments. Clinging to the board, blinking a little as a rolling swell lifted them and dropped them half a meter, she blinked. (*But . . . that . . . That'd be* cheating. *Surfing is done with the body, not with telekinesis!*)

He pushed at their surfboard with his mind, his skills considerably more practiced than when he had first tapped into them through their bond. (*I'm just saying it'd be easier, see?*)

Slightly disgruntled because it *was* easier for psychics of their strength than physically paddling, she sighed, peered behind them again, and guided their shared board into a better angle. Mentally. It *was* a lot easier, but still . . . mentally. (*It's still cheating.*)

(*You managed to get my mother into a swimsuit,*) Li'eth reminded her. (*My* mother. *Into a* swimsuit. *Admittedly, it's a private beach, but still, you got her to come out here. I am going to* insist *that you use telekinesis to protect her if you can ever convince her to come out on one of these things. Not that I'll hold my breath.*)

(He'e nalu, *not "one of these things,"*) Jackie insisted, pushing just a little bit more, until the board lifted in back, and stayed up, sliding down the slope of the wave. She grunted, getting to her feet—using a tiny bit of telekinesis to stabilize the board—and balanced while he also managed to get up behind her. Spreading her arms, she clasped his hands when he covered hers, letting her guide their bodies physically as well as mentally. (*Remind me to give you a language transfer for Hawai'ian, either tonight or tomorrow. Especially before we get into the* Terran *betrothal and marital ceremonies. You can impress and surprise my mother by reciting your lineage in Hawai'ian, not just Terranglo, you know.*)

(*Make it tomorrow night. We'll need our rest tonight, and tomorrow during the day will be filled with all sorts of Sh'nai ceremonies,*) he said, shifting a little with a nudge from her underthoughts, so they didn't bog down from too much weight near the back of the board. (*This is actually a lot of fun . . . I mean, it was fun back on Earth, but here, it's fun because it's* here. *Although I do think the waves are a little weak, compared to our day on that beach back on your world.*)

(*Look out, little niece coming through!*) She shifted their mentally linked weight, twisting them into a cutback near the shoulder of the wave, and raised her hand in a greeting sign at the hard-paddling pair. The surfing move sent them zipping away from Alani and her father Maleko as they paddled seaward to find a wave of their own. Maleko managed to spare his hand for a vague flutter, but it was little Lani-Nani, her foot and leg finally all better, who returned to them the *shaka* Jackie had given, the hand sign of one surfer greeting and encouraging another as they passed.

Since the waters around here were unknown in terms of surfing quality and concomitant possible dangers, Jackie's mother Lily—the new matriarch of the family and firmly on vacation from her duties as Lieutenant Governor of Oceania— had insisted that no one go riding the waves without a board-buddy. It was a good call, to Jackie's way of thinking. *She* had telekinesis to save herself. Li'eth could borrow hers. The others in her family, who just *had* to try the local waves, needed to make sure they would have someone close at hand for help in case of a bad wipeout.

Since they were coming in close to the shore, Jackie kicked out the board, cutting back across the foaming crest of the diminished wave. At her partner's mental urging, she gave in to Li'eth's "cheating" idea and just turned the board back out toward the open water with a touch of her mind. Using an invisible prow to cut the waves to either side, they surfed outward again, toward the line-up zone of still-rounded waves, to where she could see Maleko and his little girl working to turn their surfboard around to catch a wave of their own.

(*Alani has been catching hearts right and left all over the Imperial Court these last three days,*) Li'eth offered, catching sight of the young girl's big grin. (*Mostly, I think, because we all never thought her eyes would go back to normal, they've been so big and round and adorable every time she's looked around. She's teaching us to reappreciate the splendor of our home. Even I'm so used to seeing everything around the Summer Palace that it's only when I go away and live with the austerity of the military around me that I come back and realize how* fancy *everything looks.*)

(*It definitely is different from her home, or mine, or even my mother's,*) Jackie agreed. They slid up near her brother-in-law and niece, and got an exasperated look and a cupped-hand shout from the suntanned *kane*.

"Hey! That's *cheating*!" Maleko called out, before sticking out his hand and poking his thumb down. Like the rest of her family, he'd been given a telepathic transfer of V'Dan while riding in style—or as much style as one of the surviving V'Dan warships could provide—on their voyage here. "Boo! Booooo!"

"That's what I told *him*!" Jackie called back, poking her thumb over her shoulder at her partner, who helped balance their board while the incoming waves rolled them up and down a few feet. "He's the one who wanted to do it!"

"Well, I *was* gonna offer to race you to shore, but not if you're gonna cheat!" Maleko shouted back. He grinned at her, teasing, though Jackie didn't have to see his aura colors to know he was a bit envious that she and Li'eth could stand on their board with confidence in the relative calm of the line-up zone.

"Give us a push, Auntie Lani-Lani!" Alani called out, stretching out her arms. "I wanna fly on the waves!"

"You okay with that?" Jackie asked her in-law. When Maleko nodded, she gave a thumbs-up, and pushed carefully with her telekinesis on their board, front end canted very slightly upward so it wouldn't catch too badly on the back sides of the swells. It was one thing to "dive" the nose of a surfboard headed offshore, heading into the waves to get past them, but dipping while following them in to the shore could cause problems. A nudge of her mind against Li'eth's, and he complied as well, shifting to move their own board to make sure they didn't fall too far behind.

". . . It's still cheating!" Maleko called back, shifting carefully if quickly to stand up as they reached the zone where the rolling waves crested and could actually be surfed. "But I'm loving it!"

"I'm letting go!" she called out, and eased back on her telekinetic grip so that gravity and the joint skill of father and daughter could take over. (*It has just occurred to me that I could make a modest killing as a supersafe surfing instructor if I ever get kicked completely out of public service.*)

(*That you could,*) Li'eth agreed. (*Is that Hyacinth and Ahe coming out for another round?*)

Jackie nodded, watching her sister and nephew paddling their own shared board toward the line-up zone. Hyacinth, of course, rode in back as the heavier and more experienced surfer, for all that Ahe towered over her by several centimeters.

By rights, Jackie as the more experienced one should have been behind Li'eth, but he was heavier and could rely on the undercurrents of her thoughts to handle the waves with reasonable confidence by now. (*Why don't you take us out with a little telekinetic push since you're getting the hang of this? At least until we get a little past the breakpoint, where I can take over.*)

(*Alright,*) Li'eth agreed, and concentrated on actively joining the rolling lines of waves, not just vaguely joining them.

Free to enjoy the ride, she shaded her hand over her eyes while Li'eth guided the board, and peered at the shoreline beyond the waves. Imperial Elites still dotted the cove in their cream, scarlet, and gold uniforms. She felt sorry for them having to stand watch in formal uniforms in the late-summer heat. Ah'nan and her family were down near the waterline, busy with the very important Human beach activity of building sand castles. V'Dan-style castles, but still, castles and other sculptures made out of damp sand.

Jackie's brother still sat in V'Dan-style beach chairs on the upper beach, talking with Bale'in about something . . . which made her frown in confusion because following in the wake of Hyacinth and Ahe was her mother Lily on a surfboard with a woman in a red swim . . . suit . . .

(*That's my mother!*) Li'eth exclaimed, catching sight at the same moment—and lost his mental control of the *he'e nalu,* pearling the nose under the waves.

Jackie quickly snatched both of them off the flipping board, floating them into a protective bubble. The tethering cord tugged at her ankle from the board trying to tumble away as the crest broke and splashed under the jostling of the mishandled board.

(*Sorry—sorry!*) he apologized.

(*It's okay, I got us . . .*) Untangling the surfboard from the crest, still floating forward, Jackie brought it back under their legs. Both of them sat down on the telekinetically floating board, equally astonished at the sight of the burgundy-marked woman in the matching burgundy suit awkwardly paddling through the incoming waves under the direction of her unexpected surfing buddy. Jackie blinked a few times, then managed a semicoherent thought. (*I don't know if this is a good thing or a bad thing,*) she muttered.

(*You don't?*) Li'eth questioned. He wrapped his arms around her and hugged her as they floated above the waves, neither going back out nor heading in to shore just yet. The sight of the Eternal Empress on a surfboard was just too astonishing. It required actual contemplation to absorb. (*My mother is actually having fun. I know it's a bit shocking, but what could be bad about that?*)

(*I mean . . . well . . . The intent was . . .*) She fumbled to a stop, and shook her head wryly. (*Sorry, that was not politely thought of me. I'm just too astonished that she agreed, given the sheer formality of everything she does. And if some gossip reporter gets ahold of this news . . . but . . . yes, your mother, the Eternal Empress, is allowed to have fun.*)

(*Yes, she is allowed, and yes, it's utterly shocking and yet heartening to see her giving this sport a try,*) Li'eth agreed, squeezing a little. (*That last spill took some of my reserves away. I think I'm almost done for the day. At least where the waves are concerned. What Ah'nan and her family are doing looks like equal fun. But I'd like to stay and watch my mother surf first, if that's okay?*)

Sensing the undercurrent of filial worry, knowing he wanted both of them to be in range to bubble both of their mothers quickly if anything went wrong, Jackie nodded. Floating her tooth-and-flowered surfboard just a little bit above the waves, straddling it so that their dangling soles occasionally got smacked by the water, the two of them watched carefully. Lily MacKenzie gave her counterpart a few last instructions, then both women started paddling in earnest.

Li'eth's mother was no slouch physically, despite her advancing age. The Eternal Empress managed to match the Terran Lieutenant Governor stroke for stroke, until they slid down the face of the next wave, sliding forward because of gravity, not just to firmly stroked paddling. Lily MacKenzie popped up into her surfing stance with the smooth grace of someone who had done it since childhood, and trimmed the *he'e nalu* into the sweet spot on their chosen wave. Both Jackie and Li'eth cheered at the sight of the successful start to their ride.

As they watched, Hana'ka managed to get herself up into a kneeling position, but moved no higher than that. Still, she cheered at her son and his partner as the duo slid past, hands briefly lifted and spread before she clutched reflexively at the deck again for balance. As they slid past, Lily spared a hand from balancing long enough to cup her mouth and call out, "Stop showing off, you two! And no cheating!"

(*See? Even Mother says it's cheating!*) Jackie teased Li'eth.

(*I know, but it's fun being able to fly,*) Li'eth told her. (*There hasn't been a flying Saint in over three hundred years, you realize—and we can use* that *to distract any gossip-sellers, should they turn any long-distance cameras our way. We're already weird enough, we can handle being gaped at for that.*)

(*Yeah yeah . . . I'm dropping us into the waves, and surfing the* regular *way back to shore,*) she warned him.

(*Just for one more ride,*) he said, hugging her from behind one last time. (*Tomorrow is our betrothal ceremony. We don't want to be stiff and sore from too much water fun. Or sunburned. We'll have to do all that kneeling and bowing, and do it in public, while the Autumn Temple gives us their blessing.*)

(*Are you absolutely sure your mother would kill us if we just ran off and eloped?*) Jackie asked wryly, looking back to time their descent so they could just go straight into surfing the next suitable slope.

(*Are you so absolutely sure* your *mother wouldn't?*) he countered.

The thought of both of their mothers, raised on two far-flung worlds in far-apart cultures, being so similar despite nearly ten thousand years of difference between their two worlds, made her laugh. Li'eth chuckled with her, his under-thoughts warmer than the light of the local sun, taking pleasure at how well their families were getting along.

They were both still grinning, minds entwined in a comfortable hug, when they dipped down into a good-sized slope, so they could surf the *proper* way one last time before heading for the shore. Without cheating. Mostly.

When they finally slogged their way ashore, Jackie insisted on carrying her *he'e nalu* up to the sun shelters that had been erected, great curves of colorful canvas that allowed plenty of sea breeze to pass inside while offering a decent amount of shade. As soon as the surfboard had been stowed where the wind off the local ocean wouldn't knock it over and damage it, Li'eth tugged her toward the shelter that contained their beach picnic food.

Something about the woman who rose from her folding chair and moved to fetch their drinks tugged at Jackie's peripheral awareness. Sipping on the straw tucked into the flavorful, slightly minty mix of fruit juices, she frowned in concentration. Something . . . Her gaze snapped to the other woman. Middle-aged, dark brown hair and burgundy *jungen* rosettes, clad in a red-and-cream staff uniform, there was nothing about the woman externally that was alarming.

Nothing psychically, either . . . except that the woman's mind was wrapped in a perfectly spherical, perfectly solid, highly skilled shield.

(*Is that . . . ?*) Li'eth asked, blinking rapidly when her shock spilled over onto him.

(*That it is,*) the other woman sent back, and smiled as she lifted a tray of V'Dan crackers toward them, topped with sauces, cheeses, and artistically arranged vegetables. (*Go on, take a few and eat them. Pretend everything is normal for the nice Elite Guards.*)

Blinking a few times herself, Jackie accepted one of the appetizers and asked, (To-mi *Kuna'mi?*)

(*Technically, that personality is dead. And yes, it is me, you can call me Shey telepathically . . . and yes, I can make myself look different.* If *I concentrate hard enough when re-forming myself after I die. I'm currently borrowing—with permission—the identity of a Summer Palace chef who grew up in the Valley of the Artisans,*) she explained. (*I'm only here for a little while today, then I'll be gone . . . but I wanted the two of you to know something, and this was the easiest way to get close to the two of you.*)

(*And that is?*) Li'eth asked, munching on the cracker to hide his curiosity.

Jackie tasted one herself, finding the combination of flavors spicy-sweet with just a hint of salt. It tasted rather refreshing after spending so much energy surfing. (*Yes, any more prophecies?*)

(*Not really. Just the fact that the two of you will be remembered far into the future on a bunch of colonyworlds, both known and yet to come, for helping to smooth things over. And that you'll have some kids. And live long lives if all goes well. The war is over, but you'll still need to be vigilant,*) the oldest Human alive added, snagging a cracker for herself and chewing. (*Don't let either government slack on funding the Blockade. It needs to last for the next two centuries.*)

(*That's when the prophecies say the Devouring Ones go away by their own efforts,*) Li'eth said. (*Correct?*)

The disguised Immortal shrugged subtly. (*That's what I learned in my history classes, growing up thousands of years ago. Which won't happen for another four hundred years. And no, I honestly don't know what'll happen to* me, *the adult me, when I come into existence as a child in the years ahead. I'll probably go do what I'm about to do anyway, which is retreat to my information vaults here on V'Dan, and on Earth, and update everything that just happened.*

(*I do know I plan on enjoying whatever happens in the next few years after that.*) She popped another ornately topped cracker between her lips and smiled. (*Maybe I'll even sign up as a V'Dan soldier and go join the Blockade forces. Someone needs to keep an eye on everything while all our fleets are being repaired.*)

Not for an instant did Jackie doubt that the very strange woman standing in front of her could handle the entire Salik nation. If she put her mind to it. (*Thank you for all of your help, and for letting us know you survived. I was worried about you when I heard that wall had fallen on you.*)

The Immortal shrugged. (*I'm used to dying. I do it a lot. I still don't know what* death *is, however. I'm hoping it will be like going to bed at the end of a very long and tumultuous day. Or maybe it's opening a door to a new universe with a different set of rules. Or maybe I'll just reincarnate into something I've never been before. I think a tree would be nice.*)

(*A tree?*) Li'eth asked, distracted by the non sequitur of it. (*Why a tree?*)

(*Because trees tend to lead very peaceful lives . . . which, from all the ancient history I can remember, is what the two of you will get to enjoy,*) she told them. (*Now, have a last pair of crackers so you won't faint from hunger, and go play in the sun, surf, and sand. I'm going to spend the rest of today pretending to be a mere chef before I disappear.*)

(*Does a mere chef want to know how to surf?*) Jackie found herself offering, draining her juice dry and setting the glass on the folding table provided for such things under the awning.

The middle-aged woman who was far, far older than she looked grinned for a moment, before slightly shaking her head. (*You'll not get me out there even though I already do. My skill would be too obvious. That, and you really should go down to the shoreline now. I can see Her Eternity getting ready to ride another wave inward. She deserves some cheering for her bravery.*) Out loud, she merely said, "Go on, take an extra cracker each. Go have fun while the sun shines."

"Of course, meioa," Li'eth agreed, and snagged two crackers, tucking one into his mouth. He returned his own emptied glass to the table.

"You cook very well," Jackie added aloud, plucking a pair for herself as well. "Thank you. It's nice to meet you."

"It was nice to meet you, too, meioa," the Immortal agreed. She waited until they had turned to move away, before adding a final thought. (. . . *And aloha to you both. Always come together in the spirit of* aloha, *so your peoples will be inspired to do the same. I'd say* a hui hou, *but I'm not sure if our paths will ever cross again. You'll still be famous for some time to come, so it's best for me not to linger near the spotlight on you. So . . .* aloha'oe, *for what it's worth.*)

Jackie nodded. She didn't look back, but just twined her fingers with her beloved's and sent a shared thought with him back to their odd but likeable friend.

(Aloha'oe, *to you, too.*)

From national bestselling author

JEAN JOHNSON

THE THEIRS NOT TO REASON WHY NOVELS

A SOLDIER'S DUTY

AN OFFICER'S DUTY

HELLFIRE

HARDSHIP

DAMNATION

PRAISE FOR THE SERIES

"Reminiscent of both *Starship Troopers* and *Dune*."
—*Publishers Weekly*

"An engrossing military SF series."
—SF Signal

jeanjohnson.net
facebook.com/AceRocBooks
penguin.com

M1662AS0415